An Ordinary Odyssey

Finding yourself and your place in this world

By

Sabrina Lindner

This story is for all of you who feel like you are on a quest.

Feel free to bravely and joyfully venture out into the world, to explore who you truly are and find your place.
Embrace your free flow and enjoy this odyssey called life.

A brief foreword

Welcome to An Ordinary Odyssey!

It is an absolute pleasure to have you.

You can read this story in one of two ways: you can read it simply for entertainment, enjoying the twists and turns, the drama, the romance and the friendship, or you can go a little deeper and closely observe the actions and reactions of the people in this book. You can feel into their thoughts and emotions and ask yourself what is there for you to see in everything that they experience.

What awareness can you gain from joining Akila, her children, In Su and Ji Su and all their friends and family on this journey?

Whichever way you choose to travel through this story, let it be a journey of pure ease, joy, love and excitement.

Jump right in!

Table of Contents

The beginning of Akila

It was her father, Matthias, who told the story of her birth and how her life in this world had begun.

Eight-year-old Akila liked it, imagining how her parents were there together, waiting for a new life to appear–her own life. She smiled to herself.

Matthias began, "You were born early in the morning. Your mother, Katarina, had spent almost thirty hours with contractions, and by the time you were out, we were both so tired we thought we wouldn't have the energy to do anything for days."

In her mind, Akila imagined a grey and windy autumn day, raindrops splashing against the windows of the hospital where she had been born. She saw her mother, sweaty and exhausted, her long blonde hair untidy and wet. Her father must have held her mother's hand and encouraged her to go on.

"It didn't help that Katarina had asthma at the time, which made breathing and pushing much more difficult," her father continued. "You'd spent such a long time in the birth canal that your head was blue and slightly deformed when you were finally out. I was really shocked! We were scared that you were not healthy–but the doctor was quick to explain that it was only temporary."

Akila took a bite of the bread with the marmalade she was eating, wondering how her father must have stared at her as a baby, worrying and wanting her to be well. In her imagination, Akila saw herself, her head placed on her mother's chest, while her father was reassured by the doctor and the midwife.

"You were tall from the very beginning, and you suckled milk with determination. You knew how to let the world know what you wanted with your loud and powerful cry. You rarely gave us a moment to rest, be it day or night," he laughed.

Sitting next to her father in the kitchen and sipping cocoa, she could almost see herself then, long and heavy with chubby, rosy cheeks, demanding warmth and attention. Her mother was immersed and, at times, completely absorbed in tending to her rapid growth. Akila was like an always demanding seed that quickly became a flower–a full person.

The thought that life began just like that had always fascinated Akila. A life could begin so easily, but in a truly messy way, and a life always ended, probably also in a messy way. Or at least that's what she assumed. Akila thought about that for a while, folding her long legs on the chair next to her father, the tallest person she had ever met. She loved the fact that she had such a tall father, and she decided she would put all her will into becoming just as tall. *When you are tall,* she told herself, *you can see everything and it would be hard to get lost.*

First Steps

When Akila was two weeks old, Katarina and Matthias moved to a different part of the country further south. Steep hills, narrow valleys, and vast forests surrounded the small villages with their compact houses and fenced-in backyards.

The North had been different. Katarina would pass on her affinity for landscapes and her ability to see beauty in empty spaces to her little daughter.

Sitting in the backseat of her mother's old white Mercedes, Akila always felt like she was returning home whenever they headed north for the holidays. Later on in her life, Akila would travel alone by train, enamoured with the experience of being an anonymous onlooker as blurred images moved past the window. Akila had a special place in her heart for train rides, and whenever she travelled to her mother's old home, she would look for the changes in the landscape: the hills and valleys and the cramped towns and villages now replaced by sweeping views across the flat and open fields.

Katarina and Matthias were barely past twenty years old when they moved with their newborn baby, and there was little money to spare. They had both longed for years to break out and move away from the limitations they both felt living in their village. Katarina would eventually conclude that their desire to leave was probably the strongest force uniting them in their relationship, and, for a while, that common desire was enough.

They first moved into a tiny apartment.

Katarina couldn't help but notice how dark, grey, and lonely that small town was when they first arrived. It seemed like the environment reflected the people's mindset. On some days, the fear that she would turn into a withered, grey flower just like the other women in town overpowered and paralysed her for hours.

Slowly, the family's evenings were filled with irritation, arguments, and accusations rather than their usual discussions that left their hearts filled with warmth. Katarina, who spent her entire days looking after little Akila, felt alone. It was as if her mind was dominated by dark thoughts. Matthias, who spent his days working and studying, often came home late in the evenings where he felt judged and misunderstood.

It became evident that life couldn't go on this way, and the young couple started looking for other places to live. After weeks of fighting, this was the first thing they had agreed on, and it was nice to have something that connected them again.

One day, Matthias mentioned their struggle to find a suitable place to live to one of his colleagues in the bookshop where he worked.

The older woman told him, "There's this community that lives in the old farmhouse just outside the village I come from. Maybe visit sometime."

She then scribbled an address on a small piece of paper, handing it to Matthias.

The village, inhabited by only a few hundred people, was surrounded by hilly farmland, and further down the slopes, the forest began. While Matthias parked on the side of the road not far from the main house, Katarina noticed the large garden in the back with tall grass and ancient apple trees. It reminded her of the beauty of her homeland.

Matthias carried Akila in his arms as they walked to the wooden front door, a door bleached by the decades of changing seasons it had witnessed.

Soft music was playing inside as they rang the doorbell. Several dogs started to bark, and, a moment later, a young woman with long, black hair and dressed in a colourful outfit opened the door. She carried a small baby in her arms, not much older than Akila. The woman looked at the young family with the weary eyes of a mother who had been sleep-deprived for many nights.

"Yes?" she asked.

Matthias wasn't sure if he wanted to ask to room here. As tall as he was, he gazed over the head of the woman who had opened the door and noticed the mess inside the corridor that led into the house. Three large dogs poked their heads around the woman's legs, sniffing curiously. Matthias imagined this place would be more chaotic than he preferred. However, it didn't seem like that would matter since Katarina was already in conversation with the young mother and they were quickly ushered in.

They walked down the corridor, which opened into a spacious kitchen filled with the smells of spices and greasy fat. Clean dishes were piled high near a battered sink below a window that could use some cleaning.

The dogs had trailed behind them and were settling down below the wooden kitchen table. It was clear from the colourful array of chairs and benches arranged around the table that many people came together here.

Matthias knew that the place was filthy and, again, the thought crossed his mind that he didn't want to stay here. He wanted to be free and live his own life. But did he want Akila to crawl on these dusty and grimy floors? Did he want to eat his breakfast in this run-down kitchen with conflicting smells lingering in the air? Did he want to listen to the contemplative meditation music resounding throughout the house from one of the rooms? He wasn't really sure. But Katrina was smiling, which was a rare occurrence these days. She was fully immersed in her conversation with the black-haired woman, who had introduced herself as Andrea. Akila, now sitting on her father's lap, reached out her tiny hands for one of the dogs below the table and gave a small squeal to show how pleased she was. And Matthias decided that he would try to endure it.

And so, Akila grew up in a house that was constantly filled with people. Children of all ages mingled and spent their afternoons playing. Adults who lived there were seeking ways to live a fuller life–a life not controlled by the system. A life that had "meaning."

These were the phrases that Akila grew up hearing. There was a general understanding in this community that there had to be more to life than what was on the surface. And the best way to find it was to do things unconventionally.

There were always several dogs in the house, and when Akila was almost five, she rescued a little rabbit from a friend's farm before it could be slaughtered. A stray cat also found its way to their house, maybe realising that this was a place for unwelcome outcasts. Akila frequently fed the animal until the cat was used to her.

The spring Akila turned five, it was mild and lovely, and the days were filled with sunshine. The bees would buzz across the grass behind Akila's house early in the morning. The heavy kitchen table and chairs were moved out of the house and into the garden so that they could all eat outside, and on weekends, a bonfire would burn late into the night.

* * *

That same March, a boy was born in South Korea.

His mother couldn't hold back the screams that pressed out of her throat when the next wave of contractions rolled over her. After hours of struggle and the doctor's supportive words, the baby finally made it through the birth canal, looking at the world with glistening eyes. Opening his mouth, he released a loud wail.

"Good," the doctor said with a smile to the exhausted mother. "He has the strength needed for this world!"

And so it was. Kang Ji Su was a small child, but full of power and energy. He never slowed down for anyone, not even for a minute.

* * *

While Ji Su, in South Korea, was taking his first shaky steps at ten months of age, which amazed his mother and briefly pleased his father, who was otherwise immersed in his business, Akila walked out of the house and into the high pasture behind the farmhouse.

She was a child with many thoughts, and she often escaped into the garden to find reprieve from the noise inside the full house. At other times, she would walk across the big, cobblestone yard littered with farming equipment, striding across the fields where the cows and horses grazed, all the way into the forest surrounding them. They lived in the most forested part of Germany, and long walks beneath majestic wide-umbrella trees would shape many of Akila's childhood memories.

Moving to the farmhouse had seemed to lighten everyone's spirits. Katarina had started smiling again and the arguments had reduced significantly, but the distance that had developed between her and Matthias remained. Matthias focused on his studies but especially directed his attention to his work in the bookshop. It also served as a reasonable excuse to spend less time in the house that he still didn't feel entirely comfortable living in.

Many years later, Katarina would tell Akila of these times, when she was still a little girl running across the fields. The time when her mother and father's quest for a life that gave them enough freedom and space to breathe became two different paths.

Katarina and Matthias eventually went their separate ways, and Akila got used to growing up with her mother and visiting her father during the holidays. As a grown woman, Akila attributed her ability to accept different ways of living to her unconventional upbringing and the fact that her parents, even when separated, never spoke ill of each other.

Into the night

The car shook slightly whenever another car passed them by, even though they were moving rather quickly on the autobahn. Akila sat quietly in the back of the vehicle and gazed out the window. Their old white Mercedes wasn't exactly the fastest mode of transport, but its large, comfortable seats seemed to welcome her every time she prepared for a new journey.

The sky was painted in reds, oranges, and purples slowly running into blues and blacks of different intensities. Lights flew by, and Akila turned around to look back.

Her mother was in the driver's seat, focusing on the road. They'd already travelled for more than three hours and would soon exit the highway to the smaller country roads that led to Akila's grandparents' home.

While they drove on beneath the soothing colours of the early night sky, Akila's mother was unaware of the imagined battle taking place in her daughter's mind.

Akila's brain seemed to explode with all the images running through it. She saw herself fighting as an indigenous warrior against her enemies, the Europeans. They'd taken her people's land, with no respect for their customs and caring nothing about their way of life. Blood spilled, staining the ground of a village on fire. Horses whinnied in panic, trampling on fleeing women with their small children. Warriors ran as knives and arrows flew through the air, spears pierced through skin, causing deadly harm.

She was one of the few female warriors in the village, moving swiftly in a group of three other warriors who had been her closest comrades when hunting and were, today, fighting for the future of their people.

A burly shadow burst through the large tear in one of the dwellings to her right, screaming and swinging a sable and a bayonet. Akila froze in fear for a split second before shifting her weight to her other foot and twisting her entire body, moving past the soldier, who crumbled down into a heap of flesh.

The group arrived at the centre of their village, where most of the battle took place. Akila's ears rang. It was hard to focus on anything other than the screams of horror, but she had to stay strong and rescue as many of her people as possible. She saw a group of women and children huddled together to her left and gave her comrades a quick sign with her hand. With a brief nod of acknowledgment, they scanned the area for the easiest way to pass through. For the next hour, they battled side by side, hacking, dodging, killing, and surviving as they slowly moved toward the group of women and children. While they might have lost the chance to win against their attackers, at least they could rescue a few of their own.

When the night sky was darkest, not long before the first faint lights of early dawn they finally got to the group of women and children huddled together. Wide-eyed infants with dirty smoke-blackened faces were strapped to the backs of silently crying women and older children as the group organised them. Then they ventured away from the battle and into the night. The blinding heat from the raging fires and thick smoke made it easier to move out of the area than expected. Akila and her fellow warriors only had to win two more silent, yet furious encounters with the soldiers before the darkness and surrounding woods swallowed them up and carried them away from the heat and death of their village.

"Akila. . . . Akila! Can you pass me the water bottle, please? I'm talking to you!"

It took Akila a moment to realise that she was back with her mother in their old Mercedes. She jumped back into motion and passed the bottle of water to her mother, still dazed and high on adrenaline from what had just happened at the village.

Her mother continued talking, but Akila couldn't focus anymore. The familiar feeling of being removed in some way from the world, an onlooker in a bubble, took hold of Akila's mind and wouldn't let go.

They'd already left the highway and were now moving through the dark and narrow country road. The sun had fully set by now and only the headlights of their vehicle illuminated the street just metres before them. Occasionally, Akila could make out a large farmhouse with a few windows casting warm golden light or bulky shadows of barns and overgrown vegetation.

A small tickling itch lodged in her head, and she couldn't rid herself of it. It spread from her head down her face, through her neck, over her shoulders, along her arms, and from her chest into her legs and feet. It was an irresistible urge, a yearning that shackled her, unable to move, when all she wanted to do was open the door and jump out, flying into the night sky.

The old Mercedes turned onto the small street off the country road. It took them across the large, flat fields that characterised the landscape of her mother's homeland. Her mother manoeuvred the vehicle along the short driveway and into a parking space next to the dark shape of Akila's grandparents' house.

The small light above the entryway came to life as the wooden door swung open, giving way to Grandma Isabela. Her chestnut-brown hair was covered with an elegant silk shawl, and Akila spotted the familiar hair curlers underneath that her grandmother frequently used to force her locks into the desired form. Her grandfather followed, short and bald-headed, his round smiling face glowing with welcome and the pleasure of having enjoyed his evening martini.

Akila's mother had already stepped out of the car and Akila knew that she should get out of the car to greet her grandparents right away. She also knew that there were emotions that she should feel: happiness and excitement about being with her family, spending time with her grandparents, having aunts and uncles, and cousins close to her over the long summer holidays.

But right now, Akila was elsewhere, moving through the forest away from the burning village, urging on the group of frightened survivors with her fellow warriors. She was weary, yet extremely alert, ready to jump at anyone or anything that could pose a threat to their exhausted little flock. It was a crucial moment for the future survival of their people, and it was difficult for her to leave the scene to be embraced and spoiled by her grandparents.

She did finally move, managing to smile at the right times and offer the appropriate responses to her grandparents' questions.

About an hour later, Akila lay in bed, enveloped in soft bed sheets and the calmness of the room. Fir trees stood tall outside the window as their branches swayed gently in the night breeze, casting different forms and shapes over Akila's bed sheets. Akila closed her eyes and let herself fall back into the forest. When she'd gathered her thoughts, she was suddenly next to her imaginary fellow warrior, Wohali, finding a way through the undergrowth as silently and quickly as possible.

The next morning, Akila rolled out of bed after having spent the night in the forest fighting for survival, getting their group as far away from the burning village and violent soldiers as possible. They eventually found shelter in a small cave along the outskirts of the nearby mountain range and decided to rest before moving on.

Akila stepped into the corridor and walked towards the kitchen. She could hear her grandfather shouting in the bathroom when he turned on the cold water at the end of his morning bath, a daily morning procedure that he firmly believed had a positive impact on his overall health. Akila smiled and shuddered. Her grandfather was a lovely man, but maybe also a bit crazy given that he tortured himself willingly every morning.

Akila could make out the faint sounds of the radio in the kitchen when she opened the door, and her grandmother sat in her usual spot looking elegant and groomed. Her mother was standing by the kitchen counter waiting for the toaster to spit out the bread rolls she had put in, a breakfast routine both Akila's mother and grandmother couldn't live without.

"Akila, sweetheart! There you are. Shouldn't you have brushed your teeth before coming to join us?"

Grandma Isabela kissed her granddaughter on the cheek and motioned for her to sit down next to her. Akila just smiled at her grandma and sat down after hugging her mother.

"The weather will be lovely this week, so we'll have to go enjoy a dip in the lake! Akila, your cousins are joining us tomorrow, so you'll have a splendid time."

Akila nodded and bit down on the bread roll her mother had passed on to her after smothering it with a mound of butter and cheese.

Akila's grandfather entered the kitchen huffing and puffing after his icy treatment and sat down next to her. Her grandmother had already placed the various pills he swallowed each morning on a plate along with a cookie. No matter how hard she tried, Akila couldn't really find anything enticing in her grandfather's morning routine.

While her grandmother flipped the pages of the local newspaper, humming along to the tune being played on the radio, her grandfather spoke excitedly with Akila's mother.

Akila busied herself with her bread roll and tea, content with listening to the familiar voices around her and taking in the ticklish warmth of the morning sun. Her imagination painted the word "summer" in golden letters on the white kitchen wall, and she smiled again.

Akila spent the first day at her grandparents' lying on the daybed in the glass house reading books. In the afternoon, they took the bikes from the shed and rode along the sandy path to the little lake hidden in between birch and fir trees. It beckoned them with its cool, clear water.

Whenever Akila had time, she would return in her mind to the forest where her adventure continued to unfold. Her clan members were now making their way across the mountain range away from the pursuit of the Europeans but still faced the dangers of the wild.

The next morning after breakfast, her younger cousins arrived, ready to demand their elder cousin's attention. The two girls loved to play with Akila because she told the most amazing stories and had rather creative ideas for games.

"Akilaaaaa!" Carlotta jumped onto Akila's lap and slung her arms around her neck with a wide smile. Carlotta was the oldest of Akila's cousins. Since she had been born when Akila was five years old, the two had spent most of Akila's holidays together. There was a special bond between them and, despite their age gap, they always got along. "I am here to make you smile," she said.

And Akila smiled.

Thick skin

When Akila was twelve, she watched *Cry Freedom* for the first time. Learning about Steve Biko, who had been killed like so many others while fighting the oppression of apartheid, moved her deeply. While watching the movie, she cried like she had never cried before.

Of course, she knew that things like this happened in the world. That was one of the reasons she preferred dropping into her other worlds rather than facing her own.

Somehow watching this movie made it dawn on her that she'd be miserable if she didn't learn how to deal with the world she lived in. This realisation hit her with full force, and that was the moment Akila decided that she had to develop thicker skin.

Yes, rainforests were disappearing, people were killed because of speaking up for what they believed in, and many couldn't live a decent life because of the colour of their skin. It was completely shocking to Akila how humankind was moving towards destruction with their eyes wide open.

But wasn't she the same? She decided that the ability to ignore what was right in front of her was to become one of her strongest skills.

After a few days of milling over the whole situation, Akila slowly started practising how to block out what made her sad.

* * *

Mrs. Moon held her son close to her chest, stroking his soft, black hair. He had fallen asleep on her lap as they drove, and he looked almost like a baby doll with his chubby arms and legs, large, round cheeks, and round pursed lips. Kim In Su was a large baby, and his mother had trouble lifting him these days, even though he was only two years old. Mrs. Moon thought that his eyes shone more than any other baby's eyes. She had looked into the eyes of her neighbour's babies and the eyes of her siblings' babies, and she was sure that she hadn't spotted the same intensity in those eyes.

Her son was born to stand out. She was sure of it.

Mr. Kim sat next to her, focusing on the road ahead of them. It was getting late, and the evening sun lit up the green fields and the forests around them. Golden streaks of brilliance travelled across the rock formations that rose to the side of the road they were moving on.

In Su's parents weren't speaking to each other, which was how they usually solved their conflicts. And if they had a conversation, they both would have agreed that today was a day of unspoken conflict.

They'd been at an ancestral celebration at Mrs. Moon's childhood home, and her entire family had been present. Mrs. Moon was aware of how exhausting such family gatherings were for her husband. Her parents had always made it clear that they felt that their daughter was far too good for a small second-hand bookshop owner. They'd never understood why their precious girl had insisted on marrying such a timid man with strange views on the world. One of the only interesting things about him was that he was from Seoul, the largest and most well-known city in all of Korea–a fact they frequently mentioned when talking about the successes of their children.

Even so, Mrs. Moon's father couldn't seem to hold back his comments whenever they visited. Was living in Seoul and owning a shop really all they wanted to achieve? And a shop full of rather useless books at that? Didn't Mr. Kim want the best for his wife and son? It seemed to Mrs. Moon's father that his son-in-law lacked ambition. And ambition was needed if you wanted to achieve something great in this world.

He would mention his eldest daughter, Mrs. Moon's sister. She had such ambition and had moved to the US. She was now living a perfect life in a perfect American house in a perfect American suburb with a perfect, hardworking husband and two children. In the elderly man's view, a father should never want any less for his children.

Mrs. Moon looked at her husband, who had sat in her parent's living room silently, seemingly unaffected by the comments her father made. She often wondered how he managed to have such thick skin, completely unshaken by the accusations hurled at him. Despite his thick skin, she could tell that these words still hurt him, as she had learned to read the signs in how he carried himself and the expertly veiled irritation in the polite responses he gave. Her husband and her father communicated on completely different levels, or her father would have been furious. But he didn't catch the concealed sarcasm that coloured Mr. Kim's sentences and, therefore, had no reason to get offended.

So now Mrs. Moon and Mr. Kim sat next to each other in their small car and didn't say a single word. Mrs. Moon knew that Mr. Kim was annoyed that he had to endure his father-in-law's remarks for an entire day and, while Mrs. Moon loved her parents, she also loved her husband. It felt to her as if her love for all of them was making it hard to accept the fact that the man she wanted to be with and her parents couldn't seem to find common ground.

A thousand lights

The plane slowly descended in blue-tinged darkness, which was all nineteen-year-old Akila could see when she looked out of the tiny window. Small, twinkling lights suddenly came into view and quickly multiplied. Within seconds, Akila was looking out into an endless ocean of sparkling lights.

Akila's chest pounded with excitement, and a sense of longing she rarely experienced overcame her. It was as if something had finally been set in motion for the unfolding of her own story.

This moment remained with her as one of the most beautiful moments of Akila's life. Maybe it was because of her grasp of the magnitude of the situation, but in later years, whenever Akila would come home to Nairobi on an evening flight, she would look for the same lights and feel the same excitement with a deep sense of belonging.

That first night, Akila walked next to her mother Katarina down the corridor from the plane into the Nairobi JKIA airport, speechless. She was amazed at just how easy it was to move from one world into the next, even in this reality. It had always been easy for her to drop into other worlds in her mind, but she never realised that switching worlds was equally possible and easy for her in real life.

It was a feeling of ultimate liberation.

After passing the immigration services counter and collecting their luggage in the hall for international arrivals, they walked out through the glass doors and were instantly hit with the warm night air.

There were many people outside holding boards with names or simply shouting, "Taxi," directing the words toward the people leaving the airport.

A young woman in a tight red suit and black high heels walked in their direction. She held a small piece of paper with their names on it. With a polite smile, she inquired, "Are you Akila and Katarina?"

They would later learn her name was Lina, a connection they had made through the charity that supported the children's home where Akila would spend her next few months as a volunteer.

It was chaos on the way into the city. The last remains of the usual Nairobi evening traffic still blocked off the roads. Colourful minivans and buses with blaring music, shiny lights, and loud horns cruised from left to right, overtaking traffic and speeding in front of the taxi Lina had ushered them into. Lina informed them that these vans and buses were part of Nairobi's public transport system and were generally referred to as "matatus." Young men responsible for collecting the fare from the passengers and attracting new customers were hanging out of the open doors, performing dangerous stunts whenever their vehicle slowed down to drop off or collect passengers.

Akila was amazed by the commotion–so much life everywhere, intermingling in a colourful order that seemed to elude her. She was confident she would be able to decipher it all in time.

Life in the children's home was simple, and Akila quickly got used to the physical labour. She jumped into her new environment with enthusiasm, eager to become a part of it rather than remaining a silent onlooker. This attitude made it easy for those around her to accept and appreciate her. Although she managed to fit in fairly well, it was obvious that she wouldn't spend the rest of her life in this Kenyan "upcountry" world. Nairobi remained on Akila's mind, and she wondered what it would take to make the city her next new reality.

Akila had spent almost two months in the children's home when she met Kamau for the first time. She had only ever heard the music he played when he came home from work late in the evenings. The sounds travelled through the air over the high hedge that separated the land Kamau's family owned from the children's home next door.

That day, she'd walked over to the next small town to visit the weekly market with one of her Kenyan colleagues. Akila was busy purchasing a bundle of passion fruits when her companion greeted a tall young man who stood in front of the next vendor buying tomatoes. After shaking his hand and introducing herself, she remained silent the rest of her time in the market and on the walk back to their tiny village. All she did was look at Kamau, who carried himself with what she would describe as an almost feminine elegance, which was a stark contrast to the other men Akila had come across. She was intrigued.

Slowly, carefully, they started to know each other better, though it all happened with few words. Kamau was a thoughtful and silent person who didn't speak a lot when in a larger group of people. So as their relationship progressed, Akila learned how to hear what he often expressed with his silence.

Higher learning

When Akila visited the university grounds in Nairobi for the first time, a deep longing formed inside her. This was her opportunity to make the city her own.

When she'd started her studies in Germany and visited the university in Bremen for the first time, she remembered feeling very differently. She felt intimidated. It was clear to her that it would be hard work to become part of this community. Everyone seemed to be running around with expressions of self-importance on their faces without the time to look anywhere but where they were going.

Here it was different. The bright sunshine on the lawn marked the centre between several large buildings housing different departments. Students on break spread their beautiful scarves and jackets on the dry lawn, which had the colour of straw and only displayed lush green in a few places closer to the buildings where shade was more prominent. To Akila, it seemed like paradise, studying in one of the cool classrooms and then sitting in the sunshine on the lawn to enjoy the warmth.

It was only by chance that Akila came across the paper pinned on the noticeboard of the Institute for African Anthropology. It was a small department that didn't even have an office on the main campus and was hidden in the depths of the National Museum. A new course was being offered with the title, "Gender and Development." The two words caught her attention, and she stopped to read more. Admissions were still open, and it hit her that this was exactly what she wanted to do.

Weeks later, she'd convinced both Katarina and Matthias that she had to give this a shot and had secured the admission letter from university and applied for her student visa. It was all a lot of work, but it went smoothly. She believed that was always a sign that she was on the right path, so she kept going.

Then it was October and Akila walked along campus to meet her classmates for the first time. They were all welcomed by the head of the department in his office. It was a small first class, but a diverse group. Among them was a young woman named Joyce. She was short and bubbly, seemed friendly with everyone right from the beginning, and made life look easy. As classes commenced, Akila and Joyce started to meet before classes and studied together. It was simple for them to relate to each other, so within a few weeks, their friendship had blossomed.

* * *

Kim In Su, known to everyone by the romanization of his name, "Insoo," stood next to his coach and observed the two contestants in the middle of the hall. It would soon be his turn to step into the centre of attention, and his entire body ached from the anticipation of the upcoming fight. He knew that he had to win, and he wanted to be ready for it.

When it was finally time and he stepped forward to face his opponent, his heart was racing and it was hard for him to get his breathing right. He could feel that his muscles were far too rigid, and he was scared that this meant that he wouldn't be able to do the moves correctly.

The other boy opposite him seemed calm and composed, like a true Judo master. How did he manage that? But was failure an option? Not really. His mother was watching, and his coach too, so he better pull himself together. All those thoughts rushed through him and then the fight began. He had no time to think anymore. All he could focus on was what his opponent was doing and the fear of being defeated. So he put all his energy into gaining control.

When it was finally over, he had the strange sensation that it had lasted an eternity and, at the same time, only a few seconds. The relief of it being over and the relief that he hadn't lost was so real that he almost broke into tears. He spotted his mother looking happy and excited in the background. She waved at him. Then he saw the pleased expression on his coach's face. Dread gripped him when he realised that he had to keep stepping into the centre and win.

* * *

Joyce looked at the slightly taller, curvy woman in front of her and wondered, like so many times before, what to respond. She cast a quick glance over at Akila who stood next to her, tall as ever, her dark blonde hair untidy and her face displaying a slight frown.

"Oh Joyce, it's crazy we meet here!" the other young woman exclaimed, stopping them on the way to their usual spot below a small acacia tree opposite the university's main library. Joyce smiled back at her and thought of how they had never really been close in high school, so why make such a scene now? She felt as if the woman's eyes were all over her, ripping her apart and analysing her measures, her clothes, her hair, and her skin. It was uncomfortable, and she felt itchy from head to toe.

"It has been ages," the woman went on, flipping back her silky, fake waterfall of black hair, displaying manicured nails. "What have you been up to? Wow, you totally grew! You got true hips! Life must be good with you gaining so much weight!" She grinned, flashing her white teeth.

Joyce kept her smile plastered to her face. No need to waste energy responding to this. "Nothing much. I just study here. . . ."

The lady focused her gaze on Akila, who looked at the sky. "And who is your friend?" she asked sweetly.

Akila's gaze travelled back to them and focused on Joyce's former high school mate, and before any of them could say anymore, Akila grabbed Joyce by the arm and led her past the woman, mumbling something about needing food.

Joyce looked at her with astonishment.

"Let's go buy some snacks and then we can come back and study," Akila said and directed Joyce across campus towards the main road so that they could get to the supermarket on the other side of the street.

About twenty minutes later as they sat in the shade of their acacia tree, Joyce couldn't stop herself. The other woman's comments had hurt her, and she had to let it all out.

The frustrating thing was that this had happened quite often of late. They'd run into several of her former acquaintances and friends from primary and high school–sometimes even family members–and they all seemed to have a go at her about her looks. They commented on her hair, on her hips, and on her buttocks. They commented on her skin and on how she had been so tiny before.

Was there something wrong with her that they had to always talk about her looks?

That was what Akila felt her friend was really asking, her question hidden in all the anger she unleashed after another such conversation had taken place.

And Akila was just as puzzled.

In her eyes, her friend was just right. She kept nodding as Joyce let out a cascade of words to release her rage. Akila thought that one talent her friend had was to unleash her frustration in so many words. It wasn't easy to find so many ways to say one thing. When Joyce finally slowed down for a moment, Akila told her, "I think it's because you look awesome. Don't let it get to you." But that seemed easier said than done, and deep down, she knew that too.

A couple of weeks later, Joyce walked into the supermarket across campus to get some water before she met up with Akila. Akila had been busy the entire day, and they'd agreed to meet shortly before class and chat just a little.

Suddenly, the woman with the flashy teeth and nails was right in front of her again.

"Oh, hi. . . ." Joyce forced a quick smile.

The other young woman pursed her lips and flipped her hair back in one fluid movement. "So, now you can talk to me? The other day you seemed quite distant. Or is it because you walk with that *Mzungu* now?"

Joyce stared at her, speechless for a second. *Mzungu* was a Swahili word for a Caucasian person. "Eh, no . . . I wasn't meaning to be distant," she found herself saying, still keeping the smile going.

"Ah. I thought for a moment you think you are special nowadays."

Joyce felt a sting in her heart.

"Anyway, I'm off," the other woman said, leaving her standing, dumbfounded, not sure how to feel.

As she paid for her water and walked toward campus, disgust crept up from deep inside her. Joyce wondered why she kept smiling. The comments about her relationship with Akila followed her.

While the two women accepted who the other was from the very first day they met on campus, there seemed to be something that others saw in their being together that unsettled Joyce and made her feel as if she had to be extra polite and careful. If not, people might say that she had turned into an arrogant brat because her friend was a *Mzungu*. They might say that she didn't know how to relate to "her own" anymore.

Over the early years of their friendship, Joyce heard all kinds of these or similar expressions, and it put a stop to her speaking her mind when, deep down, she felt that she should have just said it out loud. But she held her tongue and waited for her next meet-up with Akila to show how it hurt. Even then, she would vent her anger at the world, but what usually went unsaid was the part she felt she played in it by entertaining these comment-makers. Those were the thoughts she buried deep down inside herself.

* * *

Kang Ji Su stood in front of the class, wondering how he would get out of this situation.

It wasn't that he had wanted to cause trouble. It had simply happened. Now, his teacher was furious, and Ji Su felt a little uneasy while waiting for the announcement of his punishment. Would they inform his father this time?

It had always been hard for him to sit still through an entire day of lessons, and the restlessness he experienced was almost uncontrollable. On some days, his body would start itching, and keeping his feet or hands from tapping felt like it was the hardest thing in the world. There were other days when he found everything funny and his laughter could barely be contained. And his laughter was notorious, so it was better to shackle it and make sure that it wouldn't get out while he was in class.

Many days, he looked about him and marvelled at the useless things the teachers said and how everyone seemed to walk around with serious expressions on their faces as if there was nothing else other than this world of schoolwork. It was ridiculous. And this was how he'd felt for years now.

Would this chapter of his life ever be over?

Luckily, it was his mother who came to school to discuss the latest episode of her son's lack of discipline, like she'd done many times before. It wasn't that Ji Su didn't pass his tests. He did. But he was a disruptive force in class, and he didn't seem to be able to change.

"Maybe he needs another outlet," the teacher said. "Does he play any sports outside school?"

His mother nodded in affirmation.

Ji Su had tried all sorts of sports in his short life, but nothing had kept him entertained for very long, and nothing had helped with the almost unbelievable amount of energy the boy seemed to harbour inside him.

On the way home, Ji Su observed the thoughtful expression his mother wore. She hadn't even scolded him when they left the school. She had just sighed very deeply. Somehow that was the hardest punishment for Ji Su: the tired and disappointed look on his mother's face. Didn't she see that he didn't mean to make it difficult for her?

A week later, his mother picked Ji Su up from school on a Friday. When they finally got out of the car, they were in front of the dance and music school. It was the only institution of that kind not too far from his home and Ji Su had often wondered what was going on inside the building. From an early age, he'd enjoyed dancing and music, being the most excited during the plays in school.

His mother fixed her eyes on him and said, "I have arranged for dancing classes for you. Try it out and see if you can keep at it."

They entered the school, and Ji Su was instantly immersed in all the sounds that travelled towards him. It was a colourful and enticing concoction of noises that mesmerised him and made him want to know more. His mother briefly stopped at the reception to confirm where they had to go and then made sure her son followed her down the long corridor.

They found the room they'd been told to look for, and Ji Su's mother opened the door, indicating for her son to enter. Ji Su registered that there were already a couple of other boys his age. The lean man in front of the mirror on the other side of the room, whom he assumed to be the dance instructor, noticed them. When he recognized Ji Su's mother, he quickly came over, greeting her with an enthusiasm that surprised her son. Ji Su would not have guessed that his mother was friends with a young dance instructor, but then again, he did not know much about his mother's life before he was born and whom she was acquainted with outside of the family and few friends he had known all his life.

The first lesson was a catastrophe. The rest of the group had been practising for quite a while and were used to the instructions from their teacher. They knew most of the dance moves.

Ji Su knew nothing. For the entire lesson, he felt like he was just running, trying to catch up with the others. The instructor took some time to show him part of the steps, but still . . . it was just hard. By the time the lesson was over, Ji Su was tired. And infuriated. He had looked like an idiot the entire time. What was his mother thinking pushing him right into it without any prior warning?

When his mother picked him up, he walked past her, deciding that this wasn't the time to be nice. While walking away, he heard the instructor tell her, "He has the right energy, but I'm not sure if he has what it takes to keep going."

That comment really annoyed him.

Who said that he wasn't able to catch up? Who said that he couldn't be better than anyone else in that room if he only learned the moves? *Ha!* He thought to himself. *Let them talk.* He was going to show them.

So Ji Su started to practise, and he practised hard, sometimes to the point of total exhaustion.

His mother told him that he'd only be allowed to keep going if his marks remained stable and if there was no further trouble in school. He obeyed because Ji Su was hooked.

Over the next few months, he watched himself transform and couldn't help but be amazed. He became faster and stronger. His body became leaner, his muscles firmer. He became more focused with every lesson and the steps seemed easier with every practice that he completed. And he was sure that he would be unable to stop, no matter what.

* * *

Alan walked into the kitchen. Akila and Joyce were cutting fruits for their usual fruit salad, something they especially enjoyed when the passion fruit season was on and they could squeeze the sweet-sour juice with the crunchy seeds all over the other fruits.

Alan opened the fridge with a troubled expression on his face. Joyce had noticed right away that her elder brother was here to say something, and she already dreaded the moment he would open his mouth.

"Akila," he finally said, turning around and closing the fridge without taking out anything. "I haven't seen you at church."

Akila's movements slowed down for an instant before she looked at Joyce's older brother. "Yeah. It might not really be for me. . . ."

The young man was rather short, far from Akila's height. His hair was kept completely short as well, and Akila once mentioned to Joyce that she'd never seen a day when her brother wasn't dressed in a smart, official shirt, skin, and shoes shining equally from oiling. He had a handsome face, and the girls in the neighbourhood had crushes on him.

At Akila's response, his eyebrows went up. "God is, indeed, for everyone," he said.

Akila was quick to nod in agreement. She obviously didn't want to get into any discussions about religion and beliefs today. "Of course. . . ."

Joyce could see how her friend hesitated for another split second, then pressed her lips together and looked at her feet and the tiles on the floor.

"You two should really watch out how you behave," Alan went on, and Joyce's heart dropped. Would there ever be a week when her family wouldn't barge into her world?

Akila glanced at Alan. "As in?" she inquired. Joyce could see the spark of rebellion in her eye.

"Well . . . you two are always together. People might get the wrong idea. Some say you guys are actually. . . ." He made a pause, inhaling deeply. "Lesbians."

He said the word as if it were something that shouldn't be spoken of too loudly or too often.

The two young women stared at the young man by the fridge, then at each other. They could see the same astonishment mirrored on the other's face.

"So?" Akila had crossed her arms in front of her chest and straightened her back.

No stopping her now, Joyce thought, feeling slightly uneasy.

Alan fidgeted, realising that the atmosphere had shifted.

"What if we were? Would that be anyone's business?"

Alan's face fell apart. "This isn't right!" he exclaimed.

Akila let out a sarcastic laugh and turned her back on Joyce's brother, putting her hands on the front of the kitchen sink.

Joyce quickly put her hand on Akila's arm, signalling her that it was time to stop. She knew this wasn't going to end well.

"Alan, we're just friends, and you know that. There is no reason for any rumours."

"Joyce, they say that you don't like your own people. Don't get me wrong. You can be friends. But you don't have to only spend time with her." He motioned to Akila, who still stood with her back turned on him, gazing sideways at Joyce.

"I can't believe this is even a topic," Akila spat out.

"It *is* a topic. The way you people are and the way we are is different," Alan retorted.

Akila's eyes went wide and she focused on Alan with her unwavering glare. "You aren't serious," she pressed out.

She took a deep breath to add more, but Joyce quickly moved to stand between the two of them. "Enough," she said softly.

Akila looked down at her, anger on her face.

"Let's go to school now," Joyce added, grabbing Akila by her sleeve and pulling her to the kitchen door that led to the back of the house. She told her friend to put on her shoes and went quickly to pick up their bags from the living room.

Alan observed her without another word, barely making way for her when she put the untouched fruit salad into the fridge.

Joyce's stomach hurt with anticipation. She was sure that Alan would speak to their father. And she was sure that she would be in serious trouble for not avoiding the rumours about her being the "lover of a white woman."

Akila must have sensed that Joyce was worried because, on the way to the matatu stage, she put her arm around her friend's shoulder and squeezed her affectionately.

* * *

It was a hot Nairobi evening. Joyce and Akila had settled in for their class. Their lecturer, a short man with a shiny bald head, had just entered the room, looking rather exhausted.

For weeks, dust had been whirling on the streets, and whenever Akila and Joyce waited by the roadside for a matatu, they felt as if they had been covered with a fine layer of sand. "Do we live in a desert?" Joyce exclaimed that day while beating off some of the reddish-brown dust from her trousers. "I want the rains to come!"

Akila grinned at her friend and retorted, "Now you want the rain to come, and once everything is flooded and you get drenched every day, you want the dust back."

Joyce shot her an irritated glance, but Akila was right. The weather never seemed to be just right when you relied on public transport in this city. It was either the sun was beating down on your head like crazy or the rain was trying to wash you away.

Their lecturer had started his session, but like so many other times, he was off-topic. It was a unit about gender in African societies, but the man basically talked about everything but gender. Conspiracy theories were his biggest interest, and his class frequently glanced at each other in disbelief when he shared another of his intense opinions about the workings of the world.

While Joyce knew that there was definitely a seed of truth hidden below the uncountable layers of rubbish he spewed at them, it was hard not to get upset with the teacher for wasting their precious evening time like this.

"So, have you ever thought about why so many people go crazy in our society?" the lecturer asked them.

The class didn't respond. They all knew that he would provide the answer shortly.

"Well, all the biological weapons that the West has used on people in the Middle East release gases. We all know that."

Joyce sighed silently.

"And once these gases spread and reach here, people are affected. They go crazy."

Akila, being Akila, asked, "So how exactly do these gases reach all the way here?"

Their teacher replied, "It is all due to the winds. . . ."

Joyce looked briefly at her friend. She hoped that Akila would leave it at that.

The entire class shifted a little and exchanged glances, but no one else said anything or asked a question. They all sat and listened. Was this what higher learning was all about? Listening to some old man's delusions just because he was the senior and held the title "teacher?" Joyce wondered.

When she apparently could not take it any longer, Akila excused herself to visit the washrooms. The lecturer paused, and once Akila had left, he moved on, but with a lower voice. "You know, it's really difficult to talk openly when the enemy is around."

Joyce stared and couldn't believe what she had just heard. Was he talking about her friend? Joyce was irritated, but she also did not know how to change the situation. Calling him out on his unacceptable behaviour seemed too much for her.

So when Akila returned from the bathroom and settled down in her chair and their lecturer continued as if he had never made any remark about her being the enemy among them, Joyce remained silent and wished for the whole session to be over as fast as possible.

That same evening, when Akila and Joyce slowly walked across campus to get their matatu home, she wondered if she should tell Akila what had transpired in class. But what good would it do if her friend knew how their teacher was talking behind her back? It would probably just hurt her, and knowing Akila, this might spark a conflict that would probably do them more harm than their lecturer.

Joyce looked over at her friend and suddenly knew that she should tell her the truth. Akila had been the most open and non-judgmental person she had ever had in her life, and if she wanted this friendship to continue, there was a need on her side to be open as well.

She interrupted Akila, who was still trying to wrap her head around the fact that they had been told toxic gases travelled all the way to Nairobi by wind and affected their brains. "You know, today something happened when you went to the loo." Joyce sighed and put her arm around Akila's. "When you left, he spoke about how you are the enemy. . . ."

Akila's face changed. A moment ago, her features displayed confidence and a measure of disbelief. Now, there was first surprise, and then when Joyce's words slowly sunk in and their full meaning hit her, the young woman's face mirrored pain.

"I'm sorry. I wasn't sure if I should tell you, but somehow I thought you'd prefer to know."

Akila nodded.

"Don't think too much about it," Joyce said. "He is just a crazy old man."

Akila nodded again, and when Joyce looked up and noticed the glittering lines of tears on her friend's face, she held on tighter to her arm and patted her back softly as they continued to walk towards the street.

"Don't cry, don't let him get to you."

Akila cried silently and just kept nodding at whatever Joyce was saying.

* * *

Later, alone at home in the dark, Akila wondered what had made her cry like that. Joyce was right. The short man with almost no hair was simply frustrated and delusional and projected all of his issues on others. But still . . . wasn't there something that resonated deep inside when the man unleashed his unbelievable anecdotes? Wasn't the real question why this person even thought that he had the right to talk like that? Wasn't it what had really happened to this man's family during Kenya's occupation by the colonisers that had contributed to the present situation?

It was this strange combination of inferiority that this man seemed to feel towards her, a much younger woman, simply because of her skin colour and resentment for being exactly what she was. It was an extremely unsettling feeling because the things that played into it weren't things she could change, like gender or the colour of her skin.

Yes, Akila thought. It had tasted bitter to know that only the colour of her skin had turned her into an enemy in the older man's eyes. And, she finally admitted to herself, it had tasted even more bitter that no one, not even Joyce, had spoken up in her name when she hadn't been there to defend herself. It felt lonely and Akila wished for a chance to drop into another world and not think too much, but it turned out to be difficult to stop all the thoughts rushing through her.

Mama Ntilie

There was a middle-aged woman selling local food at the end of the avenue on which The University of Nairobi was situated. The avenue ended in the driveway of a big hotel that was mainly used by large buses with tourists who had come to enjoy the less costly version of a safari and beach stay in Kenya. The clientele that stopped here wasn't comparable to that of the famous Norfolk Hotel further up the street, opposite the entrance to the university.

Akila had chanced upon this opportunity for low-cost, but tasty local food one day when she decided to explore the end of the street, and a woman with a bright head scarf welcomed her cheerfully to one of her simple benches under a eucalyptus tree. As Akila was short on money, she became a frequent customer, happy to be able to enjoy a warm meal at least once a day.

It was a sunny, dry day when Akila arrived at the eucalyptus tree to order her meal on her way to university. Somehow, something was different, but she only paid attention half-heartedly as her head was full of thoughts of Kamau. She was planning to visit the children's home one of these weekends and already felt excited at the thought of seeing him again.

She stood, still in thought, and only then noticed that there was an excited buzz among the customers on the benches.

A tall, bald man with extremely long legs and a noticeable belly stood not far from her, chatting animatedly with the woman who sold food, but also frequently addressed the customers, who responded with loud laughter every time. Akila jumped out of her thoughts for a moment into her present reality and concluded that the guy must be someone important, which was the only way to explain the excited response from the people around.

The woman in the shiny headscarf scooped food onto a thin metallic plate and handed it over to the tall man.

She then recognized Akila and waved for her to come closer. "Sit, sit!" she exclaimed and showed Akila space on a bench right at the front. "Matoke as always?"

Akila nodded, and while she waited for her plate of tasty cooking bananas, she was already back in the other world, a world in which she spent the day walking through the forest with Kamau and sitting in a small hotel sipping hot, sugary chai.

It took a moment to realise that the bald man was talking to her.

"Yes?" she asked, still a little confused because she had been so deeply engrossed in her own thoughts.

"My name is Joseph. Do you act?"

She was even more confused. This question was totally out of the blue. "Eh . . . nope," she responded, already suspicious of the man. What did he want, flattering her with such a lame opening line?

"We are actors," he went on, pointing toward a short young man standing halfway hidden behind his own portly figure. "Why don't you come for auditions? We're always looking for new talent."

Akila stared at both men, trying to figure out what he was getting at.

He seemed to have realised that she didn't really trust him and cleared his throat with a small smile. "Come and check for yourself," he said. "There won't be any harm in that, right?"

Akila dipped her head to one side and looked at the two men. She was curious, but not in the conscious way many people experience when confronted with something new. Her mind was all over the place, so what happened next felt a little surreal.

"I'm Joseph," the tall man offered again, and they shook hands.

After they had all cleaned their plates, they walked through the old, rusted gate opposite the eucalyptus tree. Several other people came down a small paved path framed with dry yellow grass and covered in dust. Old houses that Akila suspected to have been staff quarters in the past dominated the terrain.

Everyone gathered in front of one such house. Old and young, men and women, maybe around eight in total, all chatted and gestured animatedly as Akila, Joseph, and the young man, whose name she didn't know, approached. They all turned to greet them, and then the group moved inside the house, which was completely empty except for a couple of simple wooden benches.

Akila was offered space on one bench and then looked around. A short man with thick glasses took the lead after the general noise of everyone settling in had died down.

"Good to see you all here today," he began with a broad smile. "Let's get started right away. Joseph has blessed us with a guest, and I would like to know more."

Joseph looked around and said, "Why don't you introduce yourself," addressing Akila without glancing at her.

She gave a small wave and smiled. "My name is Akila. Nice to meet you all."

"Hi, Akila!" came the response in many voices.

"Can you act?" the short man with glasses enquired.

Akila thought of her high school days and the time she had been part of the theatre group. She shrugged and responded, "Maybe a little."

"Let's see that little!" the short man called out and clapped his hands in excitement.

And just like that, Akila became part of the little group of actors and actresses who were the core of one of the most watched TV series all over Kenya. It was an old-school program focused on recent political and societal issues and happenings spiced up with loads of humour and improvisation.

While she worked as an actress, she never realised what opportunities all these connections she made through her acting might offer. Maybe it was because she lived too much in so many different worlds or because she was still young and her family was far away. Maybe it was also because Akila had a natural tendency to only talk about things that came easy off her chest and kept the darker, more complicated thoughts to herself. On top of that, she wanted to make her own decisions and wasn't ready to compromise based on what others thought.

Reminiscing about that many years later, Akila thought that many things might have been different or less exhausting for her if she hadn't chosen to always make up her mind on her own and go with the flow rather than discussing her choices with others. Nevertheless, she continued on the more rocky path that she had chosen.

Even when Akila turned out to be quite busy with all her acting engagements and evening classes in university, she found time to eat a meal below the eucalyptus tree every few weeks and enjoy the simple, tasty food.

The word no

Insoo's entire body was tense. He was drenched in sweat and his ribs hurt badly. But he had a competition coming up and there was no choice–he had to keep going in order to be ready. Still, he was truly tired today. And then there was the homework that he remembered he had to complete once he was done here. How would he manage it all?

The other day, his mother had told him that they could go slow with the Judo if it was becoming too much, but he had declined. Judo had been his world, and he didn't want to stop now. And when he'd said that, he noticed the satisfied expression on his mother's face.

She had ruffled his hair and hugged him affectionately. "Fine," she said. "But if it gets too hard, let me know."

Insoo had nodded, although he knew that he would never do so. His mother's face lit up every time he brought home great marks and every time he was recognized for his great Judo skills. He didn't want her to stop glowing because of him.

Suddenly, Insoo felt the ground slip below his feet, and within seconds, he'd been whirled through the air and slammed on the ground with his back first. He'd been distracted and hadn't seen the other boy's attack coming. All the air had been pressed out of his lungs, and he gasped for oxygen.

The coach appeared in his view. "Are you okay?" He frowned, obviously not pleased with Insoo being distracted. So Insoo gave a quick nod and made to stand up. But at that moment, the pain that shot through him was so intense that he let out a scream and fell back onto the ground.

Not much later, the ambulance had collected Insoo and he'd been rushed to hospital. He was unable to move and was still in pain. In the ambulance, he was scared and cried for his parents. They appeared not long after Insoo had been dropped at the emergency room. His mother looked so scared that he broke out in tears again. His father, who was always a very quiet person, gazed at him with tight lips and a troubled expression on his face. Then he walked away.

"Where are you going?" Insoo's mother called out to Insoo's father, almost hysterically. But Mr. Kim didn't react and left the room without a word. Mrs. Moon hugged her son, patting him on the shoulder. "Don't cry. Don't cry."

A moment later, Insoo's father was back, a doctor in tow. "In Su," he addressed his crying son calmly. "Tell us what exactly happened and where it hurts."

After that, his mother seemed to come back to her usual self. She exchanged one long glance with her husband, straightened herself, and then encouraged Insoo to calm down in the composed and strong manner that was so familiar to her son. It was a relief to see her like that, and he was able to slowly stop shedding tears and begin to talk about what had happened.

* * *

Insoo wasn't able to train for weeks, and he missed the tournament. Because he was growing fast and was quite tall with a rather straight spine, he had to be extremely careful not to injure himself permanently. It was a frustrating thing, not to be able to use his body as he was used to. For the first couple of days after Insoo was back at home, he was completely lost, wondering what to do with all the hours that were ahead of him. He'd never stopped to realise how much his life consumed him–how he was totally absorbed. Now, he had all this time in his hands.

One evening, his father entered his room in his usual silent way. He had just returned from the bookshop. Adjusting his glasses,

Mr. Kim sat down on the side of his son's bed. "How is it going?" he asked.

Insoo shrugged. "Okay, I guess," he said. What was he meant to say?

His father placed a bundle of books next to him on the nightstand. "This will help put your mind at ease a little," he mumbled. "You can escape for a while and visit many other places."

Insoo looked at the books and then at his father. Books seemed to be his father's answer to any question in this world. But what else would he do until he was fine again? In this case, his father was probably right. It was the best possible response to all his current troubles. So Insoo smiled at his father and picked up the first book to begin.

* * *

Akila had spent the day acting outside of the studio and still felt elated when they all decided to go for early dinner together. "Akila, you can join me," Joseph said, opening the door of his car for her. She smiled and joined Joseph in his vehicle. It had become quite a regular thing, Joseph giving her a lift after their acting engagements were over. It had also become a regular thing that they went for lunch together, and Joseph usually insisted on paying the bills. Akila accepted it all, enjoying the noisy and busy days with her fellow actors and actresses.

Joseph was a person used to attention and used to having his way. Wherever they went, he would be recognized and people would smile as they recounted his most memorable acting; by extension, Akila also felt the warmth of that attention. She was recognized in the supermarket or on the streets sometimes, but it was nothing compared to what Joseph received from the world. People glowed around him and flocked where he was to please him and to bathe in some of the aura he seemed to possess. Maybe they felt that their life would become a little less grey and a little more polished and glittery when they got a piece of him, even just a glance.

So Akila never said, "No," when Joseph offered that they spend time together.

When did it change?

Probably when she met Joseph's fiance the day they went for another shoot outside the studio. Looking at the older, beautiful woman with the baby in one arm and the toddler hiding behind her legs, she wondered how this person would feel if she knew how many times Akila rode in the passenger seat of her fiance's Mercedes. Nothing physical had ever happened between them, but Akila had to admit that she and Joseph had also never corrected the comments people made about them looking great together. She had told herself that it didn't matter because she wasn't interested anyway. But on the day she met Joseph's wife-to-be, something shifted.

She went home feeling uneasy and told herself that it would probably be better if she avoided the free rides and lunches with him.

* * *

Insoo sat in the locker room alone with his head in his hands and his eyes closed. For weeks, he'd been working on getting back on his feet, being able to move as he wanted with ease and without pain. He'd eventually succeeded, and now he was back to training.

And he was scared.

He was scared that the pain would come back and that he wouldn't be fine if he was injured again. The thought had never featured while he had worked to become whole again. While he had done all the physiotherapy, his mind had been dominated by the thought of being mobile again. But now that he'd reached that goal and it was all about climbing to the top where he'd been before, he was paralyzed by the fear of feeling the pain again. It consumed him and made it impossible for him to flow through the Judo movements as he'd done before. The realisation that his body wasn't as invincible as he'd assumed was intense and completely unexpected.

After the first training session, he'd seen how far he'd fallen. Everything seemed hard for him. It hurt his pride and increased his fear. So, for the next few days, he milled over how he would tell his mother and his coach that he didn't want to go on.

But he never said anything.

When his mother called, "Insoo, finish your homework now. Remember, you have practice later!" Or when she drove him to the training centre. Or when his coach discussed his plan to bring him back to where he had been. He never said, "No! I don't want that. I'm scared."

And as the days went by, it became easier. The pain didn't come back and his movements became fluid like before.

But deep down, it felt different.

Before, Insoo jumped into the fight with nothing but the determination to avoid losing. He now steeled himself against the possibility of pain. So sometimes, like today, he had to sit down in a quiet place before starting his training and pull himself together.

* * *

There was a funeral being arranged for one of their fellow actresses' late father. He had been unwell for quite some time and an unbelievably high hospital bill had to be cleared along with arranging the burial. The group was coming together to collect contributions, and Joseph was in charge of the collections.

After the meeting, Akila approached him outside the building. Their relationship had shifted along with her feelings. They were meeting far less these days, and Joseph made a point of ignoring her. It was probably difficult for him to understand exactly what had happened, and Akila had no words to express what was inside her. Maybe that was because, from the beginning, they'd never expressed what sort of relationship it was they had.

It was strange, this feeling of gratitude she had towards him for encouraging her to join him for the auditions. She felt grateful for all the amazing experiences and the fun and happiness that had come with that one moment when she decided to follow him. But she couldn't ignore the fact that her gratitude was mixed with fear for what might be underneath it all–and what was to come, now that she kept her distance and declined his rides and offers for food.

What added to it was that being completely honest with herself, she had to admit that she felt a pinch of regret when he slowly stopped paying for her lunch or gave one of the pretty supporting actresses a lift instead of her. She hated herself for not being able to let the comfort that came with being close to him go so easily.

What strange combination of feelings was that? Was something wrong with her? Or was it because, somehow, with the appearance of his fiance and children in her world, she realised that there was more involved than just them? People didn't see two humans–they saw a man and a woman. Suddenly sexuality was involved where Akila hadn't noticed it previously.

On the day of the Harambee to collect the contributions for their colleague, Akila felt a particularly strong sense of unease. Joseph didn't even greet her, and when she approached him to discuss how she would send her contribution via phone later on, he seemed irritated. It made her sad to see him hurt, which again, was a feeling that seemed to complicate the situation.

In an effort to make amends, she offered, "Why don't we have lunch one of these days? And for my contribution, I'll send it to you via phone now."

He stared at her with his dark, intense eyes that he used well when he acted. She braced herself for a sarcastic retort, but he seemed to have noticed the softer and more accommodating change in her tone.

"I have a meeting right now but will be done in two hours. I'll pick up the cash on my way home. It's on the way anyway."

"I can just send it to you."

"It's no big deal. It's not even a detour. I'll call you when I get there." And with that, he was off.

About two hours later, Joseph parked the car on the side of the unpaved road outside the compound where Akila was living in a tiny, one-room house. She realised again how tall he was when he followed her inside the small room. Akila picked up the money from the table next to her bed and turned around to hand it over to him.

Suddenly, his presence seemed overpowering, and she wanted to minimise the time they spent alone here. His face was cold and his eyes intense, just like earlier–or at least that was how she experienced them when she looked at him. Her heart pounded as she thought how large he was, and his body blocked the way to the door.

"Here's the cash. . . ."

He didn't even glance at the notes in her hand. "So I come here all the way and you don't even offer me anything?"

She already felt trapped, and his comment confused her. She couldn't think properly, and without any notice, all there was inside her was fright.

"What if I take what I want?"

She was speechless. He was closer than she wanted, but maybe it was because the room was so tiny. "What do you want?" she eventually asked. She realised how weak her voice sounded.

He snorted with disbelief, grabbed the notes from her slightly shaking hand, and walked out.

It took a while before she was able to move. She stood there in her small house with her hand on the left side of her chest. Her heart gradually slowed down as she sat down on her bed, willing herself to inhale and exhale slowly. Why had she even agreed to meet him at her house? She wondered why she hadn't said, "No," and sent the money to him.

The next shoot in the studio felt even more uncomfortable than the few before. Was it in her head, or was he much more aggressive toward her? He only made comments that made her feel smaller. She took it all without a word but wished for it to go away. Without his attention and warmth around her, the studio suddenly seemed much shabbier and everyone much more distant than before. She felt vulnerable.

It was almost time for the second set of recordings for the newest episode after a short break they had taken when she stopped him in the corridor before the heavy swinging door leading back to the studio. "Are you upset with me?"

He gave a short, bitter-sounding laugh.

"Wait. Why does this feel like I did something wrong?" She didn't like that it almost sounded as if she was pleading. So she took a deep breath and looked straight at him.

"Yeah, why do you think that is?" he snapped.

Was it that her more confident attitude at that moment pushed him even further?

They moved aside to let a few crew members who were on their way back to the studio pass. Then he opened one of the swing doors to walk away.

She followed, irritated with his behaviour. "Stop behaving as if I did something wrong! You're the one with a fiance and children!"

Now they were both in the small space between the two sets of heavy swing doors that kept all unwanted noise from the studio that had all swung shut. He turned towards her and pressed her against the small piece of wall. His one hand was suddenly between her legs, grabbing her. "Do you think I am just something to play with? Is that fun?" he spat out.

Again, she was silenced by the sheer force of his body and emotion coming at her.

The next second, he moved away and disappeared through the swing doors into the studio.

She stood for a long moment, just staring at the patch of wall between the doors. Then two of her fellow actors filed into the space, laughing loudly. She jumped into motion, put a smile on her face, and joined them.

Akila didn't speak with anyone about what had happened, but she gradually pulled out of the program and all the related live shows as well, often saying that she had other commitments.

About six months later, she received a call from one of the actors she had been closest to. Akila hadn't seen most of them for months, just occasionally bumping into some of them in the city centre.

"Akila, sweetie!" the melodious voice on the phone shouted. "Joseph is finally getting married! Come and join us to celebrate. I am picking you up on Saturday."

The ceremony was to take place in one of the old churches in Karen, surrounded by tall trees and rather lush greenery.

The crowd was large, the parking lot packed to the point of chaos. Getting out of the car with the other actors and actresses, Akila looked around in astonishment–but then again, she wouldn't have expected anything less grande from him.

The ceremony was about to start and everybody was heading inside. It was a long service, and by the time it was all done, Akila was hungry. She had wondered how she would feel seeing him there with his wife after everything that had transpired. But she felt surprisingly calm and unmoved by it all and was even able to enjoy spending time with the crew after such a long time.

After the ceremony, everyone slowly filed out of the church in order to move on to the reception, which was set on expansive lawns not far away. Children ran across the parking lot, shouting and singing, relieved to be free after such a long time inside the church building. Old women in headscarves and long dresses gathered to take the provided matatus to the reception, and pretty-looking girls in high heels and figure-hugging short dresses entered cars, chatting and giggling excitedly. Golden sunlight was glossing over the scenery.

It was all quite nice, Akila decided. She turned to wait for her company when her gaze caught Joseph, who came towards them from behind the building. He was accompanied by two younger men dressed in smart suits with white roses pinned to their left chest who had been part of the lineup. "You are all here!"

There was a happy buzz as everyone congratulated the groom.

Akila stood in the back. Then, when everyone had quieted down a little, she also stepped forward and said, "Congratulations."

He glanced at her and responded, "It should have been you."

There was silence for a second, and the crew looked at their feet, not really knowing what to say. The two young men with Joseph seemed quite embarrassed. One of the older actresses smacked her tongue to show her disapproval of his comment, and Akila felt like she'd been physically hit by the statement.

But Joseph was already moving on, telling everybody to meet at the reception, and walked away with the two men in suits in tow.

Akila didn't join the others for the reception. She had the feeling that she couldn't bear to look at the bride, who would be smiling and pretty without knowing her husband had been telling someone else that she should have been in her place. Sitting in the matatu on the way home, Akila felt her chest tighten with sadness, but also with anger at herself for always remaining silent when this large man threw overwhelming comments at her. Why had she never really said, "No"?

Much later in life, Akila thought that her experience with Joseph shaped how she viewed the relations between men and women, and she was sure that it had an impact on what she sought for herself.

* * *

Ji Su ran. He was running faster than he'd ever run in his life before, or at least that was what he imagined. His feet hit the asphalt below him, and he could feel his heart pumping blood through his body with every step he took. He felt how his muscles were taut to the point of snapping, and he told them to move even faster than before. It was dark outside and there were already fewer people on the road, but still, there were onlookers casting glances his way as he sprinted past, sweat dripping down his face and neck.

The evening had begun like many others, with his mother preparing their meal, and the entire house had been blessed with the smell of a variety of savoury, spicy, hot and cold banchan, including his favourite fried fish.

Ji Su had been in his room, finishing some of the homework he hadn't managed to do earlier because of his daily workout.

Ji Su's aunt had been alone in the living room, slowly brushing her chin-length black hair which was already streaked with grey. She brushed her hair many hours each day with a vacant look on her face. Ji Su had grown up with that look, so it didn't affect him, but when he was younger, he'd noticed how uneasy his friends were around his aunt and had stopped bringing them home. It was better to separate the two worlds anyway.

When his father wasn't around, life was simple in their house, but sometimes he turned up unexpectedly and there were many things he didn't like.

Again, today, Ji Su was running like the wind because there were many things his father didn't like–like his son, who didn't follow his father's instructions and had been a trainee to become a musician and actor rather than learning how to take over the family business. Ji Su still wasn't sure how his father had found out, and it didn't matter now. His father had come home in a furious state of mind, and the meal that Ji Su's mother had already set on the table for them had come crashing onto the floor in a commotion that left Ji Su feeling paralyzed and sent his aunt whimpering into the farthest corner of the living room.

It was his mother who had stopped his father from getting physical with him. Ji Su knew that. She had stepped into the space between them and taken the slap that was meant for him.

Normally, CEO Kang was careful to not touch his wife when furious because she was the reason for his riches. She was the youngest daughter of the man who had built the company he was heading now, and without her, he might never have gotten to where he was today. So the slap she took for her son terrified Ji Su even more. But instead of taking a step forward and making sure that his father's anger was redirected at him, he turned around and left the house. Running. When he felt that he should have shouted at his father. When he knew that he should have told him, "No!" with all his might.

In the end, it was always the same. In the end, he returned home.

Although Kang Ji Su told himself every time that he wouldn't return, that he would stay away and not let his father control his life anymore, he didn't stick to it. He couldn't do that to his mother.

But was his mother truly the reason? If so, why did it feel so bitter to open that door again and walk back into the house?

Just like now. He removed his shoes in the entrance and then moved silently across the dark space through the empty living room, where the mess on the floor had been cleared, and into his room. Without changing his clothes, he lay down on his bed and stared into the shadows on the ceiling for a long time.

He must have fallen asleep eventually because the next thing he was aware of was the sunlight that floated across his room. Everything glittered with millions of particles that drifted in the beams of warm light. He thought about how beautiful the sight was, then turned onto his belly to check the time and leaped out of bed almost immediately. He would be late for practice!

Then he remembered he'd been found out, and there was no way he could go to practice today. He dropped back onto his bed and covered his face with both of his hands. What was he meant to do?

He heard the door open and someone walked quietly into his room.

"My son," his mother said softly. "Why are you still in bed? Don't you have practice today?"

He slowly removed his hands from his face and looked up at his mother. She stood in front of him, perfectly dressed, as always, with her hair shiny and her face glowing. Only today he thought that he could see the mark on her cheekbone that her makeup could not entirely conceal. Or was it all in his head?

She smiled at him and went on. "For now, you continue with practice. If you do well, you will have a little more of a breather."

Ji Su wanted to tell her that he wanted more than just a breather, but he kept his mouth shut. He knew that she had played almost all her cards to get her husband's approval so that her son could go on with his training.

"You look terrible," his mother said. "Get up and shower. You're already late."

Ji Su stared at the tiny woman in front of him. Then he went to get ready for the day. When he passed his mother, she briefly put her small hand on his shoulder.

And so it was, again, that Ji Su didn't say, "No," and lived with the constant awareness that he'd been granted a breather.

Sometimes he would look at himself in the large mirror of the practice room and wonder why he didn't stop. Still, he practised hard every day and never slowed down.

The smell of fear

It was early in the year, and the presidential elections had turned parts of Kenya into a battlefield. The conflict was described as a war between the two main ethnicities in the country, but Akila thought that it was about so much more—about the trauma and implications of colonial history and the distribution of land and other resources and about capitalism. It was scary to be in the middle of it, with gunshots ringing through the night, with news about the latest outbreaks of fights, and the feeling that anything could happen anytime.

By now, Akila and Kamau had moved in together. Kamau drove a matatu to earn money while Akila finalised her studies and occasionally acted. Where they lived, most residents came from Central Kenya. One day, Kamau came home in the evening from work and said, "I think it will be quiet at night from now on."

Akila looked at him with surprise. "How do you know that?"

"Mungiki have taken over all the matatu and bus stops. They are controlling the area. No one will dare start anything here."

Akila stared at him in disbelief. "What? They have openly come out?"

Kamau shook his head. "Not really openly, but if you check carefully, you can spot them everywhere."

Akila sighed. The sect mainly comprised people from Central Kenyan regions and was feared for its violence and focus on all sorts of criminal activities. The fact that the group was taking over the area made her feel shaky as if something much bigger had been set in motion and no one would be able to tell how this would end.

Kamau sat next to her on the couch, a thoughtful expression on his face. Eventually, he said, "I think it makes sense to close the business for a while and travel upcountry."

She searched his face for a hint as to how serious it was, but if he was as worried as she was, he kept it all well hidden. "When?"

"As soon as possible. I will speak to my mum tomorrow. We can stay at her place."

A few days later Akila and Kamau were heading in the direction of Mt. Kenya, leaving Nairobi behind. She had said her good-byes to Joyce, who was also leaving with her parents and brothers to stay with their grandparents near Nanyuki. They weren't sure when they would meet again, which was a weird feeling.

Along the highway, there were trucks of policemen wearing helmets and holding batons stationed at several spots. Otherwise, there were very few people walking, but there were many buses, matatus, and private vehicles on the road heading out of the city. Most were heavily loaded as families moved away from the conflict, not wanting to leave their possessions behind.

The future was too uncertain.

Akila spotted several columns of smoke over the rooftops further away as they sped along the highway, and she hoped that there hadn't been more casualties.

When they were almost in Thika, they had to slow down because the highway was so crowded with vehicles, and they soon came to a complete halt. Akila's heart was beating a little harder than usual, and she wondered what was causing the traffic. Kamau leaned out of the window and addressed the conductor of a bus next to them who was leaning on the side of the colourfully painted vehicle and had just finished a call with someone further down the line of traffic.

There was a huge roadblock as vehicles were searched, and some people had been pulled out and beaten up. No one seemed to know what the policemen were searching for or who would be in danger and who would not.

Akila and Kamau looked at each other. Kamu said, "Let's just do it. This is the only way."

Akila nodded, inhaling deeply. No reason to fear, she told herself.

The many vehicles on the road inched forward. There was music from several buses and matatus as people opened the windows to get some relief from the increasing heat while they waited in the sun. Conductors stood in small groups talking.

When they seemed to be quite close to the roadblock (it was hard to see because of all the heavily loaded roofs of vehicles in front of them), there was suddenly commotion ahead. Women screamed and men shouted.

On the left side of the road, a young man covered in blood was stumbling, apparently running away from where the police were.

Kamau, carefully observing the young man coming closer, said, "I know him. He was working for Peter at the car wash."

Akila couldn't take her eyes off the young man. He was maybe eighteen, slim, and lanky. He must have been hit on the head, which was why his face, neck, and shoulders were covered in blood. "They might kill him. Do you think he has done something?"

Kamau, still staring at the youth, shook his head. "I don't know, but I know him to be a good guy."

Akila took her eyes off the scene and looked at Kamau. They exchanged a quick glance. Then Kamau looked at the back of their matatu, which had not loaded passengers today, but held several bags, food they had bought, and clothes and blankets.

Without a word, Akila climbed into the back of the vehicle. Kamau put the car in first gear, slowly inching forward with the rest of the traffic. Women seeing the young man from their windows were exclaiming, some wailing in sadness, others wondering what he might have done to end up like this. Men who stood outside on the road moved out of his way, looking troubled.

"What's his name?" Akila asked.

"Mike."

When the stumbling figure was close, Akila let the sliding door on the side of their black matatu pop open and called out to him.

At the sound of his name, Mike stopped for a moment, obviously not expecting to hear anyone calling him. He glanced around in confusion and then spotted the black matatu not far from him with the open door.

The traffic moved again.

Mike started trotting, then grabbed the doorframe and got in. Instantly, Akila slammed the door shut.

Seconds later, three policemen passed them, but no one pointed a finger.

Akila sat in the front passenger's seat again and the back was filled with their luggage, hiding the fact that there was now a third passenger on board.

When they finally reached the roadblock, Akila's heart beat so hard in her chest that she felt sick.

The policemen carried rifles and pulled several buses and vehicles out of traffic, and they were parked on the side of the road. With relief, Akila noted that there were no more bleeding people. Somehow she had almost expected scenes of violence. Instead, there hung an eerie silence over the roadblock with drivers switching off the music and passengers stopping their conversations, not wanting to provoke anyone.

A large policeman with a big belly pressing against the blue of his uniform walked up to Kamau. He greeted him in Kikuyu and Kamau responded in kind. Another policeman glanced into the back of the matatu through Akila's open window.

Kamau was explaining where they were headed. From the way the two men addressed each other, Akila suspected that he knew the police officer. They exchanged a few more words, then the officers stepped away from the vehicle and they were given the sign to pass the barrier.

Akila closed her eyes and slowly let out her breath. Just after the roadblock, vehicles picked up speed, and soon the road was clear ahead of them as they flew along the hot tarmac.

They dropped Mike off at the big junction in Makutano. He had wiped the blood off his skin and wore one of Kamau's clean shirts. Akila had bought a bandage and disinfectant in a pharmacy. After cleaning the cut on Mike's head, she covered it with the bandage and put one of Kamau's woollen hats on top to make him look less conspicuous. The whole procedure hadn't taken long, and they hadn't asked about what had transpired and why he had been in trouble.

The young man reassured them that he had a safe place to stay, an aunt's place not far from Nanyuki.

Akila looked at Mike in the side mirror as they pulled away from the side of the road in the direction of Embu. He raised one hand by way of goodbye, and she wondered whether it was the right thing to do, to let him go like that.

The further Akila and Kamau drove and the closer they were to Mt. Kenya, the less tension there was. It was strange that one place could be in the grip of a serious conflict and, just a few hours drive away, it was as if nothing was going on and people went about their business as usual. *The paradox of human life,* she thought, looking at the rice fields they passed which shone in the blazing sunshine. Donkeys slowly pulled carts in the heat of the day, and when Kamau pulled over to buy rice in one of the villages along the way, hawkers came running with fresh fruit, onions, and tomatoes to sell.

The next few weeks were almost surreal to Akila. The weather was amazing and they spent their days hiking in the surrounding forests and fields and up to the near-sacred hill and waterfall. It was beautiful and peaceful.

If there hadn't been the news on TV every evening or updates received from friends and Kamau's relatives from other parts of the country, they could have fooled themselves that nothing was going on—that this was just a long break they took from the reality of city life.

But it wasn't so.

There was news of thousands of people already displaced, of homes burned, and of neighbours entering the homes next to theirs and killing families. The killings seemed to be out of control, and the rest of the country seemed to be holding its breath and stuck with the smell of fear in everyone's nostrils.

* * *

Mrs. Moon put down the phone with shaky hands. For a long moment, she was unable to move. She raised her eyes to the sky. "Please," she mumbled, then looked down at her phone. What was she meant to do?

Call her husband. Yes. First step. Then the second step–go to the hospital. Her son was there. It had happened again. Was she meant to feel guilty about the fact that she hadn't stopped him when he injured himself last time? Probably. She dreaded the moment she had to look at him and into the eyes of her husband.

She called Mr. Kim. He picked up after the third ring. "We need to go to the hospital. Insoo is there," she said without any further delay.

"Where are you?" he asked. After a brief pause, he said, "I am picking you up."

He had most likely sensed that she was in no position to drive, she thought to herself after hanging up. That was who he was in her life. The stabilising force.

When they got to the hospital, Insoo looked tired, although not in the same poor state he had been in after the first injury. His eyes were dry, and he was able to give a clear account of what happened. Coach Min was with him.

"Mother, I'll be fine. Don't worry too much," he said to her, patting her hand reassuringly. She wondered who the adult was.

The injury wasn't as serious as Mrs. Moon had feared when she first got the call. After a much shorter break, Insoo was back at training. Mrs. Moon felt a strong sense of relief, remembering how the smell of fear had coloured everything the day she had gotten the call.

But things weren't truly settled once Insoo got better.

There was Mr. Kim's face when he came home from his book-shop one evening and found his son had gone back to training. Mr. Kim had never been a man of many words, and even that evening, he didn't speak his mind. Nevertheless, Mrs. Moon saw that something was working inside of him, and, knowing her husband, she was sure that it was just a matter of time for it to surface and for her to be confronted with it. The certainty that something was brewing that had to do with Insoo brought back the smell of fear, although she wasn't sure why.

* * *

Ji Su bounced along the street on his way home after practice. His head was full of dance moves and the thought of the maths homework he still had to complete before he could call it a day.

He entered through the gate, opened the front door, and froze when he saw the two pairs of polished leather shoes that stood neatly arranged next to each other in the corridor. His heart sank. His father was home.

Ji Su stood unmoving for a moment, wondering what to do. He wasn't in the mood to be confronted with the disappointed and often angry expression his father wore on his face whenever they met. Should he leave?

His mother had heard him and came into the corridor to tell him to wash up and join them in the living room. His grandfather was there too.

So that was why there were two pairs of shoes.

Ji Su let out a frustrated sigh, although he didn't argue with his mother. He walked into the small bathroom at the end of the cor-ridor to wash his hands, neck, and face. He gazed at himself briefly in the bathroom mirror, arranging his hair a little, not wanting to acknowledge the smell of fear that welled up inside of him.

When he stepped into the living room, his grandfather sat on the sofa, his eldest daughter, Ji Su's aunt, next to him. The tiny woman seemed stiff with discomfort, the knuckles on her hands white from grabbing the fabric of her long, simple dress with all her might as if she needed something, anything to keep her steady. She had put as much space as possible between herself and her father. Her large, dreamy eyes, "owl eyes" as the neighbour's children liked to say, were focused on her feet as if there was the most interesting discussion going on between her and her toes.

Ji Su felt sorry for her. He knew that she preferred to be by herself and that she didn't react well to sudden human contact, especially when her father and brother-in-law were involved.

Ji Su bowed politely and greeted first his grandfather and then his father. The two men had been in quiet conversation when he entered the room, sipping tea as they talked. Ji Su hated it. The white collars and dark suits. The lowered voices. The self-importance and ignorance that seemed to be written all over such scenes. It was suffocating in every sense of the word.

Ji Su's grandfather let his gaze travel all over him, making Ji Su feel even more like he wanted to run. The old man was short and of small build, which did nothing to diminish his natural authority. Wrinkles covered his face, especially around his eyes–eyes that Ji Su had been told many times he'd inherited–and made them appear even more beautiful.

Ji Su often asked himself what he was meant to feel for this man who had built a successful company from nothing, who had dedicated his life to business growth, and who made decisions that were in line with the company's needs. Ji Su had never felt anything other than discomfort around him.

Just like with his father, Ji Su sensed early on in his life that he wasn't allowed to be himself around his grandfather, and, even today, he knew that he was expected to say what would please him and not what was really inside him. He lowered his head and bowed even deeper.

"There you are," the old man said, waving his hand slightly, a gesture to communicate that his grandson should sit down with them. Ji Su took a seat and avoided looking at his father, who sat across from him.

His mother entered the room soundlessly, as was her habit, and placed a few dishes on the low table between them. She shot a quick glance at Ji Su, but he was unable to decipher what she wanted to say. All he wanted was to be free of the suffocating feeling that gnawed at him.

"I hear you have been getting good marks."

Ji Su kept his eyes on his hands that rested in his lap. He nodded slightly.

"That is the basis for faster success in life, so you keep studying," the old man continued.

Ji Su nodded again, still focused on his hands.

"And I understand that dancing helps you with your energy. That is good too. A man needs to be level-headed at all times."

Ji Su gave a third slight nod. An image came to his mind from a time when he had been small, running and rushing, bursting with energy all the time. There was a day when his grandfather had been around, discussing matters with his son-in-law in the living room. Despite his mother's warning, Ji Su had opened the door and ran into the room. The two men paused their conversation and looked at him with expressionless faces. Ji Su still remembered the laughter he'd sent up to the ceiling while his mother stood by the door and begged him to come back. The whole ordeal had ended with broken glasses and plates, which his father threw at his wife while shouting, missing her only by inches, telling her that she was unable to respect him and unable to keep her own child under control. Ji Su had sat next to his aunt during the episode, his entire body rigid with fear, fear that had the stench of something slowly burning. They had had no choice but to watch, too scared to make a move.

The picture welled up in Ji Su now while responding to his grandfather's comments with another nod of his head. Again, Ji Su asked himself why this man accepted that his daughter stayed with a man like CEO Kang. Why? He was unable to make any sense of it.

His attention returned to the room and his grandfather's soft words. "Sooner or later there will be no time for your fun activities when you join your father at the company."

Ji Su didn't nod this time and continued to stare at his hands. When the silence between them became almost unbearable, Ji Su's father said, "Of course, we will plan everything well and, eventually, he will be ready to learn what he needs to know."

Ji Su observed how the knuckles on his hands turned white when he grabbed his jeans with all his might, just like his aunt was doing not far from him on the sofa. He pressed his lips together to ensure that he didn't speak. Something hot and heavy moved in his chest, and he was scared that it would press his thoughts out through his mouth and into the living room.

The evening ended as Ji Su had anticipated, with broken pieces of plates and cups and his mother on her knees on the floor collecting the sharp-edged pieces with an unmoving face. A small cut was on her throat where a small shard of ceramic had hit her when a plate smashed against the wall behind her. A drop of blood slowly made its way down to her collarbone. Ji Su's aunt was still sitting in one corner of the living room, halfway hidden behind the large couch. Her eyes were big and filled with confusion and fear. Her low whimpering made Ji Su's heart ache.

CEO Kang had gone to bed, and they knew that he wouldn't come out until the next day when it was time for breakfast early in the morning.

After looking down at his mother on the floor for a long time, Ji Su dropped to his knees next to her and started collecting the larger pieces so that they could sweep up the rest with the broom.

"Don't," his mother said quietly and gently touched his wrist with her small hand. Ji Su lifted his head to glance at her, and there suddenly seemed to be a confrontation in the air. He realised that anger boiled below the fear inside him.

His mother stared at him with wide eyes, her sadness jumping at him and making Ji Su want to cringe. Why did he feel guilty around her?

He was unable to stop the words tumbling out of his mouth, maybe because he hadn't spoken while his grandfather was still in the house. He was unable to stop the flood of anger that washed over him, gripping him and pulling him away into the ocean of emotions that he'd been fighting hard to keep under control, but that sometimes, like today, turned into a stormy sea that could barely be contained.

"What do you want me to do?" he asked, voice shaky. "I can't be who they want me to be. Maybe you can pretend to be okay. . . ." He gestured in the general direction of his parent's bedroom while shooting his words at her, knowing he was hurting her. He saw how she kept her feelings locked up inside her every day, how she fulfilled her father's and her husband's expectations, never uttering a single word of disagreement. And still, he'd seen that she had once been a different person, someone with dreams and talents and ideas in her mind. He'd seen it the day she'd taken him for his first dance class. She'd walked along the corridors with a light step, swinging her hips ever so slightly. A totally different woman.

"Why don't you fight?" he asked, his voice rising. "Why can't you be a rebel? Just do something, anything, to show you are not fine!"

He was burning, the smell of fear in his nose. Her eyes sparkled with the tears that had welled up, but before Ji Su could see them fall, she turned away from him and quickly walked to the bathroom. Ji Su heard the door lock, and an instant later, loneliness flooded through him, taking all of his energy away. With his last strength, he stumbled to his room and dropped onto the blankets on his bed.

Talida

The year Talida was born, Tarrus Riley's "Superman" turned into one of Akila's most-played songs. To her, it was a masterpiece and, along with music from Erykah Badu and Joss Stone, this was the song that she listened to most when she carried her tiny bundle of life in her arms. She had gotten pregnant amid Kenya's turmoil and often wondered why she hadn't stuck with her conviction that it made little sense to bring a child into this world. On the other hand, maybe this new spark of life would make a difference.

She'd been in her senior year at university and was eager to finalise her studies as her belly grew, and she'd immersed herself in her gender studies and spent her mornings listening to music and going through university materials. She wanted to make sure to conclude her studies with great marks.

Akila declined all offers for acting now, but when Nick, one of the directors she had worked with on two movies, called her to have lunch, she agreed. They sat in the garden of his little cottage on a sunny day.

"Children, why have them?" he asked between bites of fresh salad. "I feel we throw them into such a disturbing world and they are so much work."

Akila smiled at him. "I used to think the same. When I was young, I said I would never have children, because the world is just too horrible."

Nick took a large sip of water. "What changed?" he asked, then stopped and looked at her. "You talk like you're my age. Akila, you are only twenty-four. Don't sound too grown up–you still have time."

"Just saying," she responded, looking out at the greenery surrounding them.

Nick leaned back in his seat, observing her. "How will you make it work?'

She sighed and then focused back at him. "I guess I need a real job now," she said, only half joking.

Two weeks later, Nick called her again.

"There's this guy I usually bike with," he said. "He's desperately looking for German speakers who don't plan to leave Kenya soon. He works in tourism. I passed on your number."

The same day, Akila received the call and, a few seconds into the phone call, she had a date for an interview. Akila's heart was beating fast. She felt that this was one of those moments in her life when something was set in motion. Then she called her mother to prepare for the interview.

Shortly after that, it was early morning on the date the first doctor she'd seen for her pregnancy had calculated as the due date. It was dark outside and the usual crazy morning traffic into Nairobi city centre hadn't started yet. Akila woke up and knew that it was time to go to the hospital. She could feel a faint pulling inside her. She woke Kamau, and they hurried as much as they could to avoid getting stuck on the road.

When Joyce called later that afternoon to check on her, like she did whenever she wasn't able to go see her in person, Akila picked up the phone after a few seconds. Her voice rang with excitement. "Joyce! I just gave birth to a little girl!"

Later, this was one of the stories Joyce loved to tell most–how Akila had literally just given birth and was still being cleaned up by the nurses but was high on such an adrenaline rush that she had the energy to pick up her phone and talk to her friend.

* * *

Ji Su looked at the screen for a long time. He refreshed the page, although he knew it was ridiculous, and he got the distinctive feeling that he was a character in some cheap, soapy drama rather than a real person who had just faced utter rejection. It felt unreal. He refreshed the page again. His finger kept pressing the key, although he was sure that his brain had already sent the message for him to stop. But something wasn't operating properly anymore.

After what felt like an eternity, he finally managed to stop himself from hitting the refresh key again. He sat there, still not able to move. It was probably the first time in his life that Ji Su stopped in his tracks for longer than a few seconds.

It took Ji Su the entire evening to muster the courage to tell his parents what had happened. He'd worked hard for the auditions to get into the acting program, and he'd been adamant about the fact that there was nothing else he wanted to do–that it had to be acting and it had to be this university and not any other. Telling his father devastated him.

His father's hand had been on the way to his mouth, about to deliver a good serving of kimchi and meat. It stopped dead in mid-air, and he slowly raised his head to look at his son.

His mother, who'd been dividing the remaining food amongst her husband, her son, and her sister, also froze. Then she put down the bowl she had been holding and sat down opposite her son at the dining table. Ji Su's aunt was the only one who seemed unflustered by the news and continued to noisily slurp the meat soup she was having.

"What?" his father finally asked. "You didn't get in?" He leaned back in his chair, anger and disappointment lurking behind the mask of his unmoving face. "You said you worked hard."

Ji Su looked at the flowers on the tablecloth. "I did. I did my best–"

"Which was not good enough."

Ji Su glanced at his father briefly, then focused back on the flowers. They were black and dark blue and wound their way across the table in a never-ending entangled pattern. It was quite dizzying.

His father sighed deeply. "So what's next?" he inquired.

Yes. What next? Ji Su thought to himself but remained quiet.

"What is your plan B?"

Ji Su remained silent.

His mother fidgeted opposite him. His aunt slurped her soup. And he had no idea what to say.

His father stood up and left the table. Ji Su heard the door of his study close quietly. His mother briefly squeezed his hand from across the table, then stood up and followed her husband.

Ji Su knew that she would put herself between him and his father again, trying to keep them away from each other to reduce the chances of conflict. It was something she'd always done.

He briefly put his head in his hand, letting out his breath with a loud sigh.

His aunt had finished her soup and moved on to her favourite banchan. The sounds she made while eating irritated him today. He frowned at her.

The slim, small woman seemed to have noticed his glance because she stopped shovelling the food into her mouth and fixated on him with her eyes. Most of the time, those eyes seemed dreamy, but now they carried another intensity. She addressed him. "So your best was not good enough."

He looked the other way.

"Your best was not good enough," she repeated.

"What is it to you?" he blurted out and immediately regretted his remark. His aunt wasn't well, and most of the time she didn't know what she was saying or where she was. Why would he direct his frustration at her?

She stared at him with unmoving eyes. Her eyelids closed slowly and opened again, reminding him of an owl. "You worked hard, but your best was not good enough," she said again.

He covered his head with his hands, feeling true anger bubbling up. *Better put some distance between me and her,* he thought and stood up.

"You worked hard and were not good enough . . . and now you have slowed down," she said. "Do not slow down."

Ji Su stopped and turned to look at his aunt. She returned his gaze with her unmoving eyes and, again, her eyelids closed and opened in their peculiar fashion. Ji Su's heart pounded. The young man and the older woman with the short, already greying hair remained like that for several heartbeats. Then Ji Su sat back down at the table. He felt as if he had sprinted, his chest heaving, his heart bouncing. He gazed at his aunt one more time, then took the chopsticks and started eating his food. His aunt was focused on her food again as well. Both of them sat at the table, emptying their bowls with full dedication, not speaking a word.

It was months later when Ji Su delivered his application for the study of dance and vocals. Ji Su had worked extremely hard again for this second application. Every morning started with a vigorous workout. He watched what he ate and did his research on dance moves, vocal training, and other related topics. He was good with people, and that worked in his favour. He joined a dance practice group and looked for someone to train his vocals. He worked in a convenience store in the evenings to pay for his tuition. His mother supported him with some of her own savings.

Ji Su refused to slow down and accepted his father's critical comments and angry outbursts without saying a word. There had been something in the fact that his aunt, the woman who seemed to spend more time in other worlds than in their world, had truly seen him. It had given him the sense that he had to keep going. If *she* saw him, then others would too.

On the day of the auditions, Ji Su was unable to eat anything. His mother drove him to the venue. Ji Su was grateful that she kept her thoughts to herself.

By the end of a full day of auditions, he felt so exhausted, simply because of all the tension he had bottled up for hours, that he dropped onto his bed without changing, jeans and socks still on, and fell into a deep sleep.

The world in his dreams was all jumbled up with his aunt appearing in the shape of a large owl, flapping her wings, staring at him. He dreamt that he forgot his dance moves during the audition, which took place in his father's study. When Ji Su opened his eyes the next day, he looked at the ceiling of his room for a while, thinking how lame his dream had been and how predictable his brain was for selecting those images and putting them together like that. Couldn't he have thought of something more creative?

A few days later, he received a phone call.

Ji Su hung up and then laughed, laughter that all his family members, friends, and neighbours knew, because it was loud and intense and it could go on for minutes. Ji Su had been accepted.

* * *

Akila walked along the busy road in Nairobi downtown. She carried Talida in a colourful kanga close to her chest. The girl was looking at the world with big brown eyes, the tiny tuft of blonde, curly hair was blown this way and that by the slight breeze. The sun was still strong, but a recent shower had settled the dust somewhat, so Akila had decided that it was a good day to do some shopping in town.

Biashara Street was full of people too—expecting mothers with large bellies selecting baby clothes and other necessities, people buying gifts for newborns, and husbands who, more often than not, looked slightly overwhelmed. Both sides of the street were lined with shops for baby clothes and any other equipment one might need for their newborns. Competition was stiff, and many shop owners had hired someone to stand outside on the street to lure passersby inside.

Akila had always been put off by this practice and had specifically chosen the shops where there was no one outside trying to convince pedestrians to enter.

People stopped her on the road, asking to take a closer look at Talida. The girl was chubby with large cheeks and big, brown eyes that seemed to observe the world with a good amount of suspicion. While Akila smiled politely at an elderly couple that had stopped her to greet Talida, Akila heard someone call her name.

She turned in confusion and scanned the crowded street that lay in front of her in the heat of the approaching midday. Someone on the far end was waving. Was the person addressing her? The slim figure weaved its way through the many bodies moving along the sidewalk and on the road. Akila's eyes went wide with sudden recognition. The lanky young man was now in front of her, sporting a simple T-shirt and jeans, and worn-out shoes, not one ounce of fat on his body with white teeth sparkling at her, looking very much alive. She covered her mouth with one hand, still taken aback. Then she exclaimed his name. "Mike!"

He grinned at her. "You are surprised to see me."

She returned his smile. "Oh wow! You look awesome!"

He looked down at his worn-out clothes and gave her another grin. "You mean, I look very alive?" He said the last word softly, almost as if he didn't fully believe it yet.

She laughed. "Yes, that's it. I'm so happy to see you!"

He looked at her, then at Talida in her wrap. "I can see things have happened since we last met." He smiled and cooed at the little girl, who hid her face on her mother's chest with a shy smile and twinkling eyes.

Mike stood straight again, with a solemn expression on his face. "I am alive, and I came to say thank you. I didn't have the chance to come see you earlier, so when I noticed you, I didn't want to miss my chance." He seemed slightly embarrassed.

"It's all good," Akila said, putting her hand on his arm. "Have you had lunch? I'm tired of this crowded, hot street anyway."

He smiled. "Thank you for the offer, Akila, but I need to go. I just came to greet you."

She nodded. "Fine. Be well!"

He waved while he disappeared in the crowd, and after a few seconds, it was already hard to make him out in the bustle.

Akila looked for a small cafe in one of the many side streets close to Biashara Street and ordered lunch. She was thinking about the last time she had seen Mike, wearing Kamau's shirt, a bandage hidden below the woollen hat, and a haughty expression on his face. He had raised his one hand to say farewell while they were driving away, and she'd wondered if they would ever meet again. He had appeared so lonely and vulnerable that it hurt to look at him. After that, she'd only thought of Mike occasionally. Too many things had been going on. Or was it that she hadn't wanted to think about that day and everything that it had meant?

Akila's phone buzzed. Kamau was calling to meet up. Akila sighed and pushed her many thoughts away. Then she answered the call. What truly counted was that Mike had made it. He had survived and, although circumstances seemed tough, he hadn't lost his smile. That was something she decided to appreciate.

Talida fidgeted in her wrap and Akila untied the kanga and took the little girl out. She held her daughter in one arm as she slowly ate her lunch.

Kamau joined them at the cafe. He was in one of his peculiar moods. She sensed it as soon as he stepped in. His eyes had that certain look that usually came with the stories he'd started telling these days. It was as if a parallel universe existed around them that only he could see. But the moment he entered the cafe, his long dreadlocks were all over, shaking in all directions, and Akila thought that he made quite an impression.

Broken pieces

Kamau sat at the very edge of the seat. It was dark outside, and Akila had only put a small light on next to the coffee table. The trees in front of the house were rustling their leaves in the night breeze. She sat next to him, looking at the table.

He could feel that she had slipped out of his hands, and the sense of helplessness realising that he was unable to bring her back was overwhelming. The fear of losing her and Talida was so large that he couldn't grasp it entirely. On top of that, there were so many other thoughts inside him that made it hard for him to see clearly these days. Or was it that he finally saw the world for what it really was?

Some people wanted him dead and other people didn't agree with his views. And then there was the constant pressure of needing to make money to be someone. But now he was stuck at home looking after his daughter while his lover went to work and drifted further away from him with each passing day.

But what were they meant to say to each other?

He'd already said one hundred and more words to her, but she still didn't seem to understand. That it was people meddling with their lives. That it was all messy because others didn't want them to be happy. Even politicians from his hometown and the police had conspired against him, pulling him down and not letting him be the success that he needed to be–but most importantly, to be respected by her again. Respected like before when it was all fine.

"I can't allow it," he began.

She sighed and then looked at him briefly. "It's not like I need your permission. Do you really want to continue staying here when we're like this? That doesn't make any sense. I want you to go and stay upcountry for now."

He couldn't believe it. She was telling him to leave.

His whole body went rigid. It was like that these days. She told him what she wanted but didn't see his point at all or care about how she made him feel.

Suddenly, there was a loud bang and Akila was startled, eyes wide. Speechless, Kamau looked down at the pieces of the cup that he had been holding. He had no idea how he managed to break it with his bare hand. Hot chai dripped over his fingers onto the coffee table in front of him and on the floor. He glanced at Akila and saw fear in her eyes. It wasn't like before, when she had so much affection for him that she was never scared. Now she was trying to put distance between them and was afraid of him getting too close.

The next day, he packed his bags and left. He couldn't take another look full of fear from her. He was worried that he would really do something crazy to her if she looked at him like that again.

* * *

A couple of weeks later, Akila received a call from Kamau's brother-in-law. Kamau had become so unmanageable that they had to bring him back to Nairobi. Now he was locked up in a psychiatric clinic. Akila put down the phone and stared at her desk. She was at work, and Joyce was watching Talida for her until she had found a good house help. Her heart was running in her chest and she needed air.

She jumped up, and her chair almost fell over. The busy typing in the room stopped instantly and everyone looked at her. It was then that she realised that tears were slipping down her cheeks. Akila left the room as quickly as possible, seeking a space where she could hopefully breathe more freely again.

When she'd left through the gate and was on the small street where their office was located, Marcus called after her. He'd slipped out through the gate as well and was now standing there in the sunshine in front of her.

"Let's go have something at the place around the corner," he suggested.

She took a deep breath, then nodded slightly. "Okay, but no talking about why I'm like this," she said.

His open gaze lay on her, and somehow his presence made her feel a little better. "No problem," he responded eventually, and they slowly walked to the small cafe around the corner.

Maybe the fact that Marcus was so very different from Kamau played a role in how quickly Akila was drawn to him. She didn't pause to check herself, to check how much the whole situation with Kamau might have affected her. She jumped right into the other world that Marcus seemed to offer.

People were attracted to him, just like Akila was. He had an open face, he laughed easily and he had a tendency to turn the simplest story into an adventure when he recounted it.

So when Akila and Marcus started spending more time together, her life turned into a bright, noisy adventure. With Kamau, everything had been about emotions. It had been a relationship based on the mind–and it was beautiful.

With Marcus, it was all physicality. The house was frequently filled with people, and weekends were dominated by outings with Talida, barbecues, and parties. They managed it all, getting little Talida ready for baby class in the morning, then work, and then meeting Joyce and other friends in the evenings. It was intense and, for a long time, they went about their days like that, enjoying the sensation of brilliance and weightlessness.

When Akila realised that she was pregnant, it was exciting but also scary. A second child? Nairobi life was hard enough with yourself and one child to take care of. How would it be with two? Still, she was sure that they would manage.

Grief

Akila dropped into another world. It was filled with darkness–a velvety, heavy darkness that was hard to transcend.

Biko was there, his eyes closed and his tiny hands clenched to fists as he had always held them for the few days he had joined them. His presence seemed to occupy a large space in the darkness. But there was another presence there–something she couldn't name at first–something huge that radiated energy with an intimidating intensity.

She wanted to drop back into her reality, but somehow the world had gripped her and she couldn't remember how to exit. Akila suddenly noticed that the thing she had thought was something else was the darkness itself, which was heavy with her own sadness.

She felt so sad for Biko, for the little time he'd spent mostly in fear and pain in her reality, and for the little energy she'd been able to muster during those days to be with him.

Even years later, Akila was surprised at how painful the memory of her lost child was. Although she was able to live with it, the wound never fully healed.

* * *

A few months after Marcus, Akila, and Talida began living together, Akila got pregnant.

How did it come to this? Marcus was worried. Were they ready for it?

He thought of all the practicalities, especially the money it would cost to have a second child. Nairobi was a tough place to live on your own, leave alone for an entire family. Would he be able to provide what was needed?

Akila was glowing, though. And there was no way for him to refuse her. He wanted her to shine forever the way she did now.

Months passed and Akila's belly grew slowly.

They'd settled on a small clinic around the corner for the check-ups to make sure that it was as easy as possible for them to manage it all. Akila's first pregnancy had been very smooth, and the elderly doctor who examined her in the local clinic was sure that she would be fine. Still, he thought it odd that the baby was very active in the womb but seemed to be growing too slowly. But looking at glowing Akila, who was confident, outspoken, and strong, he didn't see the need to worry too much.

It was about 6 months into the pregnancy when Akila suddenly sensed that something was off.

Looking back, she was unable to put a finger on what it was. Something simply shifted and she knew that she needed to get a scan done. There was something wrong with the baby.

As they waited for the day of the scan appointment to arrive, Joyce and Adam, her boyfriend, invited Akila and Talida for a day trip to Naivasha to get Akila's mind off the appointment for a little bit.

Meanwhile, Marcus travelled to his hometown for a family function, although reluctantly. Akila reassured him that everything would be fine, although she had a sinking feeling when he got onto the bus after waving at her encouragingly.

The sun was casting gentle, beautiful rays across the large lake when they all arrived in Naivasha after about a 1.5 hour drive from Nairobi. They settled down on the terrace of a pretty restaurant not far from the lakeshore. Little Talida jumped across the lawn, her laughter being carried into the clear blue sky above them.

Just when the drinks arrived, Akila felt the pain in her lower back. She froze and immediately knew that they had to get into the car and drive back to the hospital in Nairobi as quickly as possible.

It was like a scene from a drama-action movie. They all got into the car, Joyce and Talida in the back, Akila in the passenger seat in front and Adam behind the steering wheel. The highway connecting Naivasha and Nairobi was a narrow, dangerous road with lots of trucks travelling and little room to manoeuvre, but Akila told Adam that it didn't matter how he got them to the hospital, it had to be quick. So he put the hazard lights on and drove like his own life depended on it.

When they encountered traffic on their side of the highway because of an accident further down the road, Adam veered the vehicle across onto the other lane. Constantly holding down the horn, Adam drove at full speed, doing his best to avoid the oncoming vehicles. It was all in response to Akila's quiet, but urgent words: "My water broke." He felt panicky, but at the same time oddly calm while putting his foot on the accelerator.

When they finally reached the hospital, all Akila could do was shout at the busily moving people around her that they had to save her baby. She screamed it over and over again as she pushed Biko into the world.

Marcus arrived straight from the night bus the next morning, totally exhausted. By then, it was clear that Biko wouldn't live. His heart was too weak. Still, the doctors kept reviving the small body every time the boy's heart failed. Seeing the little, helpless being in the incubator made Akila feel totally empty.

After four days, they signed a paper that prevented the doctors from reviving Biko the next time his heart failed. As they sat next to the incubator, waiting for the spark of life to leave Biko's tiny body, Akila felt . . . nothing.

She had stepped out of her body and was looking at the scene from outside, a spectator who had nothing to do with the scene. She felt some compassion and sadness for the poor parents who sat next to the incubator waiting for their child to die, but that was it. She had removed herself from the painful narrative.

After Biko was gone, Akila couldn't bear to speak about it with anyone. She would just talk about how important it was to move on and focus on the bright moments in life. What good would it do for Biko, Talida, Marcus, or herself to focus on this extremely dark moment and remember it?

But it took energy–a lot of energy–not to think about it and to stay focused on the light. On some nights, she felt that she wouldn't be able to go on anymore. Those were the moments she dropped onto the floor in the bedroom, wailing and rolling from one side to the other. But Marcus would never come to comfort her. He would just turn his back on her, pulling the blanket up to his neck.

She wondered if it was too much to expect. He had lost his mother only a few months ago. Now Biko was gone. Maybe it was too much for him to handle. Maybe she was too selfish, hoping for him to hold her and comfort her when she truly felt as if a part of her had just died.

This was when she started fainting. It would happen suddenly, mostly when Marcus was around and always when Talida wasn't with her. She would stand in the kitchen in the evening, after Talida was already in bed, and fix herself a small snack or wash dishes. Then there would be a sudden sensation that she couldn't go on, every-thing would turn black and she would drop to the floor. Never too hard and never in a way that she injured herself. But she would pass out for a couple of seconds or, in extreme cases, even a few minutes.

One day, she was in the bedroom and felt that she wouldn't be able to continue without feeling seen by Marcus. Everything around her turned grey, then black and she tumbled onto the small carpet. She lay there for minutes, fighting the overwhelming dark-ness and that feeling that filled her to the brim, something that drove her mad and that wanted to be released in a loud scream. But she stayed completely still on the floor, suspended in the darkness.

Marcus walked into the room. He had left his phone on the small side table by the bed. He looked at Akila on the floor, then picked up his phone and walked out. Akila, realising that, again, he hadn't come to her, stayed on the floor crying silently.

* * *

Marcus went to the kitchen and removed a bottle of cool beer from the fridge. He sat down on the bench on their balcony and stared out into the night. There were stars all over and the trees shook their branches slightly in the evening breeze. He slowly bent forward and put his face into his two hands. He felt empty and full at the same time–a frustrating sensation. It was as if his body and mind couldn't decide which way to go: break down and give up or move on.

Looking at Akila was painful these days. She was so sad, but during the day, when Talida was there or when she went to work, she put up the bravest face and just got on with it. He could only observe with amazement how she managed it all. But in the evening, she frequently turned into a mess, and it was impossible to be near her. Why couldn't she just keep the brave face on for a few more hours in the evening and hug him too?

But, no, he was actually fine. What annoyed him most was that her eyes held an expectation about how he should feel, that he was also meant to be sad and broken like her. But he wasn't like that. He was different. The strong man his mother had raised–that is what he had to be.

It turned out to be easier to be that man outside the house. What would he be able to contribute at home? Akila was in control of Talida's schedule, mostly deciding about weekend plans, how their house-help should clean, what food should be prepared, and when the shopping had to be done. It was actually quite suffocating. So leaving the place was the better thing to avoid her unwavering stares, the fainting, and the cries or the arguments that started cropping up more frequently.

* * *

Making ends meet became more difficult. Somehow their money disappeared very fast every month. Akila didn't realise what the reason was at first, but one day, when Marcus turned up past two and drunk like he had most days over the past few months, it hit her where all their money was going. They'd agreed on a shared account at the time they moved in together, and now Akila hated herself for agreeing to it.

It seemed there was no way of stopping Marcus. He was drowning himself deliberately, and every day turned into a suicide mission. And she was powerless facing him. He had completely turned away from her. Physically he was present, but Akila was sure that it was only an empty shell that looked like Marcus. The real Marcus had left a long time ago.

Later, she would wonder why they kept going for so long. Why hadn't they ended it then, admitting to the fact that the helplessness they both felt when grief had split their shared world into two and they were walking on alone? But they went on and on for months, fighting over the money gone to Marcus's drinking or the loneliness Akila felt when he left without saying a word and only turned up late at night or early the next morning, reeking of alcohol and not of any use to her or Talida.

It was one day while Akila sat in the office working that she told herself that it was all a waste of their time and she had to stop.

So in the evening, she waited for him to set them both free. But he didn't turn up and she sat there, feeling completely shattered.

Talida was outside playing in the sunshine with her friends when Marcus finally came home. When he entered the house, Akila, who was baking bread in the kitchen, sensed right away that he was even more drunk than usual. She knew that there was no talking to him when he was in that state, but she was too frustrated to hold back. So she went at him right when he closed the door, showering him with all the bitter words that were in her heart.

Slightly swaying, he looked at her and said, "Quiet." She flashed the most angry and disgusted look she could muster at him. And he grabbed her by the neck. She froze and, realising how strong he was holding her, felt pure fright rise inside her. She wrapped her hands around his arm, which was stretched out in front of him with her helplessly suspended at the end of it.

All she could think of was that Talida couldn't see them like this. "Please, if Talida sees us . . ." she whispered. It was as if he couldn't hear her. Slowly, he started walking, as if he was moving her out of his way. Eventually, he pressed her onto the couch and then let go of her neck. Akila was breathing hard, heart running like a hare.

Staring at her, still swaying, he suddenly seemed to snap out of it and disappeared through the door through which he had entered just a moment ago.

Akila clutched at her heart looking after him. It took her a very long time to calm down.

Akila duty

It was Tuesday morning and the sun had risen over the uncountable rooftops of Bengaluru City. Rose was full of energy on such a beautiful morning. She had gotten up early, taken a refreshing cold shower, and was on her way to the office. The streets were already crowded with commuters on the way to work and the usual traffic chaos had ensued, with the noisy honking and the sounds of thousands of scooters making their way across the streets of the vast city. Rose had decided to walk despite the traffic and chose the narrower back alleys to avoid being confronted with the crowds and the fumes on the main streets.

After stopping at a coffee shop for a hot cuppa, she walked into her workplace, an open space office with glass walls all around that were always slightly dirty due to the continuous exposure to all the smog the city exhaled each day. After greeting colleagues who were already there, she sat down in her small cubicle and focused on the magazine she had to get ready for publishing. It was work she enjoyed, and she was looking forward to getting it all done.

About an hour later, the office was filled with the many voices of the sales team making calls, with people chatting and laughing and with the sing-song "thank yous" from those whose turn it was to receive the small cup of sugary morning chai from the office worker that distributed it from a large metal flask around 10:00 each day.

Rose usually declined the chai. It was just too milky and sugary for her, and her doctor had insisted that she should really watch her diet. So she kept to her herbal teas and the occasional coffee.

Their boss walked in and came over. "Good morning. Let's talk briefly in my office, okay?"

Rose looked at him with a slight frown on her face. "Now? I'm trying to get the magazine ready here."

He frowned back at her. "In my office now," he said.

Rose put on her sweetest fake smile and nodded. "Coming!"

In his office, he still wore a frown on his face. "Rose, stop talking back to me in front of others. It's not a practice I want to encourage."

She sighed. "Understood. It was meant in a funny way."

He shook his head. "Others might not get that. But anyway, I want you to do me a favour. You know that we will have a colleague over from the Nairobi office for the coaching training. I want you to look after her a little. It's her first time in Bangalore, so she needs someone to show her around."

She folded her arms in front of her chest. "Why me? You know how busy I am!"

"You are good with people. Come on, you can do me that favour. Her name is Akila. Maybe you have spoken to her before?"

Rose thought for a moment. "Not really."

"Okay, then. Thanks for taking on this task on top of your work." He sat down at his desk, which was a clear sign that the conversation was over.

Rose left, wondering how she would manage. The deadline for the magazine was around the corner and there were still several things to be done and optimised. She sighed while sitting back down at her desk. And what if she didn't get along with the woman? She hadn't had many interactions with her and had no idea what kind of person she was.

Never mind, she told herself. *I can show her around a little and then let her do her own thing.*

Two days later, colleagues from all the other offices arrived in Bengaluru to join the coaching training for team leaders that the company had organised. The whole group arrived in the office in the morning to get to know their colleagues and spend some time there before heading off for the training. It was a wonderful mixture of humans with different backgrounds and there was an air of excitement spreading across the desks.

Rose stood with everyone else to shake the visitor's hands. Then a tall woman with wide shoulders, short, untidy hair, and greenish eyes behind large glasses took her hand and introduced herself. "Hi. I'm Akila."

Rose shook the sizable hand and grinned. She had to dip her head back a little because of the height difference. "Hi, Akila! Nice to meet you. Actually, I've been put on Akila duty, so rely on me to make your stay amazingly fantastic."

Akila's eyebrows went up inquiringly. "Akila duty?"

"Yup! Boss gave the order."

Their eyes met, blue eyes and greenish eyes searching each other, asking without words if this was going to be good. Finally, Akila grinned. "Awesome! I definitely need a lot of care."

Rose nodded with a smile. "I thought so."

They were still holding hands, looking at each other as the instant connection hit both of them.

Coming on this work trip had been a relief for Akila. After all the months of pain and stress she and Marcus had gone through, it was a true feeling of liberation to leave for a few days and immerse herself in another world. Talida was to spend the two weeks her mother was away with her grandmother who had come over, and Akila thought that her daughter would have a great time with Katarina.

It had been a strange mixture of familiarity and new impressions that she'd experienced when Akila first arrived in India. It was as if there were so many parallels to life in Kenya, but at the same time, so many things were so different.

When the plane touched down at Bengaluru airport, Akila seemed to be able to sense the millions of people who occupied the space. It was quite overwhelming looking at the uncountable rooftops that came closer and closer as the plane slowly descended.

After Marcus had grabbed Akila's neck, they hadn't met for days. She wasn't sure where he slept or what he was doing, and she was annoyed with herself for being unable to stop wondering and worrying. Hadn't she told herself that she would end it? Why worry about him, then? Still, her heart was too full of him, and it was difficult to not pick up the phone and check up on him.

So she welcomed Southern India with open arms–the smells, the noise, the food, the historical sights, the parties she went to with Rose. The first week rushed by in a breathless blur of warm colours and sensations of exhilaration and freedom, and Rose and Akila agreed that it felt as if they had known each other for years.

One night, Rose and Akila both dropped onto the bed. For a long while, they just lay there, arms and legs stretched out, heads next to each other.

"What's going on, Rose?"

Rose closed her eyes, taking a few deep breaths. Her heart was racing.

Akila turned her head a little, trying to look at her friend. "Rose. . . ."

"I think I have a huge crush on someone."

Akila was still looking at her. "Isn't that a good thing?"

Rose covered her face and then released a small scream of frustration. "I'm not sure."

Akila paused for a long time, then asked softly, "Why?"

"It's Kayla." Rose kept her hands over her face, realising how scared she was about her friend's reaction.

"Rose. . . ." Akila turned onto her belly and carefully took Rose's hands away from her face. Rose looked up into her friend's eyes. "I get it. She's really cute."

"But how do I even start? How do I know if she feels the same way? This is so weird."

Akila looked like she was trying to hide a small smile.

"Don't you laugh at me!"

Akila's eyes widened in their usual fashion. "I'm not! It is just . . . I guess it's just like with all the people we like, right? You show them and hope they feel the same. Or something similar."

Rose deeply frowned at her friend and turned away from her. "How dare you make it sound so easy," she mumbled.

Now Akila laughed. "I'm not saying it will be easy. I'm just saying it doesn't have to be a bad thing. If you really want to be with that person, you'll have to show it at some point." Akila put her hand on her friend's shoulder. "What do you think?"

Rose grumbled to herself but nodded at last. "Do you know what will happen if her parents find out? She's still in university and likes a girl. Her parents might lock her away. I met them once. They aren't the type to take such things lightly."

Akila sat up now, folding her legs on the bed. "You don't know that. You haven't even tried and already say it won't work. If you're looking for reasons not to show what you think about her, you'll probably find," she gestured with her hands flying around mid-air, "hundreds."

Rose stayed with her back to her friend for a long time, just staring at the wall. Akila sat next to her with her legs folded. She had stopped talking, for which Rose was grateful.

Eventually, Rose inhaled deeply and sat up. Taking Akila's hand, she said, "Okay, let's go eat something delicious."

Akila jumped up and pulled her off the bed. "Splendid idea, dear Rose!"

* * *

Akila sat on a wooden bench with her back to the large window that offered a nice view of Bengaluru's night lights. The small wooden table was loaded with different Southern Indian dishes. The idea of a breeze blew through some of the open windows that carried with it the city's sounds–voices travelling up to them, cars honking, engines running, and tires screeching occasionally.

Around the table, next and opposite her, sat two of her female colleagues. They had all met here after Akila and Saru left the hotel where the coaching training took place to end the day on a good note. Saru had given Akila a ride on her scooter, and sitting on the back of the seat, flying through the warm evening of Bangalore, she had felt a sense of freedom that made her heart beat faster and caused a rush of energy to push through her veins. It gave her the sense that many more things were to come.

After having settled for a combination of different dishes they would share, they sipped their cocktails exchanging the latest news. Akila and Saru both worked as team leaders in the sales team while Pri was part of the tech development department. They had all worked together before and were happy to be able to spend time together in person. But for some reason, the conversation didn't remain as light as they would have preferred. It hadn't been long since the shocking story of the woman being raped and killed on a bus in Delhi had made the news, not only in India but also around the world.

"It is so sad that these things are still happening. When I think about what this girl went through. Oh my god." Saru shook her head, her beautiful face filled with grief.

"I think things like this have always happened, and not in a less cruel way," Pri thought out loud. "But now that we're globally connected, we hear about all the horrible stuff going on. I just wonder what kind of a crazy mixture of issues can lead people to turn into such . . . monsters."

Akila wanted to understand. "But how come India makes headlines with such stories again and again? Is it because it's a big country? Or is there really something going on? Like that girl in the village who experienced something similar?" Realising that she might sound as if she thought India was the only country that had challenges with violence against women, she quickly added, "I mean, it's not only a problem in India. I just wonder what it is here. Or is it the same issue all over the world?"

All three women were quiet for a while, milling over their own thoughts.

"I'm not sure how it is for other places," Pri eventually said, "but I know that here it is also a problem with how we bring up our men and women. A woman needs to do so much right from the start in terms of chores and feeling responsible for everyone. A boy needs to get good grades but is generally left to do as he pleases and can feel like some sort of king in the house. Then when he grows up, he is confronted with the fact that he is not the centre of the universe and that there are actually many people much smarter and greater–and loads of those are women. It is like a shock, and some just cannot take it." She addressed Saru. "Am I not right?"

The other woman was still thoughtful. "I agree, to some extent. But is that really enough to explain how people can behave like that? To turn out to be so sick?"

Akila agreed. "In my opinion, how we raise a person definitely has an impact. And the weird thing is that it's often the women themselves pushing for those rules to be followed. The girl does this, the boy does that. When I was working as a volunteer, we also educated on the impact of female genital mutilation, and it was the women who were telling us off–and they were living with the crazy pain all their lives."

"But it's so much more than that. In my culture, for example, a woman is given a new name by her husband once she gets married. It's almost as if her identity has changed because she becomes part of the man. I never know whether I should respect this practice as part of our culture or if I should be angry about it."

Akila thought about her mother. She had always pushed the boundaries of what was expected of her as a woman, but even Katarina had a hard time making herself free of the different expectations and abilities that were attached to being a woman. Yes, she was meant to study and be smart–probably also work. But striving to become an engineer? That was something for men that was probably too much for a woman. And, anyway, she should get married before it was too late and not neglect her child.

Katarina had described to Akila the feeling of being caged in that had often gripped her as a young woman when confronted by these obligations and beliefs. It had made her angry and sad. Wasn't it all the same thing? And if this was how it was for women, how did men experience the whole thing? How did they truly feel deep down inside? How could anyone be okay with the imbalance?

Akila remembered this conversation whenever she came across situations that shone a light on the complexity and illogical construct of gender roles.

When Akila returned to Nairobi, she called Marcus. And for a while, things got better.

Mavis

Akila went to bed late, feeling restless. She had spent the evening chatting with Marcus's sister Anita. Although not completely aware of it, she had an inkling that something was going on inside her.

She left Anita and Marcus in the living room with the windows and the door to the balcony open to let in some of the late evening breeze in the hope that it would cool down the apartment a little and carefully lifted the white mosquito net draped over her bed to slip under it. As soon as she had placed her head on her pillow and found a relatively comfortable position for her large belly, she suddenly felt something wet between her legs.

Startled, she switched on her night light, afraid that there might be blood. But the fluid on the bed sheet was clear. She took a deep breath and closed her eyes for a brief moment to get her composure back. Then she slowly climbed back out of bed and removed her pants. Thinking that more fluid might come out, but also wondering why it had been so little if the water broke, she looked for one of her colourful kangas and wrapped it around her lower waist.

Helena had told her that her cervix had already started to dilate, so something was definitely going on. She grabbed her phone from her nightstand and her handbag from the floor next to it and walked back into the living room.

"Let's go to the hospital," she said in a calm voice, not wanting to alarm anyone. Marcus turned to stare at her in surprise and jumped up, almost immediately. His expression was a mixture of excitement and fear. "Now?"

"Yes, now. The water didn't really break, but a little fluid came out, so something is definitely going on. Let's go now."

She checked her phone. It was half past midnight. They would reach the hospital in less than twenty minutes.

She turned to Anita, who had remained seated, and looked at them calmly. Akila knew her well by now and spotted the excitement and slight worry below her calm demeanour. "Just let Talida know in the morning."

Anita nodded and responded, "We'll be here waiting for you."

Marcus had moved to the bedroom to change into smarter clothes and to carry Akila's most crucial belongings. Five minutes later, they were on the road, the vehicle's front lights illuminating the empty alley ahead of them. On the main road, street lights were on here and there highlighting a group of stray dogs rummaging through trash or a small kiosk closed down for the night. On the larger junction, matatus were still waiting to collect late-night passengers, and Akila could hear the conductor's shouts and the music blaring from some of the minivans with the bright lights.

Marcus was very quiet all the way to the hospital, focusing on the road. Akila sensed that he was anxious. Something wasn't going according to plan. Biko's death hung between them like an unnamed sensation.

She put her hand onto his hand on top of the gear stick. "All will be well," she said in an effort to show him that he needn't worry.

He quickly glanced at her and smiled a little. "I know."

Akila gazed out of the window and thought to herself that words often don't do justice to express what we really want to say. They usually fall short in so many ways. *Why, then, do we still struggle every day to make ourselves heard and understood?*

The parking lot at the hospital was almost empty and Akila and Marcus had no trouble reaching the elevator up to the maternity ward. It was calm all over, and only a few hospital staff and patients seemed to be awake.

Akila was resting on the bed, the curtains around them drawn. They were waiting for the doctor on duty to examine her.

Next to them, just behind the thin curtains, was another woman, already quite far in her labour, it seemed, as she was breathing heavily and moaning every time a fresh contraction hit her. Her partner was with her, trying to comfort her, but Akila got the sense that this lady had decided to be a woman straight from the American movies, being rude to her man and unreasonable in her choice of words and demands.

Breathing loudly, she mumbled, "I can't believe I allowed you to touch me again. I hate it. I really hate it."

As the contraction increased in intensity, she raised her voice, now almost shouting at her husband. "I hate it! I can't believe it. Why didn't you stop me?"

Akila and Marcus glanced at each other with raised eyebrows. Then Akila closed her eyes, trying to not let the emotions from the other side of the curtain get to her.

When the doctor finally arrived to check on her, they were all struggling to have a meaningful conversation over the loud voice of their neighbour behind the curtain. Akila was relieved when the woman was finally taken away.

Once the nurse had put the drip on, Akila started feeling the contractions growing stronger almost immediately.

She still had a very clear memory of the labour pains she went through the four hours it took before she could push Talida out into this world, and the pain that shot through her with every new contraction was unarguably much more intense than anything she had experienced. The frequency of her contractions increased rapidly, and Akila thought that she might go crazy just five minutes after being put on the drip.

Marcus, who sat next to her, looked at her with worry. "Akila, are you okay?"

A contraction hit her just that moment, and all she could do was focus on breathing calmly and not losing her mind.

"Akila?"

She couldn't respond to him. Only a moment later, when the pain had somewhat subsided, could she reply with a small, "All okay," released between tightly pressed lips. The next, even stronger contraction hit her almost immediately and, suddenly, she could feel the head of her baby between her legs.

"Call the midwife!" she told Marcus breathlessly, who left the room in a hurry to look for the midwife.

Another nurse entered the room to check the drip, and Akila, who had just been hit by another wave of pure pain, grabbed her wrist. "The baby is here," she whispered.

The nurse looked at her with a slightly irritated expression. "Are you sure? You might think it's the baby, but you probably just need to go for a long call."

"My baby is coming!" she shouted at the nurse, who took a step back and was about to respond when Marcus entered the room, the midwife in tow. Akila let her head drop back onto the pillow with relief.

"Wonderful, Akila!" Elizabeth exclaimed cheerfully. "Not even thirty minutes and you're ready!" She carefully parted Akila's legs and made a pleased sound. "Baby's here, Akila. You just need to give it a little nudge and it will all be over."

Akila pushed only two more times before it was finally done.

Marcus later said that Mavis had a surprised and slightly irritated look on his face when he was released into this world. He let out a loud scream and the midwife smiled while examining him. "A healthy baby boy, Akila. Well done! How many babies do you have? Two only? Given your perfect birthing skills, you should think of ten at the least!"

Both Elizabeth and Marcus seemed to find that incredibly funny, but Akila could only think how happy she was that the unbearable pain was over.

Turning point

Akila dressed in a comfortable, but elegant, maroon tunica that morning and made sure her hair looked a little less crazy. She wore a pair of black tights and her leather half boots.

On the way to work, she listened to some of her favourite Bongo Flava songs, singing along with Rayvanny, Diamond, and Harmonize and letting the rhythm wash over her. The strong foreboding that lay like a large stone in the pit of her stomach was momentarily pushed out of her mind, and she was able to enter the office with a smile on her face.

For months and months, turning into a year and beyond, they had been on a battlefield. The company had been acquired by a large investor and, suddenly, rules had changed. Akila was exhausted by the time she went home in the evening and exhausted when she woke up in the morning. All the sales pressure that she was suddenly confronted with and was expected to pass on to her team members, the arguments with the leadership about what the core focus of the company should be, and the responsibility she had as a coach and mentor for the performance of an equally exhausted team had worn her out. So when she walked into the office with the sense that it was over, she was almost unable to feel the magnitude of her intuition.

She was truly being let go.

It was weird–the mixture of her pride being hurt and the feeling of liberation that came over her when she left the office after she met with two of her superiors. On the way home, she shed tears but wasn't really sure why. Was it because she had been told that she wasn't a fit anymore while others stayed and had been deemed right for the new phase? Or was it because it hadn't been fun for the last few months and now the tension was falling off her? She expected it to be a concoction of it all.

Coming home, Marcus was there, shocked by the news and hugging her tightly to comfort her. And, with a clarity that she hadn't experienced for the entire day–*No*, she thought–a clarity she hadn't experienced for weeks, months, or even years, she knew that the chapter had to be closed.

After everything that had happened between them, it had been extremely hard for her to trust Marcus again. It didn't show up in their everyday life, but sometimes, when he would get tipsy, fear would grip her as she realised that she hadn't left it all behind her. Sure, life would go on as usual, but there was something inside her that had changed. The day she was told that she was jobless, she saw that she had been holding both of them back by not admitting what she felt deep down.

It took a few weeks before she finally mustered the courage to speak with Marcus.

It was a strange conversation they had the day Akila finally found the strength to say it out loud. They sat together on the couch in their living room, the sun flooding through the window and the sounds of life streaming in from outside as well. Children shouted in the courtyard while playing *catch and catch*. There were street vendors stationed outside the gate who offered their goods, and vehicles and motorcycles honked. Akila said, "I don't think we can be a couple anymore."

Marcus looked at her for a moment, then asked, "Why?"

"I don't think it makes sense if one of us, or maybe even both of us, feels it's more of a convenience than a romantic relationship. And there are some things I can't let go. I've tried, but it's just not possible for me."

He was silent for a long time, then nodded.

Akila's tears came later when it was already all decided and Marcus had moved out. She was suddenly hit by the fact that so many things that had shaped her everyday life for such a long time had come to an end, and she stood staring at the large space that had suddenly opened up inside her and wondered what to do next.

* * *

Rose was quiet for a while, listening to Akila trying to get her breathing under control on the other side of the world. "Akila, honey, if it's too hard, just get the kids and come over. We have the space. You can take some time to decide what to do next."

Akila was sobbing, and Rose, who had only seen her friend cry one time before, thought it was the most heart-rending sound.

"I don't know. . . ."

"Akila, just book the flights."

Yes, it turned out to be too hard for Akila. It was time to jump out of this world that she had created for herself and drop into another world, one that allowed her to leave the pain she felt about so many things behind.

Rose had moved from India back to her birthplace in Scotland about a year ago, and Akila decided to take the helping hand offered by her friend, although it took her several nights and days of contemplation before she could get herself to accept the fact that she needed support and was having trouble handling the situation on her own.

And so it happened one dusty, sunny Nairobi afternoon that Joyce dropped her friend Akila, along with Talida and Mavis, at the airport to take the next flight to London and on to Edinburgh.

Akila had been busy for weeks, selling all the stuff that had accumulated over the years or giving things out that she felt people would put to good use. It was a weird feeling, seeing almost everything that represented her life in Nairobi slowly disappear until two days before their flight there was nothing left but the few bags the three of them were taking with them.

At the airport, Joyce and Akila held each other for a while, and Akila felt as if they were trying to take as much as possible out of their hug and also put as much as possible into it.

Joyce kissed Talida and Mavis. Akila was relieved when they were finally at the check-in counter and their goodbye was over. It was better to look forward to their next meeting.

Looking back at that time many years later, Akila was amazed at what can happen to a human when kicked out of their life and thrown into a new one. You either drown in the ensuing chaos or you make it your own.

It was almost instantly after having lost her job that she knew what she wanted to do next: be a life coach. She wanted to be the space for people to think, feel, and say what was deep inside of them so that they could finally begin to live their dream life. Live as who they truly were. A life fully present in the moment, walking around as bright, beautiful bundles of energy that lit up the world around them.

Starting her own life coaching business was a dream that Akila had for several years. She had dreamt of it ever since her employer had sent her on a professional coaching training course, but she'd always felt that she had no energy to take the leap into it. But now, at a moment in her life where she had nothing to hide behind–no employment, no relationship, no home–what was there to lose? Nothing. The only thing was to gain something. To create something and build something based on her own values and rules.

Almost instantly, things fell into place.

How is that possible? Akila would ask herself with a sense of awe several months down the line. In all the turmoil, the fear, the pain, the sadness, how was it possible that brightness was the result–that what she had dreamt of was actually happening and all the questioning of her own abilities, of the decisions she made, and the actions that followed them, still resulted in her feeling a true sense of freedom and accomplishment. It was all very real.

As she spread the message that she had started her business as a life coach and as her first clients found her, she realised how her determination remained the strongest emotion and how a sense of trust slowly calmed down her scared mind and heart.

One day, a few months after Mavis, Talida, and Akila had arrived in Scotland and had taken the long, winding roads to the village that Rose and Edith had made their home and had settled into their friends' cosy cottage, Rose stepped through the front door of their cottage with huge excitement on her face.

"Akila dear!" she called out as she walked into the living room with her lively cheeks glowing happily. "I have the most splendid news!"

Akila, who sat at the shiny, wooden table that was placed not far from a window looking out into Rose's garden, was deeply engrossed in a blog post she was writing about the impact of "attachment" on people's lives. She took a moment to notice her friend and to pop up from the depths of her mind.

Raising her head, she looked at Rose with inquiring eyes.

"Tell me!" she said with a smile.

"You know how Mrs. Thomson's cottage next door has been empty for quite a while after she had to move to her daughter's place in Edinburgh?"

Akila nodded. Rose paced in front of her, lit up by what she was about to tell her friend. It made Akila's heart swell to see Rose like that. It was a wonderful sight that made her feel brighter too.

"As you know, Edith inquired about the cottage a while ago to see if you can get the place, and GUESS WHAT?" Rose almost jumped at the last two words. "You got it!"

Akila's eyes grew big and she felt a jolt run through her body. "Really . . ." was all she managed to say, taking in the fact that she and her children would soon have their own home, and right next to Rose's and Edith's at that. "Wow," Akila mumbled while her thoughts and her heart felt full with the realisation that things were falling into place again. *Such an amazing experience, this life,* she thought to herself.

Rose stood in front of her with a surprised and amused look on her face. "Aren't you excited!" she said in a teasing tone and winked at Akila.

Akila laughed, stood up, and hugged her friend tightly. "It's the most splendid news! Thank you!" she shouted and spun Rose, who was much shorter than her, once around like a little child.

Rose gave a little yelp but was back to her usual self as soon as Akila put her down on her feet. She lifted her finger and said, "So much to do now! Number one: Get the formalities done. I will make sure Edith can help with that. Number two: Plan the move. Luckily you guys don't have much stuff. Number three, and most important: Celebrate!"

Akila laughed and nodded.

Rose rubbed her hands together excitedly. "I can't wait for Mavis and Talida to hear the news when they come home from school," she exclaimed.

Akila thought that her children would definitely benefit from having their own place to fully settle in after several months of making Rose's and Edith's cottage their home. A couple of weeks after that, Akila and her children finally moved into their own little cottage.

"Finally!" Talida exclaimed the evening of the move after they had all settled down to enjoy dinner together, including Edith and Rose. "We have a home!"

* * *

Days later, Rose and Akila sat in front of Akila's cottage in the soft afternoon sun. Rose had come over with a bottle of whiskey, and they had moved their chairs so that they could sit next to each other covered with blankets against the cool air. They faced the garden, which was illuminated by the early spring sunlight and looked peaceful and, being Akila's garden, a little untidy and wild. Rose couldn't help commenting, "Akila, your garden needs some love."

Akila smiled without looking at her, and Rose knew that her friend had just waited for her to say something. She thought that the other woman knew how to read her a little too well. "I think it feels quite good being a little rough around the edges . . . or hedges. . . ."

Rose lifted her eyebrows at the poor joke her friend had made, but Akila found it funny. She giggled next to her and then laughed loudly when she saw Rose's slightly irritated expression.

Warmth travelled through Rose when she realised how pleased she was that they were able to sit here and that she got the chance to roll her eyes at the bad joke Akila had cracked. The last few months hadn't been easy on the woman, and now, in spring, it looked like the bits and pieces of life were finding their places again. "Hmmmhhhh," Rose muttered. "We might just have to do something about your humour, my dear friend."

Akila covered her face with her hands and glanced at her from behind her long fingers. She nodded. "I know," she said, straightening up and looking at the garden again.

Rose grinned.

"How's Edith?" Akila asked. "Still working on that case?"

Rose sighed. "Yes. It is consuming all her days and nights. I don't know what I was thinking, falling in love with a big-shot lawyer."

Akila took a sip from her glass, a thoughtful expression on her face. "Okay, she's in love with her job, but all in all it seems so much less dramatic than it was with Kayla."

"Oh my! Please don't remind me!" Rose exclaimed and shuddered in a rather exaggerated fashion to show her friend how much she agreed. "That was too much. I think we weren't ready to accept what we were feeling, and then there was the fear of what would happen if people found out." She sighed. "It's sad, thinking about how much fear there was . . . that we couldn't just be who we were."

Akila stared up at the sky, her long legs stretched out in front of her. "What's different this time?" She abruptly looked at Rose, her eyes shining in the light. "I mean, why is it easier now?"

Rose frowned slightly, thinking about it. "I'm not sure, but I think it's us. We give each other strength, and we both know how we want to live. So even if people around us aren't okay with it, it seems to matter less."

Akila glanced up. "I would want that too," she mumbled. "A silent agreement on peaceful and free living."

Rose could only smile at her friend's statement. "You are hope-lessly romantic," she concluded.

"No. I've simply seen that most of the time, I end up in a situation that is too limiting for me–almost suffocating. It's as if I and the other person suddenly speak different languages. We think we understood each other, but it turns out not."

Rose took a very long and deep breath. "Maybe that's how it is with humans. . . ."

* * *

"What–you think, you can live off the fame of the group? You know it's dead. You are the only one who still believes that we're a team. It's been over for years. Get a grip."

Ji Su was shocked by the unexpected harsh words that hit him full force, and he couldn't think of anything that would have been an appropriate response. JH was already walking away from him.

They had all met for a fan meeting in Japan. It had been a while since the five young men had come together to celebrate their past successes as boy band members. These days, they were all busy with solo projects and studies. Ji Su was the only member who still lived in Korea. All the others had relocated to Japan, Europe, or the U.S. Many of their fans still waited for their next album, but the discussions about their next project as a group were being pushed over and over again, a result of the many individual commitments the members had.

It's true, Ji Su thought. He seemed to be the only one who still held on to the dream of their group hitting the top of the charts again. Was it like JH said? He wasn't ready to live his own dream and leeched off what they had all built together.

True, it had been hard, looking for the next project to work on, accepting the nos when they came, hunting for what truly excited and consumed him so that he could give it his all. He felt as if he had been forced to slow down a little too much of late, and it made him uncomfortable to realise over and over again that he wasn't going at full speed, that the energy inside him wasn't being burned and began to fill him up more and more so that there were days when he woke up in the morning ready to scream.

What he did instead was work out. He'd always been fit, but of late, he'd taken his exercise to a whole new level. He knew it was too much–that the energy was meant to go somewhere else–but it was hard to focus and find that place. Somehow there was no visible path these days, not like before. And everyone else seemed clear about their own way and seemed successful and strong. Why not him? Where was his focus, and where was the success he was seeking?

Just two days earlier, he'd looked at the last clip he'd posted on his channel and felt sick to his stomach for the rubbish he'd put online. He had filmed himself working out in the morning without a shirt on and then prepared chicken breast and salad for breakfast. In the video, he talked about his craving for fried chicken and his eating habits.

Covering his face with his hands, he laid back on his couch, his phone resting on his chest. What had he been thinking? Was there really nothing more inside him?

So JH's outburst hurt, but most of the pain was a result of the truth that was hidden in the words. Not him leeching, but him not really being able to find his own footing and, therefore, relying on their group to be what defined him.

Or was it something else altogether, and he just didn't understand himself anymore?

Yoongi put his arm around his shoulder. "Don't take it too personally," he said with his eyes on JH, who was just disappearing through the heavy metal door into the corridor outside their lounge. "He probably has a hard time in Germany." The slightly taller man smiled at Ji Su and then walked away too.

So many memories with these four other men. And now it was all over? Was he the only one having a tough time letting their highs and lows go?

Apparently. Rae In and Mike were both sitting on the couches that dominated the lounge and were busy on their phones. They didn't seem particularly excited and had only briefly looked up when JH stormed out.

* * *

Joyce covered her face with her hands and considered picking up the phone to call Akila, but she didn't do so. Akila had too many things going on and, anyway, what would she tell her? Somehow it felt ridiculous to her that she was so affected by the news. Hadn't she grown a thick skin over the years of her childhood?

Apparently not thick enough, and that annoyed her. She wanted to accept the fact that life threw stuff her way and that she had to take it the way it came. But it was hard–really hard today. It was annoying that she, who had studied gender and knew that she shouldn't let her physical abilities as a female influence how she felt about her identity, was struggling.

It had been a few months since she had first seen a doctor when Akila was still in Nairobi. Her friend had waited outside while Joyce had her discussion with the doctor after she had taken several scans the week prior. It was an irony that she'd accepted to live with the pain all her adult life, basically since her second or third period. And that day in the doctor's consultation room, she learned that the pain she'd endured wasn't normal–that it wasn't true that some women just suffer from terrible pain and others, like Akila, did not.

No. Since her reproductive system had started being active, something genetic had kicked in and an evil growth had slowly taken over, covering her ovaries, her uterus, and spreading even to other organs. And she hadn't known, thinking she had to hold out whenever the pain took over.

The thing she felt slightly bitter about but had been trying to not think about too much, was the conversation with her mother after she had learned about her condition. Her mother had always given her the impression that menstrual pains were normal and one had to endure them. But when she spoke to her mother about what she'd learned, her mother recounted that one aunt and a few cousins had suffered from the same thing.

"So why have you never encouraged me to get checked?" Joyce asked, a lump in her throat.

Her mother had shaken her head slowly and responded, "I just never thought of it."

No need to feel bitter about it. It was what it was, Joyce told herself. But it hurt. And today she was here after the surgery to remove the growth.

All had gone well, she'd been told. The growth was under control for a while, but she needed to take measures–either hormones to control it or surgeries whenever it got too much. But would it have been best to have children first, if she was planning to have kids?

After a year of marriage, she and her husband had discussed having children.

Well, the doctors had said one of her ovaries had stopped working due to the damage the growth had caused over the years, and the other was only about forty percent working. So children were probably only possible with In Vitro Fertilisation, meaning an intense and often exhausting journey with loads of money required.

Joyce laughed and thought what a joke this life was sometimes. But, really, why did it bother her so much? Shouldn't she be stronger and see her worth in her personality and less in her body's ability to create life?

It was just . . . her family had already started asking when they would get their first baby, and her old acquaintances were asking too. A year after marriage was definitely the right time to become a mother, said the world. And it was a sad feeling inside her to know that she was practically broken–that the part that worked for basically every other woman was broken inside her.

Cold air

Insoo opened his eyes but didn't move for several minutes. The alarm continued to ring, filling his head with sound. A small pain developed on the right side of his head and steadily grew until he felt that there would be nothing else today.

He eventually moved his arm and felt for his phone on the nightstand to switch off the alarm.

It was 5:30 in the morning, and he was already exhausted.

Two and a half hours later, Insoo stood on a rooftop in the heart of Seoul holding a cup of hot coffee in one hand, which his assistant, Mr. Park, had brought him just a moment ago. He shoved his other hand deep into the pocket of his thick coat to keep it warm. It should have been spring, but the beginning of the warmer season had turned out really cold this year, and white clouds hung in front of the faces of the crew, all busily moving up and down on the rooftop.

Insoo briefly thought of a beehive with humming activity when looking at the scene, then turned to gaze over the thousands of roofs that were Seoul. Although it was only morning, there was a haze hanging across the vast city, and Insoo could feel the cold air biting his cheeks and lips. For some reason, there was a painful knot in his chest. Or was this, again, in his head? He wasn't really sure but tried to shake it off with a deep sigh that he released into the winter morning.

Someone called his name. It was time for his scene soon. Insoo nodded and gave a thumbs up in the general direction of the crew, then turned back to take another long look at the city, sipping the last coffee from his cup.

Closing his eyes, he tried to fill the cold he felt in his chest and in his head with the character he was playing in the latest series he was shooting for one of the popular studios. It was another drama, destiny and first love being the main themes.

With a sudden jolt, he realised that he was extremely bored. Another day replaying all these fake moments of love and affection, moments he knew didn't exist in real life. *What's the use?* he asked himself, a very familiar fatigue gripping him, a fatigue he experienced often these days. It was a question Insoo had never really asked himself before, but in recent weeks, it had popped up in his head like the bubbles in cartoons and confused him whenever he tried to focus. He felt that there was something that, soon, he wouldn't be able to take anymore.

Three hours later, Insoo was sitting on a small wall with a blanket wrapped around his shoulders, the cold still biting his face, the sun illuminating the Seoul haze with golden white slanted rays of light. The scene had been completed as an "OK. Cut," meaning that Insoo and the female lead had done a great job and they could move on to the next one.

Many hands had touched him today. When arriving at the scene, Insoo was greeted by the crew, and many of those he was familiar with had greeted him warmly, putting their hands on his shoulder or briefly resting them on his back. The women touched less, rather smiling and giving a small nod in his direction, but their glances and words greeted him with almost the same physical impact.

"Insoo, you look awesome today!"

"So cute!"

"Such beautiful lips!"

"Look, there he is! Isn't he super handsome?"

Why did it bother him these days? He wasn't able to put a finger on the exact reason why he hated those moments when they reached out and touched his shoulder or put a hand on his knee and commented on his looks. He didn't recall when it had started. It was as if one day he woke up being different.

The director had invited the main actors, actresses, and part of the crew for a meal after the shoot, and Ma Ru had already warned him that there would be no way out of the gathering. Apparently, a few alterations to the program were meant to be discussed.

Insoo sighed. He was exhausted and cold and would have preferred to just go home and rest a little without interruptions. But here he was, walking into the restaurant with a smile on his face, greeting the already gathered colleagues warmly. He was shown a seat right next to the director on one side and the female lead on the other, who smiled at him welcomingly.

"Great, you are here!" the director exclaimed, and food and drinks were ordered.

The restaurant was famous for its traditional Korean cuisine, and the dishes were said to be very delicious.

Insoo made an effort to engage in the joking and small talk around the table. He was sure that if anyone here would be asked later if Insoo was a nice person, easy to get along with, and well-mannered, no one would object, and they'd probably add how funny and witty he was. This was a game he usually played with himself, focusing entirely on the image he wanted to project and not giving himself a single moment to dwell on the dread that clutched his heart.

Whenever he came out of such situations victoriously, he felt elated but empty of any other emotion.

The food had arrived, and after everyone had taken a few bites of their meals, the director cleared his throat and began: "As you all know, this program is a big production with high expectations as to how it is received by the viewers. We have just gotten the update that we have an additional sponsor for the production, which is really good for us. But this also has an impact on some of the scenes for the next episodes, so I want all of us to be prepared for those adjustments. They aren't major, but still. . . ." The man went on to explain as everyone listened attentively.

Insoo suddenly felt the heat and stuffiness of the place. There seemed to be no air in the restaurant, or was it just where he was sitting?

In an attempt to make himself feel a little more comfortable, he fidgeted with the collar of his linen shirt, which resulted in a slightly displeased look from the director, who seemed to notice that he was restless. Insoo bowed his head to apologise and tried to stay still, but now he was completely sure that he wasn't getting enough air into his lungs. Without any warning, his vision shifted and he was unable to hear any sound except a loud rush in his ears.

He stood abruptly, hitting the table and taking down a whole heap of bowls and plates, including food, with him as he lost balance and fell backward. Insoo didn't hear any of the surprised yelps and screams when he fell. He'd already lost consciousness when his entire body hit the ground and his head met with the edge of the stone step behind their table.

As he lay on the floor, staff and colleagues milling around him, panicky and shocked, he was in a place where it was dark and peaceful. Someone called an ambulance and, moments later, he was lifted on a stretcher and carried away.

When Insoo woke up, he had trouble opening his eyes at first. Everything seemed very bright. Someone was squeezing his hand, but he couldn't immediately hear or see anything. In an effort to get his bearing, he tried to move his head, and a sharp pain shot through him, momentarily paralysing him.

Sound came rushing back at him, and he recognized his mother's voice.

"My son," she whispered, her voice thick with emotion. She was still squeezing his hand, almost as if she was holding onto him for dear life.

He willed his fingers to respond and managed to give a slight squeeze back.

His mother held his hand even tighter, crying silently.

His sight was getting clearer, and he was able to make out the hospital room, his mother next to him, and the nurse who entered the room, followed by his father.

* * *

Talida closed her geography book with a loud bang, making the girl who was standing by her desk jump. She stared at the book cover and sighed deeply, looking up at the pretty girl with the bouncy ponytail, blonde and blue-eyed, slim-figured—her mother would have said she was a perfect stereotype and would have warned her not to judge too quickly. But Talida had had three requests from fellow students asking to touch her hair already, and one person had actually put her hand in her dark blonde afro without asking for permission first. She was still wondering if the girl had thought that her hair wasn't real and that she wouldn't notice. Thus, Talida had a truly annoying morning, and she really didn't want to spend any more time being considerate.

"No," she finally said, her head moving left and right on her neck with her anger rising. "I do not speak *African.*" She spat out the last word. "Before you ask stupid questions and waste my time, you should Google it first. It's that simple." She packed her books noisily, making a point of ignoring the girl standing there looking quite flustered.

"Gosh, no need to get all sensitive about it," the girl mumbled, turning away. "I was just asking."

Talida could literally feel how she was rolling her eyes. Some of the other girls giggled. Talida had a hundred things on her mind that she wanted to say to that girl and to the others, who seemed to find it funny.

But what difference would it make? She'd heard many such questions–questions that were annoying and left her feeling as if she was always conspicuous, never completely being a fitting part of her surroundings. Her mother usually said that was just how many people were and that it said everything about them, but nothing about who she was. Although Talida knew that it was meant to comfort her, it actually left her feeling even more lonely. Were there really so few people that one could feel connected to? Was it such a bleak and lonely world in which most people chose to remain ignorant? The thought was depressing.

Talida stepped out of the school building and into the cold air. It was break time, and although it was freezing, the front of the school was packed with pupils standing together in small groups. The noise travelling into the winter sky was deafening to her ears, but still, Talida felt liberation after being inside the classroom the entire morning. She'd come to realise that she liked winter and that the fresh, cold air entering her lungs made her feel clearheaded and focused. So she walked down the steps and wound her way through the many bodies to find a less crowded spot.

As she walked by, she felt several pairs of eyes on her, and bits and pieces of comments travelled through the cold towards her.

". . . that hair . . ."

"Gosh! She walks as if she's . . . like . . ."

"That skin . . ."

Talida held her head high and made a point of letting her facial features remain motionless, like a mask. *Another day in Europe,* she thought to herself. She found a small wall in one corner of the yard and sat down alone with her snack. She pursed her lips and blew. A cloud of white mist hung in front of her. It looked lovely, almost like smoke slowly winding its way up into the winter sky.

* * *

Mrs. Moon sat by Insoo's bed. She slowly stroked her son's hand. It had almost become an automatism, and she didn't fully realise that she was still stroking him. He had been awake briefly and then drifted off again into sleep, pulled down into nothingness by the medication he'd been given.

The doctor had said that her son would be able to go home soon, which was a relief. When she'd first seen him on the hospital bed, she'd been frozen with shock at his pale face and the bony structure of his shoulders and chest that had been partly exposed by the hospital gown he was wearing. He looked so much weaker than the last time they had met. Or was it just that she hadn't seen it then, too excited and feeling proud of her beautiful child who had received so much recognition and praise and who had even gotten an award for his efforts?

But the even scarier feeling had been the familiarity of her help-lessness and fear. It wasn't the first time she saw her son in such a state, closed eyes, unmoving on a hospital bed.

Insoo had always been the type to be recognised. Mrs. Moon thought of it as a quality he'd inherited from her side of the family, the looks and the aura that one needed to stand out. Her husband just looked at her whenever she brought the subject up. Well, at least he'd gotten the height and the broad shoulders from his father, which did play a role in how he was received by the world.

From an early age, Insoo had taken Judo classes and had shown great skill. Just like everything he set his mind on, he'd perfected the moves, trained relentlessly, and soon joined tournaments. He'd gotten to national-level competitions and achieved several wins.

Then there'd been Insoo's first injury. It was one of the most scary moments in Mrs. Moon's life, seeing her son in pain and not being able to do much to help him. And, again, today, she seemed suspended in space, unable to help him–her son who was no longer a child and who seemed much harder to reach these days. All she could do was stroke his hand while he was asleep and unable to move away from her.

* * *

Akila hung up the phone and opened the door to her garden. Cold air hit her like a force. She stood and inhaled deeply, enjoying what the freezing sensation did with her lungs. It felt as if crystal clear liquid flowed through her and made her wide awake. It was the one thing she was able to truly appreciate about winter.

Akila had been on the phone with Marcus for a long time, and although it was slightly exhausting for her to speak with him, she was grateful for the fact that they were able to have a conversa-tion, tell each other how they were getting on and discuss when the children should visit him. Akila knew that Marcus was still not the type to share his hardships openly–in her opinion a result of upbringing–and he mostly talked about good things or made the hard things sound much better than they were.

She'd decided that she would simply let him be. Now that she had put distance between them–not the distance between Scotland and Kenya, but the emotional distance that came with their separation–she was able to accept much better that was the way he dealt with life. They had set a date for Mavis and Talida to fly over during the long summer holidays–just two weeks, but Akila felt that it was necessary for her children to stay connected with Kenya and to see Marcus and their other relatives and friends.

She stepped out into the garden while hugging herself in an effort to feel less of the cold. But the air bit her skin and after a few more deep breaths and a long gaze into the colourless sky above her, she went back inside to continue with her work.

A dog and a song

Mavis skipped along the hot asphalt, enjoying the heat that seeped through his soles every time his bare feet hit the ground. He was singing an old Popcaan party song in his mind, something his mother listened to at high volume when she needed a burst of energy to go on with her work on days when some things seemed harder than usual.

The little street was empty except for Mrs. Miller's huge striped cat, who was sprawling on the cool stone steps in front of her owner's house. When Mavis approached, the cat lifted her head slightly, ears alert and waiting for him to give her her usual treatment. Mavis stopped next to the stone steps and caressed the big cat tenderly behind its ears.

"Hi Biggy," Mavis said with a smile, to which the cat responded with a demanding, "Meow!"

"I'm in a hurry right now so I'll see you later!" Mavis continued on his way for a few more metres, then jumped over the little hedge into Mrs. Miller's garden. Since they had moved here, Mavis had discovered a hundred different ways to get from A to B in this little community, and he loved to roam about the backyards and gardens of their neighbours. Especially now, in summer, it was the perfect kingdom—his own universe of lush lawns to daydream on, bushes heavy with berries just waiting to be plucked and animals to spend time with, leave alone the different boys and girls he could choose to spend time with . . . or the adults, most of whom were really friendly.

It wasn't uncommon for Mavis to walk across someone's lawn and be called in for a cold self-made lemonade or a piece of cake. The first time this happened he'd been a little suspicious, but by now he was sure that this place was simply destined to be his paradise and that most neighbours were in one way or the other connected to him. He took several of the neighbours' dogs for walks regularly and watched cats when their owners had gone for a weekend trip.

Mavis somehow knew that the usually receptive attention he received from the world had something to do with his looks. He remembered a conversation between Edith and his mother a few months ago after an incident with the music teacher at school and how furious Akila had been.

"I don't want him to think that it's all about the looks, Edith!" Akila had exclaimed. "What kind of perspective on the world would that be? And what if one day he encounters someone who doesn't care about his looks or doesn't wish him well, precisely because of those looks? There is no way I am tolerating this!"

At the time, Mavis hadn't really understood what the fuss was all about. His music teacher, who was also his class teacher, was a kind woman who usually treated him well, and he was grateful for the fact that she had wanted to let the incident with Matt slide. Why did it matter so much to his mother *why* Ms. Pearson had wanted to let it go?

The whole thing had escalated after the preparation for the school play. Mavis' school took a lot of pride in those presentations, and playing a part was considered a big deal. Music had been one of his passions for as long as he could remember, and he'd been pleased when he was asked if he could take one of the leading parts in the next play.

Mavis was used to people's comments about his hair, and he was also particularly used to the boys' comments pointing out his "girly looks." It didn't happen often, but when it happened, he chose to ignore it for the most part and, usually, the jokes stopped with time.

But from Mavis' experience, some people simply didn't know how to stop, and Matt was one of them. He was part of Mavis' football team and part of the school band, but he seemed less interested in the latter and frequently disrupted practice–something Mavis registered as an irritating tendency on Matt's part.

Even after several weeks in the new school and being part of the football team and school band, Mavis still had to put up with Matt's comments. He actually felt that Matt was slowly increasing the frequency and adjusting his choice of words to something more hurtful by the week.

After the announcement regarding the different participants for the play, Matt had geared up even more and pestered Mavis whenever they met and no adult was around. Mavis wondered what his problem was. He didn't seem interested in the play anyway, so why make comments about Mavis' participation all the time?

It had been a warm spring morning when Mavis left school a little later than usual because he'd worked with one of his bandmates on a piece they were to present during the play. Talida was meant to pick him up so that they could go home together, but passing the school gates, he realised that she hadn't yet arrived.

"Hey, faggot!" came a shout from behind, and the next moment, something hit Mavis on the back of his head. A small stone dropped onto the pavement. Rubbing the spot, Mavis turned to see Matt standing a few metres behind him by the wide steps leading into the building, grinning widely. "Great shot, right brownie?"

Talida arrived at the school gates fifteen minutes later. Her brother stood in front of the gates staring at the blue sky, hands in his pockets, as had been his habit since early childhood. He was humming "Sheria," a song by the Kenyan band Sarabi their mother loved.

They walked down the road toward the bus stop, singing the lyrics together.

"Nalipa tax,
Na atta siwezi afford
Kupanda taxi . . .
Kwa benki sina ka kitu
Siwezi afford atta shirti . . .

"I'm paying tax,
But I can't even afford
To take a taxi . . .
I have nothing in the bank,
I can't even afford a shirt . . ."

Matt wasn't in school the next day, and Mavis enjoyed the peace he felt without his repeated pestering. Matt also didn't take part in football practice that afternoon. A day later, just after their first break, Ms. Pearson walked into the classroom with a serious expression on her face and asked Mavis to join her in the headmistress' office.

Mavis remembered the serious faces of the two women and how he wondered if he should feel guilty but decided not to. There was enough that Matt had done to deserve a proper beating. In the headmistress' office, two men sat on chairs, and although Mavis noted how differently they were dressed, he also recognized the similar features in their faces. Both had dark blonde hair and freckles on their noses, which pointed slightly upward. Mavis was absolutely sure that they were related. *Maybe brothers?* he thought.

"Mavis, please take a seat," the headmistress said. "We've already called your mother and she's on her way."

Mavis looked at the two men, who were looking at him. One wore a smart suit and tie and smiled a little when their gaze met. The other wore simple jeans and a shirt and seemed to frown at him with all his might.

Suddenly Mavis realised who these two resembled, and he couldn't help but shift a little in his chair. They did look like an older version of Matt.

This isn't good, Mavis thought.

They all sat in brooding silence for a while. Then the gentleman in the suit started polite small talk with the headmistress and Ms. Pearson.

As they talked about the weather, there was a knock on the door, and Mavis was relieved and scared at the same time to see his mother enter the room, closely followed by Edith.

"Good afternoon," Akila greeted the group with a tight-lipped smile.

The headmistress motioned toward a small couch in the corner of the already cramped room. "Thank you for making the time so quickly, Ms. Kruse," the headmistress said.

Akila nodded, sitting down on the couch with Edith.

There was tense silence for a moment. Then Akila began, "You already mentioned something on the phone, but what exactly is this about?"

"It's about your little brute hitting my boy!" thundered the slightly larger of the two men, whom Mavis assumed to be Matt's dad. The man next to him placed his hand on his arm to silence him.

Akila shot a quick glance at Mavis, who responded by staring at his shoes some more. Now he was sure he was in trouble.

"What happened?" His mother addressed him directly, and he had no choice but to look at her. Her eyes had become large and unwavering, and he knew that it was better to simply tell the truth.

"He kept bothering me," he started but was immediately interrupted by Matt's father's snort.

"Such a lie!"

"Allan," the man in his suit muttered. "Let the boy talk."

Akila smiled at Mavis. "Mavis, just tell us what happened so that we can clear this up. Don't hold back."

He took a deep breath, then began again. "He kept bothering me. That day, he hit me with a small stone and called me all kinds of names. So I told him to stop, and he still didn't."

Mavis remembered how he walked towards Matt, who'd laughed into his face and continued to call him all those names. The back of his head still hurt from the stone, and Mavis decided that it was enough. It hadn't been a conscious decision, but telling the story now, he realised that he simply hit his limit.

So he grabbed a surprised Matt by his collar and dragged him behind the school's shed where all the gardening tools and other stuff were kept. He pushed Matt to the ground and asked him whether he would stop now. After a pause, the other boy continued with his insults, although he sounded a little less confident.

That was when Mavis kicked him a few times and punched him once, leaving Matt with a bleeding nose. The boy was whimpering by then, trying to protect himself from Mavis' kicks.

"Call me anything again and you are dead," Mavis had said calmly and then walked off. The whole thing didn't take very long, so by the time Talida arrived by the school gates to pick him up, he had had enough time to calm down his screaming heart.

There was silence in the office after he finished telling his story.

Matt's dad started yelling again. "Those are lies! Matt would never! And even if, what justifies such a beating?"

Ms. Pearson, who had stood in the back quietly all this time, suddenly stepped forward and said, "I must say that Mavis has been having a hard time because of Matt. And Mr. MacCallan, we've had a few conversations about Matt's behaviour in class and music practice."

The man stared at the young teacher in obvious disbelief.

Edith leaned forward and spoke in her calm voice. "Now that we've heard Mavis' story, I suggest we discuss this without hurling accusations." She turned to Mavis. "Mavis, please wait outside."

Mavis had to wait for quite a while before the grown-ups came out of the headmistress' office. Akila walked next to Ms. Pearson while Edith stayed behind with the two Macallan men. Mavis heard Akila say to his teacher, "Thank you for your support today. Your opinion really helped in sorting this out."

"Although I agree that Mavis should receive punishment for what he did, I must honestly say that I can see why this happened. Also, I can't afford to lose him in the play. He is very crucial for its success." The two women had reached him now. "And how could you ever resist those looks?" Ms. Pearson put a hand on Mavis' shoulder, smiling at his mother and then at him.

Mavis looked at Akila and wondered whether Ms. Pearson was much slower than he'd thought or if she just didn't know how to read his mother. Thick thunderclouds built up around his mother's head, and he knew that it was better to tread carefully.

"What do you mean?" Her voice was ice cold, no emotion detectible in it, and Mavis decided that it was better to look at his feet once more.

"Ehm . . . I mean. . . ."

Good, Mavis thought to himself. She seemed to have finally spotted the danger.

"Mavis is a wonderful addition to this school. That is all I was saying," Ms. Pearson was obviously trying to rescue the situation.

"Because of his looks?" came the merciless reply, and Mavis bit his lip, wishing he was in another place.

Just that moment, Edith came down the corridor toward them after having finished her conversation with Matt's family. "Let's go home," she said, giving a polite goodbye nod to Ms. Pearson as she ushered them along. Mavis was relieved to have gotten out of the situation without having to witness his mother's full reaction to Ms. Pearson's statement.

Akila and Mavis were silent sitting next to each other in the car. Edith had taken her own vehicle, which she'd parked on the school grounds earlier. Mavis thought it was safer to glance out of the window, which he did with real dedication. But he could sense Akila glancing at him. "Sorry mama," he finally muttered in German.

Akila shot another glance at him, then sighed and focused on the road ahead. "Why didn't you say anything?"

"Because I thought he would stop."

"But he didn't."

He shook his head, still gazing out the window.

There was a pause. Then she asked, "Do you get many such comments?"

He shook his head. "Not many."

"Mavis, are you really okay? You beat that boy until he had to be seen by a doctor. Are you comfortable here or are you having a hard time? Just tell me. You know that we can always find somewhere else to stay."

"I'm fine, really." He turned to face her. "He just made me so angry!"

Akila stared at him for a second, then nodded. "I'm not surprised, now that I know the dad. The poor boy." Mavis wondered why she would feel sorry for such an annoying person, but Akila went on. "But, Mavis, just tell us next time. We're lucky that Edith knows Matt's uncle really well. Otherwise, this might have turned into something a little more complicated."

"Sorry," Mavis mumbled.

All of a sudden, his mother pulled the car over and slung her arms around him. They sat like that for a while. Then Mavis felt that he had hugged his mother long enough. "Mama, let's go home." He wriggled out of her embrace and pushed her back a little.

She smiled and nodded. "Fine."

Still thinking about the incident, Mavis had reached Mr. Anderson's backyard. The backdoor was open. As soon as he approached, a huge white furry creature shot through it and jumped at him with an excited bark. Mavis laughed, caressing Ben, Mr. Anderson's large white German shepherd, then slowly walked into the dark interior of the house.

The old man sat in front of the TV with his broken leg hoisted up on a stool. There was a plate of half-eaten sausage, egg, and beans next to him. He glanced up and nodded to acknowledge Mavis' presence and then turned almost immediately back to the quiz show he was watching.

"Hi Mr. Anderson," Mavis greeted over the noise of the TV. "I'm going to take Ben for a walk now."

The old man waved his hand vaguely as if to tell him to stop bothering him, but Mavis had decided to not take any of his strange behaviour personally. Since he'd fallen down the staircase a few weeks earlier, Mr. Anderson had changed a lot, and Mavis had a feeling that it had much to do with his frustration about his immobility and less with anything else. He fetched Ben's leash from the hall and left with the excited dog by his side.

They roamed the backyards and gardens together, avoiding the direct heat from the sun, and looking for cool places to take a rest. The afternoon progressed with the sound of the buzzing bees and the occasional bark of another dog or high-pitched laughter of a child. Otherwise, it was almost completely silent.

Their roaming had taken them close to home, with Mavis humming "Sheria" under his breath. The song had stuck in his head, probably because of him thinking about the thing with Matt.

When they'd just jumped the hedge into Miller's garden, Ben suddenly stood alert next to him. The lush green lawn climbed up a slight slope and ended at high creepers heavy with rose flowers that marked the beginning of Mrs. and Mr. Williams' place. Before Mavis could act, Ben was already flying up the slope and disappeared into the creepers.

"Ben!" Mavis followed the dog, but because of the thorns he encountered when trying to take the same path Ben had taken through the foliage, he took a moment longer. Once he had made his way through on all fours, he became aware that he was right on the Williams' porch. Ben was there wagging his tail and whimpering in a low tone. Mavis now noticed the two feet in pretty leather sandals next to him, and when he glanced up, he looked right into Mrs. Williams' dark brown eyes. Deciding that it was no good staying on all fours on the floor, Mavis jumped to his feet.

"Hi, Mrs. Williams," he muttered. For some reason, he felt like an intruder. Ben was still whimpering, and Mavis moved to calm him down when he noticed that something wasn't quite right with Mrs. Williams' face. He froze and slowly lifted his head to take a better look at her.

Although he'd made direct eye contact with her just a second ago, he only noticed now that her one eyelid seemed different, hanging somehow down over her eye, and there was a strange colouring on her cheekbone. The woman held a wet cloth to her mouth, and when she moved it slightly, he could make out a tear and dry blood. Mavis' heart seemed to skip a beat and then resumed its rhythm at a much faster pace. Mrs. Williams glanced over her shoulder toward the open door that led into her cottage, then turned and gazed at him directly. Very slowly, she lifted her one hand and placed one finger over her lips.

Mavis stared at her in disbelief and opened his mouth to say something, but she shook her head quickly and placed her hand on his naked arm. Her skin was dry and hot and she pulled him a little closer, shaking her head again. Her eyes seemed to plead with him and his heart beat even faster. Out of impulse, he shook her hand off and took a step back. Looking at her, he saw that she had been crying and was probably about to do so again.

"Mavis," she whispered.

Mavis lowered his gaze and grabbed Ben by the collar. He pulled the large dog away from Mrs. Williams and the porch, then hooked the leash onto the small ring on the collar and left the garden through the gate without looking back.

Once he was outside the gate, he sprinted down the street, Ben by his side. He only stopped at the next corner where he leaned his back on the warm stones of the wall, closed his eyes, and stayed there until his breathing was back to normal. Ben sat patiently on the pavement, tongue out, waiting for Mavis to regain his composure.

That night, Mrs. Williams appeared in his dreams. After all his attempts to find sleep failed, he walked down the small corridor, opened the door to his mother's room, and climbed into Akila's bed.

"Mavis," his mother murmured, still half asleep. "Did you have a bad dream?"

He nodded, although she wouldn't be able to see, given the darkness. She put one arm around him, and he curled up as closely as possible and eventually found sleep.

The end of it all

Lee Tae Oh was on his way to the set. He was excited and in a great mood, having gotten two days off shooting and being able to see Insoo, whom he hadn't spent time with in quite a while. Their careers had experienced a steady upward trend, and they'd both worked on several film projects and commercials. Insoo had even worked on a couple of theatre productions. Therefore, their time for social interactions had been very limited, particularly this year.

Tae Oh arrived at the set, a pretty, slightly old country schoolhouse with a large garden and a view of an unpaved road that was lined with a row of Magnolia trees. He took note of the beautiful scenery while parking the car next to the production van and a few other vehicles in the driveway. Getting out, he took a deep breath and stood in the sunshine for a brief moment, embracing the feeling of freedom. Then he turned to glance at the wooden house with the traditional windows and roof and wondered where everyone was. He slowly walked to the right around the building and, after a few steps, he was able to make out voices coming from the garden.

The majority of the crew was gathered on the open lawn facing a large pine tree and with a breathtaking view over lush green hills in the backdrop. "Wow!" Tae Oh muttered to himself, amazed by the backdrop they'd chosen for the production.

Insoo stood below the tree with one of his actor colleagues, an elderly, sturdy man they all respected as their senior, as he'd been in the film industry for years and had been part of several successful productions.

Keeping his distance, Tae Oh observed the scene. It seemed to be one of the more impactful moments in the drama. There was complete silence among the crew as everyone focused on getting the shot right. Cameras moved slowly across the tracks laid out on the lawn around the tree, and the crew members all seemed to be holding their breath a little.

The old man below the tree displayed slumped shoulders and simple clothes while Insoo's character was dressed in a fine linen shirt and elegant summer pants. They were both crying, and the younger man covered his face in distress. The older man said between sobs, "How can you be like this? Aren't I your father?"

Insoo was still crying. And was quiet.

As the silence progressed, Tae Oh sensed a change in the atmosphere. Was something wrong?

"Not again," someone not far from him muttered. Tae Oh shifted his weight from one leg to the other, suddenly feeling uneasy.

"Cuuuut!" came the shout, and the buzz started instantly. People shook their heads while others walked away from the set or adjusted their equipment with frustrated expressions.

"Does he want us to spend our days like this?" one man muttered.

Tae Oh walked across the short grass and could make out the director, who had left his position behind the monitors and was approaching Insoo. His friend was still standing below the wide branches of the pine, head high, his face blank. Tae Oh knew his friend well enough to recognize the tension by how he squared his shoulders and kept his back completely straight.

Tae Oh wasn't able to hear the exchange between Insoo and the director, but he saw how the younger man shook his head vehemently. They obviously had a disagreement, which was not part of Insoo's usual habit. However, the director seemed to have made up his mind. He turned and briefly spoke to one of his crew members who went ahead to shout across the lawn with a megaphone. "That's it for today, everyone! Take a rest. Let's resume tomorrow!"

Another burst of low noise broke out, and Tae Oh could feel a general sense of relief, but he was sure he also recognized something like disbelief among the people around.

After briefly greeting the director, Insoo's father in the series and some of the crew members Tae Oh had worked with before, he slowly moved toward his friend. Insoo stood alone at the edge of the garden facing the panorama of green hills and blue sky. "I guess I came at the right time when you can actually take me for a meal," Tae Oh said after hesitating for a few seconds, wondering how to begin.

The tall man turned around with a surprised expression and broke into a wide smile when he recognised his friend. "What are *you* doing here?" he exclaimed and they hugged briefly, clapping each other's backs and laughing.

"I missed you. What else?" Tae Oh responded and stood next to Insoo. Letting his gaze wander over the hills and small white clouds in the sky, he added, "Not a good day today?"

Insoo seemed to freeze for an instant before shaking his head slowly. "Not a good day. . . . The great thing is that we are both free now."

Tae Oh grinned. "Anywhere around here for a proper dish?"

A while later, they sat facing each other in a small restaurant with many tables that were full of noise from all the customers slurping their soups with noodles and conversing loudly. Luckily, they'd managed to sit by the open windows so the afternoon sunshine fell on their faces and the noise was a little more bearable.

Tae Oh made an effort to keep the conversation light and focused on what they'd been up to. Insoo looked tired, which was even more evident in the direct sunlight which highlighted his general paleness and the darkness below his eyes. His face seemed drawn, and even after several minutes together, there seemed to be a wall that Tae Oh was unable to break down. With a heavy heart, he noticed that his friend wasn't truly speaking his mind.

The sense of unease evaporated somewhat once they were outside again and walking along the main road of the small town.

Insoo seemed more like himself here–less tension in his back and shoulders more relaxed.

He's probably just exhausted, Tae Oh thought while listening to Insoo talk and observing his face carefully. *He also ate very little. He must be under a lot of pressure.* "What happened today?" he dared ask, interrupting Insoo mid-sentence. There was a long pause, longer than Tae Oh would have anticipated, and just when he thought that he probably wouldn't get an answer, Insoo finally responded.

"I have been forgetting my lines."

It was one of the true horrors for both of them–the fear that things wouldn't go as they should and that they weren't able to meet expectations. Tae Oh knew well how that terrifying feeling gripped one's heart and wasn't easily shaken off. He still got nervous whenever he had to shoot a scene.

They continued on their way in silence, both of them lost in their own thoughts.

"You've been doing a lot. Maybe you just need a few days off," Tae Oh finally offered and turned to look at his friend.

Insoo looked away. After a few more strides without any response, he nodded. "Yes, a few days off will be great."

"Hey, let's go on a trip once we're both done!" Tae Oh was excited by his own idea and grabbed his friend's arm. "Let's take some time and just enjoy the moment."

Insoo's face didn't mirror his excitement. Tae Oh noticed that at once. Still, he smiled at Tae Oh and gave a little bow to show his agreement. "That would be awesome," he said.

Something in his voice made Tae Oh feel deflated. For the rest of the afternoon, he was unable to shake off the feeling.

* * *

They spent almost the entire rest of the day outside in the sunshine, Insoo mainly listening to his friend, only sharing a few anecdotes of his own. He was happy to have his friend around, but at the same time, it was exhausting. By the time evening approached, he was worrying about dinner and asking himself how to navigate the situation. He was sure that he wouldn't be able to eat anything. The pressure had simply been too much. But what would his friend say when he saw him avoiding food? Would he notice? Would he ask? All these thoughts went through Insoo's mind and made it much harder to appreciate the time he was able to spend with Tae Oh.

It was dinner time when Insoo received the update from the director that they would start with another scene early the next morning, so the two men called it a day and went to bed early, with Tae Oh being anxious not to sidetrack his friend and Insoo hoping to escape his exhaustion for a few hours. As they settled down in the room, with Insoo in the bed and Tae Oh on the couch, they both took a while to fall asleep. Without knowing it, the two friends felt a similar kind of soft sadness pulling at their hearts.

* * *

Early the next morning, there was a general buzz on set when Insoo and Tae Oh arrived. Insoo was immediately ushered into one of the smaller rooms they were using to fix makeup and hairstyles, and Tae Oh remained on set, enjoying the fact that he could observe the early morning craziness without being directly involved in it.

Insoo's manager arrived thirty minutes later, greeting him with a tight-lipped smile. *He must have heard about what happened yesterday,* Tae Oh concluded.

Insoo and his colleagues were just getting ready on the pretty terrace of the house and everyone on the team was running to make the last adjustments to cameras, lighting, and makeup before the shoot began.

The call came and there was instant silence while the entire focus shifted towards the scene.

Tae Oh moved slightly to get a better view of Insoo, who he thought looked awesome this morning, although still a little tired.

The first few minutes went great and Tae Oh felt the relief going around the room. He could see the director wearing a satisfied expression while focusing on the screen in front of him.

But just then, there was a sudden pause around the set and prolonged silence until the call to end the scene cut through the air like a knife. Tae Oh moved closer, concern making his heart beat faster. He spotted Ma Ru hurrying towards Insoo, who stood frozen on the terrace with one hand covering his face and the other on the wall, seemingly to prevent himself from falling over. By the time he was at the terrace, Ma Ru had already gripped Insoo by one elbow and led him through the set and down one corridor deeper into the house, away from the stares.

Tae Oh followed, trying to ignore the frustrated comments being muttered all around him. The crew was tired of it all, that much was obvious.

Insoo was leaning on the wall further down the corridor, with Ma Ru talking to him frantically. But it didn't seem as if his friend was listening, having closed his eyes and his head resting on the white wall.

"Lee Tae Oh!" the manager exclaimed when he spotted him.

Insoo didn't move.

"Please take him to his room. I need to speak with the director first."

Someone called from down the corridor, probably the upset director. The man was known for his brilliance, but he was also known for his temper on set, and having his shoot interrupted in this manner not just once, but on two different days was certainly not good for his mood.

Tae Oh took Insoo by the arm and pulled him away from the wall. His friend followed him with shaky steps but didn't object. It was almost as if he wasn't aware of what was happening.

They reached the first floor over the staircase at the back of the house. Tae Oh made it to open the door when Insoo put his hand on his shoulder and moved him aside.

"Just . . . I will call you later. Please go back to Seoul for now."

Tae Oh stared in disbelief, not sure if he had understood correctly. "What. . . ."

"I will be fine. Really. I just need a moment."

"Insoo, this is crazy. How can you expect me to leave now?"

Insoo shook his head, covering his face again with one hand. Then he looked at his friend. "Can't you just respect me?" he shot at him. "Don't make this harder!"

Tae Oh was still dumbfounded when Insoo unlocked his room and closed the door with a loud bang, locking it immediately from inside.

* * *

Inside the room, Insoo froze with his back against the door, staring straight ahead. There was a burning sensation in his throat and his chest was pained, making it difficult for him to breathe properly. He slowly slid down to the floor, stretching out his long legs in front of him and clutching his chest on the left.

There were no tears. He felt completely empty.

Panic gripped him, and he turned to the right to throw up. There was nothing to leave his body, and the bile had an extreme stench that made him gag even more. Tiny blotches of blood had found their way onto the floor, too, and he looked at them for a while trying to feel something about them. He knew they weren't a good sign.

Someone was knocking and the noise was disturbing, so Insoo gathered all he had left in his limbs and moved away from the door. He stretched out on the carpet in front of the large glass door leading to the balcony and let his gaze wander across the ceiling.

It felt good, being completely still–feeling like something was coming to an end.

The longest summer

Talida hit the pedals of her bike as hard as she could to speed up as much as possible. When she gathered good speed, she let go of the handles and spread out her arms. The warm summer wind blew across her face and let her hair billow. Rushing down the hill, she felt a sense of freedom that made her heart jump and filled it with excitement and eager anticipation. *What else is coming my way?* she wondered.

It was their first summer in Scotland, and she was in love. She loved the rolling hills and breathtaking sunsets. She loved how the wind blew the clouds at an unbelievable speed across the countryside on some days and how the little flowers by the roadside attracted all the buzzing and humming creatures that she was so interested in.

When they'd moved, Talida had been furious at first. She was furious with her mother for uprooting them, for breaking up their small family, and for forcing her and her brother to start all over again so soon–making friends, getting used to the new school, looking for the right clubs to join.

But it hadn't taken Talida long to become aware of the fact that Scotland suited her, that the wide skies and wild wind blowing through her curls quieted her burning heart, and that she was able to be at peace in this empty space and be herself.

In early spring, Talida stood on the pavement in front of the small convenience store, waiting for her mother to pick her up. A shower had covered everything with tiny raindrops that twinkled and glittered in the pale sunlight breaking through the grey cover of clouds above the town. Talida raised her head to catch as much sunlight as possible on her face. It was a rather beautiful moment.

A group of teenagers strolled down the road towards her, pushing and shoving and laughing excitedly. Judging by their uniforms, they belonged to the local high school. Talida moved a little in an attempt to avoid getting caught up in the ruckus the girls and boys made while filing into the store.

One of the girls suddenly stopped and turned to look at her, although she was already halfway inside the store. Peeping around the muddy glass door, she looked at Talida.

"Hey, don't I know you? I think I saw you in our Taekwondo class."

Two boys of the group came to an abrupt halt behind the girl and also looked at Talida.

Feeling a little uneasy with the unexpected attention, she shifted and nodded. "Might be. I just joined Taekwondo."

"Ah!" The girl made a satisfied face and then grinned at the two boys behind her who were complaining about her blocking the way. She was of medium height and had straight brown hair caught up in a simple ponytail. Her strong legs were clad in white kneesocks that were now covered with dark brown patches of mud. "Hey, Michael, stop making a fuss and say hi to our Taekwondo mate!" she shouted at a boy who was arguing with another while trying to get out of the store. Then she turned back to face Talida, smiled, and stretched out her hand. "The name's Suzie," she said.

Suzie had grey-blue eyes that looked like aquarelle colours mixed with too much water. The beauty of the colour had been diluted and could only be guessed. But Suzie's smile was energetic and mischievous, and while the two boys pulled her out of the way to get into the store, Talida took hold of the offered hand and shook it.

More girls and boys spilled out from the store onto the pavement, tearing open packages of flavoured crisps and opening chocolate bars and juice bottles. To Talida, the noise seemed deafening.

A boy appeared next to Suzie. He was still occupied pushing one of his friends who had tried to trip him on the way out. "What,

Suzie?" He turned and seemed to freeze for an instant. Talida understood why. They looked at each other in astonishment.

"Hey, Michael, you didn't tell us you had a twin!" came a shout from behind. "Where have you been hiding her all this time?"

Same height, same colour and texture of hair, same long legs and arms, same wide, full mouth, same skin, same large brown eyes.

"Eh . . . hi." He offered his hand abruptly. "I'm Michael. You joined our Taekwondo class?"

Shaking his hand, she nodded. "Talida," she said.

The entire group surrounded them, making her feel like she was in an enclosed space and had little room to breathe.

"Wow! You guys really look like twins!"

"This is so weird!"

"Michael, what have you been keeping from us?"

Suzie, who stood right next to them, laughed loudly.

Talida felt a little shaky in her knees, and her head was pounding. She wished for all these people to go away.

Just then, she heard her brother's voice above the comments and laughter. "Talida!"

Looking over the heads of the girls and boys, she spotted her mother's car pulling up on the curb and her brother waving out of one window.

"I gotta go," she mumbled and let go of Michael's hand quickly. The others parted to let her through, and she was in her mother's car within seconds, letting out a sigh of relief after having escaped the noise and proximity of so many strange bodies.

"Hey, honey," her mother said and then focused on the traffic while pulling away from the pavement and joining the other vehicles on the road.

"Hey," Talida responded, still keeping her eyes shut but putting her hand on her brother's, which he'd placed on her shoulder, reaching over from the back.

"What? You already made like a hundred new friends!" he teased her, but kept his hand on her shoulder, which was extremely comforting.

Looking at him in the rear mirror, Akila rolled her eyes at her son. He grinned back at her. Talida saw the exchange and, looking straight ahead, she said, "Yeah, lovely noisy friends!"

"Who are they? I can't believe you stayed in that crowd," Mavis commented.

"Some are in my Taekwondo class. I think they're from the local high school."

Talida continued to hold her brother's hand and looked at the wet houses and streets and then, as they left the small town to drive along the winding roads toward home, at the muddy fields.

Two days later, Talida went for her second Taekwondo class. After walking into the practice room, she spotted Suzie and Michael almost instantly sitting on the low window sill, chatting. Michael saw her too, and Suzie seemed to notice his shift in attention because she turned around to follow his gaze. Recognizing her, she waved at Talida enthusiastically and motioned for her to come over.

"Hi," Talida said to both of them as she sat next to Suzie on the window sill.

The brown-haired girl stared at both of them with open amusement. "Wow, this is like a movie!" she finally said. "Are you sure that neither of you is adopted?"

"Suzie!" Michael hit the girl on her shoulder. "Are you crazy?"

"What? Man, that was a joke. Don't be so sensitive!"

Talida looked at her feet.

The instructor called for the class to join him in the centre of the room. They all stood up, with Suzie still arguing her case as she followed an irritated-looking Michael, who was trying his best to ignore her.

The three of them ran into each other again outside after practice. Talida was in a bit of a hurry to catch the next bus to go home, so at first, she thought of pretending that she had not heard Suzie's call. But then she changed her mind and stopped to wait for them.

"Hey, Talida, you are super fast!" Suzie was out of breath and laughing when she stopped next to her. "Why in such a hurry? Are you going somewhere?"

"Home," she responded.

Michael had caught up with them by now.

"We're going to have milkshakes at this really cool place. Why don't you join us? You can always go home after that." Suzie grinned at her, making her eyes really large and moving her eyebrows up and down in a gesture of excitement.

Talida couldn't help but smile a little.

"Or are your parents tyrants?"

"No. I'm just not sure if I want to join," she said.

Suzie's face changed instantly, her jaw dropping down, her water-colour eyes almost popping out of her face and her eyebrows shot up, fully expressing her disbelief. "My, you are something!" she said in a thick Scottish accent.

Michael, who stood next to her, burst out laughing, and he continued laughing so hard that he had to hold his ribs. "Ouch, that hurts!" he exclaimed, wiping tears away.

Suzie stuck her tongue out at him, not looking amused.

Talida smiled again, then took out her phone and called Akila.

Not long after that, they all sat at a table by the floor-to-ceiling window in the small corner cafe, slurping on their milkshakes.

Suzie did most of the talking, chattering away with no apparent full stops between any of her sentences. Talida was wondering how she managed to breathe with all that talking. Eventually, Michael put a hand on the girl's shoulder and said, "Suzie, just slow down for a minute."

She stopped herself immediately, muttering, "Sorry!" and put her mouth on the straw.

The ensuing silence was a relief for Talida. She was actually able to hear the low music playing in the background and the muted voices from the other customers.

"So, you just moved here?" Michael started the conversation.

She nodded. "This winter."

"How do you like it?"

"Not so sure yet. The nature is nice."

"And the people?" he asked with a small grin and glanced at Suzie. She stuck her tongue out at him again.

Talida laughed. "That's what I need to decide on."

Michael looked at her curiously. "You have an interesting accent. Where are you from?"

"Kenya and Germany. And you?"

"Ghana and Scotland," he responded.

Later, Talida flew down the hill. The summer air rang in her ears with a loud swish. Just before the sharp corner close to home, she put her hands back on the handles of her bike to take the right turn at the small junction. She was already able to see the first roofs of the houses on Greenwood Street, not far from their own street.

Talida had spent most of her afternoon at Michael's house in town, where she spent much of her free time these days.

Michael's home was a fascinating mixture of African and European influences, and Talida loved walking up the staircase to Michael's room, looking at all the photographs of Mrs. and Mr. Smith smiling at the camera while on a tropical beach, squeezed in with a group of colourfully dressed family members, holding hands at an airport or sipping fresh juice on a crowded market street. There were artefacts all over the house and, because Mrs. Smith worked as an anthropologist, every corner of the ground floor seemed to be packed with books and papers on the different languages, ethnicities, and the history of Africa.

Compared to this obvious celebration of "Africanness" in a burst of colour and an unaccountable array of items related to Mrs. Smith's heritage, Talida felt that her home was rather empty and cool, filled with too little colour and left with far too many open spaces.

The first time Michael had brought her home, Mrs. Smith had walked over to say hi, and after looking at Talida with obvious amazement, she had clapped her hands and announced, "Time for proper cooking!"

Mr. Smith, who had been sitting in the living room which was equally crowded with stacks of books, looked up from behind his paper and whistled cheerfully. "Today must be a special day! Michael, you must have done well."

Michael looked at his mother pleadingly. "Mum, please! I asked you not to be weird!"

The large woman swung her wide hips and adjusted her orange-red headscarf with a dignified look on her face. "Your mother is on her best behaviour," she said, to which Mr. Smith snickered from behind his paper in the most childish way.

Talida loved both of them instantly.

"I hope you're hungry." Mrs. Smith smiled at her warmly, and Talida simply nodded her agreement. At that moment, she would have agreed to anything this wonderful woman asked her to do.

Michael coaxed her up the staircase. "Call us when dinner is ready."

"Behave yourselves up there!" Mr. Smith called from the armchair he occupied.

"Daaaaad!" Michael released an exasperated sigh and muttered, "Sorry."

Talida laughed. "They are really sweet!"

He just rolled his eyes, muttering, "Yeah, right," under his breath.

Later, Talida rode on through Greenwood Street, then took another right to pass Rose's and Edith's cottage before coming to a halt in front of their own cottage. Now, in summer, light pink and yellow roses climbed up the wall outside their house, and dark green ivy covered the little roof on top of the entrance.

Mavis sat on the pavement, his naked feet covered with black soil and his knees covered in scratches from all the climbing he must have done today. Ben lay next to him, pink tongue hanging out of his mouth. As Talida approached, Ben wagged his tail a little but concluded that it was still too hot to move, so he stayed put next to his favourite human.

Talida dropped her bike in front of the house and then went over to sit next to Ben and her brother.

"Hey," she said by way of greeting as she sat down on the hot tarmac.

Mavis looked up at her in surprise. "Hi, Talida," he muttered.

"Wonderful spot," she commented, enjoying the warm golden light of the evening sun on her face.

When no response came, she looked at her brother. "You okay?"

"Hmmmh?" He gazed at her briefly with his large brown eyes, then nodded. "Yeah, all good."

Talida cocked her head to one side, observing Mavis for a few minutes, but not pushing him to speak.

"How was Michael's?"

"Great! He might pass by tomorrow. You want to join us for the lake?"

Mavis smiled briefly. "I would love to."

"Where's Mama?"

He pointed over his shoulder to the house. "She had a session earlier. Must be over by now."

"Kay. See you."

He nodded.

Talida stood and walked to the front door. As soon as she opened it, she could hear loud Algerian beats blaring across the living room. Soolking was going all out with "Melegim," and her mother was at the kitchen counter with a cup of coffee, looking at her laptop with a frown.

Talida waved. She doubted that Akila would have heard a word she said over the loud music.

Noticing her daughter, Akila reduced the volume. "Hey, Talida!"

"Hi! Tough day?"

Akila laughed. "Is it that obvious?"

Talida walked over to take a sip of her mother's coffee. "Loud rap music, coffee and you frowning at your laptop," she said by way of explanation.

Her mother gave a short snort that Talida found quite amusing and smiled tightly. "This client is just pissing me off. Why does he ask for coaching if he thinks he has all the answers anyway?"

Talida looked at her mother and wondered why her clients would ever want to cross her. Akila was quite adamant about what she believed. But that was the funny thing about her. Akila was so open and understanding when it came to people around them. Even with her brother, she appeared to be much more patient than with Talida.

But Talida felt that it was hard to say things sometimes and difficult to really start expressing her feelings to Akila. It was different with Mrs. Smith, with whom she was at ease. It was simple to talk about how it felt when someone suddenly touched her hair or made a comment about her looks. With her mother, she couldn't start talking, not wanting to see her mother's sadness and also not wanting to hear some of the explanations she tried to give for what people did. Who cared if the problem was really with them and not with her? It still upset her how they behaved. Why was she always the one who needed to be understanding?

This was how she felt with her mother these days.

Only Akila possessed a skill that Talida guessed she also used on her clients or Rose when she had a bad phase. She would shift her focus suddenly, often when things were pent up inside Talida when she hadn't had an outlet for her emotions for a while.

Akila would sit Talida down on their couch, or get her ice cream and take her to the garden, or stop the car on the side of the road when they were the only ones inside. And then she would look at her daughter and coax every single piece of frustration out of her, giving her the feeling that she was the only thing that mattered in the world, and she would say exactly those things that soothed the ache that Talida had been feeling.

That was when Talida felt strange about having wished that her mother was a little more like other mothers, and especially a little more like Mrs. Smith. Was it guilt that she felt? She wasn't completely sure what it was, but she knew that she didn't want her mother to spot those thoughts when she looked into her eyes.

"Have you seen your brother?" Akila asked. "He left hours ago and I haven't seen him."

"He's sitting outside with Ben. I think he was here, but you were working, so maybe you didn't notice him."

"Oh," Akila said, nodding.

Talida briefly considered mentioning that Mavis did seem a little off but then decided against it. She didn't want her mother to start thinking about things that Talida had maybe only imagined. She'd already discovered that she often saw things in her surroundings that were different from what others saw, and she avoided setting things in motion if she wasn't absolutely sure that what she had sensed would make sense also for someone else.

* * *

Talida spent most of her first summer in Scotland with Michael, often accompanied by Suzie and Mavis. It was an amazing feeling to walk around with someone whom everyone instantly recognized as a part of her. When people commented on how much they looked alike or when strangers assumed that they were siblings, they just smiled mysteriously. And when they held hands and got even more confused looks from strangers, they would enjoy the confusion they caused, feeling indefinitely and irrevocably connected.

When they were out with Mrs. and Mr. Smith, Michael's mother would sometimes ruffle both their hair affectionately and mutter, "My beautiful children!" and then release a happy sigh that made Talida feel all warm inside.

When Michael and Talida were out with Mavis and Akila, her mother would cock her head slightly at the comments about how amazingly good-looking her family was. But Akila wouldn't smile as happily as Mrs. Smith did, and she wouldn't walk around ruffling their hair affectionately. She would give a tiny smile and not respond to the comments at all. Somehow, that annoyed Talida.

When she mentioned the fact to Michael that her mother did seem a little cold when people commented, Michael said, "I really like how she never makes a big deal out of it."

Talida looked at him in surprise. She hadn't expected that kind of response. For some reason, she expected him to feel the same way.

Michael stared at the ceiling. He lay on Talida's bed with his arms folded below his head.

"Actually, I like how she just gives you space. I wish my mother did that sometimes." He looked at her, seemingly embarrassed about how he felt.

Talida was quiet, but thought, *There it is again. How I see the world so differently.* It made her slightly sad that it was also happening with Michael. Them looking the same had given her the sense that they also felt and thought the same way. But apparently, that wasn't the case.

Talida lay in the bean bag that was squeezed into one corner of her room. She observed Michael and wondered how much more there was that, in truth, was different and not the same.

* * *

Rose stood in the garden behind her cottage. She was clad in a dark blue apron and their kitchen chairs were lined up neatly in front of her, waiting to be beautified. Rose had been feeling a little restless of late, so she decided that repainting these wooden chairs might remedy the urge she felt to pack her bags and leave.

It was something she experienced from time to time, this sudden need for movement, and it was hard not to follow the call she heard inside her heart. Or was it inside her head? She wasn't sure. But because Edith was here in this small cottage, and she wanted to be where Edith was, she found ways to bury what she felt inside her. The energy that resulted from that flew into many projects, not only her writing work but also into their garden and into their furniture, most of which Rose had refurbished with her own hands.

It was the end of August, and the weather already carried the first signs of autumn. This was the time when she got especially restless with the knowledge that the colder and much shorter days were approaching–days that made her feel lonely and empty, even with her loved ones around.

Talida entered the garden through the little gate on the right side of the cottage and, as always, she smiled, taking in the beauty of what Rose had created in the space behind their house. She'd told Rose many times that, in her view, she had a true talent for making things beautiful, and Talida spent many afternoons with her working on repainting furniture or maintaining flower beds. It was a way to unleash what was inside them, knowing that they weren't able to explain how they felt to the people they cared most about, let alone to the world at large. There was just too much fear that someone wouldn't get it or that someone would look at them sadly, hurt by their words. So they worked together, making things pretty.

"Hey, sweetie." Rose smiled at the tall girl with the blonde afro and pointed at the second apron that hung on a hook next to the glass doors that led into her cottage. "Want to join me?"

Talida only nodded and went to fetch the apron. Then she took the paintbrush that Rose held out to her and, without further delay, they started working on the chairs.

September

It was late September in Scotland, and a cold autumn wind blew across the hills. Akila sat at her desk preparing for the next session with one of her clients. It was a Tuesday, and the cottage was filled with silence after the usual morning bustle when her children got ready for school and she had to leave the house on time to drop them at school.

A message lit up the phone next to her, and she stole a quick glance to see who sent it. Her eyebrows went up and she released a pleased, "Ah!" into the quiet when she saw that it came from Antony. It was a short message, asking her to get in touch about an interesting assignment.

She responded immediately, inquiring when he had time to tell her more.

He sent back a laughing emoticon a few minutes later, teasing her that her current assignments must be rather boring if she was that quick, and then called her an instant later.

They smiled at each other on the video call and then settled down to do the serious talk. Their relationship had always been like that. They briefly joked or talked about other things, but their friendship was built on the mutual love for problem-solving and deep thinking, and that was what they mostly dwelled on whenever they met.

Antony had connected her with a few clients in the past, so it was nothing new that he reached out. She usually looked forward to him making these connections, because she liked working with international clients from different backgrounds.

"It's a job in Seoul," he said. "I remember you mentioning a while back that you are interested in the South Korean film industry."

Akila stared at him in disbelief. "How did you get that assignment for me, Antony?"

"Well, I think you are better suited for what they are looking for. To me, it sounds more like a life coach assignment, and that is your specialty."

"Tell me more!" She beamed at him, and he couldn't help but laugh at the sight of her excitement.

"I am setting up a meeting with the manager of the guy who is looking for a coach. The rest is up to you."

"Yes, yes, yes," she replied. "I'll make you proud!"

Two days later, Akila was set to have the first meeting with Mr. Kwon Ma Ru, the manager Antony had mentioned. There was always a mix of anxiety and excitement before the first meeting with a new client, and Akila was restless that Thursday morning. She had dropped Mavis and Talida at school and came back to the house in time to arrange the kitchen after breakfast and set up her laptop for the video call.

A middle-aged man Akila had seen countless times in the Korean series she watched popped up on her screen at a minute past 10:00 in a smart, official shirt, with soft facial features and a polite haircut.

"Ms. Akila," he said in strongly flavoured English, bowing his head. "It is a true pleasure to meet you today."

"Mr. Kwon," she responded with a warm smile.

Now that the meeting had started, she was able to let go of all her anxiety and focus on what this client needed. "I am very pleased to meet you too. Has the weather in Seoul been as terrible as here in Scotland?"

Akila had learned that a little small talk was very healthy for her business, and although she was otherwise rather poor in making small talk, she found it easy to break the ice with a few general comments and questions before getting down to business.

The man on Akila's screen looked satisfied with her way of making conversation, and they exchanged a few pleasantries and thoughts on this year's weather around the globe before she asked, "Mr. Kwon, are you okay with me inquiring what coaching experience you are looking for and for whom? I understand that you are not the primary client I would be working with."

The manager ran his right hand through his hair and nodded slowly, bearing a thoughtful expression. Time for serious talk. "You are not mistaken, Ms. Akila," he responded politely. "I am the manager of an established, but still growing, South Korean actor and model who is looking to overcome a few . . . obstacles. He requires guidance as to how exactly to overcome what hinders him."

Akila gave a nod and went on. "Tell me more so that I can grasp what the real needs of your client are and what coaching experience would work best." The man hesitated. Something seemed to be complicated about the whole thing. "And don't worry. By way of my profession, I am bound to treat everything we discuss with the greatest confidentiality. I can assure you that I will do everything in my power to support you, but I can only do this once I understand your client's situation and we agree on the best way forward."

What followed was one of the most unusual conversations with a new client that Akila had to date. Kwon Ma Ru wasn't really willing to discuss the details of his client's situation but made a lot of inquiries about her work and opinions on different topics. By the end of the first forty minutes, they had talked about many things but not really anything about the details of the coaching she was to do.

"Ms. Akila," the Korean man said eventually. "I would like to offer you a contract for a three-week intense coaching program for my client, requiring your presence here in Seoul. Is this something you could manage? I would like us to start once you are ready, probably in mid-October. If this is something you are willing to consider, I will send you further details in an email, including the payment and other benefits we are offering for you to think about. I will also send you the name of my client."

Akila was a little surprised. She hadn't expected that this would require her presence in South Korea. Her head started spinning a little, thinking about what that meant. She had been wanting to visit the country for a long time, but so far, life hadn't offered her the opportunity.

"I usually prefer to discuss details personally and openly, but I can sense that you would be more comfortable if I studied the contract and other details and then reached out. Am I correct?"

Kwon Ma Ru smiled at her and bowed his head. You are correct, Ms. Akila," he agreed. "Please know that our situation is very delicate, and I require you to fully respect the rule of confidentiality."

"I'm sure you heard that I'm great at what I do. And part of that is to respect the privacy of those who reach out to me," she replied.

By evening, Akila had received the email the manager had mentioned.

Her children sat at the kitchen counter eating dinner and talking about the day. As usual, they put on some music and were humming along while exchanging the latest news from school and the neighbourhood.

Mavis, who hung around with a colourful variety of neighbours of all ages and genders, was usually best informed about what was going on in their little community, and mother and daughter were often speechless at just how many personal details he knew about everyone.

They heard the front door open, and Rose walked into the house with a bottle of whiskey in hand. "Hellooooo sweethearts!" she chirped, her round cheeks glowing red from the cold wind outside. She was instantly greeted with energetic hugs and pecks on the cheek from both children. "Ahhhhh, wonderful. This is what I needed."

Akila, who sipped her hot tea by the kitchen counter, pointed to the bottle in Rose's hand. "Are we going to have this for dinner? It's Thursday evening, just in case you got confused."

"Honey, I am totally aware of the time and day, but I had an awfully tough week and need to sit on your couch with this bottle in hand."

Akila motioned toward the sofa. "Do your thing," she said.

An hour later, both children were in their respective rooms, each tucked in comfortably with a great book. Akila let herself fall onto her couch with a pleased sigh and took the bottle from Rose's hand to fill her small glass with whiskey.

"Now, now," she said after taking a generous sip and grinning at her friend. "Before you tell me your story, I need to check something out."

Akila took her phone, opened her email account, and clicked on the unread email that had been sitting there, waiting all day long.

She quickly flew over the words, looking for the piece of information she'd been wondering about since her conversation with Kwon Ma Ru.

When she finally found the name, her jaw dropped and her eyes grew big with momentary disbelief. She grabbed Rose's hand and then turned to look at her friend.

"What?" Rose asked after seeing her face. "Akila, what is going on?"

Akila turned her gaze back to her phone and read the name again. No doubt this was real. She hadn't made this up.

"Rose, this is crazy," she finally muttered, turning to her friend again with a very excited expression. She felt like jumping rather than sitting on the sofa.

"Akila, dear, I can't help you in your obvious distress if you don't talk to me," Rose said.

"This is unbelievable. . . . What are the odds?" She was trying hard to digest the fact that the contract she was about to sign (once she checked the terms) involved a very promising young Korean actor. This was definitely one of the most exciting assignments she had received so far.

"Rose?" Akila shook her friend's shoulders gently.

"This is amazing! Kim Insoo! Can you believe it?"

"Nope, because I don't know the guy," Rose responded dryly, and Akila couldn't help but laugh.

"Right. I'm being annoying," she conceded and gave Rose a peck on her soft cheek.

Then Akila took a deep breath and whispered, "This is going to be great! I am going to coach Kim Insoo!" She gave a small squeal of real excitement that resulted in a flustered-looking Rose, who seemed to have a hard time adjusting to her very animated friend.

"Just who is this guy?" Rose enquired. "I have rarely seen you like this, honey."

"True, true. . . ." Akila opened an app and selected an episode from the series with Insoo in it. "This is the guy," she said after she had found a part she liked, and they watched a few minutes in silence.

Rose glanced at her friend. Akila looked truly excited, and her heart went out to this woman with one hundred different facettes. "You are going places, honey. I am so happy for you."

Akila grinned and then suddenly hugged Rose with all her might.

"South Korea, get ready for the storm!" Rose shouted.

Laughing wildly, they clinked glasses and emptied the whiskey in one go.

"Why the whole bottle today, by the way?" Akila asked her friend.

Rose shook her head, avoiding Akila's inquiring eyes. "Not so important. Let's just celebrate today, that's much more fun."

Akila leaned in on her. "Rose, talk to me!"

"Nope honey, not today! It's all good anyway." Rose squeezed her eyes shut to show Akila how serious she was about it.

Eventually, Akila let herself drop back, giving in. "Fine, let's talk another day."

Rose opened her eyes and smiled at her. "Where's that bottle?" After pouring another drink, she said, "By the way, what are you going to do with your two lovely babies?"

Akila fixed her eyes on her, putting on her sweetest, pleading face.

Rose couldn't help but laugh. "You crazy woman. Okay, I will be here, but call your mum as well. Let's split responsibilities."

Akila nodded. "I love you!"

Rose shot a tight smile at her friend. She felt shaky and lonely tonight, and Akila's excitement didn't make it better. Edith had travelled to London for an important case and would only be back late the next day. Rose felt scared being alone in the house. It was her mother's death anniversary and, like every year, it was a tough time for her.

The other world

The plane touched down in Incheon Airport and Akila's heart beat wildly in her chest. She'd had many interesting encounters throughout her coaching and mentoring career so far, but travelling to South Korea for a three-week coaching intervention with a Korean actor was one of the more exciting opportunities she'd been presented with. Of course, she was extremely nervous as well, wondering if she would be able to fulfil her client's expectations, especially when she wasn't exactly sure what they were, given that she had only spoken with the manager and not the person who really wanted to be coached.

What was it that Kim Insoo wanted to achieve? What was it that held him back? She kept milling over such questions, knowing that it didn't really make any sense to ask them until she was able to pose them to him directly.

* * *

Insoo stood and looked at the woman next to his manager. She was surprisingly tall, something that wasn't very common with the women around him. Her shoulders were straight and broad, almost like those of a slender man. She had long legs and arms, and when she offered him her hand by way of greeting, he took note of her very long fingers and sizable palms.

Her hair was short but still seemed to be all over. It was wavy and framed her marcant face in a wild explosion of brownish blond that he wasn't sure he liked.

She obviously wore no makeup, and her eyelashes and eye-brows were very light blond and harder to notice against her skin. Shaking his hand, she seemed to search for something in his face, observing him intently from behind silver-rimmed, large glasses. "Mr. Kim Insoo," she smiled.

He was taken by surprise when a light suddenly seemed to travel across her face, with her eyes and her mouth being the centre of the sparkle.

"Nice to finally meet you in person. I'm looking forward to working with you."

She seemed totally convinced by the words she'd used, while he felt that she had made use of a phrase too common in English movies and that seemed to hold no weight in reality. But still, he shook her hand politely and smiled with a slight bow of his head to respond to her greeting.

Kwon Ma Ru stepped past them and ushered her further into Insoo's house. "Ms. Akila, let me show you around!" he exclaimed and directed her toward the kitchen space, which was the centre of the house, then into the living room with a view of the city be-low and down the corridor toward her room. All the while, Kwon Ma Ru chattered excitedly, eager to make their visitor comfortable, Insoo noted with a hint of irritation.

Insoo followed slowly but then decided that he wasn't really needed and sat down on his couch in the living room. He heard Akila laugh in the corridor. She had a loud laughter, obviously not worried about what others might think of the noise she made.

Kwon Ma Ru and Akila came back into the kitchen.

"Coffee or tea, Ms. Akila?"

"Coffee would be lovely, thank you!"

While he was busy preparing a cup of coffee for Akila, he said, "I would like to invite you for dinner tonight, Ms. Akila. Will you have the energy to go out for a Korean meal?"

"That sounds wonderful," Akila responded.

Insoo decided that it was time to leave. He wasn't ready to spend his evening with this woman that his manager had brought into his house more or less without his consent. His manager was the person who had wanted her here so desperately, so he should be perfectly capable of taking care of her.

"Insoo, what do you think? Should we go for an early dinner with Ms. Akila?" Ma Ru addressed him directly when he entered the kitchen.

"Sorry, but I need to prepare for the interview we talked about earlier. You two can go ahead and enjoy the meal." Insoo felt an almost savage sense of satisfaction looking at his manager's face. But when his gaze wandered over to Akila, who was observing him again with a curious expression on her face while sipping the coffee Ma Ru had handed her, his strong resolve to make this difficult for everyone lessened and he wasn't able to go on.

Looking at his feet rather than her, he added, "I guess we will still have the chance to talk more," then took the opportunity to disappear down the corridor and into his room.

Insoo made sure to stay in his room for the rest of the evening. For some reason, he couldn't muster the energy to face the tall woman again today. He went to bed early, wondering what he would do the next day when Ma Ru had clearly told him he had to attend his first coaching session with her.

Insoo felt a familiar sense of dread grip him.

What would she want to talk about? For the hundredth time, he wondered what his manager was expecting as an outcome of the whole thing. How could he force him to accept such an intense intrusion for three weeks?

It was already enough for Insoo that he frequently had so many people around him that the agency provided. His stylist was with him wherever he had to go for work. On most days, he was chauffeured around when going anywhere. There was even a time when Ma Ru had insisted an assistant stay with him day in and day out. Ma Ru had said that it was only in Insoo's best interest, but he hadn't been able to deal with it.

When his manager noticed that it affected him, and more importantly, his performance, negatively, he'd taken to dealing with

Insoo personally. Insoo knew that he was getting special treatment and that he had more freedom than most people in his position could ever hope for. It wasn't common for a manager like Kwon Ma Ru to handle an actor's appointments or to let an upcoming star drive his own car and live alone in his house without constant supervision and support. But they had worked with each other for many years, and both of them knew that they'd only reached this far because Ma Ru had understood that Insoo worked best with enough private space to breathe. Thus, bringing Akila into this house, something that was also quite risky because of the press, felt like even more of a breach of their mutual agreement with Insoo.

Yes, there had been an official announcement by Kwon Ma Ru through the agency that Insoo would be working with a life coach to prepare for his move into the international market to avoid any negative rumours. But would that really work? Would no one question it? And the most uncomfortable thought was that Akila would look at him, like she'd done today, and see right through him.

The thought was terrifying.

It was a restless night for Insoo, and he woke up the next morning with an even stronger sense of irritation–something very close to anger.

First session

"Hi, Insoo. Thank you for making the time to meet for our first session." Akila smiled warmly.

After yesterday, this was the first chance Insoo had to examine her more closely. Again, he noticed how tall she was and how her broad shoulders underlined her generally confident manner. Her small eyes, an undefinable colour between brown and green, observed him from behind the large glasses that made her look like a professor from the movies. She folded her legs on the spacious leather seat and, just like the day before, he noted how long her limbs were. Everything about her seemed long.

He settled down on the sofa and briefly glanced at her. She had a small notebook decorated with green leaves in her lap and a small pen in her left hand, which she now put down.

What was he to think of this situation? Suddenly a fully grown woman lived in his house, and she was actually waiting for him to talk.

Kwon Ma Ru had mentioned that a coach usually listens and Insoo would only have to chat with her. But her smile made him feel uneasy, and how she gazed back at him was definitely something he didn't want to experience each day for the next three weeks.

He slightly bowed his upper body and added a nod, replying, "I am still not sure what it is we are meant to be doing."

She observed him through her silver-rimmed glasses. "I'm just here to be here." She looked at him still, searching for the best expression. "It's really up to you exactly what we'll be doing."

Somehow, this elusive response annoyed him. "Is that so?" He was tired. He stood up and walked over to the desk behind the sofa. Coming back, he dropped a large set of bound papers in her lap. "I need to practise my lines for the next show I'm shooting. Turn to page four. You are the female lead."

It seemed to him that it took a moment before she composed herself. Then she picked up the script and turned to page four. He was surprised and a little disappointed to see no emotion on her face when she adjusted her sitting position.

"I can't read that," she said calmly and glanced up at him. The entire script was in Korean. Her face was still calm, but her eyes widened, almost double their usual size, and they carried an intensity that seemed to fix him into his spot.

His heart sank. Why was he being rude? He stood up abruptly and left the room.

* * *

"Mr. Kwon. Can we talk about our contract, please?" Akila asked.

"Yes, of course," he replied.

"You told me that he was ready for the coaching experience I offer, but he isn't ready to talk to me."

Kwon Ma Ru and Akila stood in the kitchen. Her arms were folded in front of her chest, and, although her general demeanour was calm, he noticed the frown she wore. He sighed and put his coffee down. It was still quite early in the morning on the second day after Akila's arrival, and the autumn sun was illuminating the city outside.

"He *is* ready to talk to you, Ms. Akila. He just needs a little more time to realise that." Akila's stare was the most unwavering thing he had ever seen.

"I told you exactly what I offer, Mr. Kwon! I'm not a trained therapist, and I might not be able to help him in any way. His condition is quite serious, and you might be playing with his future by getting a coach instead of a therapist."

"Do you think I don't know that? But he would never accept that. The fact that you are in his house and he came for his first session is more than I imagined might happen."

Ma Ru stepped closer to Akila and gave a slight bow, avoiding looking into her stern eyes.

"We have three weeks. Please, Ms. Akila. All I am asking for is for you to try."

She continued to stare at him, not moving, and he wondered how long she could keep this up. He continued to bow.

She finally inhaled sharply and said, "I'll observe how it goes this week," before she turned and walked out of the kitchen.

Still bowing, Kwon Ma Ru closed his eyes and exhaled slowly.

Ma Ru knew that he was taking a huge risk by hiring this coach and making the decision that she should stay in Insoo's house. But what else could he do? No one, himself included, had been able to discuss what was really going on with Insoo. There had been too many incidents lately, and their agency had to deal with an increasing amount of questions from partners and fans. Ma Ru saw that all their work, all the dedication they had all put in for years to make Kim Insoo the star he was becoming, would go down the drain if he didn't try something different–something that would hopefully lead to the turn around they needed with increasing desperation.

* * *

Akila sat on the sofa and waited for Insoo to show up for his second session. Mr. Kwon had informed her of the time for their session, but after what had happened the day before, she wasn't sure if he would show up. She wasn't sure if she actually wanted him to show up. This man was unwell. You could see it physically. How could they think all he just needed was a coach?

Insoo walked into the room, slowing down slightly when he noticed that she sat on the sofa. After a second of hesitation, he greeted her with a slight bow and sat in the seat she had occupied the day before.

She braced herself and smiled. "My contract with your manager goes for three weeks. Let's make it as pleasant as possible for everyone. We don't even have to talk. That's up to you. How about you show me the city first?" She stood up and walked towards the front door.

He took a moment, then stood up and followed her.

Without saying a word, they both got dressed in their boots and coats. Then she opened the door and they left the house through the front yard. Standing outside the house on the steep driveway, she briefly closed her eyes and turned her face to the sun. She inhaled deeply, enjoying the sense of warmth on her cheeks, and asked, "What should I see first in Seoul?"

He had worn a pair of large sunglasses and stood a few steps away. "What do you want to see?"

"Anything," she responded. "Just take me to all the sights people usually visit."

"That's not possible in just a few hours."

"I know. But we have three weeks. You can make a plan now so that we finish by the end of those weeks."

She wasn't sure if he was looking at her from behind his sunglasses, but then he removed his car keys and the car doors unlocked with a small beep as he got into his vehicle with the tinted windows. She followed and sat in the passenger seat next to him.

About three hours later, Insoo dropped Akila in front of the house. Mr. Park, Insoo's assistant and chauffeur, was already waiting outside. Insoo got out and took her place in the passenger seat, and Mr. Park got in the driver's seat behind the steering wheel.

"Will you be fine, Ms. Akila?" the burly man inquired politely. "The shoot might take several hours."

"I have some work to do and have calls to make, so don't worry."

It felt nice once Akila was alone in the house. It was a peaceful place with comfortable furniture and warm lighting, something she appreciated a lot.

After a hot shower and a warm meal, which she made from the containers in the fridge and smiled at how much the food reminded her of all the Korean series she'd watched, she sat in the living room facing the large windows and worked. She got a good amount of things done, stopping once in a while to think about today's "session" with Insoo.

He was good at being quiet. Most people she knew feared silence, but she and Insoo sat in the car without saying a word to each other until they reached their destination.

Insoo parked the car and pointed to where they would be going. Still not saying a word, they walked. After a while, he pointed some things out, explaining in simple terms what he apparently felt she needed to know.

She just listened. Han River Park was a large area with paths winding along viewpoints with various groups of trees and lawns. Akila enjoyed the sense of open spaces and being out in nature. There were only a few people out, probably due to the time of day and the low temperatures.

After wandering for a while, he asked her if she wanted some hot coffee. She smiled and nodded, and they walked over to one of the coffee shops nearby. It was good to be in the warmth for a moment. Akila's hands were already stiff and her fingers were white for the lack of blood. This usually happened to her in the cold, even when wearing gloves, which was why she preferred warm weather.

While she went to the washroom to let hot water run over her fingers and let the blood circulate, Insoo went to the counter to buy the coffee.

Most of the people in the coffee shop were out for a run or doing other sports and minded their own business. Still, Akila noticed that several customers recognized Insoo and a few phones were held up to take pictures of him. Akila wondered how he felt about turning into public property anytime he stepped outside his own space. Did he like it? How did it feel to never know whether your moment was private or not?

He soon joined her with two takeaway cups in his hands, and she accepted hers with a small smile and bow, as she had seen others do here, and they walked on. A middle-aged woman was still taking pictures from the window of the shop, but Insoo didn't show signs of noticing.

They eventually got back to where Insoo had parked the car and he said, "There is a shoot I need to go to. I will drop you at home."

* * *

It was dark when Insoo came back, his manager with him.

Akila sat on the kitchen counter with a hot cup of chai next to her and a book in her hand. Stew simmered in a pot on the stove, and her music box, which she carried everywhere, was playing some Bongo Flava tunes.

She looked up at them and smiled. Kwon Ma Ru entered the kitchen noisily and greeted her. "Ms. Akila! You are still here!"

She gave a small nod, then asked, "Would you like some stew? I found it in the fridge, and it's really tasty."

Insoo's manager took a look at the food and smiled. "This is the best food you can hope for, Ms. Akila. All of these dishes have been prepared by Insoo's mother, Mrs. Moon." The short man put the lid back on the pot and left to drop some documents he'd been carrying on the desk in the living room.

As soon as he left, Insoo mumbled, "Good night," and disappeared down the corridor toward his room.

Akila followed him with her eyes, sipping her chai. "Has he eaten anything today, Mr. Kwon?" she asked when the manager came back through the kitchen.

"Eaten? Yes, a little snack during the shoot."

"Did he go somewhere right after the meal?" she inquired, still looking down the corridor.

"Leave? What do you mean?"

She turned to fix the manager with her eyes. "I'm asking if he usually goes somewhere right after his meals."

Kwon Ma Ru was flustered for a moment and hesitated. She could see that he was trying to make sense of her questions.

"Let's talk tomorrow, Mr. Kwon," she said with a smile. She gave a slight bow with her head and added, "Have a good night."

After Mr. Kwon left, the house was quiet. Insoo had closed the door to his room and there was no sound. She had paused the music and finished her meal sitting on the kitchen counter.

She cleaned up and switched off the lights. Her heart pounded and there was the familiar sense of excitement and longing for home that she'd felt a few times in her life. She associated that feeling with Nairobi, but sometimes it showed up in other places as well.

It was time to turn the page and let the jump into the new world happen.

The next day was sunny again, but smog hung heavily over the city. Seoulians were covered up smugly in heavy jackets, and white clouds of breath could be seen as they walked.

Akila and Insoo got out of the car and walked through the park.

Their third session brought them to another sightseeing spot in Seoul–a beautiful panoramic view above the city. Again, Insoo wore sunglasses and they didn't speak.

Today, she'd filled the thermos she discovered in the kitchen with hot coffee and, after an hour in the cold, she removed it and sat on a bench, pouring them both a cup of steaming brew. He accepted his cup without a word, giving a light bow of his head before looking around. It was mid-morning and fewer people were out, probably not willing to brace the cold. Mr. Park stood discreetly a few metres away from them. The large man had joined them but kept a respectful distance.

Insoo had a second photo shoot for a new collection later that day, so they'd left early for sightseeing.

Insoo came out of his room early that morning for his usual workout and found her sitting on the kitchen counter responding to messages on her phone. She looked up and smiled, "Good morning! Coffee?"

He'd shaken his head and left for his run.

Sixty minutes later, he was back, freshly showered, and his assistant was there to discuss the day's schedule. "Your session with Ms. Akila, first thing in the morning. This afternoon, your second round of the shoot for the collection."

"How much time do we have today, Mr. Park?" Akila had chimed from the living room. She sat at his desk with her laptop, fingers flying over the keyboard.

Insoo frowned slightly. When had she gotten so comfortable? Sitting on the kitchen counter with folded legs and using his desk as if it were hers after only three days in his house. This woman was surely interesting.

"You have about three hours if you start soon," Insoo's assistant responded.

"Insoo, where is today's session taking us?" she asked while still typing.

He didn't immediately reply. He'd finished the cup of tea Mr. Park had handed him after he'd come out of the shower and wondered where he should take her today.

"Not sure," he said, picking up his phone in search of inspiration. A moment later, he had his next spot for their sightseeing.

Now, they stood at the viewpoint high above Seoul, and she smiled while taking in the view. "I've seen this place many times," she murmured, then turned to search for his eyes behind his shades. "This spot is part of so many Korean series."

"You watch Korean series?"

"Oh, yes! Apart from books and music, they're my secret joy when I want to wind down after a long day or don't want to think too much," she responded with a twinkle in her eye. "Don't tell anyone, though."

Had she just winked at him before turning back to enjoy the view again? Insoo frowned and checked the time on his watch. It was time to leave. "Are you fine taking a taxi home?" he asked. "I have a lunch date soon."

She continued watching the city for a while, then said, "Let me join you today. I really want to understand what your days look like." She turned to smile at him, and again, there was a twinkle in her eyes. "I will be pleasant company and won't say a word."

"Why would I agree to that? It's all work." Insoo was irritated by the good mood she seemed to be in and the way she spoke to him as if they were familiar with each other.

"I might never get another chance to experience how a Korean actor lives, and you aren't letting me do the work I came here to do anyway. I'm a guest in your house, so consider it proper treatment of someone who would otherwise be busy as well. It's you who doesn't want to talk."

Insoo frowned but didn't argue.

Kwon Ma Ru had already arrived at the restaurant when they walked in, and everyone at the table stood up to greet them politely, bowing, nodding, and shaking hands the Korean way Akila had observed many times over the last few days.

She was introduced as the coach Insoo was working with, as had been reported in the media, and she also bowed her head politely and smiled.

"Please don't mind me," she said. "I'm just here to get a glimpse of Mr. Kim's work routine and experience as much of Seoul as possible on such a wonderful day."

Food was brought and the discussion in Korean ensued. She enjoyed the meal as she observed the group. The different dishes were amazing.

A young man sitting opposite her whose name she couldn't remember (something that happened to her all the time and was an annoying shortcoming) explained the different dishes to her and how to eat them.

Insoo sat next to her with a beautiful array of dishes arranged around him. He smiled and seemed to engage in the conversation just like everyone else, but as Akila expected, he barely touched his food the entire time. Even the older-looking man opposite Insoo noticed and pointed at the chopsticks next to his hand. Insoo looked a little embarrassed for a moment and then took several bites of the food while everyone else encouraged him with smiles, comments, and nods.

When the meal ended and Mr. Kwon ordered coffee for the entire group, Insoo excused himself and disappeared toward the washroom. Akila followed him with her gaze, and she suddenly had a sinking feeling that left her stomach hurting. In the same instant, she realised Kwon Ma Ru was staring at her. After a quick glance at him trying to figure out what he was thinking, she turned to focus on her coffee, which had just arrived, until Insoo returned to the table.

When everyone finished, their goodbyes were hearty and warm, and Akila liked how Insoo smiled. The meeting must have been successful.

On the way to the photo shoot, Akila sat in the back of the car with Kwon Ma Ru. Mr. Park drove quietly as Insoo leaned back in the passenger seat, engaged in conversation with Mr. Kwon, and Akila observed the city flying by as she thought of the barely touched food Insoo had left on his plates.

Their destination was a studio in one of the more modern highrise buildings in Seoul. From the moment they stepped through the door, Akila felt as if she had jumped into one of her other worlds. Bright, warm lights filled the large room where photo equipment centred around a group of large white blinds close to big, tinted windows.

A flock of people came toward them as soon as they entered the room, and a lot of greeting and laughing followed that felt so exaggerated that Akila couldn't help but retreat a little, hoping she might be ignored. A tiny, muscular woman with a short haircut and wearing jeans and a t-shirt greeted Insoo with a, "Hi, sexy," in an accent Akila couldn't place and put a hand on his butt for a second. In response, Insoo displayed a smile Akila thought was more of an insult than anything else.

There was a tall, thin man who seemed to be important, judging by the way everyone seemed to centre around him. He greeted Insoo as well, but more politely, and then ushered him towards the changing area.

Mr. Park introduced Akila, and she was given a chair close to the set and someone put a cup of steaming coffee in her hand. She made a mental note to take less coffee for the next few days and removed her bottle of water while waiting, slowly taking a few sips.

From where she sat, she was able to observe the stage where a group of people was running back and forth setting up lights, adjusting the large blinds that now had different colours on them, and setting up camera equipment.

She was also able to see Insoo and two of his stylists who were already busy applying makeup and styling his hair. A while later, he stepped onto the set wearing a light blue shirt and slim jeans, his hair gelled back in a way Akila decided was outright disgusting.

The masculine woman and the thin man both held cameras, giving instructions to their crew. A hush fell across the room, and other lights were dimmed while last adjustments were made on stage.

The first poses when the cameras went off were simple, with Insoo moving from one pose to the other. But apparently, this was just a warm-up.

A stylist came onto the stage and unbuttoned Insoo's shirt, exposing his lean, muscled upper body, and pulling his jeans a little further down to expose the label on the underwear.

For some reason, Akila looked away.

He was beautiful. She'd known that from watching his series. But everything was just too physical for her, and she sensed, again, that he was public property–not a man who could just be himself.

She looked for Mr. Kwon and found him chatting quietly with another gentleman closer to the entrance. She asked him to message her when they were almost done and then left.

She walked for a long time and was already on her way back because her fingers and toes were ice cold when she got the message that they would probably wrap up in the next thirty minutes. Entering the room, she was momentarily blinded by the bright lights on stage.

Insoo was still posing, although his hair had changed and his clothes were different.

She sat back down in the chair she'd left behind and waited.

After a few more clicks from the camera and a loud shout, followed by collective clapping and cheering, the session finally ended. Insoo smiled, gave a small bow, and left the stage to change.

It was already dark as Mr. Park drove home, Insoo sitting in the passenger seat with his eyes closed and Akila in the back with his manager. She quietly took in the many lights of the city moving past.

At home, Insoo left to shower and Akila warmed some of the food from the fridge. "Do the next days all look like this for him?" she asked.

Mr. Kwon briefly looked up from his phone which had kept him busy since they'd entered the house. "Yes. We just signed a deal for another commercial, and it was confirmed today that he will join season two of one of the programs he acted in recently. He will be busy."

"You know he's unwell," she responded.

The manager looked up from his phone again and frowned. "He did well today," was all he said. Akila hated the whole situation on Insoo's behalf.

She'd Googled some of the images of Insoo that afternoon and asked herself why they nearly all seemed suggestive. Was it that she was growing old and felt uncomfortable when everyone else was just fine or was her sense of fashion, modelling, and art just different?

Insoo stepped back into the kitchen with wet hair, looking pale and tired. "Let's discuss tomorrow's schedule," he said and flopped into the seat in the living room.

Akila filled three large bowls with food and placed one next to Insoo on a small stand. He looked at her, slightly flustered, but then focused back on Kwon Ma Ru, who spelled out the next day for him: "There's a session with Ms. Akila at 10:00–you will have two hours tomorrow. After that, lunch. Then a 15:00 meeting with a blogger," Kwon Ma Ru recited in English.

Akila sat on the kitchen counter with her legs on the raised chair in front of her and enjoyed her tasty meal, already looking forward to her hot shower before bedtime.

A little while later, Mr. Kwon excused himself and left, placing his emptied bowl in the kitchen sink.

Insoo stood up as well and went to his room, giving her a little bow with his head as a way of good night, which she responded to in kind.

Only after he left did Akila see the untouched bowl with food on the stand next to his seat. She picked it up and looked at the now-cold dish for a while before she placed it in the fridge and switched off the lights.

A bookshop encounter

The next day, Insoo took Akila to Bukchon Hanok village. They'd left a not-so-happy-looking Mr. Park at home. Having observed Insoo and his team for the last few days, Akila gathered that Insoo took a lot of liberties and that his manager and the team had learned to accept it, although they weren't very pleased with it. She guessed how much was at stake for an agency with such a rising star moving about as he wanted and wondered how Insoo had managed to achieve such an arrangement.

She was amazed by the part of the city they visited today with the small, winding alleys and the traditionally built and designed houses.

* * *

Insoo, who was even more pale and quiet this morning, couldn't help but notice her excitement. She had the twinkle in her eyes again. Today, it was directed at her surroundings, and she seemed at home while looking at the wooden carvings on the roofs and carefully touching the old wooden gates in front of the buildings they passed.

"I am meeting a friend before my next appointment," he heard himself say. "Would you like to join?"

She turned around to glance at him and nodded.

It was a new feeling studying a woman almost as tall as him, especially a woman who smiled so openly and never avoided his eyes but stared right into them as if she was searching for something every time.

When they entered the bookshop which also included a cosy cafe, she noticed the tall young man right away. She'd seen him in several Korean series she watched and had read online that he and Insoo were best friends. He shook her hand with a crooked smile and offered her a seat next to him.

"It is great to meet you," he said in English which was flavoured with the now-more-familiar Korean accent. "He never mentioned how tall you are–and how good looking."

She couldn't help but smile and raise her eyebrows at his choice of words. "I could say the same thing," she retorted. They gazed at each other with a sense of familiarity she'd only experienced with a few people before. Insoo had a good friend she realised with a sense of relief.

"How has he been treating you?" Lee Tae Oh asked her after they had placed their order. "I am worried that I did not check on you before. He can be extremely rude and selfish."

"I'm used to it," she responded, already enjoying the conversation. "This is day five in his house."

"I'm actually surprised that you lasted this long," he replied, and their smiles were equally mischievous.

Insoo observed them and was surprised to realise how pleased he was that they seemed to get along well. At the same time, he was confused by the fact that he couldn't talk to her like that. When he was with her, he didn't have many words to say.

Cakes and coffee arrived at their table, and Akila and Tae Oh ate while they chatted away about the Korean series she liked and their favourite actors and actresses. They laughed at her stumbling over the pronunciation of some of their names. Insoo was intrigued by how she was a real fan who even listened to some of the soundtracks.

Ma Ru had mentioned that Akila had lived in Kenya for most of her life and had a Kenyan-German family. How was it possible that she was also so familiar with the Korean film industry? Life sometimes felt strange.

He was content just sitting and listening to the two of them talking. Akila asked many questions and listened with her particular intense stare. It seemed like Tae Oh was the one person on this planet she was really focused on, and Insoo could see how much his friend was enjoying it.

"Oh by the way," Tae Oh suddenly mentioned. "Some of the guys are also stopping by. I was chatting to Hae In, and he has not seen you in ages." Tae Oh glanced at the time on his phone. "They should be here soon."

Not long after that, a second table had been added to theirs, and the cafe was filled with the Korean chatter of four more young men and two women all sipping shakes and coffees and eating cakes. Akila had never seen Insoo smile so much, and she was pleased to see him that way, despite the paleness and the dark shadows below his eyes. He had even finished his coffee and a whole piece of cake, something she hadn't seen in the five days she spent in his house.

Akila had been introduced as the coach who was here to support him with his next big move in the international market, and everyone had asked a few polite questions in English before the conversion moved on in Korean. The two women seemed a little reserved toward her, but Akila was used to that. She'd experienced this kind of initial guard from fellow females many times before and had learned to give them time to warm up to her and not take it personally.

Despite being familiar with the feeling, she had never been able to fully grasp what happened when this took place, and she made another mental note to try and uncover the mystery one day. She wondered whether this truly had to do with the social nurturing she'd studied so much about in university or if the reasons had nothing to do with gender.

It was at that moment when Insoo moved to stand up.

"Please don't go," she said, putting her hand on his. Their eyes met when he looked down at her, as he was already halfway up from his chair. Glaring straight at her and realising how the conversation around the table had come to a halt, he slowly sat back down.

His friends probably hadn't heard what she said, but they noticed the physical contact she made and the tense look on both of their faces. Glancing around uncomfortably, they fell silent.

Tae Oh interrupted the growing silence. "Wow, I am so sorry! We have been really rude, speaking Korean all the time, and you cannot even take part in our conversation."

Akila broke her eye contact with Insoo and, feeling shaky, smiled at Tae Oh thankfully. She shook her head and let go of Insoo's hand. "That's totally fine, really! I'm just a little exhausted from the last few days and felt dizzy."

"Do you need anything?"

"We should get her some medicine!"

"I can't believe how impolite we were."

"Let's order something sugary. That will help with your dizziness!"

The table erupted in activity, the waitress was called to get water and juice for Akila, and the awkwardness of the moment passed.

Insoo remained silent, but he also remained seated.

Akila was acutely aware of his presence for the rest of the time they spent at the cafe. While Korean was still spoken most of the time, several of his friends engaged in courteous conversation with her, and they all tried to ensure that she wasn't left out again.

When it was time to leave, warm goodbyes were offered in Korean and English and bursts of laughter filled the cold air outside the bookstore. Hugs and bows were exchanged.

Tae Oh had asked for her number right before they left the cafe, and she handed him a few of her business cards. He sported his mischievous smile and said goodbye. She smiled back at him. Pedestrians had started to stop on the sidewalk to take pictures, especially of Insoo and Tae Oh, and everyone else hurried away.

Mr. Park suddenly appeared and said, "Let's hurry. We are already late for our next meeting. Ms. Akila, are you joining us?"

Insoo looked the other way and said calmly, "Get her a taxi home."

She nodded at Mr. Park reassuringly, who seemed slightly taken aback by Insoo's tone. He hailed a taxi for her while Insoo was already walking away. In the cab, she leaned back in the seat. Closing her eyes, she slowly exhaled. She only noticed that instant that she hadn't taken a proper breath the entire time.

Her heart was racing and she didn't feel very well when she entered the house. Taking water and sitting down to think about what had transpired didn't help either. She'd been gripped by a sense of restlessness and couldn't think straight. Her phone rang, and she moved to pick up her children's usual morning call.

"Mamaaaaaa!" Mavis chimed, awarding her with his usual broad smile on the video call. "I'm going to dance practice again today!" he shouted.

Talida's head popped up behind her smaller brother's wild blond afro and she commented, "As if she didn't know."

Both children gazed at each other with a mixture of irritation and affection. Then Talida looked at her mother, waving. "Hi, Mama! We hope you are well! Almost leaving for school. Oh, and I managed another A in maths!"

It was good to speak to them, having to focus on their stories and giving them her full attention. She felt slightly more calm after a few minutes of chatter had passed. In the end, Rose came into view on the video call. "Hey, honey. How are you doing?" she asked in her usual British singsong.

For some reason, that made her feel emotional, and Akila had difficulty holding her tears back, which was unexpected. Hadn't she been in control of her feelings just a few seconds ago?

"Honey, my dear, what is going on over there? Are you having a hard time?" Rose moved away from Akila's children's noise and focused back on her. "Akila, what's going on?"

She was crying now, only able to shake her head, not able to explain her reaction even to herself. "Let's talk later," was all she could manage, forcing a smile at Rose before hanging up.

It took a long time for her to calm down. Sitting on the seat in the living room, looking across the city through the large windows, she tried to get her breathing back to normal and her emotions under control.

She had crossed a line today–meddling in Insoo's life, like no good coach would dare do, and almost exposing him in front of friends with whom he'd clearly chosen not to share how he was truly getting on. She felt sad just thinking about it. Why hadn't she held the line like a professional coach should? Now, she remembered the feel of his cool fingers below hers. She covered her face with her hands and curled up in the seat. She had no tears left, and she felt hot and dry in her heart and head.

* * *

Insoo got home after dark and wasn't surprised to find the kitchen empty and all the lights switched off. He wasn't sure how he felt about her avoiding him. A part of him was relieved that he didn't have to face her unwavering eyes. Another part was slightly disappointed. He walked to his room and silently slipped in, closing the door behind him.

Day six

It was day six in Insoo's house. Akila hadn't slept very well and was relieved when the night was finally over. But when she'd gotten dressed and walked into the kitchen to brew her coffee and warm her milk, she felt sore and sad and couldn't shake off the feeling of doom.

There were several messages from Rose on her phone that she had no energy to read and respond to. She put on some music at low volume and quietly sang along with the Swahili lyrics while removing a few food containers from the fridge to warm the contents for breakfast. She already loved Korean food and decided to enjoy these great breakfasts for as long as she was around.

The front door opened and Insoo stepped in, still panting from his workout in the crisp morning air. She noticed how he hesitated for an instant at the entrance when he saw her and, only then, removed his shoes.

He strode into the kitchen, not saying anything. Again, she was acutely aware of his presence in the room, and her heart and head started to pound.

Insoo walked past her to the fridge and took out a bottle of cool water to drink.

"Have breakfast with me," she blurted out, forcing herself to look straight at him. It was no use avoiding it. They would have to talk about what had happened anyway.

He lifted his head and seemed to study her for a while before he opened his mouth to respond. They heard the front door open, and Kwon Ma Ru, closely followed by the large shape of Mr. Park, entered the house with a joyful, "Good morning!"

Insoo and Akila stared for a second longer before he disappeared down the corridor to his room, probably to shower as usual. Akila closed her eyes briefly and slowly exhaled.

After getting ready, Insoo sat on the sofa and listened to the day's schedule. It was Friday, and a few appointments for marketing were scheduled–one radio show and one TV appearance he'd been preparing for.

He looked extremely tired and Akila wondered how he would get through the day and how anyone could fail to notice how unwell he was. His skin seemed thin and papery, and the dark shadows below his eyes seemed to have gotten even deeper.

"There's a 9:00 session with Ms. Akila," she heard Mr. Kwon say, moving through the timeline for the day. She was warming the food for breakfast. Next to her, Mr. Park sipped his coffee and noisily turned the pages of the newspaper he'd brought with him. Akila was relieved and scared at the same time to learn that their session was the first item of the day. No use in avoiding the conversation.

Akila prepared the bowls and small plates with the side dishes and placed them all on a tray. Mr. Park bowed his head politely when she placed his food in front of him. Then she carried the tray over to the living room and looked at the clock. 7:30. "Let's eat before we start," she said, not looking at anyone in particular, but addressing Insoo. She wanted him to sit and eat and talk to her. What was so painful was that he looked like that and no one did anything, least of all himself.

He glared at her, and she could almost see the air change in the room. The tension emanating from him was intense.

Akila put the dishes on the side table beside the sofa, close to where he sat. She was startled by the sudden burst of energy rushing through the space between them when he abruptly stood and marched through the front door without another word, pulling his shoes on as he went. The dishes came tumbling down and food splattered on the wooden floor, the small table, the couch, and the carpet. She froze where she was.

"Ms. Akila!" Kwon Ma Ru's voice shouted next to her. Mr. Park gently held her by her arm, a worried expression on his face. She had no idea how they'd gotten there. Insoo's assistant led her around the mess of food and broken ceramics on the floor and sat her down on the seat. Only then did she become aware that her hand was bleeding. It was a deep but clean cut, which was good news, she told herself. Mr. Kwon got a towel for her to press on the wound while he frantically searched for the first aid kit. He talked constantly, muttering to himself, calling out to her, and looking seriously worried. Mr. Park stayed next to her, not saying a word the entire time, watching Mr. Kwon.

Failing to find anything to use on Akila's wound, Mr. Kwon asked Mr. Park to rush to the next pharmacy and get bandages. The burly man left without any delay.

Akila sat in the seat, pressing the towel on the cut, and stared into the space before her. It had been a long time since she'd felt unable to gain control over a situation. Mr. Kwon walked up and down the room, looking unsettled.

Mr. Park returned not long after he had left and put a bandage on her cut. "Oh, Ms. Akila. I can't believe this has happened," was all he said, his eyes sad.

Mr. Kwon kept apologising while preparing a cup of tea for her.

Eventually, Akila couldn't take it anymore. "Mr. Kwon, you need to stop talking for a minute!" she burst out. "Just give me a minute of silence, please."

He looked a little hurt but closed his mouth and handed her the cup without another word. Mr. Park continued to clean up the worst of the mess next to her.

"I'm sure you're both busy," she said after a while, taking a deep breath. "If Insoo doesn't turn up soon, can you please let me know once you know that he's okay?"

Mr. Kwon looked at her and bowed slightly. "I definitely will, Ms. Akila."

Mr. Park didn't seem very comfortable leaving her alone. "Are you going to be fine?" he inquired. All she could do was nod, feeling exhausted.

Avoiding any further conversation about what had happened, they parted ways in front of the house with Akila leaving for a walk to clear her head and the two men heading for the agency to figure out what to do next.

Insoo didn't return home.

By midday, Akila sat at Insoo's desk in the living room trying to focus on her work and trying not to cry. She felt extremely lonely and homesick in the empty house. She had talked to Mr. Kwon on the phone, who was seriously worried by now as there was no sign of the young man.

It was late afternoon when Akila picked up her phone to look for Tae Oh's number.

He picked up after a few seconds. "Akila, hi."

She hesitated for a moment, then inhaled deeply to muster the courage to speak. "Tae Oh, something happened to Insoo this morning. Do you know where he is?"

There was a slightly longer-than-expected silence on the other end.

"He is fine, Akila," Tae Oh said. "I picked him up a short while ago. He seems a bit of a mess right now, so I am giving him time."

Her relief was almost physical, like the rush of energy she got when running fast. "Can you let Kwon Ma Ru know? He's worried as well."

"I am calling him next thing."

Insoo didn't come to his house that night.

Mr. Kwon passed by in the evening to have dinner with her. It was a sweet effort to help her avoid feeling lonely, but the reality was that they both struggled to make any real kind of conversation, often remaining quiet for long minutes lost in their own thoughts. Insoo hadn't shown up for any of the appointments that had been planned for the day, and his manager was seriously upset about it.

She wondered what missed appointments meant for an actor like Insoo. Was it very harmful to his career?

When Akila switched off the lights and settled into her bed, she was glad that she still hadn't read Rose's messages. Lying on her back, she scrolled through them and smiled at the many love hearts she had received and the, "You can do it!" reassurances. She sent a few hearts back and told her that she would call soon.

It was late afternoon the next day when Akila and Insoo stood glaring at each other. She'd waited hours at home that day trying to work on her other assignments but not being able to focus.

In the morning, she'd received a short message from Tae Oh, emphasising that all was okay and he would drop Insoo as soon as possible. However, it was only after many hours that had left Akila more and more worked up that she finally heard the front door open and shut.

Without a word, Insoo marched past her and down the corridor into his room. His door slammed shut. "Kim Insoo!" she shouted, giving in to the feeling of frustration that had been gnawing at her the entire day. She followed him, pushing his door open with such force that she almost fell over.

It was her first time entering his private space, and judging from the expression on his face when he turned around to glare at her, he wasn't pleased with her invasion.

"Speak to me." Her voice broke as she wondered why this whole thing had to be so dramatic.

"About?"

"Everything."

"What are you even talking about?"

"I apologise for Thursday. Please. Just speak to me!"

"WHAT YOU ARE TALKING ABOUT?"

She instantly shut her mouth. As if a curtain had been pulled open, Akila suddenly noticed how quickly he was breathing and how stiff his entire posture was. He seemed barely able to hold himself back. Again, she felt like crying. What was she doing here?

After a moment, he pointed at the small bandage she was wearing. "What happened to your hand?"

She lifted her hand, momentarily perplexed. Then she remembered. "The dishes yesterday morning . . ." she murmured. Was this a new way to evade a topic? First, running away, then just talking about something else? "Are you ready to talk?" she inquired, inhaling sharply to get her reeling feelings under control.

"Were you trying to test me?"

His voice felt like ice slicing through her head, freezing her to nothing. "What?"

"Placing all that food. . . ." He interrupted himself and let one hand run over his face. "Were you trying to see what would happen?"

She was confused, wanting to figure out what he was getting at. Then it dawned on her, and her eyes went wide with emotion. "What kind of person do you think I am? I came to coach you, not to make you miserable. But I want to know: When was the last time you ate a proper meal, Insoo? And didn't throw up immediately after? YOU tell me what you expected to happen when you agreed to this contract with me! Did you expect that I would close my eyes and keep my fucking mouth shut when you're slowly dying? You're such an idiot!" When was the last time she had shouted like this? It had been ages. She didn't usually raise her voice.

"I am not dying."

"You *are* dying," she retorted forcefully. "It will be a few more horrible years, and then you'll be dead."

She couldn't help but notice how his dark eyes went dim at her words. It was as if a light had gone out. He blinked several times, being otherwise completely still, then sat down on the edge of his bed. He covered his face with his hands, his long body slowly bending forward. He looked utterly defeated.

Akila stood fixed in the same spot. She could feel their emotions whirring around the room, charging the air with agony and exhaustion. He still covered his face, but tears found their way down his cheeks and fell on the carpet. *What to do?* she wondered.

Another few seconds passed, then she walked to the bed and sat down next to him. Very carefully, she placed her hand on his back. He was crying hard, although making almost no sound. She sat even closer and put her left arm around his shoulders.

They remained like this for a long time.

Eventually, he calmed down a little, straightened up, and wiped his face with his hands. He took a deep breath, despite his chest still trembling, then stood up without looking at her. Silently, he disappeared into the bathroom and, a second later, she heard the click of the lock.

She stayed where he left her, feeling too tired to move. She didn't want to leave him alone, but at the same time, she didn't want to be overbearing. There was an inkling that something was unfolding, but it was still very fragile and she didn't want to break it.

In the end, Akila simply crawled onto his bed, pulled up one of the blankets, placed her head on one of the pillows, and closed her eyes. She could hear the shower running in the bathroom. For an instant, she was worried that he would do something crazy in there, but judging from the fact that her sense of alarm wasn't strong enough to make her open her eyes again, she decided to give him his space.

Akila woke up and recognized pale sunlight playing on the blinds covering the window. She felt wonderfully warm and smug and decided that it was best to close her eyes again. Where were her children? Only then did she return to the world and the images of the past days flooded into her brain. Her eyes popped open and she let out a small gasp at the force of her arrival back in Seoul.

It was then that Insoo stirred slightly, and she realised that he was right behind her. It was his body heat that made her so comfortable. He had placed his arm around her and his warm breath blew into her hair at the back of her head.

Akila's muscles tensed, and she tried to remain completely still. With wide eyes, she listened to him breathing, experiencing the regular up and down of his chest close to her back with an intensity that got her heart pounding strongly. After long minutes like that, she adjusted her arm so that she was able to weave her fingers through his and hold his hand. He didn't wake up, and Akila closed her eyes and willed herself to drop back into her other worlds.

Wandering aimfully

When she woke up again, she was alone. Which day was it again, and where was she exactly?

Even now, it took a moment for her to focus and accept the emotions and images of her first week in Seoul.

She turned to lie on her back and stared at the ceiling. It was Sunday, which probably explained why the house was so quiet and Kwon Ma Ru hadn't called through the house and Mr. Park hadn't popped his head in through the door to inform her of today's schedule. What would they say if they found her in Insoo's bed? Judging from all the Korean series she'd watched, spending the night in the same bed seemed to be a big deal in this country.

Akila sighed and sat up. Not sure how to feel about it all and worried how Insoo would feel about it too, she put her feet on the floor. She checked the clock on the nightstand: 8:00 in the morning. She walked to the window and glanced out into the front yard after opening the blinds. It was a hazy day, like many others she'd seen since she arrived, and snow was falling. It was a beautiful sight, and the delicateness of the motionless morning with only the snowflakes dancing down onto the city filled her heart with a sense of calm and determination.

She took in the view one more time and then looked around. Where did he go?

* * *

Insoo sat on the sofa in the living room. He had recently woken up with Akila in his arms and the fingers of his one hand interlaced with hers. She'd been so completely still and peaceful that he carefully lifted his head to check and see that she was breathing regularly.

It had been warm and comfortable, and he'd inched closer, inhaling her scent and putting his face into her hair, feeling the softness of the skin on her neck.

She still hadn't stirred and he found himself wrapping his arms tighter around her and letting his lips touch her neck just below her ear. Thinking about that now, a wave of heat washed over him, and he absentmindedly rubbed the back of his neck, frowning. "What is going on?" he murmured to himself.

The last few days had been exhausting enough, and he experienced a mixture of fear and exhilaration thinking about the fact that she'd seen right through him. How had she noticed what he was doing?

The impact of the realisation that he wasn't fine had hit him hard, especially last night. The anger he spotted in her unwavering eyes stayed with him even now. All the months he'd carried on working, meeting friends and family despite feeling so tired every day, working more and eating less and less until he literally ate nothing most days.

And still, he felt that he wasn't good enough.

Looking into the mirror had turned out to be more difficult over the past year, especially on those days when he'd been forced to put food in his mouth. It was as if he instantly changed and gained so much weight that he was inadequate.

But today he suddenly felt like he couldn't go on. He wanted to be free of it.

Insoo had been so occupied with his thoughts that he didn't notice when Akila came down the corridor. Her hair was ruffled and she was a little pale, standing there looking at him. After a moment of hesitation, she walked over, sat down next to him, and folded her legs. She looked like she was having a silent dialog with herself, gazing straight ahead, followed by a sigh and a slight nod as if concluding on something. Then she reached out and simply took his hand into both of hers.

He could barely hide his astonishment. She seemed so calm and steady, holding his hand. Something inside him shifted, and although the general feeling of weakness that had been his companion for a while now didn't lift completely, he felt a small rush of energy run through him. They remained seated like that for several minutes until their hands were warm, and Akila's stomach growled.

Turning to him, she said, "I need to eat and have my coffee. Will you keep me company?"

She jumped to her feet and moved into the kitchen. Music played moments later and the clattering of dishes and the sound of the water heater filled the air. Insoo stayed on the couch and observed her warming food and preparing coffee while humming along to the songs that emanated from her little portable speaker.

Just like on Friday, she arranged all the dishes on the tray and came over. Insoo stood up to move the low side table in front of the sofa for her to place her load. She smiled at him, and after getting two cups of steaming coffee from the kitchen, she sat down on the carpet and arranged the small bowls and plates on the table.

"I'm not going to force you to eat," she said, pointing at a small bowl with a few spoonfuls of rice. "But why don't you try just the rice? My grandma used to tell me that she ate only plain rice for a week whenever she wanted to lose weight."

He was a little irritated by her comment. What was she trying to say?

She probably realised it, because she went on to say, "Insoo, I can't really know how you feel." She looked straight into his eyes as was her habit, and he noticed how they were light green today. "But I can promise that I'll stop you every time you want to run away after your meals and that I'll celebrate every time you manage not to do it. If you want, I will do that."

He didn't know what to say. Did he want her to do that? Would she be able to? He would rather avoid eating than not be able to stop himself after food.

"I stopped you once," she added, as if in response to his doubts. "I can do it again." She faced the table with a satisfied expression and started loading her bowl with food.

He studied her profile while she was eating, many thoughts pulsing through his head.

She chewed unhurriedly and drank some of her coffee with milk in between, which he found odd. Given the savvy taste of the warm food, which for him was a contrast to the taste of coffee, he preferred his coffee after the meal. Startled, he wondered what those random thoughts meant. "How? How will you stop me?" he picked up the conversation she had started. "What if I am somewhere else and you are not there to stop me?"

She didn't look at him, but carefully placed her almost empty bowl on the table. "For now, I will be wherever you are to make sure I can stop you. My contract is still on anyway. After that, we'll find a way."

She glanced up at him and smiled. Sitting there on the carpet, she was so calm and confident that he didn't know what else to say. He felt as if there was a real possibility of breaking free, and it frightened him to even acknowledge that there was a spark of hope nagging him. That spark was pushing and pulling at his heart, willing him to accept her offer.

She finished her coffee, gazing out of the windows, when that spark won the battle. He reached out and took the bowl and metal chopsticks from the table. After a moment of hesitation, he began to eat.

They sat in complete silence until his bowl was empty, the music still playing on low volume in the kitchen.

* * *

Akila stared straight ahead, her heart pounding strongly in her chest and her hands trembling. She sat in awe of this moment, a moment she was sure she would never forget in her entire life. The moment he had accepted her help and had torn down the last barriers between their lifelines. She was responsible for keeping her promise now, and there was no option of letting him down.

He took the last bite from his bowl and placed it on the table. He looked as if he was in disbelief at what he'd just done, and fear was on his face.

She unfolded her legs and, with great care, she settled down right next to him. She moved so close that she was sure that he could feel her quick heartbeat and wrapped her arms around him. His muscles seemed so tense that she thought they might snap. She pulled him towards her, and his head dropped onto her shoulder. He had a vacant look on his face, and she was unspeakably scared that she wouldn't be able to stop him. Physically, he was much stronger than her, and if he really wanted to go, he could leave. She placed her fingers on one of his cheeks and wrapped her legs around him, afraid that he might jump up from the couch.

Looking out over the city beyond the front yard, she started talking. Her children were the first thing that came to her mind, and they'd never really talked about their families. It was easy for her to describe their usual ways, the breakfast routines on weekdays, the loud music in the evenings, and their likes and dislikes. She realised how much she missed them.

Insoo was completely motionless in her arms, his forehead resting against her neck.

When would it be safe to let him go? If she let him go too early, would he jump and run?

It was a long time before he finally moved. Gently, he peeled himself out of her embrace. He was very pale, but when she searched his eyes for a clue about how he was feeling, he gave her a tiny smile. "I think we should go out for a bit," he said. She nodded. A walk was a good idea.

* * *

They dressed in their winter coats and left the house as they were. Outside, they stopped on the steep road to take in the cold air. The sun was making an effort to break through the cover of grey clouds. A few snowflakes drifted down to them. Insoo and Akila strolled uphill, Akila taking the lead through the smaller, winding alleys she liked so much.

It was late lunchtime when they stopped at a small cafe somewhere in the city to get a hot drink and for Akila to take a small bite. Feeling overwhelmed by the variety of snacks to choose from, she asked him to select what he thought was best for her.

They sat in the small cafe among a few other customers, sipping hot coffee from simple, already quite beaten-up cups and Akila chewing away on her snacks. It was Sunday, so the usual lunchtime buzz food stores experienced during the week was missing, and nobody seemed to recognize Insoo, which he registered with some relief. He wasn't in the mood to wear a cute smile for anyone today.

There was an old-fashioned TV hoisted in a metal cage over the entrance of the cafe that presently showed the trailer of a local drama. Akila's eyebrows shot up in recognition, and she pointed her spoon at the screen.

"Oh, I've seen this before! I like this actor." She grinned at him.

"I can't believe that you are really a fan," he commented while watching the end of the trailer.

"Why not? I enjoy Korean productions so much. Do you want to know why? They take time to tell the story, which is awesome."

He glanced at her. They were sitting next to each other at a small round table, and he was able to observe her without the fear of getting caught staring. When she smiled, a ray of wrinkles appeared around her eyes and suggested that she'd smiled a lot in her life. She had thin lips and a thin, straight nose that ended in a small tip. Her nose underlined her serious looks whenever she was upset and her eyes widened to about double their usual size to glare at the other person unwaveringly. He thought she was quite intimidating at times.

"Have you watched any I was part of?" he asked without truly thinking about it and instantly regretted the rather silly question. To someone like her, he must come across as obsessed with himself. They had just managed to hit a small milestone on his path of turning it all around, and here he was, asking if she had ever seen his programs. But she smiled cheekily and nodded, her mouth full of the last of the snacks he'd selected for her.

"Yup, I have. My favourite was the corruption and crime story where you were the young gang member who joined the prosecutor. You were absolutely amazing in that."

He was a little surprised by her taste at first, but letting it sink in, it did completely fit in with who she was. He remembered now that Tae Oh and Akila had discussed this topic in the bookstore the other day. However, he hadn't been able to listen properly, feeling too exhausted then.

Today, he wanted to take it all in, keep every word she uttered with him, no matter how trivial. "That was also one of the programs that was most fun shooting," he found himself saying, something he'd never told anyone else. As an actor, you were expected to not judge the roles you took on and the programs you appeared in. But you especially didn't say anything negative about romantic dramas and comedies. They were by far the most popular, and a big part in a romantic drama could make a new star overnight. "Which other programs do you like?" he wanted to know.

She placed her chin in her hand, thinking for a moment. "So, for crime stories, I really enjoyed *Bad Guys*, the second season. *The Lies Within* and *Strangers*. Oh, and I thought, for romantic dramas, *Where Your Eyes Linger*, *Something in the Rain*, and *To My Star* were awesome. And I really loved *Itaewon Class*. And I cried the most when I watched *My Mister*."

She lifted a finger, remembering something else. "Oh, and for action-hero dramas or whatever you call that, I loooooved *The K2*. That was simply great! So lavish and dramatic. And *Descendants of the Sun*. Oh, and I thought *Semantic Error* was super sweet."

She laughed, obviously amused by his baffled expression. "Shall I go on?"

He looked at her twinkling eyes, the wrinkles like rays of sunlight around them, and listened to her laughter. "What about American or European actors? Or African actors?" he inquired.

"Mmmhhh. . . . Bae Doona is awesome, of course. Oh! I think she's Korean too." She winked and then went on to list actors and actresses she liked, and for the first time in months, he felt content to simply sit and spend his time with someone else.

They were outside most of the day, walking across the big city.

By late afternoon, Akila needed another snack, and she asked him to choose something he felt he could stomach too. "I am a social eater. My food tastes best when I enjoy it with another person. Plus, we have been walking a lot in the cold, so you would benefit from food as well. And let's make use of this day. You have time today, and we can test how much we can accomplish."

She smiled her warm smile at him and, unlike with others, he didn't feel it was too much. She talked as if it was the most natural thing for them to discuss the fact that he had to learn how to keep food down again. It was a little unnerving, but at the same time, it was probably also the reason why he was able to agree to her suggestion and got a light snack for him and a wider selection for her.

They strolled along a wide park after that, nibbling on their eatery, talking, and avoiding the busier areas of the park.

It was a short while after he was done with his snack that he noticed the change. It came all of a sudden, and he couldn't stop feeling sick to his stomach. He wasn't sure if he would be able to keep his food down. Instantly, the fear of being in a public space without full control over how he felt hit him with overwhelming force.

Akila was still chatting animatedly, obviously not yet aware of the shift in him, and he could do nothing to alert her.

He bent over, trying to regain his composure and trying not to think about throwing up, but it was hard to do. His body seemed to be screaming at him to remove everything until nothing was left inside him.

"Insoo," Akila called. "Insoo!" She looked scared, holding his arm and patting him on the back. "Are you feeling unwell?"

All he could do was nod his head, still gasping for air and closing his eyes in an effort to overcome the growing urge to puke.

She suddenly pulled him up and put her hands on his cheeks, locking her gaze with his. Her eyes were wide with fear. "Insoo, look at me! You can do this, just look at me. Just focus on how to respond, okay? Okay?"

Everything had gone blurry, and even making sense of her words was difficult. His inner organs were rebelling. But she kept looking into his eyes, and he noticed the green amid the brown that shone brightly, now that her eyes were open wide.

"What program did I say I liked most?"

"What?" he mumbled, trying to push her away and get some space to breathe. All he wanted to do was to get rid of what made him feel so sick.

"Think!! What programs did I say I loved the most? Insoo! This is important!"

Important? Why was it so important? She looked really worried, and he wondered what would happen if he didn't help her with the answer to her question. He should at least try to help her, even if it was out of a selfish wish to get rid of her. She was too much in his personal space right now. "If I tell you," he uttered between shallow, fast breaths, "Will you leave me in peace? Will you finally leave me in peace?"

She nodded. "Yes, yes!" Her eyes were teary. "I will leave you in peace!"

He walked to the side of the path they had been strolling on and, trying to straighten up, he made an effort to think about her question. Programs. They had talked about programs sometime back. When was that? There was the TV in the cage. The round table. Her laughter. "*The Lies Within* . . . and *Stranger*," he spat out, still gasping for air. "You said you liked those."

She was still close to him, her body too much of a presence in his personal space. "True, true," she said breathlessly. "You're right. But there were more. Can you remember?"

"What for?" he raised his voice. "Are you crazy? Get out of my way!" He pushed her, this time with more force, and she stumbled, almost falling backward. He turned, wanting to walk in the other direction and put some distance between them, but there was a small wall in the way and he tripped and fell over onto the lawn covered by a thin layer of snow behind it. Pain shot through his right shin and all he could do was stay on his back and stare at the sky above him.

* * *

It was past midnight when they left the hospital.

Akila was extremely sleepy, wanting only to drop onto her bed and rest forever. Kwon Ma Ru had brought the car to the front of the hospital and opened the doors so that she and Insoo could easily get in.

The last few hours seemed like a proper Korean TV drama to Akila, including hospital visits that shake everyone up and a turning point that leaves the hero even more determined to overcome their personal boundaries.

She had to smile a little at the thought and remembered a conversation she'd had with Joyce a few years back. They'd talked about all the crazy things that had happened to them since they met on their first day at university and agreed that it was all the very best TV drama material. Again, today, Akila had the same thought. Those TV dramas that she usually thought were a little over the top could actually be real.

After the ambulance had dropped them at the ER entrance of the nearest hospital, it had been chaotic for Akila. The ER was busy that Sunday evening and doctors and nurses were running back and forth without noticing them. The team from the ambulance put Insoo, who still wasn't able to move and was just regaining his consciousness, on a stretcher and finally got a nurse to take over.

Seeing Insoo's pale face and the vacant look in his eyes, the nurse organised a bed to rest straight away and put a drip on Insoo to avoid dehydration.

After the nurse had pulled the curtain around them, Akila had sat on the side of Insoo's bed for lack of a chair in the tiny space. He was almost too tall for the small bed. It was one with wheels that could be pushed. Insoo was sleeping by now, the drip slowly suspending the liquid, and his feet in dark socks without the boots were poking out from under the thin blanket the nurse had draped over him. Somehow, the sight of his exposed feet made Akila feel sad.

Akila sighed and then thought that she should probably call someone to help. Communication with the nurse had been a little challenging, both of them struggling to decipher each other's accents.

When she called Mr. Kwon, he picked up almost immediately. She explained briefly where they were and that Insoo needed to get his leg checked.

Thirty minutes later, the short man was with them, buzzing around the ER like a busy bee, organising for the X-ray to be taken and making sure that a doctor would see them soon. She could see how stressed he was, but also how diligent and efficient he was in handling this situation, and she was grateful that he was taking charge.

However, when the manager wanted to organise for Insoo to be moved to a room, she put her hand on his arm and stopped him. Pointing at the young man sleeping on the small bed, she told him, "Let him rest here, Mr. Kwon. It's been a hard day for him, and waking him up now would be a crime."

Smoothing down his thick black hair with one hand, as was his habit, Kwon Ma Ru glanced from her to the sleeping Insoo, then bowed slightly to signal his agreement. "Fine, Ms. Akila. But please keep the curtain closed at all times. It is my job to ensure that rumours do not spread."

She nodded and sat back down on the chair that Mr. Kwon had organised for her shortly after he had arrived.

It was already 20:00 hours when Insoo was finally taken for the X-ray, and another hour passed before the doctor saw him.

Insoo had been very quiet the entire time, from when the nurse had woken him up so that he could get checked to the moment when they had been called to go see the doctor. He told both Akila and Mr. Kwon to wait outside and entered the room on his own. Akila saw how unhappy the manager was with having to wait outside, but he accepted Insoo's preference nonetheless.

She leaned on the other side of the door from where Insoo was sitting, asking herself what the outcome would be. It took a long time before the door opened and Insoo stepped out, followed by the doctor.

Kwon Ma Ru came forward and politely listened to what the doctor had to say. The elderly man in the white coat turned and shook Insoo's hand with a final remark and walked back into the consultation room.

Insoo had been told to get another drip for a few hours and something to support his shin until it had healed. It was nothing serious, and his leg would be fine if he was careful. This was as much as Mr. Kwon shared with her about the exchange with the doctor.

Akila hadn't been able to follow what the three men had talked about, but the fact that Insoo's manager didn't say a single word on the way back gave her the sense that there was more she didn't know.

Insoo lay down on the bed with a sigh after the nurse had put the drip back in. Mr. Kwon mumbled that he would get some drinks for them all and disappeared, pulling the curtain completely shut.

Akila settled onto the chair and focused on Insoo. She was sure that both his manager and Insoo himself were milling over something.

"Are you ready to tell me what the doctor said?" she asked him after letting a few minutes of silence pass between them.

He had closed his eyes momentarily, but she knew he wasn't sleeping. Keeping his eyes firmly shut, Insoo responded sooner than she had expected. "I am underweight and lack a whole list of nutrients. I need to do something if I don't want my inner organs to be damaged."

He opened his eyes and looked at her. "It's the worst for my food pipe. Because I haven't kept food inside, it is already damaged from the acid."

Akila kept her eyes on him as she inched forward in her chair and then took his hand with both of hers. His gaze wandered from her face down to their hands, and she wondered if he would cry. She couldn't read his expression.

Still looking at his hand embraced by hers, he murmured, "Can you still keep your promise? I gave you a hard time today."

At that moment, the curtain was pulled back and Kwon Ma Ru entered with drinks and snacks in his arms.

Squeezing his long fingers gently, she quickly responded, "Yes," then smiled as broadly as she could muster. "Let's do this."

Her heart beat with unusual intensity, filled with a mixture of fear and determination.

He nodded, still wearing a solemn expression on his face, then looked up at his manager and accepted the small snack and bottle of juice the other man held out to him. Mr. Kwon excused himself as he had to get the medication and the splint Insoo had been prescribed.

Akila was deeply impressed when she observed how Insoo slowly opened the snack and started eating it in tiny bites. In between, he sipped from the small bottle of juice, his face completely blank. When he was done, he leaned back into his pillow, and then reached out for her hand. "Don't let go," he said once their fingers were intertwined and closed his dark eyes.

Battle plan

The next couple of days were intense. Insoo insisted on following his schedule as usual, plus making up for the interviews he'd missed on Friday.

Once again, Akila got a taste of how good a manager Mr. Kwon was. He was efficient in sorting out the schedule, made sure Mr. Park picked them up at the right time and place, and prepared for each item on the agenda, which was a bigger part of Insoo's daily routine than she'd expected.

Being an actor and model meant putting hard work into every shoot, and being a public figure meant that he had to live up to his image and continue grooming relentlessly. What Akila realised was that there was barely any negative press on Insoo. His image was that of an approachable, hard-working, and polite talent with an intense sex appeal, and this image was cultivated in everything Insoo did. In the background, with Kwon Ma Ru coordinating most of it, the agency that had signed Insoo supported this image in order to continuously grow the income he generated.

Therefore, Mr. Kwon didn't hesitate to pull some strings to get the interviews back on the schedule and manage the situation in a way that earned Insoo sympathy points for rescheduling so soon after his unexpected leg injury. Although the small, busy man tried to carry a display of worry, Akila spotted the satisfaction beneath the surface that his "asset," Insoo, wanted to continue work without any delay. She hated him a little for that and was wondering how she'd bring up the subject when it was just the two of them.

Insoo's determination to work left her lost for words, but also a little unsettled. Where did he suddenly get all that energy from? Was this a healthy way to go about it or was this just a short fight he put up before he had to give up, utterly defeated?

She worried a lot but tried to let him take the lead without making any discouraging remarks.

Thus, Akila's second week in Seoul passed in a blur of photo shoots, business meetings, interviews, and attending a radio program and two TV shows. This included hours of preparations for these events on Insoo's part.

Lunch dates were rarely of a personal nature, and by Friday, Akila asked herself how Insoo had managed his schedule without eating proper meals.

On Friday, late evening, Akila stood in the kitchen fixing herself a hot cup of tea after another busy day. She'd connected her speaker to her phone and, presently, "Tadow," the wonderful song by Masego and FKJ, filled the room with the sound of the saxophone.

Akila thought about the days she had spent in Seoul. After making their agreement in the hospital, she went wherever Insoo went. At all appointments, Mr. Park was with them too, like a shadow who made sure that they got to where they had to be at the right time and took care of their other needs as well. He made sure Insoo sat comfortably. He made sure he got his refreshments and ensured the stylists were ready on time. He made sure that Akila had a good place to sit and wait. Sometimes, Akila found it almost suffocating, although Mr. Park seemed to be honestly concerned about Insoo. But after a couple of days, she began to truly grasp what it meant to be surrounded by people whose job it was to ensure that you stayed in line and were protected. And due to the circumstances, Akila thought how much she had suddenly become part of that system, keeping her eyes on Insoo all the time. What was she meant to feel about that?

With the exception of her children, it had been a long time since Akila had spent so much time with another person. Sharing all these hours with Insoo, she realised quickly how close he was with his own family and friends, and it hurt Akila to see how he tried to hide his exhaustion and distress when speaking, especially to his mother on the phone.

Akila put the kettle on and washed the fresh ginger, humming along with Masego's vocals.

Accompanying Insoo to the various shoots, shows, interviews, and meetings, she observed how easily other people related to him. He wasn't aware of his effect on others, and he usually seemed truly embarrassed when someone mentioned his looks or sex appeal. He was very focused and diligent at shoots, but during break times, he wasn't shy to joke with the crew and make everyone laugh.

Still, Akila felt uneasy about the physicality of his image. Looks and, more or less subtly, sensuality and sex were almost always popping up as terms that defined him, no matter if it was a photoshoot, a discussion about the next program, or compliments he received.

Online, comments were all about how beautiful and sexy he was and why hundreds of girls and women were crazy about him. Uploaded images often showed those scenes or pictures with him having less, rather than more clothes on.

Korean culture was definitely much more reserved and less direct than European or North American cultures, Akila reflected, but when it came to fandom, South Koreans went all out in following and supporting their stars–commenting online, uploading the latest images and news, and nurturing their crushes on their favourite actors and actresses. She was impressed by this dedication but was also worried. What happened if something didn't go according to expectations and the whole machine of online conversation about a star turned negative? She guessed that the impact must be devastating. Also, was this all Insoo was?

The water was boiling, and she dropped the pieces of fresh ginger she had cut into a large cup, adding honey and hot water. The next song on the playlist was Erykah Badu's "Tyrone." She smiled.

Akila wondered whether anyone could remain free of public opinion once they became a public figure. She guessed it wasn't completely possible, and changing an already created image must be difficult. "He's the best in crime stories," she mumbled while stirring her tea with a small spoon. "Why would he do so many shallow romantic dramas?"

In the afternoon, she had joined Insoo and Mr. Kwon for a meeting with a director who was set to shoot a new drama for one of the big TV channels. It was an interesting opportunity, Insoo told her, because the program would be aired during prime time in Korea and would eventually reach millions of viewers across Asia, Europe, and the Middle East.

It was a story about love and destiny and involved many heartbreaking moments. Many episodes would pass by before the lovers would be able to be together. Akila didn't doubt that it would be good–a proper Korean TV drama–but she didn't like the fact that Insoo seemed reduced to that while he seemed so much better at playing multi-faceted characters. But was she to say so? Even after these two weeks, or maybe especially because of all that had happened since she had arrived in Seoul, she was never certain about how much of her personal opinion she should share and how much she should keep in as a coach would do. After all, she had been hired as a coach–but in the end, the whole thing turned out so differently. So what was she to do?

Wherever they went, Akila was introduced as Insoo's life coach, and Kwon Ma Ru continued to spread the news online that the young star was always focused on improving himself and was currently working with a specialised coach to achieve further international growth. The comments on that were almost all positive. As was their job, Mr. Kwon and his team had placed selected bits of information strategically and achieved a spike in Insoo's popularity.

Many of the meetings took place partly in English and Korean, so Akila got a glimpse of what was discussed. She also noted with satisfaction that she had started picking up words and phrases while being with Insoo and meeting so many different people in such a short time. Grasping a simple conversation in Korean was still hard, but not impossible. This trend reminded her of her early days in Kenya when she had made an effort to learn Swahili and started picking up the meaning of words in a similar fashion.

Akila shook her head in an attempt to clear her head of the overwhelming thoughts in her mind. She blew her tea absent-mindedly and took a small sip. "Ouch!" she muttered, touching her mouth and frowning. The tea was burning hot and had burned her lip and the tip of her tongue.

She left the steaming cup to cool on the counter. Walking over to the living room, Akila stretched her entire body by lifting her arms to the ceiling and making herself as tall as she could to remove some of the tension in her neck and shoulders. She was grateful that the week was over and that Mr. Kwon had told them to rest over the weekend.

Insoo was already stretched out on the sofa, his hair still a little wet from showering. He was scrolling through his phone, responding to messages.

Akila let herself drop into her favourite seat next to the couch and folded her legs, then leaned back and watched him. He was, indeed, beautiful. "You did really well," she said after observing him for a while.

He glanced up briefly and smiled a little. "Thanks."

This whole week, he'd forced himself to have a small bowl of light food each morning, during lunch meetings, and snack times at shoots. He hadn't avoided the food and always accepted something, although in tiny quantities. And he managed to keep it all in–although not without a struggle.

There'd been several occasions when he had to fight the over-powering urge to escape to the washroom, but somehow they navigated the moment every time and came out victoriously. She would either grab his hand under the table, which happened at one lunch meeting with a famous journalist who wanted to do a feature on him, or she would suddenly start a conversation about her favourite actors and actresses, forcing him to focus on her questions and find the right answers by remembering their exchange from Sunday. Somehow, this method worked, and by Wednesday it had already become a secret code to signal that a tough moment was approaching.

He would say, "Akila, let's talk about your favourite actors," and she knew that she had to keep going and not let him slip away until the internal battle was won.

Seoul nights

She stood up to get her cup of tea from the kitchen, which she thought should have cooled down by now. Insoo's phone rang and she could hear him picking up. Judging from the way he was talking, it wasn't his mother speaking–probably a friend. By the time she was back, he had hung up and looked at her.

"Tae Oh is going to stop by with some other friends," he told her. "There is an event we have been invited to."

She stared at him in disbelief. "Another event? I thought we were done for the week."

He smiled at her reaction. "It's a party organised by a director who recently turned fifty. It is something like his birthday celebration, and we should pass by. So nothing serious."

She popped her head to one side. "Does that mean there will be music and dancing?" Then another thought occurred to her. "Do Koreans dance at parties?"

He raised one eyebrow at her comment and couldn't help but laugh. "Only one way to find out," he responded. "Are you going to go like this?"

She glanced at her yoga pants and simple shirt. "I don't know. What do people wear at such parties?"

"Smart but comfortable, I would suggest," he responded.

Eight hours later, they stood in the elevator on the way down. Everything in the lift was golden and Akila randomly asked herself who had thought of this decadent design. She stood at the back with her head on the wall, gazing ahead. There was total silence, although there were seven people in the small space.

Insoo stood at the far end, his hands in his jeans, a frown on his face, looking at the ceiling. He was still a little out of breath– she could see his shoulders moving up and down from where she was. In front of him, Mr. Park looked calm and unmovable. Tae Oh stood right next to him, staring at the ceiling just like Insoo was, frustration written all over his face.

Akila folded her arms in front of her chest and shifted slightly.

The night started quite well, with Insoo's whole crew meeting at his house to get ready for the party.

Akila was a little nervous getting ready in her bathroom. What did one wear going to a Korean birthday party accompanied by people who were a decade younger, or more?

"Don't think that way," she scolded herself. "Since when do you care about age or any of that?"

She ended up in one of her favourite black tunics with black tights and a dark turquoise woollen jacket on top. Better to be comfortable.

There was a happy bustle in the corridor as everyone put on their coats and shoes and spilled out onto the street, getting into two of the vehicles parked in front of Insoo's place.

Insoo sat in the front of the car Tae Oh was driving and one of the girls got in next to Akila in the back. Her name was Seo Hui, and her English was quite good, so it was easy to have a proper conversation on the way. The second car was driven by Mr. Park, who would accompany them as per the agency's directive but would remain in the background.

They eventually slowed down in front of a modern highrise building with shiny glass walls and entered the underground parking.

The group took the elevator up after the other vehicle arrived as well, and when they opened on the twentieth floor, the noise of people talking and laughing and music playing somewhere deeper inside the large apartment hit Akila full force. She hadn't gone out to party in a while and needed a moment to adjust to the wide array of sounds jumping at her.

Insoo was ahead of her. He turned to smile at her, then motioned for her to follow him. They wound their way through the crowded flat, with people stopping Insoo and Tae Oh many times for a brief conversation or a quick hi. Akila looked around to get her bearings and decided that she would probably need a whiskey or a gin tonic to survive this party. It was loud and full, and she was definitely underdressed. Women in unbelievably high heels and short dresses passed her, their sleek black hair falling to their butts and their faces done perfectly with luxurious red lips and shiny eyes. One of Insoo's friends, Hae In, asked her what she wanted to drink, and she asked for a whiskey on the rocks or a strong gin tonic. He gave her a thumbs-up and disappeared into the crowd to get the drinks.

A while later, they made their way further through the crowd to an arrangement of bean bags and sofas, and Akila instantly recognized a handsome tall man sitting there who greeted Insoo and Tae Oh with affection. He was one of the really big actors in South Korea, and she had watched several of his programs before. They all settled down around him and some other people, finding space to squeeze in, and conversation ensued.

Akila sat next to Seo Hui, who chatted away with another girl she had met in the crowd, and Insoo and Tae Oh sat opposite her, talking to their colleague, laughter travelling up to join the general noise level in the place. Akila folded her legs, as was her habit, and slowly sipped her drink, looking around. Several smaller groups of people had started dancing and singing along to the songs being played. Still, this was very different from the parties she had been used to in Nairobi, where dancing took place anywhere and everywhere and made an evening worthwhile. Back in Europe, Akila had often missed the Nairobi party culture. Almost no other place was comparable. Scotland wasn't the best place to go out to dance, and she was sceptical as to whether Seoul could live up to her high expectations.

Suddenly, a cheer from the crew dispersed on the seats and sofas emerged, and several people jumped up to dance. Akila smiled.

This turned out to be more to her liking than she'd expected. Seo Hui nudged her and asked, "Akila, do you dance?"

"I do, but I'm not sure if I can dance the 'Korean way,'" she responded, laughing.

Seo Hui pulled her up, already a little tipsy, and shouted through the general noise, "Show me how people dance where you come from!"

Akila briefly imagined herself imitating a stiff German dancing out of rhythm, then discarded the thought. She'd always been poor at imitating others for fun. "I can show you how *I* dance," she said, smiling as she started swinging her hips with the beat. American and Korean pop music played, so it was easy to dance along.

For the next few hours, Akila and Seo Hui, together with her acquaintance, danced and sang their hearts out. They were joined by several of Insoo's friends, as well as others from the crowd, and the group was rocking, cheering, and clapping whenever the DJ, who operated from the far corner of the large room, played a song they especially liked.

Insoo, Tae Oh, and their handsome, famous colleague remained seated, still in conversation, but after a while, they turned to watch them all with amusement on their faces.

Seo Hui laughed. "Akila, why didn't you tell me that you are a great dancer?"

"You are too!" Akila responded and they swung their hips and moved their shoulders in unison.

Akila was just thinking about how much she enjoyed this moment when someone touched her buttocks. She didn't think clearly the second after that. It was as if her instincts took over, and she whirled around to slap the man across the face with as much force as she could muster.

He stumbled backward, falling back and pulling several other dancers with him. But he was quick and straightened up an instant later, looking at her with anger and coming extremely close. His aura frightened her, probably because she felt more vulnerable after having had a few strong gin and tonics.

"Akila," Seo Hui whispered next to her, staring at the tall, angry man in front of them. "Hey," she shouted at him, then went on in Korean. Suddenly, he grabbed her by the neck. Akila, afraid that he might seriously hurt the young woman, was about to kick him when Insoo appeared in front of her.

He twisted the man's arm onto his back in one fluid movement. Akila stood speechless, then turned to put her arms protectively around Seo Hui, who was gasping for air. There was a brawl going on now. Apparently, the guy had come with his friends, who moved to free him of Insoo's grip, but now Insoo's crew was there, plus some of the other people they had been sitting and chatting with, holding them back.

By now, the DJ had noticed the disturbance and lowered the volume of the music. The party came to a halt as everyone glanced around the room, trying to understand what was going on.

Someone threw a bottle at Insoo's head. Insoo let the man he'd been holding go, pushing him completely to the floor, then went for the person who had attacked him with the bottle.

Oh shit! Akila thought, looking around in the ensuing chaos for a safe place to keep Seo Hui. She quickly moved her to a corner next to the large window front with the view of the many lights of Seoul shining, then went back into the crowd.

Insoo had already punched the other man, whose nose was bleeding profusely. She saw Tae Oh pulling him back, and the famous actor stepped in between Insoo and the angry men, gesturing to Insoo's friends to put an end to the fight.

Another group of men made their way through the crowd. Akila recognized the large figure of Mr. Park among them.

Tae Oh was talking to Insoo without a pause while holding him back, and Insoo looked like he had difficulty calming down.

Akila wound her way through the people around them and said, "Let's go right now," as soon as she reached them. Tae Oh looked at her, nodding. "Can you get him out of here?" she asked. "I'll take Seo Hui."

He inclined his head in the affirmative, then started pushing and pulling his friend away from the other men who were shouting and taunting him, but not willing to start a conflict with Insoo's entourage.

A few minutes later, they all reached the elevator from different directions. Insoo seemed less pumped up, but Tae Oh kept holding him and pushing him closer to the elevator doors. When the doors slid open, everyone got in. Mr. Park had arrived silently and took over from Tae Oh, making sure Insoo was at the very back of the lift.

Akila, who had her arm around a quiet Seo Hui, had never imagined that Tae Oh could get angry, but he clearly wasn't pleased now, releasing a cascade of Korean words that couldn't mean anything good and looking at Insoo. Insoo stared silently at the ceiling. His frown was deep and his chest was rising and falling fast.

There was dead silence in the car on their way home. Seo Hui had closed her eyes and rested her head on Akila's shoulder. Insoo sat in the passenger seat gazing out of the window as his friend drove.

When the two vehicles arrived in front of Insoo's house, there was a short discussion about who would stay with Seo Hui for the night and who needed to be dropped where. Hae In and the other girl agreed to stay at Seo Hui's for the night. Mr. Park was sent to chauffeur the rest of the group home, who were all too tipsy to drive.

Akila hugged Seo Hui and they smiled at each other. Then everyone got into the different vehicles and took off. Before leaving, Tae Oh lowered his window and told Akila, "I will pass by tomorrow."

She nodded. "See you then. Get home safely."

"Take care of this idiot and make sure he doesn't cause any more trouble," he told her but looked at Insoo, who looked at the sky.

Akila couldn't help but smile and gave Tae Oh a thumbs up.

They entered the quiet house, removing their coats and shoes without a word. Akila was suddenly very thirsty and walked into the kitchen to get some water. Taking out two large glasses, she poured some for Insoo first, then poured some for herself.

Glancing up at Insoo, who had followed her into the kitchen, she said, "Are you okay? The bottle must have hurt."

Avoiding eye contact, he nodded. "I'm okay." He took several gulps of the water she had poured for him.

"Thank you. And sorry for causing trouble, but–"

"He attacked you," he interrupted her. "That was wrong."

She stood facing him and felt something inside her move. It was an intense feeling, and she quickly pulled herself up and sat on the kitchen counter with her legs folded in an effort to get what she was feeling under control.

Insoo briefly glanced at her, and there was a look in his eyes that made her wonder what he was thinking. The air was thick with something she couldn't name, and she sat in anticipation of what was coming.

Insoo finished his water, then turned abruptly, mumbling, "Good night."

Akila sat in disbelief. Was he really going to leave like that? Before she knew it, she jumped off the kitchen counter. He had just reached the corridor when she caught up with him and held him by his light leather jacket.

Insoo came to a halt and she could sense the intense emotions emanating from him. They hovered around him like thick clouds. "Why are you running?" Her heart beat fast and she felt out of breath. The words came out hardly audible, with her voice already tending to be the type that was easily overheard. She wasn't sure if he had heard her.

A fierce battle raged in her brain with the gin tonics she'd had earlier contributing to her tangled thoughts. Should I show him what I really want to do to him? Or draw the line and stay safe with no risk of rejection? But she wanted so desperately for him to feel better.

Their eyes locked. She let go of his jacket and was ready to retreat, suddenly feeling she didn't have enough strength.

But he grabbed her shoulders and put his lips on hers. An explosion went off in her head and spread through her body.

Colours and heat intermingled in unspeakable chaos. Through it all, she felt his presence and held on to him to keep herself from drowning.

* * *

Insoo had gone for an early morning run as usual, although it had been more of a walk, owing to his still slightly injured leg. He had woken up in Akila's bed at around 6:00 with her next to him, completely motionless, her face peaceful. Just like the first time they shared a bed, he moved very close to her to confirm that she was breathing properly. *How can a person be so still in her sleep?* he wondered.

Lying on his back and gazing at the ceiling, he wondered how his life had been turned upside down in only two weeks.

No. It had started earlier. The whole thing had been set into motion the day he fainted at the gathering after the rooftop shoot and Ma Ru decided that they needed a quiet, but effective intervention. Quiet? No. Effective? Most certainly.

He looked over at the tall woman with the ruffled hair, and warmth ran through him like liquid. She seemed different without the large, silver rimmed glasses–undressed and, therefore, more approachable and vulnerable. When she wore her glasses, she looked smart and unbeatable–especially when she was annoyed and her eyes widened in their peculiar way. It was almost as if those glasses were part of her armour.

He reached out and touched her brow softly, not wanting to wake her up, but also feeling the need to confirm that this was a real situation and not some movie he was in. In his life, reality and fiction were intertwined and the lines had gotten blurred a while ago, so confirming that this was real was necessary.

She stirred slightly at his touch, and he pulled his hand away quickly. The reality of it hit him. She'd already spent two of the three weeks defined in her contract in his house. She lived in Europe with two children and was ten years older.

He knew for a fact that his parents, his mother in particular, wouldn't approve of a relationship with a much older, foreign woman with children. And he was sure that Ma Ru would want to kill him if he found out. This wasn't at all in line with the image they'd been grooming for years. He was well aware of that.

Insoo closed his eyes for a moment, deciding he needed to clear his head before it got worse. A few minutes later, he wore his running gear and was out the door, deeply inhaling the crisp morning air while making his way uphill.

When he finally got back to the house, feeling much freer, although not completely free of the many questions that whirled around his head, he had several missed calls on his phone. He'd left it on the kitchen counter when he went out earlier. Checking the display while sipping his water, he knew that something was wrong. There were several calls from his mother and about ten alone from Ma Ru. Tae Oh and Hae In had also tried to call him several times. What was going on?

He was about to call Tae Oh when Akila walked into the kitchen. He placed his phone back onto the counter, not sure what to do. She came up to him and wrapped her arms around him, resting her chin on his shoulder. He felt her warm breath on his neck and ear and was amazed at how easy it seemed for her to embrace him. It was as if she was also embracing all the questions on his mind, quieting them down gently, telling them that there would be answers later.

He hugged her too, one arm around her lower back, the other gently around her shoulders, his hand on the back of her head. She'd already showered and her wet hair smelled of shampoo. Again, he noticed how small her head was, something that was usually concealed by her often untidy hair.

He hesitated. What should one say in this situation? It was extremely comfortable to hold her. At the same time, he knew he needed to call everyone without further delay.

"I'm hungry," she finally said, looking up at him. "Can we have breakfast?

He nodded. And gazing into her eyes, he resolved not to hold himself back anymore. He'd already come so far. There was no stopping it. "Let's have breakfast," he echoed. Shifting slightly with her in his arms, he picked up his phone and showed it to her. "But I have about fifty missed calls, so I need to find out what is going on."

She raised both eyebrows and her eyes grew larger. "Uh oh," she said. "Then make your calls. I'll prepare breakfast."

He moved over to the living room, dialling Tae Oh's number. Waiting for him to pick up, he could hear Akila connecting her speaker to her phone, and a second later, she was already singing along to her Bongo Flava tunes while putting on the kettle and opening the fridge to remove some of the food containers.

Tae Oh picked up after a few rings. "Insoo." Judging from the sound of his voice, his friend was probably driving.

"Hey, what's going on? Are you guys okay? I saw all the missed calls and wondered if something happened."

"We are okay. Have you spoken to anyone today?"

"No. I just came back from my run and had no time to check my phone. What's going on?"

"I will come over. I'm on my way already."

"Wait . . . now? Hey, Tae Oh, what's really going on?"

"If you don't want to wait until I am there, check the latest news on Kim Insoo," he said. Insoo's stomach dropped when it dawned on him that the thing he'd always dreaded so much had happened–there was a scandal relating to him.

He hung up and stood frozen in his spot for a moment, staring into the space before him. Did he want to know what it was?

Akila walked over from the kitchen, a curious expression on her face. "Are you okay?"

He forced himself into motion. "I'm not sure. Something has happened." Lifting his head, he stared at her and was scared. If Ma Ru and his mother had called him so many times, whatever it was must be serious.

"What?" she asked him "What is that?" She was close to him now and wrapped her fingers around his hand, not taking her eyes off him.

He realised how the brown in her eyes was more pronounced today and wondered if this was due to the light. Why did her eyes have such a different look each day? Maybe those random thoughts helped because he was able to slow down all the confusing worries and remembered what he told himself just moments ago–he wasn't holding back or avoiding her anymore. "It must be some kind of scandal about me. I want to check what it is."

He could see that she was startled, but almost immediately, she gained control of her face and said in a firm voice, "Check now."

He unlocked his phone and typed his name in the search engine. Almost instantly, several new posts came up. Because he hesitated, she reached over and clicked on the first link, which also showed an image. When the page opened, they both stared at the images right at the top of the post in disbelief. After a pause, she said, without any emotion in her voice, "Translate for me, please."

Insoo flew over the content and felt a little sick. There were additional images and already over a hundred comments below. Additional comments were being added as they looked at the post and the number rose with unbelievable speed. Someone had even uploaded a video.

Scrolling through the comments, he felt his head spin. This was what he always worked so hard to avoid. The most sickening part was that the meanest comments were directed toward Akila. How could he even begin to translate?

"Insoo. . . ." She observed him carefully. Her green-brown eyes behind her glasses displayed a sense of calm, and he had an inkling that she already knew.

Still, he avoided saying anything by clicking on the next link and being confronted with similar images and commentary. He was about to open the next link when they heard the password being keyed in at the front door, and a moment later, Tae Oh entered the house.

* * *

He spotted them standing by the large windows in the living room, the phone between them, and instantly came over. From the looks on their faces, he could guess they'd seen the posts and articles because he slowed down after glancing at both of them and sat on the sofa. "Do you have any coffee to spare?" he asked.

Akila reacted first. Inclining her head, she responded, "We were just about to have breakfast. I'll get the coffee."

They looked at each other and forced a smile as if they both wanted to encourage each other.

Insoo's phone rang. It was his mother. He was torn for a second, then picked up as he walked out of the living room and down the corridor. He didn't want them to listen to his conversation with his mother, which he expected to turn out quite emotional.

Akila arranged the two cups of coffee on a small tray and carried them over to the living room. Tae Oh accepted his cup with a slight bow. She sat next to him and took a first sip, wondering how to begin the conversation. "I can tell that this isn't good," she finally said. "But can you tell me what exactly the story is? Insoo didn't want to translate for me." Tae Oh stared at her for a moment, and she realised that he hesitated, just like Insoo had. "Just tell me the truth. That will be easier than me putting the bits and pieces together for myself. I can handle it. I am sure it's worse for Insoo than it is for me."

"So you know that he fears scandal?"

"It was my guess, given everything that's been going on."

He nodded thoughtfully, then said, "It is bad for him. There is a lot of negativity already, and the story is spreading like wildfire. But the real issue is that it involves you."

"Yes, I saw the images, and there's even a video." She shook her head. "Where did that come from?"

"You were in some park."

She froze and it dawned on her that it had to be last Sunday when Insoo had suddenly thrown up. Her hand instinctively covered her mouth as she remembered how terrible that moment had been for both of them. Someone had filmed it and uploaded it now? A week later?

"Oh no," was all she could manage. How humiliating for Insoo. "Oh no." She imagined how many conclusions one could draw from looking at that video without understanding the context. "What's the story? Tell me the truth now, Tae Oh. There's no use avoiding it," she said weakly.

Tae Oh shifted next to her.

"Tell me!" She looked him in the eye and put as much determination into her voice as she could manage.

He rubbed his face, then began slowly. "The story is that Insoo has trouble, maybe due to drug use, and being supported by a life coach made it worse. They say he seems to have something going on with this much older, foreign woman. You. There is a video that looks like you are arguing, and someone also leaked last night's incident, so he looks like a crazy, violent guy now."

"Whaaaaat? I can't believe it! What an asshole. . . ."

Tae Oh lifted both hands to calm her down and to show that he agreed. Then he quickly went on. Akila got the sense that he wanted to be done as quickly as possible now.

"Most posts imply that you manipulated him and are using him . . . derailing him. They dug up some personal information. The fact that you are older, had two children without being married, and lived all over . . . well, it is perfect fuel for gossip."

She covered her face with her hands. "Oh shit!" she exclaimed. "Poor Insoo."

"Akila," he said with an intense look on his face. She was somehow frightened seeing it. "It *is* bad for Insoo, yes. But the worst comments are about you. And there are many. . . ."

She saw pity on his face and didn't like it. It irritated her, because it made her feel vulnerable, and she didn't like that feeling at all. Her natural tendency was to never show she was shaken–to never lose her composure in front of others. Even now, that mechanism set in, and she sat up straight and looked into Tae Oh's eyes to signal that she was in control–to show that this was a small thing for someone like her. But deep down, she felt shaken and was grateful for the fact that her children were somewhere far away and could be protected from all of this.

"Well," she finally said. "Isn't it always the woman's fault?"

"Akila, this isn't right. Don't pretend that it's not affecting you."

She closed her eyes for a second and turned her face away. Why was he doing this?

"Akila. . . ."

She shook her head and motioned for him to be silent. A tear found its way beneath her eyelid and was travelling down her cheek. She'd become much weaker recently, she found herself thinking as she tried to stop the other tears from falling. It was no use. They were falling anyway, so she let them run. Tae Oh placed a hand on her back but didn't say anything further.

After a while, she was able to get her breathing under control and dried her eyes with one of her sleeves. Facing him again, she said, "Insoo has worked so hard the past two weeks. It frustrates me that he has to deal with such rubbish. How can we help him?"

Studying her briefly, he seemed surprised at her reaction. She knew how people thought. They expected everyone to focus on themselves first. She disagreed with the common notion that was "human nature." But, truth be told, she was being selfish. She wanted Insoo to be fine for himself, yes, but also for her. Insoo being fine would mean she was fine as well. It meant that she had succeeded in this crazy venture that had been out of control almost from the start.

"Well," he responded after giving it some thought. "You can counter with clarifying information and with a story good enough to turn public negativity into sympathy and understanding. Kwon Ma Ru will know best how to do it. He also has the necessary connections."

"All he'll think about is how to protect his brand and not lose money. You know that," she retorted. "Is he really interested in Insoo as a person?"

"The person being well means his brand, as you call it, is well, so, yes."

"To some extent, I agree, but not totally. I think there are things Mr. Kwon would never want Insoo to do if it affects the profit."

Tae Oh suddenly smiled. "You know him well," he said. "But in the end, he will have to go with what Insoo decides. Ultimately, Insoo will have to make the call on how he wants to handle this, as it's going to affect his life and his career. And yours."

"Is that how it works between them?"

"In the end, yes. That is the kind of agreement they have."

She slowly nodded her head, letting that piece of information sink in. "Good to know." Then it hit her that Insoo hadn't turned up in quite a while. Was he still on the phone? "Let me check on Insoo," she said as she got up and left the room.

She knocked on his door before carefully opening it. Insoo was just coming out of the bathroom, rubbing his hair with a small towel and already dressed in jeans and a woollen pullover. Seeing her, he came to a halt, and after she closed the door behind her, they both stood for a moment in silence.

She eventually attempted to find the right words. "I want to say so many things," she said. "I want to say I'm really proud of what you have done the last two weeks. And I want to say don't let this stop you now. And I also want to say that I'm fine. I can handle it."

Insoo walked further into the room and dropped the towel onto his bed. "Akila, this isn't a joke. The comments about you. . . . It's just . . . I don't want you to be in a mess because of me, and I also don't want this scandal to affect me and my career." He let his hand run through his hair at the back of his head. "I'm not sure what to do," he muttered with a sigh.

She wondered if he wanted her to hold him, which she desperately wanted to right now, but his words made her unsure of what he expected of her and how close he wanted her to come. Maybe space was what he wanted more.

So she stayed where she was, wondering what she could say to make him feel more confident. While she was still thinking, she heard the front door open and voices filled the small corridor leading to the kitchen and living room.

Insoo heard the voices too and, after pressing his lips together tightly for a second, stepped past her and out of his room with determination.

Akila couldn't help but feel a little abandoned after he had walked past her without a word, but at the same moment, she told herself to stop being so self-absorbed. Insoo had far more to deal with than her, no matter how nasty those comments about her were.

Akila heard a woman's voice ringing out from the direction of the open-plan kitchen and wondered who was there. She left Insoo's room and walked down the corridor toward the voices. Coming closer, she recognized Mr. Kwon's familiar voice as well and thought that he must have come with someone else from the agency.

A beautiful, short woman with sleek black hair and dressed in a neat costume fell silent and turned to look at her as she approached. The resemblance was striking. She and Insoo were both simply beautiful people.

"Ms. Akila," Insoo's manager said, obviously avoiding awkward silences. "This is Insoo's mother, Mrs. Moon. Mrs. Moon, this is the life coach we have been working with, Ms. Akila."

The small woman didn't acknowledge the introduction in any way but seemed to inspect Akila thoroughly. Akila was sure that she spotted anger and a very strong will in her eyes. Of course, Insoo's success-focused and determined mindset had to come from somewhere. Maybe she'd found the source. "It's nice to meet you, Mrs. Moon," Akila said, not taking her eyes off the woman.

"Under different circumstances, I might have said the same," came the reply, the hard edge audible in Mrs. Moon's voice. Her English was strongly flavoured, but she seemed like a woman who had seen a lot of the world.

"Mother," Insoo said in Korean. He used the respectful term to address her, but it sounded like a warning. Mrs. Moon looked at her son and rapidly went on to speak to him in Korean, Akila only grasping a few words.

The discussion ensued with Mr. Kwon jumping in frequently and Tae Oh, who had been standing in the open space between the kitchen and living room, maintaining a respectful silence.

In the whole exchange, Insoo said only a handful of words and seemed to be interrupted every time by either Mrs. Moon or his manager.

Akila grew increasingly agitated, feeling that this wasn't going in the right direction for him. Hadn't Tae Oh said it was best if Insoo took the lead?

"Excuse me," she finally blurted out. "But if you're discussing what to do about all the rumours, I'd appreciate it if we could all talk about it together, as it also affects me."

Everyone looked at her for a moment. Then Mrs. Moon said, "Yes, of course. Unfortunately, your . . . unique lifestyle and choices have fuelled the whole thing immensely."

Insoo stared at his mother with a strange expression on his face. Was it anger? "Mother, please stop!"

She glanced at him only briefly before moving on. "We are here to discuss damage control and decide which way is best to clean up this mess you both have created. I can't believe you two weren't more careful about it. Insoo, your image is extremely important to your career. You know that! You have worked so hard for everything!" She looked so worried that Akila could completely relate to her–to her fear for her child and her wanting to make sure Insoo was fine and well-protected.

Mr. Kwon chimed in. "Insoo, I agree. We need to make sure that there is no confusion about your well-being and that there are no further rumours about your being unstable in any way. We need to turn the negative commentary around. The best approach is for you to make a statement. You would publicly show everyone that you are fine. And you have to make it clear that your relationship with Ms. Akila is only professional. I will ensure you get the interviews and airtime you need."

"What about the video?" Insoo asked after a pause. "How will you explain that?"

"We will not explain. I will make it go away," his manager responded forcefully, and Akila's heart sank. Would they just force him to continue on like he had for all these months?

As Mr. Kwon went on to explain how they would ensure Insoo's image was put back together and what steps were required for Insoo in particular, she looked over at Tae Oh in an attempt to get his help, but he was currently observing Insoo, worry written all over his face.

Mrs. Moon was talking as well, adding to Mr. Kwon's explanation.

Insoo was quiet. He didn't seem to be ready to say anything further.

It was probably instinct that took over, Akila concluded later on. How else could she explain her outburst when she was normally the one person in control of her emotions in front of others?

She found herself taking a step closer to everyone, her heart pounding painfully in her chest and her head spinning like a rollercoaster. Did they even know how strong Insoo had been these last few days, slowly but deliberately freeing himself of the shackles of the perfect picture, as they called it, that kept him paralyzed? She interrupted Kwon Ma Ru with such force that her voice almost failed. "Are you fucking serious? Do you know for how many months he didn't eat a single proper meal during the day? Do you know?"

* * *

Her usually soft voice had an edge now that Insoo had only experienced once so far. She was seriously upset.

Tae Oh, who'd been very silent, looked up and stared at her in confusion. "What?" was all he could muster, and his eyes moved from her to Ma Ru, to Insoo and his mother and back.

"I'm wondering what you're thinking! Do you want to carry on and pretend like nothing is going on? Is it really that important to uphold the perfect-picture image you're creating? Is that more important than his health? Are you all CRAZY?"

"Akila!" Insoo took a small step toward her, but a gaze from her wide, intense eyes stopped him instantly, and he stood, feeling helpless. "What are you doing?" he asked quietly.

She turned her back on them and quickly wiped her eyes. Was she crying?

There was dead silence. Tae Oh looked at Insoo and knew that the expression on his face meant that he would demand answers and not back down anymore. He was surprised at how guilty he felt seeing that look on his friend's face.

Akila spun around and spat at them in a shaky voice, "I am a COACH! I came because I thought I would be coaching." Tears ran down her cheeks. "Instead I've watched you all pretend and ignore. . .." She motioned in his general direction. "How can you all be there but still leave him SO ALONE?" She screamed the last two words.

In the ensuing silence, she first stood unmoving, then stormed out of the house, barely putting on her boots and coat before pulling the door open.

At her scream, his mother, Ma Ru and Tae Oh all flinched and stared in astonishment at the front door being slammed shut. Insoo simply remained where he was, wondering what to do next and worrying about her. Was she truly leaving?

"Insoo. . . ." His friend broke the shocked silence. "What was she talking about?"

Insoo gazed at his feet for a second, then looked at him. "Give me a moment," he responded, then quickly walked to the front door, put on his shoes and coat, and left the house.

He heard his mother call out to him with a desperate voice, but he left nonetheless, thinking that Akila shouldn't be out on the freezing winter day alone. She got cold so easily.

Insoo came to a halt on the road, wondering which way to go to find her. He collected himself and decided to turn left, up the hill and into the labyrinth of winding alleys and small roads that Akila loved.

He found her about an hour later sitting on some stone steps heading further up. Her head rested in her hands, and the few pedestrians out on the crisp winter day were looking at her curiously. While he had walked uphill, he called her phone until it dawned on him that it was probably at home, and was glad he'd run into her on one of the roads.

When Insoo finally reached the steps, he was so relieved that he had to lean on the stone wall that ran along the narrow alley. He hadn't admitted to himself how worried he was about not being able to find her until the moment he spotted her blond hair illuminated by the orange street light.

He crossed the alley and sat down next to her. It was freezing, and he hid his hands deep in the pockets of his coat.

It took a few minutes before she lifted her face, acknowledging his presence. He didn't know what to say, so he waited, trying not to feel the frosty stone they were perched on through his coat and jeans.

Eventually, she sighed heavily and then dropped her head on his shoulder. He put one of his arms around her and pulled her toward him. She didn't resist, and he felt how she inched closer, pressing her body onto his.

"Your hands," he mumbled into her ruffled hair. "Are they okay?"

She shook her head ever so slightly, and he wrapped his other arm around her as well, embracing her completely. Again, he was caught by surprise at how much he felt at ease holding her. It was comfortable and comforting in the midst of all the turmoil the last weeks had brought.

When they arrived at his house, the lights were on, casting golden light across the front yard on the pale winter afternoon. Tae Oh was waiting, sitting on the wide seat in the living room.

There was no sight of Insoo's mum or manager, and Akila was thankful for the quiet house. It was time for Insoo to talk to his friend. In her opinion, he'd waited far too long.

Insoo held her hand all the way back down to the house and, once inside, he took it again, not giving her the chance to slip away to her room as she intended.

Tae Oh weakly responded to her smile as she and Insoo dropped onto the sofa.

She pulled the blanket from the corner of the couch and stretched out completely, covering herself and resting her head on Insoo's leg. He momentarily seemed taken aback by her open display of intimacy. But then he settled down and shifted his attention to his best friend sitting opposite him.

Akila heard their low voices from afar as she drifted into her other worlds. The conversation seemed hesitant at first, but judging from the sound of their voices and the increase in words spoken as minutes passed by, she suspected that it was going well.

* * *

Tae Oh had once taken Insoo on a weekend trip to Busan, where he'd been born. It had been a great trip. Neither of them had leisure time for a long time, and excitement had gripped Tae Oh when he'd seen Insoo waiting for him in front of the train station. They'd made silly jokes the entire train ride, listened to music together, and exchanged thoughts on books and movies. Tae Oh had felt as if all the tension from the many days of acting and smiling at cameras was falling off him. And he'd been astonished at how deeply connected he felt to this handsome, tall man who went along with his lame jokes, no matter how bad they turned out, and who seemed perfectly fine with long silences.

Sitting in Insoo's living room now, years later, he remembered that trip vividly.

In Busan, they walked along the promenade, taking in the view of the ocean with the high-rise buildings of the town as their backdrop. Eventually, they'd stopped by a coffee shop, and Insoo ordered cake and iced Americanos. Tae Oh had noted how many people recognized his friend despite the large shades that covered most of his face. Sitting close to Insoo with cake and coffee, he noticed how much more beard Insoo had now. It was as if his friend had grown up, and he hadn't been there to witness it. For some reason, that made him a little sad.

While they chatted, Tae Oh had been playing around with the small fork he used to eat his cake. He turned it this way and that between his fingers while talking to Insoo and absentmindedly let it hit the large glass that contained the remains of his iced coffee. The impact created a small clang. And then again. Clang! He continued this while talking, trying to create a small melody.

Eventually, Insoo took the fork away from him, asking him to stop making noise. Tae Oh laughed at him, looking slightly embarrassed. Insoo rubbed the back of his head, then said, "Since people began recognizing me on the road, I can't stop myself from always being scared of people looking at me for the wrong reasons. I am always conscious of them seeing me and thinking negative things. Sorry." He mumbled the last word, staring out of the window in front of them, seemingly focused on the ocean view.

Tae Oh stopped laughing and observed his friend. He often felt the same, but Insoo seemed much more intense about it than he thought he needed to be. Afraid that the mood might be affected, Tae Oh changed the subject.

Listening to Insoo today, realising that his friend had been living for years without him, his so-called "best friend," knowing how bad it had been, he couldn't help but feel a deep sense of regret for letting that comment slide and not responding to it. Maybe things would have turned out differently for Insoo if he'd been able to share how he felt that day.

* * *

"Mama," Akila said in German. "I'm basically stuck here and need a little more time. I'll explain everything in detail later, but for now, all I need is for you to stay with Talida and Mavis a bit longer so that I can finish what I need to do here and come home. Can you give me more time?"

Her mother was quiet for a moment, then asked, "How long do you need?"

She sighed. She had no idea what to expect. "I'm not sure," she finally responded. "Maybe two more weeks? If it's too long, I'm sure that Rose can also help out."

Katarina was silent again. "We'll figure it out," she eventually said. "Are you sure the children will be fine?"

"I'll speak to them every day," Akila said, feeling awful at the thought of not seeing her children for such a long time. This guilt was a reality for mothers–she knew it all too well. But there was no way she could leave Insoo alone just now. He'd worked too hard and made too much progress in such a short time. She wasn't ready to let it all be for nothing.

Her mother seemed to have made up her mind as well. "Call them every day, and I'll figure out a way with Rose."

"Thank you," Akila breathed, trying to hide the emotion in her voice. They said their goodbyes and Katarina hung up.

Akila had experienced several moments throughout her life when her mother accepted her situation without many words being exchanged between them. Her mother had been there as Akila went through it all and came out at the end of things–often with ruffled feathers, but stronger, nonetheless. Maybe this was what all mothers did. Akila was not sure, but she was incredibly thankful for the fact that her mother worked that way and was there for her no matter what was going on.

After they hung up, Akila sat on her bed for a while, waiting for the overpowering sense that she should be with her children to pass. She'd always made an extra effort to raise Talida and Mavis as independent individuals, and she knew that they would be fine, even after not seeing her for more than a month. Still, she hated being parted from them for such a long time. It left a void only her children could fill.

Insoo knocked on the half-open door and walked into her room while looking at her curiously. He let his long body flop onto the bed then stretched out his arm and placed his fingers over hers.

She gazed down at his hand on hers and wondered how this whole thing had happened and where it was going.

She lay down on the bed as well, her legs up on the wall and her head next to his. There would be enough time to worry about that later, she decided. *For now, let's not overthink,* she told herself. "Have you guys decided what to do?" she enquired eventually. "Or rather, have *you* decided what to do?"

The look on his face showed that he knew exactly why she was making that distinction. He stared at the ceiling and responded slowly, "I am not sure. I do not know what would be best. I do not want to suffer because of this–and I want you to be fine, too." He turned his head to face her completely. He was so close to her all of a sudden, observing her with his dark eyes. She felt unable to look at him. She sensed that too much would be visible in her own eyes if she glanced back at him, so she continued facing the ceiling.

He had inched closer, and he was so close that she couldn't put a coherent thought together. Heart pounding, she closed her eyes, not sure why she partly feared his closeness.

He kissed her ear softly. Then her temple. He shifted slightly and propped himself up on one elbow, kissing her lips. She had no other choice but to respond to all of it. She slung her arms around his neck and, a moment later, he had moved his entire body over to where she was and they were totally entangled, their hands and lips seeking each other's warmth.

* * *

Later, she asked him, "Why don't you just tell the truth?"

He looked at her, raising his eyebrows by way of a question mark.

"No, I really mean it. Why lie about what has been going on with you? Why not talk about what you have experienced and show how strong you have been to get out of it? Wasn't Kwon Ma Ru talking about a way to turn negativity into sympathy and under-standing yesterday? Tae Oh said a similar thing, but he didn't talk about hiding everything–and hiding means more and more lies to protect the image you have. Isn't that exhausting? Telling the truth would make life just so much easier, don't you think?"

Insoo shook his head carefully. "I doubt it."

Akila lay on her belly, looking at him intently. "Why not? Just think about it for a moment. You might believe that hiding what has been going on is easier because that's what seems to be common practice. You don't talk about your real challenges. You make sure you always look perfect. That is how it works all over, I guess, but my sense is that especially here, everyone needs to be very perfect and pure in certain ways. Forgive me if I'm judging wrongly. . . ."

He inclined his head a little to acknowledge her admission that he probably understood South Korean society and the film industry much better. Still, there was truth in what she said.

"It is true that we need to be perfect and . . . what did you call it?. . pure, in certain ways, to be considered stars and to be called for certain programs and commercials."

"My question is this: Do you know for a fact that you would be disadvantaged if you talked about your real struggle and how you managed it so well? Or is that an assumption that you have not yet put to the test?" Her eyes sparkled in their peculiar way, observing him.

He shifted slightly, not sure he liked the turn the conversation had just taken. "It is an assumption. But there's also the reality of things that have happened to others in the past." He thought for a moment. "And it is probably also influenced by expectations–expectations from my mother, my family and friends in general, Ma Ru and the agency. . . ." He stopped himself and stared at her in surprise. Why was it so easy to say those things to her? He usually did not even think such things to himself. "These are not bad expectations. Just expectations people have of each other like parents have of their children," he hurried to add, "but. . . ."

"But they're expectations that influence how everyone, not only you, thinks about what can be done and what not," she concluded. "Am I getting it right?"

"Yes," he said.

He realised, yet again, that once he started talking to her, it was easy to continue because she wasn't judgemental. From the very first time they had met up until this very moment, she had never given him the feeling that she judged him or his surroundings. Yes, she had her opinions and she shared them. But even in the most heated moments, he had never felt that she looked down on him for not being able to keep a meal in or at his mother and Ma Ru for wanting his image to remain intact. It was a quality he truly appreciated about her.

"I also don't know what the best decision would be," she went on. "But I just wonder whether it might not be really liberating to just let go of the image and be yourself." She turned and smiled at him mischievously. "It's for only selfish reasons. I might be able to get you to act like in that crime drama every day and experience your true talents full force."

This last comment stuck in his head and he found himself milling over it. He had yet to give Ma Ru his update on how he wanted to proceed, and while following the experienced manager was certainly the easiest and safest option, he wondered if it was the best option for him. Was easy and safe the best way to go right now? Or was it just appearing that way because he wasn't used to doing things any other way?

When Akila talked about his role in the crime drama she had enjoyed so much and how that somehow reflected his true talents, he'd known exactly what she was referring to. Acting as a young gang member had been fun and exciting, although it had also been extremely challenging at times. He knew that he was most interested in twisted and less obvious plots and roles that portrayed the diversity of humanity. But these roles were less popular and, therefore, often paid less or were harder to come by because they were part of the smaller productions, away from the mainstream productions he'd been focusing on of late.

So, again, Insoo wondered what path to take.

* * *

"Ms. Akila."

Akila looked up from her laptop, slightly surprised to see Mr. Kwon in front of the desk in the living room so early. When had he entered the house?

She found it hard to stay in bed after Insoo had left for his morning workout and had decided to get work done–work that had begun to pile up over the past few days.

"Mr. Kwon! You're here even earlier than usual!" she exclaimed and smiled at him. He didn't return her friendly gesture and, studying his face more closely, Akila knew that something was going on.

"Ms. Akila, can I have a few moments of your time?" Insoo's manager asked politely and motioned towards the couch.

Akila hesitated for a second, wondering what was on the short man's mind. Then she nodded. "Of course. Would you like some coffee?"

For some reason, that question seemed to spark something in Mr. Kwon. He stopped on his way to the sofa, looked at her with an irritated expression on his face, and then replied curtly, "If I would like a cup of coffee in this house, I can surely fix one for myself."

Akila stopped and observed his smart suit, the neatly combed hair, and the serious expression he wore. It dawned on her that he had planned the timing for this conversation. Insoo was out of the house and there was something he wanted to discuss without him around. The cool atmosphere in the room spoke volumes.

Akila took a deep breath and sat down on the leather seat next to the couch. She waited for him to settle down and begin.

"Ms. Akila," Mr. Kwon started eventually. "I will be frank with you because I feel our relationship has been like that. Open and honest."

Akila gave a tiny ironic smile, which he chose to ignore, and moved on. "Insoo's situation is tricky right now. You know that he is blessed with amazing potential and that his big breakthrough is imminent. What is happening is only harmful to him and it has to stop. Immediately." He took a very deep breath and glanced over at her.

She'd folded her legs in the seat and listened without making a sound but focused her full attention on him. She saw that he was uncomfortable and angry, so she bit back the comment she'd wanted to make about how he was talking about his asset–the brand "Insoo"–and had neglected the person–Kim In Su.

Instead of speaking her mind, she just gave a small nod, encouraging him to go on.

"Your behaviour when Mrs. Moon was here made me very uncomfortable, and it also got me thinking that probably it was not a good idea for me to hire you like that–forcing Insoo into living with a life coach in the same house. At the time, I thought it would help him to overcome some of his challenges. And the recommendations you have are more than convincing. But now. . . ." He paused and then continued with more force. "I feel that you have not been carrying out your duties as agreed, and on that ground, I would like to ask you politely to leave this house." He glanced at her with an unmoving face.

She studied him intently, telling herself that there was no use in getting upset with him. He was making an effort to protect what they had all worked very hard for. And, of course, he was right in the sense that she had not had any professional coaching sessions with Insoo since the day she had arrived. He was also right that he'd been wrong to force Insoo into accepting a life coach into his house when he, as the person who was meant to receive coaching, hadn't bought into the idea.

She finally moved, stopping herself from glaring at him too much. "So you want me to pack my bags and just leave?"

Kwon Ma Ru nodded. "I ask of you to please cooperate. Mrs. Moon would also be more comfortable with that."

Akila couldn't help but feel a sense of bitterness creep into her heart, and her smile was probably displaying the irony that she saw in the whole situation. "So you two choose to ignore that he was unwell for months . . . no, wait. Probably for years." She lifted her gaze and stared straight at him with unwavering eyes, the bitter taste on her tongue reflected in her words. "You choose to ignore that he is unwell, which was something I pointed out right away, by the way!" She struggled to keep her voice steady. "And now, when it's the toughest for him–when he is finally trying to break out of it, you tell me to leave?" She only realised when she spoke the last words that she had raised her voice and was shouting at him.

Astonished, she closed her mouth, but she didn't drop her gaze from Mr. Kwon.

He observed her carefully, probably trying to judge if more shouting was coming his way. "This is exactly what I am talking about," he said. "You are emotionally invested and cannot separate your feelings from the situation and are probably guiding Insoo in a harmful way." He raised his hands to stop her from interrupting him. "Please listen! This is a delicate situation, and as the professional you are, I urge you to take a step back. Your story being mixed with his story is only dangerous for him!"

Akila stared at him in disbelief and slowly leaned back in the seat she occupied. She was unable to say anymore because what he said was true. She had crossed the line and hadn't kept the professional distance a coach should. Her emotions were completely intertwined with the situation, and her personal opinions flooded the scene.

But what did "better" really mean?

"Naturally, you not fulfilling your professional obligation as a coach, means that there will be no payment. But of course, your flight back will be taken care of, and we have been covering all your expenses here anyway, so I assume this is in order. And we will refrain from making an official complaint," the man added. His posture had changed, and he looked like someone confident of winning the battle.

Akila felt helpless and empty. Listening to Insoo's manager, she suddenly felt defeated. Being told that she hadn't done a good job was something she wasn't used to, and she was surprised at how hard it hit her.

Mr. Kwon looked at her for a long minute. "I think that is settled then."

Akila hated the satisfied expression he wore. And the fact that she felt she had no right to argue with him.

Just then, they both heard the password being keyed in, and the next second, Insoo opened the front door, striding into the small corridor. He was sweaty and panting from his workout. From where he was, he was able to overlook the entire kitchen space and the living room beyond. Seeing both of them there, he froze in the entrance. Something moved in his face, but Akila couldn't tell what he was thinking.

Kwon Ma Ru was already moving toward the young man. Akila wondered if he was trying to divert Insoo's attention. Would he really go this far to hide why he'd come this early?

* * *

Insoo removed his shoes with deliberate slowness, wanting to make sense of the scene. Both Ma Ru and Akila wore weird expressions, and he was sure that something had happened between them. After placing his running shoes in the shoe rack next to the door, he stood up straight, returning Ma Ru's gaze. He'd worked with his manager for many, many years and had learned to read most of his gestures. Right now, something unspoken was in the space between them, almost like a thick wall that made it difficult to communicate properly. The older man was too intense in his demeanour, almost staring him down, making an effort not to appear uncomfortable.

Insoo briefly looked past Ma Ru at Akila, who was staring the other way. Focusing his attention back on his manager, he said, "We need to discuss the next steps. I will come by the office. When is good today?"

Ma Ru seemed slightly taken aback by Insoo's curt words, but he accepted the statement and they agreed to meet at 10:30 at the agency.

Without saying another word, Insoo walked down the corridor to his room. He needed to shower and think of what to say to Akila. He was sure that she'd been told to leave.

Spotlights

The assistant gave him the sign that it would be his turn in a few seconds. Insoo nodded in acknowledgment then thought of taking a last look in the mirror but suddenly changed his mind and searched for Akila. She stood next to one of the cameras by the stage with her arms folded in front of her chest, her ruffled hair reflecting the spotlights slightly. She wore a serious expression. Ma Ru stood next to her, looking straight ahead at the stage.

The assistant appeared again and gave him his go-ahead. It was his turn to step into the spotlight and take his seat next to the host of the show.

It was a program he had been on a few times before–the first time after his appearance as a high school rebel, which got him noticed nationwide. But today felt different, and he acknowledged that he was nervous.

It had been three days since the media in South Korea, and a few other parts of the world had started discussing his health, his state of mind, and, of course, his relationship with Akila, extensively. It was mostly online news, but also in several TV shows and a few magazines people took turns taking wild guesses at what was going down. He had decided to join this show to clarify things, but more importantly, he wanted to let it all go and, hopefully, act in a thousand crime dramas in the future.

The last few days had passed in a bustle of activity including some intense, and often exhausting, conversations. As Insoo expected, the discussions with Ma Ru and other representatives of his agency had been the toughest, followed by the talk with his parents.

While his mother had been the most emotional, she turned out to be one of the most supportive once Insoo had made it clear that he had chosen his path. His father, as was his nature, had remained quiet. All he had done was put his hand on his son's shoulder when they said their goodbyes at the front door of his parent's house.

Although he'd decided to talk about what had been happening to him, he spent part of his nights wondering if he'd made the right choice. What if he ended up not getting any offers for shoots or commercials after that? What, if no one else believed that his true talents would show in more complex roles? The fear of rejection was real and it was hard to stop the flood of what-ifs in the evening when he finally got some time to slow down.

His conversation with Ma Ru after they had briefly met at his house had been extremely emotional. They'd never had such an outright disagreement before, and it was painful for both men to realise that the other wasn't willing to back down and now there was something that divided them, where before there had only been one common goal: making Insoo a true success.

Ma Ru had stared at him with angry eyes, his upper body extremely straight and rigid. "What are you talking about?" he finally inquired, almost as if Insoo hadn't been talking for the last few minutes.

Insoo paused, sighed, then went on to start his explanation again, but Ma Ru raised his hand abruptly, gesturing for him to stop. "Just be quiet, please." Ma Ru's voice was ice cold.

They sat in silence for a long moment, Insoo looking mainly at his shoes, wondering when it would be the right time to look at his manager and begin again. "We agreed that I always have the final say," he finally told the neatly dressed man. "This is me making clear what I want to do."

Ma Ru glared at him, shaking his head in disbelief. "Is that you speaking or Ms. Akila?" He gradually raised his voice, his anger taking over with every second that passed. "Insoo, do you think I do not know what is going on between you two?" he shouted. "How can you risk everything we have worked for so hard? For

THE TRUTH? What rubbish is that?" he scoffed, not able to contain his frustration anymore.

Insoo remained silent, looking at his shoes again.

Ma Ru still glared at him as he jumped up and marched around the room. The short man seemed in desperate need of an outlet for all the emotions pent up inside him. After a few rounds, he stopped. Gazing at Insoo, he said, "First, Ms. Akila's contract is terminated. She has not fulfilled her coaching obligations at all, and she has angered me in many ways. I have already discussed this with her. Second, I have discussed with your mother how we will position what has happened. We both have agreed on the best way forward."

Insoo rubbed the back of his head slowly. This wasn't going like he had wanted, but at the same time, he had known that it would not be easy. He took a deep breath, then pursed his full lips and raised his eyes to face his manager. "First, you will pay what Akila is due. If you do anything to her or urge her to leave one more time, you and I will not be on good terms. And you make that video of me and her in the park disappear as you promised." He stood up and squared his shoulders, making sure his full height was displayed. "Second, I've made it clear what I want to do. I expect you to honour our agreement and follow my instructions." Insoo was relieved that his voice shook only slightly while he spoke.

The short man stared at him without saying another word. Insoo picked up his phone from the low table in front of him, then bowed politely and walked toward the door of Ma Ru's office. He already had his hand on the doorknob when he turned around to add, "I am going to have a conversation with my parents, too, so don't worry about my mother."

Insoo strode out of his manager's office, determined to ignore the many glances and the loud silence that followed him to the elevator. Mr. Park appeared, ready to follow him as usual, but Insoo gave him a sign indicating that he would drive himself. The burly man hesitated before giving a small nod signalling that he would respect Insoo's preference as he had always done.

Inside the elevator, Insoo was thankful to be alone. Suddenly feeling faint, he leaned against the mirrored wall and closed his eyes for a brief moment, making an effort to regain his composure before he had to leave the enclosed space of the lift.

He headed straight for his father's bookshop. It took him a while to get there, given the usual Seoul weekday traffic. First, Insoo thought that it was probably better that he had some time to reflect on how to start the conversation. But when he parked the car in a tiny space that he was lucky to find only a few steps away from the old bookstore he didn't feel that he was any clearer on how to begin the talk.

The little bell chimed when Insoo opened the glass door to enter. His father sat behind the counter, stacks of books all around him. As usual, he was reading. The shop was filled with books to the brim, and it was hard to make out how large the space was. It was a place novel lovers appreciated as much as students and professors from the nearby campus seeking specialist literature. All of them loved his father's shop for the fact that you could find almost everything you were hoping for in the tightly packed, often slightly dusty shelves.

As always, Mr. Kim seemed a little out of place, as if he had been dropped into this world by mistake and belonged to another age. His height was concealed by the fact that he had spent so many years bent over, sitting and turning the pages of books. For a long time, Insoo hadn't been aware of how tall and broad-shouldered his father was. For most of his childhood, it had been his mother who was the strong force, the person who made the decisions, gave direction, and was reliable–someone Insoo could depend on. All of that had changed to some extent the day Mr. Kim had turned up at Judo class and had taken his son home. It had been the last day Insoo had participated in any form of competitive sports and the first day he had seen his parents fight, ending with his mother crying in the bathroom.

After that day, he began to see his father in a different light. He had seen how much strength there was hidden in the bent back when it was straightened. It had been a comforting feeling, and at the same time, a feeling of guilt. He felt guilty for the relief he felt when his father stood at full height and said that he wouldn't let his son ruin his body any further just for some trophies.

A customer placed a book on the counter, waiting for Mr. Kim to notice her so that she could pay. She was used to the elderly man's unique ways because she started browsing through some of the books stacked on the counter rather than trying to attract his attention.

Insoo stood by the entrance for a moment, observing the scene. Then he walked over to join his father behind the counter. Bowing slightly to the customer, he took the book she had selected and sorted the payment. His father noticed his presence by now. Adjusting his reading glasses, he wore a pleased expression on his face when he saw his son serving his customer.

"You are here," he said, straightening his back with a little grunt and putting down the book he had been holding.

Insoo looked into his father's face, a face marked by the years that he had lived and spent focusing on written words, probably more than on the spoken words around him. Would he be able to listen to his son's spoken words today?

Insoo hadn't been fully prepared for the guilt he felt in the face of the pain his family and friends, or even Ma Ru showed when he talked to them about what he had gone through. It was a weird situation, him knowing that he was the victim, someone who needed support, but at the same time constantly worrying about the reactions of the people in his world and mostly fearing the pain on their faces and their lack of understanding for the choice he was making in talking publicly about it all.

It was also difficult not to start skipping meals again because eating required his determination, and he often felt that all his energy was already going towards digesting the reactions of the world.

The host had taken her place next to him and Insoo snapped out of his thoughts and smiled back at the long-haired, pale-skinned woman. His heart performed somersaults in his chest, and he momentarily felt as if he wouldn't get enough air to even speak when the first question was shot at him.

* * *

Akila, who stood in the back of the studio, moved closer to Mr. Kwon to get his help with the translation of what was going on on stage. The host displayed her dazzling white teeth facing the camera, introduced the show, and then turned to Insoo with her first question.

Akila saw the tension in his shoulders, all squared and displaying none of the usual smoothness that he carried himself with other times.

Mr. Kwon was almost motionless next to her, fixated on the scene in front of them. He only sporadically responded to Akila's initial inquiries, and she soon realised that it was probably better to let him be.

Insoo's manager had remained clear that he was extremely opposed to this interview up to the very end. There had been a huge conflict about it at Insoo's house. After Insoo had come home from his meeting with Mr. Kwon at the agency and with his parents, his manager had turned up unannounced in the evening, screaming his frustration at Insoo. There were threats of huge fines–threats of Insoo losing everything he had worked so hard for since he was a teenager.

Akila felt helpless in the face of the short man's anger and eventually left the room. Sitting on her bed, hearing Mr. Kwon's voice over the low music she had put on, she realised how shaken she still was by the conversation he'd had with her. He had struck a chord with his comments. She couldn't deny it. Somehow she felt as if he had exposed her true colours when he called out her unprofessional behaviour, which was selfish and didn't put the client first. It left her wondering how well she carried out her tasks with other clients and what she should do about future clients.

She only stayed because of what Insoo had said when he had come out of the shower that morning. Or that was what she told herself. If it wasn't for that promise, as a professional, she would have left right away.

When she told him that, he'd looked at her, unimpressed by her emotions, and asked, "So what? I don't care about lines crossed. You promised to stop me when I need you to stop me. So keep your promise." He picked up his phone and called his father, something she hadn't witnessed in all the days she had spent with him. Most of the days, he'd spoken to his mother and his father had only featured in a few sentences.

Akila stood glaring at Insoo, who suddenly seemed undefeatable. Like so many times before, she wondered where he found the momentum, the rush of energy that seemed to catapult him forward. It almost felt as if he was unable to stop himself, despite his terror about what lay ahead.

When she had gone back to the living room much later that evening, Mr. Kwon was gone and Insoo was stretched out on the couch, his phone in hand.

The preparations for the interview started the very next day.

Kwon Ma Ru showed up with a colleague responsible for Insoo's PR and they spent the day discussing strategies.

Akila met up with Tae Oh instead and spent the day sightseeing. They smiled a lot at each other, saying only kind things and avoiding the topic of Insoo altogether. Somehow neither of them felt ready to talk about the things that were on their minds.

* * *

The day Insoo gave his exclusive interview, Ji Su stood in his small kitchen getting ready for a day of recording. While having breakfast, he shot a video for his vlog, hoping that this would psyche him up for the day ahead. It would be tiring, and he wasn't fully convinced about the song they had selected, so he wondered what to do to remedy the whole thing. After the success of the latest mini-series he'd recently starred in, he had been on the lookout for the next exciting step, but so far nothing really convincing had turned up.

Before he left his flat, he stood in front of the full-length mirror in the corridor, making sure he looked great.

After recording all day, he sat with a group of friends in the large airy cafe close to the studio. The flatscreen on the wall was on and suddenly someone said "Hey, turn up the volume!"

The attention in the room moved to the interview being aired. The actor Insoo was talking about his eating disorder and sharing his thoughts on beauty ideals and pressure prominent in the industry.

"Wow, I can't believe it!" one woman at the table next to them said, staring at the screen in disbelief. "I love this guy! I can't believe he has been through so much!"

"I know, this is just shocking," another responded.

Ji Su put his juice down and listened to Insoo's words over the general comments erupting around him.

Insoo seemed tense and he wore a troubled, but determined expression on his face. Ji Su thought that saying all these things out loud must have taken Insoo a lot of courage. He was one of the upcoming next big shots in the industry. Why was he willing to risk it all by exposing himself like this?

Ji Su frowned, intrigued. He went home wondering what Insoo might have thought before he took the seat in those spotlights.

An interview

"I wonder what he's thinking.

"You know, as women, we already work so hard to make our challenges and needs visible and be heard. We fight a serious fight every day. And again, now that we have managed to move forward quite a bit to free ourselves of the many limitations that come with being a woman in this country, a man comes along and uses a very feminine issue to gain attention. I just can't believe it! In my view, this is ultimate selfishness."

When Akila watched the first few minutes of the interview, she wasn't sure what to think.

Someone had added English subtitles and she was able to follow the whole discussion.

It was painful to see the smug expression on a stranger's face—a person who didn't really know Insoo and had no idea how much he struggled each day to break free of the patterns that had dominated his life. It hurt to see how someone else passed judgement on this young man's actions while she had to watch him in the evening, pale and silent, holding onto the kitchen counter like a drowning sailor, willing himself not to do what he had been doing for months and to rewrite his own behavioural programming.

Akila was surprised to feel anger rising in her. She wanted to go and slap the woman across her face and ask her why she was so arrogant—why she felt she could disregard a person who had been brave enough to go out there and tell the truth.

And why are societal issues related to gender either women's or men's issues and not human issues? Akila demanded in her silent dialogue with the woman on the screen and with everyone else who was currently discussing the "Insoo matter." *Why can't you all support a man who has shown so much courage, more than most people ever would?*

"Why does it upset you that Insoo revealed his eating disorder and openly spoke about beauty ideals and related pressure?" the female reporter on the screen asked.

"Well, as I explained just now, as women we deal with a lot of obstacles in society. This is not only true for South Korea, but many other places around the world. The stigma that Insoo spoke about is in my view *nothing* compared to what a female actress, singer, or model will go through in the industry. Just think about it a little more. Women face the constant objectification of their persona. They are often reduced to their bodies and appearance alone and end up with the exact issues Insoo talks about. But just take a close look at what is happening. . . ."

Akila increased the volume. She could already see where this line of argumentation was heading, and this woman made sense.

"Take a close look," the woman repeated. "Can you see how much attention Insoo has received since he revealed his challenges? Can you compare the impact that his revelation and commentary have had on the industry, what debates this has sparked as compared to when a female talks about these things?"

The woman glared at her host, who was leaning in toward her guest, listening attentively.

"As a society, we still recognize what men say as the bigger truth, as something that holds more weight," she continued.

The interviewer nodded encouragingly.

"As women, we often struggle alone, seeing other women suffer, but we can't ever pass the glass ceiling if this continues. We don't listen to women, giving what they say equal weight. The change starts with us women recognizing each other, but, of course, men also need to make a change." The woman sighed and it was obvious that she needed a moment to compose herself.

"This is why this upsets me," she finally continued. "That a man can just stand up one day and say, 'I have been struggling with the beauty ideals portrayed by this industry and as a result, I am suffering from an eating disorder,' and the entire nation is discussing it and supporting him! Women have been facing this for ages all over the world and did anyone listen? Did anything change without us having to put up a real fight? No!"

There was a pause.

"Wouldn't you agree that this is hurtful?"

Akila turned off the TV and sighed, folding her legs on the sofa.

She understood why this woman was worried about men, again, claiming a space that women had had to fight so hard for. It was a phenomenon that she'd observed many times herself, and she could relate to the fury that seemed to jump out of the woman's face when she spoke–fury about the fact that someone else always seemed to have it easy, to receive recognition and power while others had to suffer so much in order to taste only a tiny piece of it. Or worse. Fury about having to dream of how it all tasted but never getting the chance in real life. She had seen so many women like that, and she was angry with the woman for attacking Isoo, but at the same time, she connected to the underlying ideologies on which she based her points on.

Rubbing her face, she moaned and let herself drop back onto the couch. "What to do?" she whispered to herself, staring at the ceiling.

It had only been three days since Insoo went public and she already felt like running. There were reporters around the house all day up until late night, and moving freely was difficult.

Kwon Ma Ru was going crazy over the phone calls he received and the increasing amount of attention the whole story was getting. Whenever he stopped by the house, the room was thick with tension, and the short man seemed to be getting angry at anyone and anything these days.

What Insoo's manager had been fearing was happening. The interesting part was that the majority of comments from Insoo's

Korean fanbase were sympathetic and encouraging toward the young actor, which was a real relief to Akila. Still, Insoo's open announcement that he questioned the current beauty ideals and practices in the industry had also resulted in negative reactions from some of the big mainstream companies he had been working with, because loads of interviews and debates had been sparked by Insoo's words and these companies felt directly attacked.

There were also many comments online that questioned Insoo's true intentions. Was he trying to just cover up his unacceptable relationship with a foreign, older woman? Did he simply want to hide his violent and weird tendencies? In the end, he had been part of a fight only recently. These comments were fewer, however, and coloured how Insoo felt about everything. Akila could see that. They also influenced how some of his partners reacted to his going public. So, while there was an overwhelming amount of support for Insoo, the critical voices remained loud enough to spark a real storm in Insoo's private life and turn his agency's work into a real task.

Akila knew that Mr. Kwon made her partly responsible for what was going on, so she tried to stay out of his way as much as possible.

Akila's phone started buzzing. Tae Oh was calling.

"Hey Akila," he said. "Get out of there. I have tickets for a concert you might like. Some of the other guys are joining too."

Insoo walked into the living room. "You should go," he said to her. "You can't stay indoors the whole time just because of this craziness."

Still holding the phone to her left ear, she asked him, "And you?"

"I need to work on some stuff. Just go. . . ."

To Akila's relief, there were only a few reporters outside when Tae Oh and the others picked her up in Hae In's little van and it was easier to get out of the house.

Tae Oh had gotten tickets for a small concert produced mainly for TV and, therefore, only a few people had received seats. When Akila saw the names on the poster, she looked at Tae Oh with astonishment. He grinned in his usual mischievous way. "You said you liked the movie. This is a mini concert including all the soundtrack songs. I thought you might like it."

Their group walked into the studio which was set up for an intimate live performance. The light was welcoming and the cameras and sound equipment gave Akila a sense of familiarity.

Other people had already taken their seats or were just settling in when they went to find their places. Akila felt elated and it was a great feeling to be out and think about something else after all the overwhelming days they had been through.

To Akila, it felt as if she had dropped into one of her other worlds. The warm light shone on the musicians on stage, the small crowd swung left and right with the rhythm and there was laughter when the lead singers joked in between the songs. How long had it been since she had been at a concert? It felt like ages, especially given how her time in Seoul seemed to have pushed everything else into the background. At times, it was hard for her to imagine that she usually lived in Scotland with two children and had to make sure they ate, went shopping, went to school, and so on.

Realising all that while being absorbed by the music, she decided that it would soon be time for her to unite the different worlds she lived in at the moment.

The concert was over and looking around, Akila saw happy faces and smiles. It was extremely soothing. Seo Hui, who had joined them, hooked her arm around hers and they grinned at each other.

Tae Oh walked on her other side. "Did you like it?"

Akila nodded her head in an exaggerated gesture to express her ultimate happiness. He laughed.

"Hey!" Hae In suddenly said. "Why don't we say hi to the band? I know the drummer, I'm sure that there is a way to greet them!"

They all looked at each other.

"Oh, that would be really cool!" Seo Hui exclaimed and the rest of the group agreed.

Hae In went to speak to one of the technicians who was packing up the equipment. Then he motioned to them to follow him through a heavy door in the back of the studio. They could hear the musicians talking excitedly from the corridor as they entered through the door. The audience wasn't the only ones in high spirits after the performance. Hae In knocked on the doorframe and walked into the room, the others in tow.

The musicians were packing up, now slowing down as they looked at them. Recognizing Hae In, one of them grinned and the two greeted each other.

"Long time!" Hae In said.

"You watched our performance? Cool!" Everyone bowed, shaking hands and greeting each other.

"You did so well!" Hae In replied. "It was a great concert!"

"Hey, we have a real star with us tonight!" said one of the band members, pointing at Tae Oh, who bowed politely, looking slightly embarrassed.

Akila thought that he really perfected the modest look. She stayed in the background, still only halfway through the door. When it was her turn, she also bowed her head politely.

Her heart beat hard in her chest, and she got the distinct feeling that something had shifted. She would have rather left the room, scared of what was coming her way. There was already so much going on, another shift seemed too much for her at that moment. Then Kang Ji Su stood in front of her. He had been greeting everyone else, leaning on a table that stood on the right side of the room. His face was curious and open. "You *are* tall," he commented in English. It was true—she was taller than he was and he lifted his chin to be able to look into her face directly.

His was the air of someone who was used to getting the attention of people in the room, and he was definitely aware of the impact he had on others. She didn't like that she was just as affected by it—his pretty face beneath the black bob, the broad shoulders, and slightly O-shaped legs that gave him a confident stride. So she hoped that she managed the indifferent face well, the mask that she wanted to show him.

Seo Hui put her arm around Akila's shoulders and said, "This is Akila. She is a coach from Scotland."

"Hey, why don't we all go out and celebrate today?" Hae In interrupted, and Akila was extremely grateful for the shift in attention.

Once they were eating, Kang Ji Su turned to Akila. "So what exactly is it you do?" he asked between bites of food.

"I coach and mentor people."

He looked up from his plate "Like, you tell them how they can get better?"

She shook her head, focusing on her plate. "No, it's more like I provide the space for them to think outside the box. Unless they specifically ask for my opinion, I will be completely neutral."

Ji Su leaned back on the bench he occupied with Hae In and some of his band members opposite her. "How does that work? And does this also work for people like me?"

She was still staring at her plate, the spoon in her hand shifting the food back and forth. "You mean artists? Yes, it works for artists. Actually, I specialise in coaching artists or people who want to get their creativity flowing. And it's hard to explain how it works. Someone has to experience it to really understand. It's all about asking the right questions. And silence."

Tae Oh, who was sitting next to her, pulled out his wallet and removed something. He handed it to Ji Su. It was the business card Akila had given him on the day they first met. "Spread the word," he said with a smile.

Ji Su turned the business card with his slim fingers. He had a thoughtful expression on his face.

Oh no, Akila thought, quickly putting a full spoon of food in her mouth, not sure what was coming.

"So, Insoo coming out with his issues like that. . . . Was that after he had coaching from you?"

Akila froze and looked up at him. His gaze was intense. Did he want to provoke her?

She slowly straightened herself, thinking how to respond.

The conversations around the table quieted down. The change was barely noticeable, but it felt like an extreme difference. "And what if it was?" she asked him.

Ji Su studied her face for a moment, then he grinned at her. Helplessly, Akila observed how his eyes turned into sparkling stars and how the traces of wrinkles that ran around those very eyes made him look like the representation of "happiness."

"I was just curious. No need to get offended," he said before turning his attention to the rest of the table and changing the topic.

Akila took a deep breath and focused back on her food.

"Are you okay?" Tae Oh said next to her.

She nodded, her mouth full of food.

When she was back in the house later that night, Ji Su's questions kept bouncing up and down in her mind. She already had ideas–working with him would be very interesting.

She covered her face with her hands. *Nope,* she told herself. *Don't do that.* There was no need to make things more complicated than they already were.

She sat down with her laptop on Insoo's kitchen counter, folding her legs. Akila stared at the screen for a long time. Then she opened the app she used for music and started compiling a playlist for Ji Su. While choosing the songs, she saw how it could work for him, how she felt he could bring out the strengths she had spotted. When she was done she went through the songs she'd selected and, swearing under her breath, slammed her laptop shut. Korea turned out to be too tumultuous for her.

The next day, Insoo and Akila locked up the house late in the evening when most of the reporters had left and the steep road was finally peaceful beneath the streetlights. Insoo's mother had arranged for a stay outside Seoul to take off some of the pressure while things quieted down.

Insoo drove with Akila in the seat next to him. She had put on her Soul playlist and "Soulful" was playing when they left the large city behind. It felt as if they were driving towards the moon, which hung bright and big in the dark sky above them, almost full. They drove away from this world and into one of Akila's other worlds, one that was calm and empty, Akila imagined.

It was very cold by the seaside, but the air was so crystal clear that Akila thought she could almost see it when moving her gaze over the grey-blue rolling waves. They wore thick pullovers, heavy coats, and scarves. The sand seemed to be shifting slightly with the cold wind that was blowing across the beach, seemingly in rhythm with the rolling waves. Seagulls rode the breeze, screeching above.

Four days at the beach, eating food and drinking hot coffee. Four days looking at Insoo, who stared at the ocean. Here, no one seemed to be aware of the ruckus that Insoo had caused, and it was almost as if they had imagined it all.

Every afternoon, Akila chatted with her children on video call. They missed each other badly and she knew that it was time to go home.

Today, Insoo and Akila walked on the beach and eventually sat down in the cold sand. Akila let her hands run over the tiny grains and imagined how she would lie in the warm sand on a hot beach. She closed her eyes and lay down on her back. The sky was extremely light blue, almost as if the colour had flown out of it.

Then she looked up at Insoo next to her. He had his long arms on the knees of his long legs.

"You know that you have grey hair just like me," she finally said.

Pulled out of his thoughts, he glanced down at her. "Yeah, I am probably much older than you at heart. I haven't noticed your grey hair. Mine is obvious."

"I need to go to Scotland."

He didn't look at her but nodded.

"Talida and Mavis. . . ."

He glanced at her. "I think it's better if you leave."

She sat up and touched the small spot of grey hair on the side of his head softly with the tips of her fingers. He looked down at the sand, then quickly looked back at the ocean. He rubbed his nose. "I am wondering . . . will this get easier?"

She didn't know how to respond to that. "If it gets too hard, send me a zero on our chat. I'll know it's too hard and come over."

"Another code?" he asked.

"Yes. Sometimes it's good to use codes. Less struggle to explain."

Insoo nodded. "Maybe you are right."

Akila took a deep breath and said what she had been wanting to say for days. "Insoo, please see someone professional about your eating. There's no harm in trying."

There was a very long pause between them after that. But on the way back to their place, he put his arm around her and put his face into her hair.

The same evening, Akila booked her flight back to Scotland. Looking at the departure details, she experienced a strange mixture of excitement and fear. What would happen to Insoo, alone in his house? Would he be able to eat properly? Would his career go on? Would she be fine without him around?

They packed their bags the next afternoon and hit the road back to Seoul. Akila was responding to messages from Talida and Tae Oh when a chat popped up from an unknown number. Frowning, she opened the chat window and read through the lines. Then she read the lines again, her head and heart exploding. She closed the chat and stared out of the window. *Kang Ji Su, you idiot,* she thought. Or was it Tae Oh she should blame for giving out her business card that evening?

That was exactly why she had wanted to keep her distance. She was unable to suppress the excitement she felt reading his message, already knowing that she would work with him now that he had asked.

* * *

Akila had been back in Scotland for more than a week already and Insoo's house felt empty. He had just completed his morning workout and stood in the kitchen. The morning sun cast long lines of bright light across the floor of the living room and into the kitchen space.

Insoo picked up his phone and put his earphones in. He opened the playlist on his phone and, a moment later, the first sounds of "Mikrokosmos" pulsed through him. The poppish beat gave him energy and he grinned, remembering how she had shared the playlist with him before she left. "This is you . . . in music." She had looked quite embarrassed when saying that and had avoided his eyes. So he'd remained quiet and had just focused on his cup of coffee.

Winter in the hills

It was early morning in the small cottage by the little road. Akila had just woken up and taken the stairs down to brew her first cup of coffee. It was 6:30 and completely dark outside.

She had switched on some of the small lights in the large living and kitchen space and sat on the kitchen counter with her legs folded, slowly sipping her coffee and waiting for the day to start, but also enjoying the quiet before it all began.

The flight from Seoul would arrive later in the afternoon.

Mavis walked into the kitchen an hour later, and Akila had already set breakfast at the counter and was sitting on the sofa in their living space, typing away on her laptop and listening to Mafikizolo's beats on low volume.

Mavis let himself fall onto the couch next to his mother and put his wild hair on her lap, forcing her to stop what she was doing and turn her attention to her son.

Talida turned up a few minutes before 8:00 and joined her mother and little brother at the kitchen counter.

"When is the flight arriving again?" she asked between spoonfuls of muesli.

"14:25," Akila responded, chewing on cheese and bread, wondering how she would survive all the hours until then.

Akila could feel her daughter's eyes on her and tried to avoid the stare by focusing on the preparation of her next slice of bread. But her daughter was the type to not let go if a thought had caught her attention. "Are you nervous?"

Akila looked up from her plate with raised eyebrows. She was still the type of woman who struggled to speak openly about her own insecurities and worries. "Nervous? About?"

Talida shrugged and continued to spoon in her muesli with an incredible speed that amazed Akila every time. "Not sure," she responded. "Somehow it seems to be a big deal."

Mavis, who had just changed the music to some older Bongo Flava songs and was humming along to the melodies, glanced at both mother and sister. He then decided to increase the volume slightly and exclaimed over the beats, "This will be a cool Christmas! Insoo and Tae Oh are staying the whole time. Sure it will be fun!"

Talida rolled her eyes at her little brother. "I'm not saying it won't be fun–"

"Hey," Akila interrupted before the conversation could take the wrong turn and end up in an argument. "Let's just make sure we have a great time, okay? Rose and Edith are also going to be around, and for them, a happy time will be really important."

As Talida and Mavis adored the couple tremendously, both nodded without any hesitation and the discussion was over.

Afternoon arrived with grey, heavy clouds billowing above the hills and a few drops of icy rain, something close to hail, splattering the windscreen of her vehicle as Akila set out toward the airport.

Rose had come over for lunch and helped Akila prepare the guest room. She had been a little quiet and Akila had made a mental note to check up on her once their visitors had settled in. There was a high chance that Rose just suffered from the winter blues that hit them once in a while during the long, cold season. They all loved the sun and colour, and being in the grey and not able to see the shiny blue sky for days was tough at times. Akila could relate all too well and she was happy that she could fill the cold season with enough people and activities to look forward to and think less about the lack of colour in this part of the world.

Akila kissed her friend on her cheek before getting into the car. "Let's meet for dinner, my dear, just as we planned," she said.

"I already look forward to it, honey!" Rose sang, then pushed her toward the vehicle. "Now get going! You should not be late when picking up the guy you sleep with."

Akila gave her friend a look of exasperation, while Talida, who stood next to Rose in her blue winter jacket, let out a little snort of amusement.

Akila quickly got into her car, put on the seat belt, put in gear one, and drove off, muttering, "Crazy woman," to herself. She cast a glance in her rear mirror and saw Mavis, Talida, and Rose standing on the side of the road in the increasing rain, hair blown in all directions by the gusts of wind that rushed through the street. They were all waving and Mavis was dancing on the sidewalk in his usual clownish manner. Akila smiled.

By the time Akila arrived at the airport, the few drops had changed into proper snow-rain, with heavy wind blowing the snowflakes across the country at an almost vertical angle.

Wonderful! she thought while driving onto the parking lot outside the airport. The last beats of an Anderson .Paak concert hit her eardrums and made her bounce her head with a tiny smile. She looked around and found a parking space a little closer to the buildings. Akila was suddenly worried that the plane wouldn't be able to land because of the snow. She grabbed her bag and jumped out of the car, almost taken off her feet by a strong gust of wind that hit her at exactly that moment. She tightened her scarf and zipped up her coat, then quickly walked toward the building for arrivals.

She was almost certain now that the plane wouldn't be able to land, and a sense of panic came over her. She had willed herself to stay composed and calm. And when the flights had finally been booked, she had felt such a sense of relief, just to realise that she would have to hold out only so many more days. Cold fear sometimes gripped her before picking up his call or reading a message—fear that it all turned out to be too much and that he wouldn't be able to go on.

Seo Hui regularly chatted with her and Akila was often in contact with Tae Oh too. That was how she stayed updated because

Insoo mostly refused to speak about the latest developments in terms of his career. Since she had left Seoul for Scotland, he hadn't really spoken about what was going on but focused their conversations entirely on her, the children, the weather, which commercial or shoot was upcoming for him, but never how he felt in the midst of it all–being in the centre of the debates on equality, of better support for actresses and actors, and dealing with people that still questioned his intentions.

There had been increasing international interest in Korean film and music recently, and Insoo's revelation in combination with the debates and additional revelations, especially from female film stars and musicians, surrounding it all were feared to have an impact on the industries' future. Speaking about his struggle had set something in motion and the entire nation seemed to be involved in trying to figure out what this should and would mean for South Korea's rapidly growing film and music industry.

Fans were in strong support of Insoo and so many others who had gone through similar struggles. Agencies promised to focus more on the human being and not just the image. Female actresses discussed their personal limitations as women in the industry. And in the midst of it all was Insoo, someone whom Akila knew would rather be alone in a peaceful place.

Weeks after the first interview he had given, his name was still featured in the top celebrity headlines. As a result of the whole story, he had lost a few deals. These deals weren't lost because of Insoo revealing his eating disorder but because of the controversy around his other behaviours. Did he have an affair with an older woman from outside the country? Had he been in a fight? If so, he probably had even bigger personal issues than an eating disorder.

Deep down, Akila felt that it was a result of the debates that some of his interview comments had sparked–debates about beauty ideals, racism, gender roles, and industry practices. Akila had watched it all unfold and was still shocked at how intense these debates got, especially on social media, and how malicious some comments turned out to be, while others were sweetly supportive and completely reasonable. It was obvious that people's emotions had been set into motion by Insoo's story in many different ways.

Again, the sense that the public property, the brand "Insoo," was leaving too little room for the actual person "Kim In Su" made her want to tell him to stop and not care about his career–to just leave it all behind.

Akila made an effort to control all these thoughts while hurrying through the arrival hall in search of the next display board to check for the status of their flight. When she finally stood in front of the large board and had digested that the information displayed meant that Insoo's and Tae Oh's plane had already landed, she needed a moment to slow her increasing heartbeat. Then she stood there for a moment longer to make sure she got her bearings to be able to find the correct place to go and wait for them.

* * *

Insoo and Tae Oh were walking down the corridor leading them from the plane toward the luggage band and exit. They had already gone through customs upon arrival in London before boarding their connecting flight to Scotland, so they both expected to get out of the airport fairly quickly. It had been a long journey and the time difference was making them both feel slightly drowsy.

"Let's just pick up our luggage as quickly as possible and get out of here," Tae Oh muttered. A few of the passengers from the flight from Seoul to London had joined them on the connecting flight up North, and while they were few, it had already been hard enough to keep people from commenting on Insoo throughout the journey to London. Tae Oh had no patience for any more comments about his friend, and he felt that he might react in a truly impolite manner. He wanted to make sure he spared everyone the embarrassment.

Insoo, walking next to him, was quiet. Tae Oh was torn every day, one moment thinking that he looked much better than before, thanks to the small but regular meals he was now able to consume. But the next moment, he would look into Insoo's eyes and feel sure that he read despair and exhaustion in his friend's gaze. It made him want to kick butts and take all the arrogant know-it-alls down with one big blow.

The two men reached the luggage belt, and it didn't take long before one of their suitcases showed up. While waiting for their other bags to show up, Insoo fidgeted slightly and Tae Oh wondered what was going on in the young man's mind. Was he nervous? Was he excited? Anxious? It was hard to tell.

Insoo had turned into a much more private person over the years he had known him; although he'd never been a person to reveal it all, he'd been more open when they first met. Tae Oh felt a slight pain in his chest thinking about how everything had changed and how he had simply been blind to Insoo's struggle, too busy enjoying his own life. Would it have been different if he'd been around more often—if he'd been realistic about the fact that things could change any minute and a beloved person could be by your side one day and suddenly be gone the day after that instead of thinking that Insoo was someone who would always be around.

Their other two bags arrived and they hoisted them off the luggage belt and made their way to the exit.

Tae Oh couldn't help but release some of the excitement that now boiled in the pit of his stomach. "I can't believe we are here!" He put his arm around his friend and shook him a little. "Can you believe it?"

Insoo gave him a quick smile then slowed down to look around. They had just passed the gate and stood in the airy hall. Tae Oh looked around too, trying to spot the tall, crazy woman with large glasses and wild hair who was meant to be their host.

Seemingly out of nowhere, she appeared in front of them, rooted to the spot and staring at Insoo. Tae Oh had seen this kind of reaction from her before. It happened when she came close to his best friend and, after all the weeks they'd been separated, this was expected, he told himself with a grin. Insoo stood too, one hand on the handle of his suitcase, the other motionless on his side, looking at her.

People walked around them to get to the exit. It was almost like they were little islands in the ocean with the surf of people breaking on their rocks and swelling all around them. Tae Oh decided it was time to get things moving.

He left his suitcase and bag on the floor next to Insoo, walked over to Akila, and hugged her with all his might, lifting her and spinning her around once, laughing while she squealed with surprise, a sound he hadn't expected from her.

"Akila!" Tae Oh exclaimed, still laughing. "It is so good to see you!"

She had regained her composure and was laughing right back at him. "It's so amazing that you are here! I really missed you!"

He flipped his hair back in a mocking gesture of attitude and said, "I know you can't live without me."

Laughter spread across her entire face and her eyes glittered with amusement. "You know me too well," she said, grinning.

Insoo, who still wore his solemn expression, suddenly walked past Tae Oh and put both arms around Akila. Her eyes grew large for a moment, then she closed them and hid her face on his shoulder. Tae Oh noticed how tightly she held onto Insoo's coat and saw how his friend hugged her even closer, pulling her so close that she was almost bent backward.

Neither said a word, but still, passersby cast quick and curious glances at them. Tae Oh couldn't bear to look at them for too long. His heart ached, thinking that Insoo appeared as if he had barely kept himself from drowning all these weeks and had finally found a log to hold onto in the stormy sea.

* * *

Twenty Minutes later, they were on their way to Akila's place, their bags and suitcases in the trunk, and some of Akila's Mafikizolo all-time favourites played while they slowly drove through the whirling snow.

"You get a proper winter welcome!" she exclaimed, squinting momentarily to be able to see better. Luckily, the wind had reduced a little, but the snowfall had increased and it was difficult to see ahead.

Akila had called home before they left the airport and told them that they would be late. Talida had picked up and, with her usual teenager-serious voice, had informed Akila they would be fine. Mavis had been the disappointed one but was only slightly audible in the background. When Akila hung up after the short conversation, she asked herself why she often thought she detected boredom or a slight irritation in her daughter's voice. Was it that she really felt like that or was she not aware of the sound of her voice? Or was it Akila who read more into it than there was?

Sighing, she dropped the phone into her bag and smiled at Insoo and Tae Oh. "Let's do this!" she said and the two young men nodded and grinned at her.

Now, they were finally on the small, winding country road that led them deeper into the highlands and toward their little village. The roads were covered in snow, and it was hard to make out where the road ended in some parts, but there were far fewer vehicles here and Akila knew the way by heart, which made her much more comfortable driving in this snowstorm.

Rose called, probably because she was worried after seeing the snowfall increase further, and Akila glanced over at Insoo who sat next to her looking out at the snow and laughing at one of Tae Oh's jokes.

"Can you pick up, please?" she asked him. "I'm sure that she just needs to know that we are fine."

Insoo nodded and picked up. "Hi, Rose! How are you doing? Akila is driving so I am picking up for her."

Akila could hear Rose's voice from afar but couldn't make out what she was saying. Insoo was about to say something when his eyes grew large and he shouted, "AKILA!" grabbing the steering wheel with his free hand and turning it with all his might. By now, Akila had reacted as well and jumped on the brakes. There was something large in front of them in their lane.

The car slid through the wet snow on the small road, off to the left, and into the other lane. The stone wall that marked the beginning of the fields beyond came into view.

"Hold the brakes!" Insoo shouted and turned the wheel even more. They flew across the street, Mafikizolo's "Khona" providing the soundtrack and Rose screaming on the phone. Somehow, the loudspeaker must have been put on.

But Akila didn't take anything in other than the slithering car that had lost control and the stone wall rushing toward them. She continued to step on the brakes, releasing them and then stepping on them again in intervals.

The car changed direction and, by force of the turned steering wheel and the brakes, slid around to point the front where its back had been seconds before, and by the time they hit the stone wall, they didn't hit it head-on at full speed, but with their side and had slowed down considerably. The impact still shook the entire vehicle, and the screeching sound when stone hit metal made Akila flinch.

* * *

When the car had come to a halt, there was complete silence for a moment. Insoo was still holding the steering wheel and breathing shakily. Then he quickly turned to both Tae Oh, who sat with a shocked expression in the back of the car, and Akila, who panted and, very slowly, put her head on the steering wheel to exhale with closed eyes.

"Are you both okay?" he wanted to know.

A weak, "Yeah," came from the backseat. Tae Oh looked shaken but otherwise seemed okay. Akila could only nod, her eyes still closed and her forehead resting on the cold wheel.

"Akila?"

She turned her head a little and opened her eyes, looking at him. "I'm okay," she managed to say, then closed her eyes again.

He switched off the music, which was still playing, and picked up Akila's phone, which had fallen onto the small mat between his feet, and spoke into it. "Rose, we just had an accident, but it seems we are all okay," he said.

"Ohmygodohmygodohmygod–"

"There was something on the road." Insoo glared out of the window, trying to make out the road and whatever sudden obstacle they had encountered. "We'll check out what is going on and see how the car is. It might still be operational," he went on.

"Where are you?" Rose asked, her voice still more high-pitched than usual.

Insoo looked at Akila questioningly.

She took the phone from him and explained to Rose where they were.

"That's not too far. I'll come over!"

"No, Rose, the roads are really bad. Stay put until we have checked how the car is and what's actually on the road. We'll call you back in a few–"

"Akila!"

"Wait just a short while. I will definitely call you back."

Akila hung up and looked at Insoo and Tae Oh.

"Let's go," Insoo said.

A moment later, they all stood in the whirling snow, staring at the vehicle on the other side of the road. It was resting motionlessly on its roof with the wheels pointing toward the covered sky.

"Call an ambulance," Insoo said to Akila, not taking his eyes off the car. "Let's see if someone is inside."

While Akila dialled the emergency number, Insoo and Tae Oh made their way to the vehicle.

"Shouldn't we somehow secure the place?" Tae Oh asked as they carefully walked over the slippery snow cover around the silver car. The windscreen was gone and parts of the bumper had come off. When they reached the other side, Insoo and Tae Oh could make out a large dent in the front door and a long scratch that went across the entire side of the metal body.

"Not sure if anyone would see anything with this snow, even if we put the warning sign up," Insoo responded, still observing the car attentively. He kneeled to look inside, but couldn't make out anyone in the interior.

Sitting up, he said, "There's no one inside."

They both looked around. With the heavy snowfall, it was hard to make out where the car had come from and where it had hit whatever obstacle it had encountered.

Akila appeared around the back of the vehicle and bent down to take a look inside.

"They are on their way," she told them, and suddenly she froze. She went down on all fours and inched closer to the damaged door, trying to get a better look. Noticing that something was going on, both Insoo and Tae Oh came back closer to her.

"What is it, Akila?" Insoo already had an inkling of what was going to come next.

Akila turned and stared at them, distress in her eyes. "This is Mrs. Williams' car!"

She turned back to stare at the brown manila paper cat dangling from the rear mirror, already wet from the snow blowing inside through the broken windscreen. Mavis had given this cat to Mrs. Williams a while ago because they both shared a deep love for cats. "She lives across from us. . . ."

Akila jumped to her feet, almost falling over due to the slippery ground. Insoo caught her by her arm. She looked around wildly, grabbing Insoo's sleeve. "If she's not inside her car, does that mean she is somewhere around here? Maybe she was thrown out through the windscreen? OH NO!"

Insoo and Tae Oh stared at her, then looked at each other.

"You said, she lives across from you? Call Rose and ask her to check if possible. Could someone else have used her car?" Insoo said.

Akila fumbled with the pocket of her coat, removing her phone with trembling fingers.

"Let's take a look around," Tae Oh suggested, "We might be lucky."

Insoo thought that it was probably of no use. It was getting dark quickly, and with the snow, it was just too hard to make anything out. But he kept his thoughts to himself and followed his friend to the side of the road where they started to look out for anything unusual.

They could hear Akila's voice through the fall of the snowflakes only a few metres away and circled the vehicle, increasing the distance between them and the car with every new round, making their way slowly through the snow. After several freezing minutes, there was nothing.

Exhausted and, by now, feeling extremely cold, they all stood very close to each other by the turned-over silver vehicle. Insoo had managed to get one door open and put the hazard light on, which they also did with Akila's car. It was completely dark, and they couldn't go on searching.

"They are here," Insoo said quietly, and Akila and Tae Oh were able to make out the short line of blinking lights coming down the hill.

They left the little hospital late that night after being examined by the local doctor, whom Akila knew because they had bumped into each other a few times on the weekly market and who lived two streets down from where they stayed.

"Why do we always seem to end up in some hospital when we are together?" Akila had muttered when they had been dropped by the ambulance. Insoo hadn't known how to respond. It was true, their time together hadn't exactly been marked by calm moments.

Two officers from the local police station had offered to drive them home as they visited Mrs. Williams' house. No one had been able to reach or locate Mr. Williams, who presumably wasn't aware that his wife had been in a serious accident.

While Akila, Insoo, and Tae Oh waited for the doctor to release them, the officers informed them that Mrs. Williams had been found. "Alive, but in awful condition," one of the officers, a large, red-haired man, explained. "They aren't sure if she's going to make it."

"Carl–" His partner shot the burly officer a warning glance, obviously not happy with how freely he traded the latest news on the case.

Insoo had already passed the point of total exhaustion hours earlier and was in a state of acute awareness. His senses seemed extra sensitive and he felt as though the bright lights of the clinic and the intense body odour of the large officer next to him affected him more than usual. He took a few steps back, trying to keep his face straight, and wondered how he would manage to sit in the same vehicle with this man and his smell.

Tae Oh, who sat on a chair by the wall a few metres away, rested the back of his head on the white paint and closed his eyes. Judging from the steady rise and fall of his chest, he'd dozed off.

Akila, who had left for a short while to call Rose and let her know that they were coming, returned, looking pale and worried. She managed a small smile at the sight of Insoo that made him feel warm. She walked over and said, "The kids are asleep, thankfully." Then she turned to face the two police officers. "Are we ready to go? Our visitors have gone through quite a lot since they arrived. I'd love to give them the chance to rest now."

"Yes, yes. Of course!" Both officers were ready to move.

While Insoo woke Tae Oh, Akila exchanged a few words with the doctor. Insoo heard him reassure her, "I will update you if I hear anything. But I'm sure Edith will hear updates through her connections anyway."

"Thank you so much. Good night!"

There was a thick layer of snow outside Akila's cottage, and it was difficult for them to get the suitcases and bags to the front door without falling over.

Once they made it all the way, a little out of breath, they stood there in the cold winter night, looking across the street to where the police car had stopped in front of the Williams' house. The two officers were ringing the bell and calling Mr. Williams' name. When there was no reaction, one of them disappeared around the house. A dog started to bark further down the road.

Akila sighed and turned the key in the lock. Before she could push the door open, it was pulled from inside and she almost toppled over into the corridor of the little cottage. By now, the light in the small entrance had been switched on and Rose stood there, soft cheeks covered with red blotches, probably from the anxiety the evening had caused her. Further in the back, Insoo made out another woman with short blonde hair and an equally exhausted and worried expression.

"OH MY GOD!" Rose said, staring at them. "I am soooo glad you are here, I cannot even begin to express. . . ."

Akila stepped into the house and hugged her friend tightly. "We're okay, Rose, I swear. We just need to sleep, that's all. But we are okay," she mumbled into her friend's hair. Rose hugged Akila back and closed her eyes. The two women blocked the entire corridor, holding onto each other.

"Are you two serious?" Edith's voice came from the back. "Let them in! They got off the plane to drive straight into a blizzard and become part of some kind of accident drama. Just let them in already!"

"Yes, of course!"

"Yes, yes!"

The two women, sniffing a little and standing close to each other, gave way and both Insoo and Tae Oh moved into the warm house.

"Help them with their luggage!" Edith commanded and a minute later luggage and humans were finally inside with the front door closed. There was shuffling and confusion as the three of them pulled coats, scarves, and boots off. Then Insoo and Tae Oh walked into the spacious living room to be greeted warmly by Rose and Edith.

"It's so wonderful to finally meet you in person!" Rose sang, shaking Insoo's hand vigorously.

"Hi, I'm Edith," Edith said, shaking both their hands.

"I am sorry that we kept you waiting," Tae Oh responded with a little smile, and both Rose and Edith couldn't help but laugh.

Insoo smiled, already looking around and taking it all in. This was where Akila spent her days.

"Would you like something to drink?" Rose inquired as Mavis appeared on the staircase.

"Mama!"

They all turned in surprise to look at the boy in pyjamas, his big, dark-blonde afro all over the place and his eyes blinking sleepily.

"Mavis!" Akila rushed to hug her son only to notice that he had his sister in tow.

"Mama. . . ." The tall girl displayed an equally crazy array of hair, slightly darker than her brother's, with wild curls pointing in all directions.

Insoo hadn't seen prettier beings in a very long time.

Akila hugged both her children and then turned around to introduce them. "Now that you are here, say hi and then go back to bed!"

"Hi," they both said, almost in unison.

Insoo smiled warmly. He was already in love. Glancing briefly at Tae Oh next to him, he recognized similar feelings on the young man's face.

Insoo echoed what Rose had expressed just a moment ago. "Nice to finally meet you in person."

The children observed both of them with curious faces but didn't say more. They just smiled and nodded politely.

"Now off to bed!" Akila demanded and ushered her children back up the little staircase to their rooms.

"Rose, Edith, can you show them around?" she called as she disappeared upstairs.

"Sure!"

It was almost 2:00 in the morning when Insoo finally put his head on a pillow and wrapped his arms around Akila. He'd been imagining this happening for weeks, and slowing down, step-by-step, after being in motion for so many hours, he realised how stunned he was. It was unexpected how it had turned out to be, their first day together in the same space after such a long time. But he could feel the warmth of her skin seeping through his and filling his entire being with a sense of light.

Later, when Insoo surfaced from an unsettling dream about spinning vehicles and being caught in a tiny space below layers and layers of snow, he needed a moment to realise that he was actually in a small village somewhere in Scotland and had just made it through a blizzard the previous evening. Someone was looking at him, and Insoo jumped a little when he recognized Mavis standing by the door in his pyjamas, still sporting his amazingly untidy afro and an unsure expression on his face.

"Morning," Insoo said after collecting himself, keeping his voice down and trying not to wake Akila, who appeared to be deep asleep next to him.

Mavis looked at Insoo. "Is Mama coming?"

Insoo glanced over at Akila and made up his mind. "She's still sleeping," he responded. "Should we go downstairs and prepare breakfast?"

Mavis took an instant before responding but then nodded. "I'm hungry!"

Insoo got out of bed and, a few minutes later, the two stood in the kitchen, which was part of the larger living room. The floor-to-ceiling windows that faced the garden showed them a completely white and shapeless world in the dull morning light.

"Wow," Insoo muttered.

Mavis glanced up at him, then said, as if in agreement with his statement, "So much snow. . . ."

Insoo turned back toward the kitchen and asked Mavis, "What do you like to eat? Show me everything, and I am sure we can fix breakfast!"

Mavis came over, a funny look on his face.

"What?" Insoo enquired.

"You have a weird accent," the boy said with a smile that presented Insoo his one dimple, and Insoo finally felt that he understood why Akila was always so worried about Mavis' looks playing too much of a role in how the world reacted to him.

Insoo grinned. "You too. Is that how people talk here?" he responded.

Mavis nodded and they both laughed.

When a hungry Talida came downstairs later, she could smell coffee and eggs and found Mavis sitting on top of the kitchen counter, legs folded just like his mother would. He was wolfing down bread and fried egg while chatting away with Insoo, who was munching on a bowl of muesli with fruit.

"Morning," the tall girl said.

* * *

Edith put down the newspaper and looked at them. "I got a call from the station today," she finally said with the usual serious expression on her face. "Mrs. Williams passed on last night. They investigated the case and it seems like Mr. Williams has been violent against her for many years. He's already been arrested."

There was shocked silence. Akila, who had been cutting carrots for the salad they were preparing, looked at Edith and slowly put down the knife. Rose froze by the kitchen stove, where she stood holding a pan on the stove.

"So that means she was probably on the road after a fight?" Akila inquired after a prolonged pause.

Edith nodded. "It appears so. There were several signs that she had been hit . . . and more." She quickly glanced over to Mavis and Talida who were lying on the carpet in front of the glass doors to the terrace reading books. Mavis was showing off his favourite stories to Tae Oh who was sitting next to them with his back on the door frame.

Akila tried to wrap her head around the fact that their ever-smiling neighbours appeared to have been living a different life from what they thought. The middle-aged couple had always seemed very pleasant and satisfied. "So this has been going on for ages, he has been doing that to her for a long time? And now she is dead?" She had a hard time accepting the fact that she had completely misjudged the situation and that the woman was no more.

Edith nodded again. "Yes, apparently."

Insoo, who had remained silent on the other side of the kitchen counter, looked at Rose. She held the pan, completely motionless, and the eggs started burning. She stared at the wall in front of her, her back turned on the others, and a very small tear slid down her cheek.

Insoo, who had been washing some herbs in the sink next to her, put down the rosemary and parsley and very carefully reached out for Rose's hand on the handle of the pan. He slowly put his hand over hers and, gripping both her fingers and the handle of the pan tightly moved the eggs off the flame.

Rose, suddenly aware that something was happening, blinked a few times and stared at the burning food. She quickly wiped away the tear and muttered, "Sh–" under her breath. Insoo looked away, focusing on the herbs again.

"Akila, can you take care of these eggs for me?" Rose quickly asked, trying to hide the quivering in her voice. Then she quickly walked out of the house, avoiding everyone's eyes as best as possible.

Edith and Akila exchanged a glance. "I'll go." Akila finally said. She handed the pan to Insoo, then followed Rose.

Edith stayed at the table, staring at the newspaper in front of her for a long time. Then she sighed deeply and stood up. "How can I help?" she asked Insoo, walking over to the kitchen space.

Outside, Akila walked into the cold and along the sidewalk still covered in ice and snow to get to Edith's and Rose's cottage, which stood just a few metres further down the narrow street.

Rose had already disappeared inside the house, and Akila wasn't sure that she would open the door. Good thing that she had a key.

"'Rose?" Akila called softly after entering through the front door and walking into the living room. There was no response, which didn't surprise her. She walked through all the rooms on the ground floor, but there was no sign of Rose, which began unsettling her a little. She quickly took the old, creaky stairs up to the first floor and called again, with more urgency. "Rose!" No response. Something gripped her and she sprinted up the last flight of stairs to Edith's and Rose's bedroom. She pushed the door open and rushed into the bathroom that was connected to the bedroom, just like in her own cottage.

Rose sat on the floor. At Akila's entry, she looked up, pale and wide-eyed.

"Rose. . . ." Akila said her friend's name with a sense of relief and quickly moved over to her.

Sniffing and wiping away the tears that seemed to cover her entire face, Rose responded, "I'm glad it's you. I wouldn't want Edith to see me like this. Oh, I am such a mess." She wiped her face again.

Akila carefully sat down next to her and wrapped her arm around the shorter woman's shoulders. Looking over at her, she spotted the small pillbox hidden next to Rose's left thigh. Her heart sank, but she didn't speak. She hugged her friend for a few seconds and, while moving back to her original position, picked up the pillbox and placed it above her next to the sink.

Rose saw it and started crying again. "I just wanted to calm down a little. . . ."

Akila held her.

After a while, Rose whispered, "Isn't it the saddest thing in the world? To think that we were all around her and never noticed anything? It is so heartbreaking."

Akila thought that Rose probably felt the pain even more. Everyone had looked the other way and not noticed anything while Rose's mother had beat Rose up whenever she was drunk. That was why Rose was unable to look away. It hurt to realise that she hadn't spotted what was going on. Akila hugged Rose closer and stared at the space ahead of her, wondering how responsible they were for what had happened.

* * *

Insoo looked at the snow. It glittered ever so slightly in the faded light of the winter day. He wore his thick coat, and his scarf covered his face up to his cheeks, but his nose hurt from the cold anyway. Mavis, Talida, and Ben, the dog, ran, slithered, and jumped alongside him.

Before, he had thought that Korea got cold, but now he'd changed his opinion. Korea was warm compared to what he felt here, with the frosty wind blowing through the hills, looking to gain control over every spark of life that still resisted the reign of winter. But the surprising thing was how beautiful it was, despite being so freezing that it was hard to stay outside for more than just a few minutes.

Ben jumped through the high heaps of snow on either side of the road. He had his tongue out and released the occasional bark of excitement, especially when Mavis threw another snowball for him to catch. The energetic boy seemed just as excited, squealing and shouting as he slithered down the road. Talida, who walked next to Insoo, laughed at the sight of the two bouncing figures.

Insoo thought how little his stay with Akila resembled the joyful time he had longed for. It was meant to be a time of rest and a time away from all the exhaustion from his recent rather dramatic appearance in the limelight. But it turned out to be a heavy, emotionally charged time. *Life never gives you a breather,* he reflected.

Still, looking at Talida next to him and at Mavis, who was currently rolling down the icy slope of a small hill to their left with Ben hopping next to him, he couldn't regret making his way here.

They managed almost an hour in the cold.

Talida and Insoo found common ground by talking about books. He had liked many of the books she also cherished. She looked at him in amazement when he mentioned his father's bookshop. "What? You grew up with a bookshop?" she exclaimed. "Did you always love reading?"

Insoo took a second before he responded. "Sometimes I loved the books, and sometimes I hated them," he said.

Talida stared at him, then asked, "How can you hate books?"

He smiled, feeling almost shy in front of this girl, who was almost a woman. "It is possible . . . under certain circumstances."

She frowned, obviously troubled by his statement. But she didn't say anything further, and he was grateful for that.

It was only when they were already on their way back home that she picked up the subject again. "If you hate books, isn't it more like hating the characters? Because the book just tells the story."

Insoo looked up at the icy blue sky and felt something pull at his heart. He thought of his father and mother, too. He nodded. "Yes, you are probably right. It has to do with the people."

By now, they'd reached Ben's house, and Talida and Insoo waited outside while Mavis rang the bell and then opened the front door with the key Mr. Anderson had given him some time ago. The old man had never fully recovered after he'd fallen down the stairs and was unable to walk Ben as much as the dog needed. So Mavis helped out as much as possible.

Mavis came out again, closing the door behind him. He wore a thoughtful expression on his face, but just said, "Let's go."

They hurried along the street, feeling the cold biting their faces, toes and fingers. It was getting dark–time to get somewhere warm and cosy.

When they entered the cottage, Edith and Tae Oh sat on the couch, each with a drink in hand. Rose, who was better after the two days she spent mostly in bed, stood next to Akila preparing food. The entire house smelled of Indian cuisine.

"Woohoo!" Talida exclaimed after they had removed their winter coats and boots and strolled into the living room. "Rose, I've missed your Indian food!"

Akila smiled with a sideways look at her friend. Rose was immersed in her preparations and looked up only briefly to acknowledge Talida's comment. "Then come over and help!" she sang and held out a hand to Akila's daughter.

Insoo sat down in a seat next to Tae Oh and Edith, who were deep in discussion about current political issues. They were obviously not on their first drink.

Insoo watched Akila. She stood next to Talida, hair as untidy as ever. Both cut vegetables for Rose's feast. Mavis sat next to her on the counter, already so much like his mother, with his legs folded.

Insoo hadn't told Akila that he had lost several deals following the controversy surrounding him. Also, there was a big program he recently started recording. They'd already completed four episodes, but the production company had halted all his shoots for now, stating that they had to make up their mind about whether they would be comfortable continuing with a male lead who was attracting too much attention by being involved in questionable actions. As much as they repeated that they understood the challenges coming with his eating issues, it was their way to not anger the fans who were mostly in support of Insoo, but to also safeguard their interests. The program was meant to go international. If they decided against continuing with him, he might be sued for billions of Won. Insoo had left a furious Ma Ru back in Seoul cleaning up the mess. That was how his manager put it when they spoke last, shortly before Insoo and Tae Oh left for the airport to catch their flight.

Regardless of everything that was going on, or rather precisely because of what was going on, he had to leave. He had not been sleeping well, and there was a week when he had his phone in his hand too many times, thinking of sending Akila a message–a 0. He wanted to say that he couldn't do this anymore, but in the end, he didn't say anything, like so many times before in his life.

How much was she able to see in his face? One moment, he wanted her to see it all–how empty and tired he felt, how hard it was to eat, and how his heart ached. The next moment, he was disgusted looking at himself in the morning and wanted to make sure that she didn't get even the tiniest glimpse of what was going on.

Something was happening with Mavis and Akila, and Insoo frowned, pulled out of his thoughts. The boy with the large blonde afro had just mumbled something and his mother stopped chopping the cheese for the salad, freezing in mid-motion, looking up at her son. Talida and Rose suddenly stopped working too, both staring at Mavis. And then, as Mavis slumped down on the counter, covering his face with his two hands, the three women all jumped, rushing at the boy. Akila, who'd been right next to her son, slung her arms around Mavis and pulled him off the counter.

Mavis cried hard and Edith and Tae Oh turned around on the couch staring in disbelief. Talida wrapped her arms around her brother and her mother, and Rose did the same. They all stood there, Mavis wailing loudly, face hidden behind his hands. Insoo thought it was the most heartbreaking sound.

Mavis had taken a long time before he was in a state to explain why he thought that he was partly responsible for Mrs. Williams' death. He had seen her one day, in the garden, and she had put her finger on her lips and he had kept quiet. And then there was Mr. Anderson's comment about Mrs. Williams' death–a comment about how people always looked away when it got hard, and it had Mavis shaken to the core. He had looked away too.

* * *

Later that night, after Mavis had finally calmed down and gone to bed without eating anything, Akila lay on her back staring into the soft darkness surrounding her. Insoo's regular breathing next to her had a soothing quality and the warmth of his skin was radiating, giving her a sense of comfort, but still she couldn't find sleep. She thought about her children and how scary it was sometimes to have to release them into the world—a world in which they were confronted with all sorts of things. As a parent, she could only hope that she could teach them how to be strong enough inside to face the world, but couldn't shield them from everything. She did believe that it was best to try to show Talida and Mavis how to live in the world as it was and not to sugarcoat it too much, but at times, like today, she felt that it was too much for children to handle. All across the world, all the things these young personalities had to handle–it wasn't right.

Akila's heart was filled with a concoction of different emotions: mainly anger, sadness, and pity. Most of all, she didn't want Mavis to carry that sense of guilt with him. She wanted him to be able to let it go.

The days that followed were quiet and cosy. Akila and Insoo did a bit of sightseeing, but the majority of their time was spent simply being together, taking walks, reading, and listening to music. Mavis and Insoo played football inside the living room for hours until Akila said she couldn't take it anymore and chased them out. So they played football in the snow, which had started to turn into brownish mud. They slithered down the icy sidewalk, trying to catch the ball. Their laughter and shouts could be heard along the entire street.

All of them cooked and baked and spent long evenings with Rose and Edith on the couch. Michael stopped by most of the days, spent nights in the house, too, and Akila felt as if she was living on a tiny, warm planet, separated from the rest of the rather cold universe, which they only visited when absolutely necessary.

Everyone made a special effort to make Mavis feel better. He got extra cuddles and sweets from Rose and Talida and Michael had taken him for hot chocolate and a movie. Edith brought a new pair of sneakers from London. Tae Oh practised dance moves with him.

Akila was unsure if this was the right thing to do, but she didn't stop them. Maybe extra affection and attention were exactly what he needed.

After a couple of days, she was sure that he would be able to handle it. It was after she had seen Insoo and Mavis in the garden. They'd been playing football when she went into an online meeting with one of her clients. When she was done and walked back into the living room, she saw them sitting next to each other on the terrace outside, ignoring the cold. Mavis was talking and Insoo was listening, only uttering a few words occasionally.

That evening, Akila sensed a shift in Mavis, and although he woke up from the same dream for months afterward, a dream featuring Mrs. Williams, he seemed less shaken and unsettled as the days passed.

"Sometimes it's not the closest people who can help us," Akila reflected when she discussed the situation with Rose. "Sometimes those with more distance are the better support."

Rose nodded and grinned at her. "Well spoken, coach!" she teased her affectionately.

Akila rolled her eyes at her friend and put her arm around her.

The house seemed empty on the day Talida, Mavis, and Akila returned from the airport after dropping Insoo and Tae Oh off. The children had insisted that they all had to squeeze in–they didn't want to let the two men go without saying goodbye. That evening, Akila sat in her living room by herself, unable to take the stairs up to her bedroom.

Glances

Akila was set to be back in Seoul by early March. The excitement she felt at going back gave her a rush of energy weeks before the actual flight took off.

Rose teased her frequently, and it was obvious to everyone that Akila was in a good space. She worked with a higher-than-usual number of clients. She repainted Talida's and Mavis' rooms. She repaired the bathroom light, which had been broken for months, and fixed the chair that had been standing in the corner of the living room because anyone sitting on it risked their life. She moved furniture around to make the cottage more cosy.

On the day she dug up the garden and rearranged all the flower beds, Rose stood next to Talida and Mavis and said, "Akila darling, you need to slow down now."

Akila straightened up and let out her breath. Wiping her brow, she looked around at what she had done to the garden and knew Rose was right. But she couldn't help feeling elated at the thought of travelling back to Seoul. Insoo was there and she wanted to spend time with him; she wanted to see Tae Oh, Hae In, and Seo Hui. On top of that, she had booked flights for Talida and Mavis, too, and they would be joining her during their holidays–and maybe even beyond that. She was still in discussion with their schools about possible ways to extend their stay with her.

Again, Katarina had agreed to come over to stay with her grandchildren for a couple of days, and Rose and Edith were covering the rest of the time. What would she have done without such wonderful people in her life? Wasn't the world suddenly very beautiful?

Akila had observed moments before in her life when the world turned into the most wonderful place for her and nothing could reduce her positive outlook. She enjoyed the sensation. It was amazing to be able to focus entirely on the blue between the clouds rather than the grey clouds covering the blue.

But in the evenings, when she was alone, she had instances when she felt something pressing against her mind–a thought that she had shut out consciously. Over the years, Akila had become a professional at shutting out unpleasant thoughts. She was great at not speaking about what was on her mind if it was something that she hadn't milled over on her own. In the past, she had often denied that fact, but these days, she accepted that she was good at shutting things out that she wasn't ready to face. So this time, as was her habit, she went about her days smiling, riding her wave of excitement without clarifying to anyone, even to herself, that something was lying beneath the surface.

Akila hadn't spoken to anyone about the sessions she'd had with Kang Ji Su. To most people, he was known as the formerly successful boy band member who was now a solo musician, dancer, vlogger, and actor. He was energetic and impossibly rash at times, especially when he had set his mind on something, and Akila often felt this persona was less the person Ji Su and more the public figure Kang Ji Su. What seemed burdensome to Insoo many days appeared to be what Ji Su craved and what he looked for almost desperately. He was used to getting attention and he wanted more of it.

It was during their third session when it hit Akila that she had to speak to Insoo about her work with Kang Ji Su.

Ji Su had driven her crazy the entire hour they'd talked. They were working on content for his personal channel and vlog and had already agreed on the basic concept, but Ji Su kept diverting, absorbed in what he'd seen others do, and Akila felt irritation rise inside her. Ji Su was several years older than Insoo, but he often seemed like an energetic child, overflowing with all kinds of thoughts and emotions, and he didn't always take time to sort those out before he released them into the world.

"Ji Su, can you stop!" she finally said, staring at the beautiful face on the screen, wearing a frown on her own face. "Why do you keep focusing on what others do? How is that relevant?"

He looked at her for a brief second, then asked, "How is that not relevant?"

She sighed. "This is about you and how you can turn 'Kang Ji Su' into the brand you want. Stop being shallow by focusing on others."

There was a pause that stretched into silence. Akila put her head in her hand, suddenly feeling exhausted. It had happened again—crossing the line. What was really going on with her these days?

Ji Su looked to one side. Then, when Akila was about to apologise, he glanced at her with a twinkle in his eyes. "You are the rudest person I have worked with," he stated. Then he laughed his loud laughter, a fearless and shameless laughter that shook Akila to the core. It shook her because, when he laughed like that, she was helpless, seeing his glittering eyes, observing how those wrinkles around his eyes made his face even more impressive, and she was unable to stop herself. It was almost as if he was a place she had to reach.

The thing that irritated her most about it was that she knew she wasn't the only one who felt that way. Kang Ji Su wasn't a big brand like Insoo, but he'd done many different things as an artist and had a strong following as an influencer. Online, Akila had found numerous videos from fans who added sequences of Ji Su's laughter together. It amazed her what people did in their free time, looking for clips of Kang Ji Su's laughter and making videos out of that. She was annoyed with herself for falling for it too—for selfishly wanting him around her. It was ridiculous, and the conversation with Mr. Kwon about how she'd been unprofessional with Insoo many weeks before popped up in her mind with increasing frequency. Thus, after that third session with Ji Su, Akila decided that it was time to speak with Insoo about her latest Korean client.

"Insoo, are you busy?" she texted quickly.

It didn't take long for him to respond. "Preparing for a shoot. Can we talk later?"

"I'm coaching Kang Ji Su. (emoticon with face covered with hands, followed by emoticon celebrating)"

"Ok . . . sounds like great news! Let's talk later. Have to go! (several emoticons winking and releasing kiss)"

Akila stared at the chat conversation and sighed deeply. She had said it, although she felt that she was still avoiding the real conversation. Insoo was the one person she wanted to be open with—but how, when she didn't even know what to make of herself these days? If she didn't understand herself, how would he?

* * *

"You have a big nose!"

Dead silence followed Akila's comment and everyone in the room turned to stare at her.

Ji Su looked at her too, with this particular way of his, as if he was studying a rare species he hadn't expected to encounter in his world. A tiny frown had shown up on his face, and he squinted ever so slightly. "What?" he asked in Korean.

"You have a big nose," Akila repeated, still in English, but with less force this time. She felt shaky, unable to handle her frustration, so she walked away from him, pushing the doors open violently. Outside in the corridor, she had to stop and bend over with her arms around her tummy. Trying to catch her breath, she closed her eyes. People passing her in the small space of the corridor observed her curiously.

She jumped at the touch of his hand on her shoulder.

"Hey, Akila. . . ." He looked worried, which made her feel worse.

What had gotten into her?

"Let's have some coffee," he said and took her by the wrist, guiding her down the corridor and through the entrance out onto the street.

There was a small coffee shop in the next building, and Ji Su sat her down at one of the tables next to a large green plant with a view of the street outside. He went to order at the counter and came back with a glass of water for her. She accepted the large glass with both hands and drank half of it in one go. Ji Su had made himself comfortable in the chair opposite her. He was studying her again.

When the waitress brought their coffees, Ji Su continued. "So, what's going on?" he asked with a confused, but amused smile on his face. "Why are you attacking my nose?"

Akila mourned and covered her face with her hands.

* * *

Like so many times before, Ji Su tried to make sense of what she was doing. She often confused him. She was strange in so many ways. It amused him, how she went about her life, and he couldn't deny that it intrigued him how she seemed to be afraid, but still jumped right into what she deemed necessary. Apart from his aunt, who had he met who was so scared and yet so fearless?

Looking at her, he wondered why she didn't make her hair look a little less crazy and why she never put on makeup. Why did she always wear those wide clothes that didn't flatter her figure in any way?

She was obviously working on how to best put her emotions into words, so he waited.

Eventually, she put both of her rather large hands on the table in front of her and, taking a deep breath, asked, "Why do you accept their empty flattery?"

"Huh?" He didn't understand what she was getting at.

She raised her eyes to look at him and, in that instant, all the fear seemed to have seeped out of her gaze. All that remained was that unwavering stare from two large green-brown eyes fixing him in his spot. It was a truly intimidating sight.

"Dance practice today was rubbish," she went on. "You didn't manage to put your vision into the dance moves, and the crew didn't do a good job because they're not getting you." She took another deep breath. "And still, when they smile and tell you how great everything is, you accept it. . . . Why?" She had a frustrated look on her face, which Ji Su didn't like at all.

She gestured animatedly, wanting to express what she had on her mind, but he wasn't feeling comfortable with what she appeared to communicate between the lines. "You're great at so many things! Why do you rely on other people telling you how things are going if, deep down, you know best?" She ended her outburst with her left palm slapping the round table that separated them and sighed, staring at her coffee.

Ji Su shifted, glancing at her. It wasn't a good feeling, seeing how he was the reason for her frustration. At the same time, it angered him that she spoke as if he was shallow and unable to handle things on his own. He looked at his untouched coffee and decided he needed to put more distance between them than just the width of the table until he'd come to a conclusion on how he felt about the comments she had made.

"Still no need to talk like that," he mumbled, almost to himself, but she'd heard him and looked up–and what she saw worried her.

She straightened and opened her mouth to speak. Before he could hear anything she said, he stood up and strode out of the shop. When he briefly glanced through the windowfront of the coffee shop while walking by, he saw Akila sitting motionless at the table, her head resting on her left fist.

* * *

Insoo had been relaxing on his couch with his phone in hand after a long day of shooting. It was early evening and he wondered where Akila was. She'd had a session with Kang Ji Su earlier that day, but she said she'd be done by afternoon and come home to get some of her other work done. Just when he dropped her a message, he heard the password being keyed in at the front door, and a moment later, Akila walked into the living room. Spotting him on the sofa, she came over without saying a word. Her face seemed sad and Insoo looked at her in surprise when she released a deep sigh and let herself drop half on top of him, slinging her arms around him. He could feel her breath on his neck, where she was hiding her face, and, wondering what had happened, he slung his arms around her too.

They stayed like that for a long time and Insoo was almost sure that she had fallen asleep when she stirred and held him even closer.

"Akila–"

The sound of someone else keying in the password at the front door interrupted him, and a second later, Tae Oh called out while entering the house. He walked into the living room and, seeing them stretched out on the sofa, he grinned and asked, "Looks cosy. Can I join?"

"Of course," Akila mumbled with a tiny smile as they sat up and made space for him on the couch.

A while later they had put music on at low volume and Insoo got some drinks from the fridge. They all sat on the couch next to each other, glancing at the slanted rays of late evening sunlight that illuminated the living room. It was the most beautiful sight.

"What happened today, Akila?" Insoo finally inquired.

She took time before she responded, and when she did, both Insoo and Tae Oh noted the coat of sadness that covered her voice. They briefly glanced at each other as they listened to her recount her exchange with Kang Ji Su.

After she was done, there was silence except for the music playing in the background.

Tae Oh made an attempt first. "So you told Ji Su that he had a big nose. . . ."

Insoo closed his eyes and dipped his head back on the couch to avoid her seeing the twinkle of amusement in his eye.

Akila sighed deeply. "I think I'm just not good with people who are called Su. They really get to me."

Tae Oh grinned at her. "Wait! The last time I saw him was at the concert with you. That was months ago. Let me check quickly.

Does he really have such a big nose?" He pulled out his phone and, a moment later, showed them Kang Ji Su's images. "He has a nose, but I think it suits him rather well," he exclaimed. Focusing on the screen, he added, "He is really good-looking!"

Insoo was beaming now, not able to contain his amusement any longer.

Akila looked at both of them with obvious irritation. "It's not funny!"

They burst out laughing.

She wore a real frown on her face and crossed her arms in front of her chest.

But, somehow, observing the two young men next to her holding their bellies and laughing lifted part of her sadness. And suddenly the meaning of the moment hit Akila with full force. She looked at Insoo with amazement and wondered when the shift had taken place. He was still underweight and had to steel himself every day to make sure he kept eating his meals. He still went to therapy. Some days were easier. Many were still very hard. But he was sitting here, laughing. She felt warmth spread through her and decided that there was almost nothing more important than this moment, being able to see Insoo laugh out loud.

Later that night, when Akila slipped under the covers of her bed, she picked up her phone and opened her chat with Ji Su. She left her door ajar and was able to hear the low mumble of Insoo's and Tae Oh's voices from the living room where they were still chatting. Staring at the last messages they had exchanged, she asked herself how to best begin her message to Ji Su.

Ji Su didn't respond to Akila's messages that night or the next morning. As the day passed by, she kept glancing at her phone, wondering what to do if he chose to completely ignore her. Insoo was out for a whole day of shooting and would only be back late that evening. Akila told herself that this was a great opportunity to get pending work for some of her other clients done.

But by midday, she had to admit to herself that she wasn't as productive as she would have liked to be, increasingly worrying that Ji Su had decided to terminate their working relationship. What had gotten into her for behaving so unprofessionally? She sat at Insoo's desk in the living room, holding her head. Finally, not being able to keep waiting any longer, she picked up her phone and called Ji Su. Her call went unanswered. She waited for another ten minutes, then picked up her phone, her purse, and her coat and left the house to get a taxi to the dance studio.

In the back of the taxi, Akila kept thinking about what her next step would be if she didn't find Ji Su at the studio. There should be a way to find out where he lived and go find him there. But what if she didn't meet any of his fellow dancers?

Having reached her destination, Akila paid for the taxi, got out, and walked into the building. Moving along the narrow corridor toward the particular room that Ji Su used for practice and shooting some of his dance videos, she told her heart to slow down a little and stop jumping in her chest.

The practice room with the large mirror seemed forlorn when Akila opened the door. The piano was almost in the centre, and today, the heavy curtains were drawn open and daylight flooded through the big windows, casting everything in a bright, almost white light that seemed harsh and unforgiving to her.

Just when she was about to turn around, Akila noticed something on the floor in front of the windows, the sight halfway obscured by the piano because of where she was standing. She moved to the right, closer to the mirror, and froze. It was Ji Su, she realised, lying on his back with his arms and legs spread out.

She walked closer quickly, not sure why she felt the urge to confirm that his chest was moving. It wasn't as if she expected that their argument would push a person like Kang Ji Su to do anything crazy. Being closer to him, she could see his chest rising and falling quickly and she could see the sweat on his face and his white t-shirt. He had probably been practising.

Akila remained where she was. How would she start the conversation? Her heart hadn't listened to her and was still jumping in her chest.

Ji Su had closed his eyes and, although he was lying still on his back, it seemed like something ran extremely fast underneath the stillness.

Without thinking about it, Akila put down her bag and walked over to Ji Su. She didn't make an effort to be quiet, so by the time she lay down on the floor with her head next to his and her feet pointing the opposite way, he had opened his eyes and was looking at her.

"Sorry," she said, then repeated the same in Korean, "Miane," while staring at the ceiling.

After glancing at her for a little longer, Ji Su turned his head to stare at the ceiling as well. He was still a little out of breath, and Akila felt the heat that was emanating from him.

"Don't you get tired of it sometimes?" she finally asked.

He didn't respond for a long time. Then he inquired "Of what exactly?"

"That they all just behave like they think you want them to? And never say, 'No,' or 'I don't like it,' or 'That's crap.'"

He frowned slightly as he let what she said sink in, still focusing his gaze on the ceiling above them.

Akila suddenly thought of Joseph, in Kenya. Why? She hadn't thought of him for a very long time. Why did he pop up today? Was it because he was an example of how someone could turn out when given too much attention? And when no one ever said, "No," or, "I don't like it," or, "That's crap?" She thought about that for a while. Then she said, "There's this guy I was close to in Nairobi. I acted with him. . . ." And just like that the whole story emerged. She hadn't even told Joyce or Rose or her mother about it. When it was all told, including her bitter thoughts and all the details that still upset her a little, even after all these years, they were quiet again.

Eventually, Ji Su sat up. "I'm cold," he said and then jumped to his naked feet. "Just give me five minutes to change. Then let's go for a drink."

"Crossing the line again," Akila mumbled to herself as she waited for Ji Su, sitting on the small stool in front of the piano, her bag on her lap. But she decided to drop it and let the reality wash over her. She was unable to feel any regret. All she felt was relief that she had found him so easily.

So she took out her phone and messaged Insoo that she was going out for a drink and would come home later.

About thirty minutes later, Ji Su and Akila had settled in a small bar Ji Su had chosen and had ordered a snack and drinks. As the evening turned into night, they talked about everything else, but not about their conflict the day before, and also not about Joseph's story. Akila wondered if he'd decided to let it all pass and was undecided about whether she would like that more.

Just before midnight, Insoo dropped her a message that he was home. She smiled a little, imagining how he probably walked into the house, switched on the lights as he went through the kitchen, took his bottle of water from the fridge, and moved on down the corridor. She was slipping her phone back into her bag when Ji Su asked, "So, did you comment on my nose because you are worried that I will turn out like that guy in Kenya?" He slowly turned his whiskey glass from left to right between his slim fingers, a thoughtful expression on his face. He glanced up at her.

"Not sure," she responded. "Of all days, I thought about that time today. Maybe it's what you are saying, but maybe I was also annoyed with those who don't say that they don't like something. Like your crew yesterday. I can't say that I said, 'No,' to Joseph. That's bugging me." She quickly took a large sip of whiskey from her glass, suddenly afraid of the way the conversation was going.

Ji Su's glittery eyes were on her and he still wore that thoughtful expression. Akila thought that she'd said way too much. He had stopped turning the glass between his fingers. And with the confidence that she had seen so many times in him, he told her, "Sometimes it is hard to say, 'No,' or, 'I don't like it.' No reason to get worked up forever. Just try harder next time."

Why did it touch her somewhere deep down, a place nothing she didn't allow to get there usually reached? It was nothing that hadn't been said before. But she was balancing tears that wanted to jump over the brim and slide down her cheeks. *How ridiculous!* she thought. She couldn't look down because the tears might fall, so they sat there with their eyes locked.

"Let me take you home now," he said and turned to ask for the bill. And just like that, the moment was over and Akila got a chance to quickly wipe her face to make the tears disappear.

Ji Su ordered a cab and they waited outside the bar without saying much. He had insisted that he take her home first, then go to his place after that. She only managed a few weak objections, too immersed in her musings.

In the cab, they sat silently next to each other, and it was only when they finally reached the steep road with Insoo's house towards the end of it that he asked, "When are we meeting for our next session?"

She was confused by the sudden question, then realised that he still wanted to work with her. "Send me a few suggestions that work with your schedule and I'll make it happen," she replied, slightly out of breath because of the excitement that had gripped her.

Inside the house, there was pleasant darkness. She stopped by the fridge and took a whole bottle of cool water while sitting on the kitchen counter. She was feeling as if she was floating. There was alcohol, relief, excitement, and a pinch of fear all mixed up in her mind and heart.

She knew it would take her some time to be able to fall asleep, so instead of opening the door to her room, she carefully opened the door to Insoo's. But his bed was empty. Akila stood in the darkness, feeling how her heart beat hard in her chest. He'd said that he had come home, so where was he? Frantically, she left his room and hurried back down the corridor to the living room. But Insoo wasn't on the couch. Akila stared at the empty sofa, which was slightly illuminated by the city's skyline that cast faded lights through the windows, and the terror that rose in her was real. Where was he?

Then it hit her that she hadn't been to her room. Running down the corridor, she opened the door and saw the figure below the blankets on her bed. She had to lean on the doorframe of her room for a moment so that her heart could calm down a little. When she finally felt that it was fine to move, she walked over to her bed. Insoo's skin was warm and soft below her fingertips. Realising that she was close to him, he turned and wrapped his arms around her. Akila briefly wondered what had frightened her so much before drifting off to sleep, into her other worlds.

Insoo and Akila spent the next couple of days absorbed in their projects. Ji Su was working hard on his dance project and the number of followers on his channel, where he provided the videos as well as the interest from sponsors, was already growing. Akila and Ji Su met several times a week, and all their energy flowed into their exchanges. For all three of them, there was little time for anything else but to focus on the next point on their agenda. The only other thing constantly on Akila's mind were Talida and Mavis, who were due to join them in early April.

* * *

It was Tae Oh who brought up Insoo's birthday. It was coming up at the end of the month and Tae Oh was of the clear opinion that it had been too long since they last celebrated properly. And when he offered to organise everything and assured Insoo that he would just have to be there and have a good time, there wasn't anything that Insoo could say to change his friend's mind.

Insoo wasn't sure how he should feel about a party after all the intense times they'd been through of late. Would it truly be the great thing that Tae Oh praised so adamantly? Or would it overwhelm him and make him feel uneasy? He'd made good progress on his eating but still had many days when he woke up and didn't think that he could go on. He didn't want anything to suck up the energy he needed so desperately to stay on track.

"Then let's just not do it," Akila said when he briefly mentioned how he felt. "It's your birthday and your decision in the end. Just think about it a little more and Tae Oh will have to go with what you want."

Insoo walked over to where she was standing behind the kitchen counter preparing their morning coffee before they went their separate ways for the day. He carefully put his arms around her and hid his face in her unruly hair. Insoo closed his eyes and took a deep breath.

Several days passed without Insoo saying anything about the party, and by the end of the week, Tae Oh had already organised a good portion of what needed to be done. He had gotten help from some of Insoo's other friends and Insoo felt uncomfortable telling them how unsure he was about having so many people around. So it happened that Insoo decided to celebrate his birthday with more than just a handful of people.

* * *

There was already a happy bustle in Insoo's kitchen and living room. Delicious finger food of all sizes, colours, and shapes on pretty platters had been placed on the counter and the fridge was stocked with drinks.

Akila had connected her speaker to her laptop and music was playing. She was excited because it was only a few days before Talida and Mavis would join them in Seoul and she was looking forward to having her children with her.

Insoo wore a smile on his face that made her feel like everything was slowly coming together. He had spent the morning with his family to celebrate his birthday and then stopped by the agency to record a video message for his fans and take a couple of images with all the birthday gifts that had been sent by supporters, partners, and fans. Akila had been shocked to see the images of Insoo standing in a large room surrounded by uncountable gifts. The sense of support and appreciation was overwhelming.

Now it was early evening and people started filling the house. Hae In and Seo Hui were already there, and Tae Oh had done a great job organising everything. He looked extremely pleased while glancing over at Insoo, who was smiling and chatting with his first guests.

The sun was setting and the fairy lights that they had draped along the large windows in the living room were switched on, creating tiny shiny sources of warm light all around. The doorbell rang and Hae In went to open the door. Akila recognized the drummer who had played with Ji Su last year at the concert. They'd recently met again at the dance studio where Ji Su was working on his videos. What was his name again? Akila frowned, irritated that she hadn't managed to get rid of the annoying tendency to forget names.

Ji Su strode into the small corridor, following his bandmate. He greeted Hae In in his usual enthusiastic manner then put his hands in the front pockets of his jeans, letting his gaze wander around the place. Not for the first time, Akila asked herself how someone could have such a strong positive aura. It was as if nothing could take Ji Su down. He seemed to look at the world knowing that there was no option of retreat–that all there was was moving ahead.

Tae Oh walked over and, after exchanging greetings, the two men entered the kitchen space. Ji Su was offered a drink and food. It was good to be able to look at him from a distance, not having to wonder if he noticed how much he managed to shake her up inside.

He laughed at something Tae Oh said and the sparkle in his eyes lit up his entire face. Just then, Insoo walked into the kitchen to get a drink for one of his other guests. Tae Oh called him over and introductions were made. Ji Su stood in front of Insoo, shoulders relaxed, O-shaped legs confidently apart. Insoo was so much taller, but at the same time seemed much more delicate. Ji Su smiled up at Insoo and they shook hands. Tae Oh made a comment and still holding the other's hand, both Sus burst out laughing, their voices ringing across the room. Ji Su's laughter was unbelievably loud, and staring at him in astonishment, Insoo continued to laugh, apparently carried away by the other man's fearless outburst.

Seo Hui appeared next to Akila, putting her arm around her shoulders. "Akila, let's go say hi!"

Akila felt as if she had been caught.

"Kang Ji Su!" Her friend with a heart-shaped face pointed over at the kitchen. Judging from Seo Hui's grin and flushed face, she must have already had a couple of drinks without Akila noticing. Pulling her along, Seo Hui made her way across the room, smiling at the other guests sheepishly when she bumped into them by mistake.

All three men turned to look at them when they arrived and Akila braced herself, silently begging that no one would notice how her heart was sprinting and how warmth crept up from her chest and spread to her ears and into her cheeks. Seo Hui was talking and Ji Su said something while looking at Akila. Insoo was next to her, his long body leaning against the kitchen counter, short hair shining in the light above him. For some reason, Akila was unable to decipher the language spoken. She closed her eyes for a moment, then opened them again, realising that she needed air. Mumbling something, she walked away from the group quickly through the open front door, where two more of Insoo's guests had just been welcomed by Hae In.

Outside in the cool-but-not-cold night, she took a few deep breaths. Then she sat down on the steps leading down to the yard in front of Insoo's house.

"Wow," she said to herself, pressing one hand onto her chest where her heart was still racing and trying to make sense of what she was experiencing.

* * *

Inside the house, there was a quick exchange of glances between Tae Oh, Insoo, and Ji Su. They all followed Akila with their eyes. Then Seo Hui diffused the moment when she squeezed herself in between Tae Oh and Ji Su and started chattering animatedly.

"I better go check on her," Insoo said, and, shooting a small smile at Ji Su, excused himself and left.

Insoo almost walked into her on the steps in front of the house. He settled down next to Akila, stretching out his long, thin legs and gazing up at the sky. "Walking out is becoming your trademark," he commented.

She looked at him with a confused expression on her face then smiled weakly. "Sorry," she responded. "It suddenly felt as if the space was too small. . . ."

He observed her in the dim light. Something was working inside her, he could see that clearly. Suddenly, she moved very close to him and kissed his neck softly. "I'm fine, I swear. Give me a moment and I'll be back."

Back inside, it was almost like another world with light, music, voices, and laughter rolling over him. Insoo spotted Ji Su in the kitchen, Seo Hui by his side. He'd obviously not managed to escape.

Where was Tae Oh? After a moment of hesitation, Insoo walked over and gently moved his tipsy friend to the side. "Ji Su, let's have another drink," he said while winking at Seo Hui, who didn't look pleased at all. He guided Ji Su over to the already crowded couch in the living room.

* * *

It was five in the morning when the house was finally silent. The kitchen counter was filled with empty bottles and glasses. Stacks of bowls and plates with remains of food were piled up in and around the sink. The fairy lights in the living room were still on, but in the first light of approaching dawn, their light appeared faint.

On Akila's bed, Seo Hui had slung her arms around Akila's waist. She was snoring slightly, mumbling in her sleep from time to time. As always, Akila was completely motionless in her sleep.

On Insoo's bed, Tae Oh, Hae In, and the drummer had all squeezed in together, legs and arms intertwined for lack of space. Snores travelled up to the ceiling.

There were three more bodies in the living room. A girl, Ha Na, was stretched out on a thin blanket on the floor in front of the desk. She was Hae In's latest love. She had covered herself with one of Insoo's coats. Sitting upright on the couch, arms folded in front of his chest and legs stretched out to full length, Insoo was deep asleep. His head rested on Ji Su's arm which was wrapped around his shoulder.

When Akila walked into the kitchen two hours later, she stopped abruptly at the sight of the two men sleeping. Silently and very slowly, she lifted her phone, which she'd been carrying in her left hand, and took a picture. Akila stood a while longer, letting her gaze travel over Insoo and Ji Su next to each other. Then she moved on to the kitchen and started clearing some of the dishes to make space for her morning coffee ritual.

Later, they'd removed the old wooden table from the basement and placed it in the sun in the middle of the front yard. It was still a little cool outside, so they wore coats, but the sunlight was tickling their faces and the smell of coffee filled their noses. They had warmed all the remaining food and loaded the table. Lack of sleep made them hungry, and for a few minutes after they had all settled down, only the sounds of food being consumed were audible.

Gradually, the conversation returned. Akila fetched her speaker from the house and selected some of her soul playlists that she thought went well with the mood.

"Ji Su, I saw your video. Awesome dance moves and a really cool idea!" Tae Oh gave a thumbs up to Ji Su over his plate loaded with food.

Ji Su smiled. "It was hard work!"

"Did that come out of coaching with Akila?" Hae In asked while shovelling more food onto his plate.

Ji Su nodded.

"How is it, working with her?" Seo Hui enquired. Her voice was scratchy from all the whiskey she'd consumed the previous night and all the singing she'd done while they danced, but she started looking like her usual self now that she had eaten something and taken the cup of strong coffee Akila handed her.

Ji Su had a twinkle in his eye, and Akila thought that wasn't good for her. "She is the rudest person I have ever worked with," he said dryly. When he noticed the irritated expression she wore, he laughed his fearless laughter. It travelled up into the blue sky above them, whirled around, and made Akila's heart swell.

Tae Oh grinned, then said, "Finally, we see her true colours. . . ."

But Hae In, Seo Hui, Ha Na, and the drummer looked at Akila in surprise. They obviously couldn't imagine the older woman being rude.

Ji Su motioned to Insoo. "You spend the most time with her. Tell us–how is she treating you?"

Insoo smiled but remained silent.

"He is a changed man!" Tae Oh called out, and everyone but Akila and Insoo laughed.

Ji Su looked over at the young, tall man on the opposite side of the table. "Insoo, that was cool, the way you took it all head-on last year. Must have taken a lot of courage."

Akila focused on the food on her plate, not sure if she was comfortable with where the conversation was going.

Insoo returned Ji Su's gaze. His face was calm and, after a long pause, he nodded. "I feel freer."

Ji Su smiled. He seemed to like that statement. "So what's next for you?" he inquired between mouthfuls of food.

Insoo had a contemplative look on his face after hearing Ji Su's question. "Not sure yet," he said. "I guess I am waiting to see what's coming my way. What about you?"

Something about the energy around the table made the conversation between the two seem incredibly intimate. Akila felt as if the rest of them were mere onlookers who weren't important to the scene. A strange sense gripped her because neither Insoo or Ji Su seemed tense at all. There was a casual quality about everything they said, but still–every word seemed to carry weight.

* * *

After Insoo's birthday party, Ji Su stayed. It happened without any of them speaking about it, but instead of going back to his house, he spent the entire day with them and the three of them were deep in conversation by the time everyone else had left and evening was approaching. So Ji Su spent the night in one of the empty rooms of Insoo's house and they all went about their activities as usual the next day.

Insoo couldn't help but notice what Akila had mentioned to him–the ball of energy that seemed to live within Ji Su and that seemed to propel him forward. Where Insoo hesitated and spent his nights turning thoughts and feelings around and around, Ji Su just seemed to run ahead.

So that day, when Ji Su said that he would cook his favourite dish for them for lunch, Insoo couldn't keep from glancing at him.

Ji Su stood at the kitchen counter, cutting vegetables for the meal he wanted to prepare for them. He wore simple jeans and a white T-shirt, and his still slightly wet hair fell into his eyes. He kept pushing the strands away with the back of his hand. Sunshine from the windows in the living room filled the kitchen space.

Insoo tried not to look too much, afraid that Ji Su would notice. He was confused by what was going on, but his gaze kept travelling back to the man. He felt a little weak in his legs. Not knowing what to make of it, he moved back into the corridor and walked down to his room. He slowly closed the door behind him, deciding that it was better to wait until he had calmed down.

Waves

Insoo and Akila had agreed to make time to travel through the country with Talida and Mavis. Although they didn't say so, they both knew that they wanted the children to have a great time in Korea. It seemed to be one of the factors that would have a great impact on how their lives would continue in the future. Based on Insoo's suggestions, they agreed on a few places and made reservations. It had been some time since Akila had travelled without the purpose of visiting specific people, either family or friends or clients, so she felt elated at the thought of being on the road exploring.

Ji Su had left after spending another night in the house and Akila had seen something taking shape between Insoo and Ji Su that she didn't want to ignore. Therefore, when the stars had come up and they were in Insoo's bed that night, she said his name softly. "Insoo. . . ."

Suddenly, Akila's heart beat very hard in her chest. She was sure that he could feel it against his chest too. But she had told herself that he would be the one person she would not hold back with. So she closed her eyes and inched closer, pressing herself against him. He held her tighter, his skin warm and comforting.

"Hmmh?" he inquired when she didn't go on.

"Let's ask Ji Su to come with us."

Insoo didn't move–didn't say anything. But from his breathing, she knew that he was wide awake.

* * *

Talida and Mavis sprinted across the beach. It was a slim stretch of sand and the narrow road that wound its way along the coastal strip ran parallel to it for many kilometres. It was slightly hazy and the green trees covering the rocky formations at the end of the bay seemed a little unreal.

Insoo stood and looked at the ocean. Every time he did so, it soothed whatever it was that burned inside his heart. He hadn't visited the ocean for far too long. Was the last time really with Akila the year before?

Ji Su suddenly appeared next to him, hands in the front pockets of his jeans as always. He let his gaze run over the waves and inhaled deeply, a smile spreading over his face. Insoo noticed the sparkles in his eyes. Every time Ji Su smiled, he seemed so content that Insoo felt a little jealous.

Then Ji Su's arm was around Insoo's shoulders and he grinned up at him. "It is beautiful!" he exclaimed and ruffled Insoo's short hair. Surprised by the unexpected physical contact, Insoo froze and could only stare at Ji Su, who laughed his loud laughter.

A second later, Ji Su was serious again, standing close to Insoo with his arm around his shoulder, taking in the view of the waves that dominated the entire space before them.

* * *

Akila sat in the sand observing Mavis and Talida, small bouncing figures further down the beach. So far, they seemed to be enjoying their time in Korea, which she registered with a great sense of relief. If her children could be comfortable here, it would be easier for her to find a way to reconcile the different worlds her life consisted of at the moment.

Then she looked at Insoo and Ji Su who stood close to each other facing the ocean. Ji Su had put his arm around Insoo's shoulder, and Akila liked that Ji Su made contact so easily. Where Insoo hesitated and observed from a distance, Ji Su went right in, not giving Insoo a chance to retreat.

They had left Seoul two days ago in Insoo's car, heading for the ocean. Akila felt that her days were filled with light, now that she had her children with her. Talida and Mavis had arrived at the airport and jumped into both her mother's and Insoo's arms. They had been tired but were too excited to slow down, and both Mavis and Talida had talked non-stop from the airport to Insoo's house.

* * *

"Do you think that it affects your people every day that their country is divided?" Akila had asked as they drove.

After a moment of silence, Insoo responded. "I think so. Maybe not consciously every day, but yes, it affects them."

"Has it affected Germans that their country was divided?" Ji Su inquired.

"Yes. Even today you can see the traces of it."

He nodded, thoughtful. On the other side of her, Insoo glanced up at the crystal clear sky.

Travelling through Korea, Akila thought about the randomness of it all–of borders and boundaries. Of conflicts that came from how a line was drawn. The absurdity of it. And then the beauty that managed to exist right next to where the pain was. She was reminded of the time they had left Nairobi because of conflict and thought of Mike, who had shown his beautiful smile when they met again much later. The determination to live was almost always the most prevailing, it appeared.

Akila also thought about a conversation she had had with Seo Hui a while back when they'd started getting closer. That day, they sat by the water, Akila with coffee in her left hand, Seo Hui with a large shake next to her. For a long time, the short woman with the heart-shaped face just looked at the water and then at the people passing by. Her mouth had been set in a tight line and she frowned until her eyebrows had almost met in the middle above her tiny nose. Akila knew that something was going on, but she had waited and hoped that Seo Hui would say it out loud eventually. It took a long time before she spoke. Akila sat next to her, observing how the other woman milled over what was burning inside her.

"Don't you think that this planet is just one confused place?" she finally asked.

Akila inhaled slowly, wondering what had happened for Seo Hui to talk like that. "You can say that," she responded.

"And this place is especially confused!" Seo Hui added. "Confused about everything. I am so tired of it." She violently turned to her shake and sucked at the straw with an even deeper frown.

"What happened?" Akila attempted to understand.

But Seo Hui wasn't ready to say more. Eventually, she stopped slurping and went on, as if Akila hadn't asked the question. "I'm confused about what tradition means. What modernisation means. What women and men should be." She gestured wildly and several pedestrians passing by looked at her with curious expressions.

Seo Hui never elaborated on what had transpired to raise those thoughts, but when Hae In visited a day later, he mentioned that there had been a conflict at work. It had something to do with how much Seo Hui was paid compared to her male colleagues and how she was expected to behave at company outings and team dinners. Hearing Hae In's conversation with Insoo, who looked troubled, gave Akila the chills. Could one never escape the imbalance? Even then, listening to Hae In and Insoo discuss the matter, Akila had felt uneasy because of how random the entire thing seemed, so lacking in logic.

* * *

Akila sighed and returned to the present. Insoo lay right next to her on the large mat that they had removed from inside the house and placed on the wooden deck that offered a great view of the night sky. Here, there weren't many lights at night and the darkness was splattered with uncountable shiny dots. It looked amazing, and Akila's heart ached a little. Ji Su was on the other side of her, shifting slightly to find a more comfortable position. It was past midnight and Talida and Mavis had gone to bed a few hours earlier after they had enjoyed another long walk along the beach and through the little town they had stopped at. They had grabbed some food at a local restaurant and then headed to the place they'd rented.

Akila had enjoyed the light mood, the frequent laughter, the running and jumping, and she had quietly appreciated the many times an arm was around someone else's shoulders. Talida had come up to her, skipping, and put her arm around her with a smile. Ji Su put his arm around Mavis while the boy balanced on top of a short wall and, a moment later, put his other arm around Insoo, who was strolling next to him. Akila observed and appreciated it all, willing herself to keep those moments inside her and remember them later.

Now, on the wooden deck that was still a little warm from the sunshine of the day, the mood had shifted. It was heavier, and she felt as if tension was in the air, although nothing noticeable had happened. Maybe it was inside her? But Akila was sure that Insoo and Ji Su felt it too, even if they might experience the sensation differently.

Deciding that it would be better if she removed herself from whatever it was that was taking shape around her, she sat up. "Getting some water," she explained as she slipped through the glass doors into the house.

She filled a big jar with cool water from the fridge and removed three glasses from the cupboard. When she carefully walked back through the dimly lit living room towards the deck, carrying the jar and glasses on a tray, she could see Insoo and Ji Su sitting in the moonlight. Something made her stop and stand where she was. Insoo had turned away from the other man, and it seemed as if Ji Su looked at him intently.

Akila carefully placed the tray on the small table that stood not far from her, keeping her eyes on Insoo and Ji Su. Suddenly, quickly and unexpectedly, Insoo stood and pulled open the glass doors. He entered the room and came to a halt not far from her, but he didn't seem to have noticed that she was there.

In the same instant, Ji Su jumped up and followed. He grabbed Insoo by the arm, pulling him around with such force that the other almost fell over when he turned.

"What the. . . ." By now, Insoo's shoulders were squared and his back rigid. Akila put a hand over her mouth. Knowing him, she could sense the anger emanating from him and wondered what he would do next. It was rare for him to lose his composure, but he seemed close to exploding.

Insoo was much taller than Ji Su, but the shorter man was fit and muscled, and Akila had already found that he had far fewer mental barriers than most people. He seemed completely fearless at times.

Insoo stepped close to him, their faces almost touching, pushing him, daring him to hold him back from leaving.

But Ji Su did not budge. "What?" he asked. "What? Are you afraid that you will like it when I kiss you?"

There was dead silence for a moment, and Akila could almost hear Insoo's racing heartbeat from where she stood. The two still stood extremely close and appeared to be struggling to hold back what was boiling inside.

Then Insoo pushed Ji Su away with a physical force that Akila hadn't seen in him since the night at the party when he had fought the man who had hurt Seo Hui. The next second, the door hit the wall and he was out in the night.

Akila stood frozen. Then she looked at Ji Su, who was looking at the door, which was still open. She walked over and closed it quietly, silently thanking her children for sleeping so tightly. She had been worried that they had heard the commotion and woken up.

When she turned around, her eyes were on Ji Su again, who looked a little defeated. She felt there was nothing she could say to make it better, so she just hugged him.

"Let's go to bed," Ji Su simply said. Akila was surprised to hear how firm his voice was, almost as if he was saying, "Just wait and see. . . ."

They slept in one bed, with the door to the bedroom open, because Akila was concerned that Insoo would return and not be able to come in. It was only an hour or so later when he turned up outside and softly knocked on the front door. She climbed out of the bed and went to let him in. He stood there in the cool dark, looking embarrassed and apologetic, with his shoulders hunched and letting his hand run over his short hair, as was his habit when unsettled. Akila smiled ever so slightly when she pulled him into the house and shut the door.

They spent the entire next day by the water. First, Akila had been apprehensive that it would be awkward, but although Insoo was very quiet and avoided Ji Su's eyes during breakfast, he was careful not to show too much of his emotions. Akila was grateful for it and announced that it was a beach day, which was welcomed by cheers from Talida and Mavis and made Ji Su smile. They walked along the ocean line and jumped into the water, which was quite chilly. They sat in the sand and looked up at the blue of the sky. They ate seafood and held their faces into the sunshine with closed eyes. Insoo bought a ball in one of the shops in the little town and spent hours playing football with Mavis. Ji Su joined for a while. Talida and Akila strode to a lighthouse that stood high and pretty at the end of the bay.

When evening came and Talida and Mavis had said good night, Akila stood up from the couch where she had been sitting between both Insoo and Ji Su and said "I think it's time you two talk." And with that, she went off to bed.

She was sure that she'd seen fear in Insoo's eyes before she left, and in her mind, she asked him not to run again.

* * *

There was silence between them after Akila had left and Insoo felt how stiff his own back was. The sound of his heartbeat rang in his ears.

He wasn't sure how much time had passed when Ji Su moved over and reduced the space between them to nothing. They sat so close together that Insoo could feel the warmth coming from Ji Su. He thought that the other man's eyes were on him, and Insoo had to look the other way, afraid of what Ji Su might be able to see. Or was he afraid of what he would spot in Ji Su's eyes?

For a brief moment, Insoo considered putting distance between them, but he didn't move.

Then Ji Su gently put his fingers on his cheek and forced Insoo to face him.

Insoo's chest was heaving by now, and he pressed his body against the sofa, not sure if he wanted to run or push him away . . . but again, he didn't move.

Ji Su's lips carefully made contact with his skin, kissing his left eyebrow, then his right eyebrow gently. And Insoo helplessly clutched the couch when their mouths met.

So many reasons why

Insoo sat in the folding chair staring across the lake.

It was a slightly gloomy day and they were having trouble shooting the scheduled scenes with the desired lighting. The director had called for a break after being too frustrated with the fact that the scene he envisioned didn't turn out the way he wanted, mainly due to the many clouds covering the sky today. He was someone who preferred as natural lighting as possible for his shoots, but this Friday's weather hadn't wanted to cooperate.

However, Insoo felt that the rather grey atmosphere and the sense of frustration that hung over the crew matched his mood.

He didn't mind just sitting in the folding chair with his light coat around his shoulders, his gaze wandering across the water. The silver-grey light seemed to be casting a desolate sense of empty spaces across the landscape, and the whole scene was beautiful in its own right. One could sense the sun just behind the cloud cover, and there were places where it pierced through the greyness with sharp, bright bands of light that travelled over the waters of the lake in front of Insoo and changed every second as the shape of the billowing clouds above changed.

There were so many reasons why this wouldn't work and why stopping was probably the better choice. He milled over that thought for a while, but eventually, he stood up, having decided instead to go fetch the book his father had gifted him for his birthday and which he hadn't started reading yet. Today seemed like a good day to cultivate his love for books. He was thinking of Talida and her deep affection for books when he arrived in front of the trailer he used as his dressing room while on these outdoor shoots. The way she had been full of amazement and gentleness when they visited his father's bookshop one afternoon had made him think that he should probably revisit how he felt about his family at times.

On the way to the trailer, he met several of the crew, greeting them all with a warm smile and a polite nod. Most of them seemed slightly restless, not happy with the sudden halt in shooting simply because of the light. His fellow lead had disappeared, mumbling that she needed rest.

He'd been content, being left alone with the view of the lake to himself, and he was still somewhat in a different mind space when he was about to open the door and suddenly noticed Ji Su.

A jolt went through him at the sight of the other man who stood confidently, hands in the front pockets of his jeans.

They hadn't really talked since the trip they had taken with Akila and her children. One reason was that Insoo had to leave for his next shoot almost immediately, but probably more so because Insoo didn't know what to say or what to do around Ji Su just now. After what had happened between them, he was confused, not sure what it was he felt amidst all the other emotions he harboured these days. The storm around him had quieted down, but inside Insoo it was still howling with deafening intensity and he was afraid that Ji Su's presence would just add to the noise that wore him out. So seeing him here on set, more than an hour's drive from Seoul on a random Friday, shook Insoo in ways he had not anticipated.

Ji Su's eyes seemed to scrutinise him, his expression serious with his chin slightly to the front, as if he was chewing on something he didn't like at all. Was he here to argue?

Insoo stood rooted to the spot by the door of the trailer, only able to return the gaze.

Then Ji Su moved, striding over to him so quickly that, by the time his lips met his and his hands were all over him, Insoo had had no time to decide on anything. But Ji Su's lips were warm and soft and his hands seemed to respond to the emptiness and exhaustion Insoo had been feeling so acutely whenever left alone. Somehow, the two of them managed to enter the trailer and Insoo wondered later how that had been possible. The only recollection he had was of how it had felt to be with Ji Su again.

* * *

Ji Su was on his way back to Seoul. It was getting dark and the lights of his car illuminated the road in front of him. He had put on some music to accompany the feeling in his heart. His heart was filled to the brim, almost exploding.

When he finally walked through the gate of Insoo's house, having spent some time in the evening traffic, the windows were throwing squares of warm yellow light at him. It was as if the house welcomed him with open arms.

Inside, Akila sat at Insoo's desk, still working. Music played here too.

Akila looked up from her laptop and smiled "Hey. How was it? How is Insoo?"

Ji Su smiled back, but instead of responding, he looked around. "Where are Talida and Mavis?"

"Mavis went for a sleepover at Ji Min's house and Talida is in her room, reading. And chatting with Michael, I guess."

He nodded. His heart was so full, that he wondered if it would burst. He looked down at Akila, with untidy hair, wide tunica, and large glasses on her nose. She glanced back at him and shifted on her chair. Her eyebrows went up questioningly. What was she seeing on his face?

For a moment, Ji Su just stood, realising what he was feeling—that he was finally conquering it all. And then he stepped around Insoo's desk and bent down. Their faces were so close. Her eyes were wide and unwavering, almost as if she was about to kick him. She did not. Even when he put his arms around her and let his lips touch her neck, she did not.

"I wonder if this is a mess," she said the next day in the morning. "I mean, the three of us."

They were clearing the kitchen after having had their breakfast with Talida. Mavis was still at his friend's place and would only return later that Saturday.

There was a girl from the neighbour's house who was roughly Talida's age and who had stopped them on the road just a few days back, shyly and politely making conversation with Talida. And today, the two of them met for the first time. The two girls sat outside in the morning sun, talking in a mixture of Korean and English, which seemed to work just as well.

Ji Su, who was wiping down the counter, briefly glanced at Akila. "I don't feel like it is a mess."

Akila agreed. She didn't feel like it was a mess, either, but she could see how it could turn into one. "You know that we don't live alone in this world," she mumbled, trying to explain what she was thinking.

"We never do," Ji Su responded.

He straightened up, having completed his task. "I am leaving for practice. Do you still want me to pick up Mavis later on?"

"That would be awesome."

"Cool. We'll see you in the evening then."

And with that, they parted ways and jumped into the new day.

* * *

Akila stood with her phone in her hand and looked over the small front yard of Insoo's house and the steep road beyond the gate. There were millions of rooftops stretched out across the hills of Seoul, and somewhere further down in the valley were the skyscrapers. She hadn't allowed her tears to fall while on the call, but now that she was by herself, she couldn't contain them and they flowed freely, winding their way down her cheeks.

In a hospital in Nairobi, Joyce held her phone as well, holding on very tight until her already exhausted hand hurt and she had to let go. Her phone dropped to the floor and she looked down at it, startled. A nurse passing by quickly bent and picked it up for her. With some relief, Joyce registered that the screen hadn't cracked. "Stupid," she told herself the next second. "Who cares about a cracked screen?" But she tried to hold back the tears that filled her to the brim. She blinked quickly a few times and it seemed a little easier.

Sometimes in moments like these, Joyce wondered why her life unfolded the way it did. Was it that, if someone was strong, the world threw all kinds of rubbish at them, knowing they would probably be able to handle it and go on? Or was she just one of these unfortunate people who always ended up in situations that turned out dramatic?

No need to dwell on it. Akila and Joyce had talked about it before. Her life was great material for a soap opera, so she would just go on acting. Now that she'd managed to survive for more than thirty years in this world, she could manage a few more.

One of the nurses called her to come in. She stood up slowly, still feeling extremely sore, especially around the area where they had cut her open for the emergency caesarean. Joyce passed the sliding doors and followed the nurse up to the incubator that contained the small spark of life that they'd removed from her a few hours ago.

Gazing through the glass box, her heart ached like it had never before. Her baby was so tiny and delicate, forced into this world far too early, obviously not ready for what he had been confronted with. There were tubes and needles, and Joyce asked herself how such a small body would be able to take it. The small fingers were folded into fists, and his arms and legs had absolutely no fat–not like most other babies she had seen when they were born at full term. Where would he find the strength to fight?

"Joyce. . . ."

She was startled when she suddenly felt her husband's hands on her shoulders. She hadn't realised that Adam had walked up to her. Together, they stood there for a very long time. To Joyce, it felt as if they were together, but still utterly alone.

* * *

Akila was still on the rooftop, with her tears. What to do? she wondered, like many other times in her life. Fly straight to Nairobi? It seemed very hard for some reason. Maybe because of the emotions that she knew would linger in every corner around her friend because of the pain she would have to face, that fear when your child is not fit to live. Akila knew too well how frightening that was.

After Talida, Mavis, and Akila had moved to Scotland, Akila went back to Kenya not too long afterward. It was for a friend's wedding, and she went alone for a short week, leaving her children with Rose and Edith.

The wedding was in the middle of a nature reserve, with the most amazing sweeping views over the golden grass on the plains and the silhouettes of umbrella acacias completing the scenery to perfection. It was an outside garden wedding below a beige canvas, and on the day of the wedding, cars flocked down the reddish dirt road and released women, men, and children in colourful suits and dresses and smart leather shoes, high heels, and glittering sandals. But everyone had spotted the black clouds billowing across the endless sky, and by the time the ceremony began, the first drops fell.

When the wedding congregation arrived at the reception, the canvas, flowers, and tablecloths were all drenched and covered in mud. So were the wedding guests. Colourful floral dresses were covered with splatters of water and soil, and suits and shirts were dark from wetness. Toes in sandals were covered in mud that concealed the shiny nail polish. Umbrellas that were meant to shield from the sun now came in handy to protect from the water that poured from the sky.

The bride's long wedding dress was reddish-brown all around the hem. She had tried to keep it away from the ground but to no avail.

The wedding congregation gathered in a small cottage that the owner of the grounds allowed them to use because she was probably pitying the young couple whose big day was about to be drowned mercilessly. "Rain is always a blessing," she tried to comfort them. "Look at it as a sign of your fertile relationship!"

The crowd squeezed into the small house and what food had been rescued from the downpour was served to the guests. The DJ put up his portable speaker, and soon after, music was playing and drinks were passed around. It took less than thirty minutes before the clapping of hands, slapping of thighs, and tapping of feet on the floor had turned into a full-blown party. People whistled, shaking their bodies, singing along. In the general noise, Akila and her friend Joyce sat next to each other on a small sofa in one corner. Akila had her arm around her friend and Joyce's head rested on her shoulder. Her hands covered her belly protectively–her belly in which there grew a tiny speck of life, so tiny that she was still afraid to believe that it was there.

She had looked into her tall friend's eyes when she and her husband had picked her up from the airport and asked her, "Can it be true?"

Akila had gazed at her with the usual intensity and without a hint of a smile on her face, only determination, when she responded. "It must be true."

This was the third time.

First, there had been hormonal treatment for weeks on end that made Joyce feel like she was a stranger in her own body. Then the procedure to remove the evil growth inside her. Then came the removal of the eggs, hoping, and praying for them to be strong enough to stay alive. Waiting for them to grow. Then planting the egg. Waiting for the signs of pregnancy. Feeling elated–feeling sure that there was something . . . but no.

Two times she went through the whole thing and nothing happened. It was as if she was simply not right for it.

It was so hard to keep the self-loathing at bay–so hard to smile at the reassuring words of her husband. So hard to stay positive and to go about her everyday life. To keep a straight face when people asked when the first baby would finally arrive.

There were days when she felt so exhausted that she just wanted to drop down exactly where she was and not ever move again.

She didn't know what kept her going, but she did keep going. Now was the third try, and there had been a flicker of life within her that had refused to be rejected, and Joyce told it constantly to hang in there, to keep growing until it was strong and big and could overcome anything and everything.

Sometimes, on days when she didn't feel so down, she would call Akila and they would talk and agree on how important it was to stay positive. Still, when Joyce hung up the phone, she felt full of sadness, not determination. Akila must have known, because sometimes she simply told her, "If you can't take it anymore, just stop. It is your body and your choice." But even that was hard because it didn't feel as if her body was only her own or as if the choice was just hers.

The two women sat on the small sofa in the middle of the noise and dancing and talked. They hadn't talked like that for a very long time, and it was like warmth spreading through their wet and cold limbs and flowing into their hearts.

Akila remembered that moment at the wedding that had been blessed with rain, and she had to abruptly sit on the stairs of Insoo's house and ask the hazy Seoul air to please, please, please let the little boy live.

* * *

"Mama, I don't want to change schools again," Talida said. They all sat around the table in Insoo's front yard eating lunch. Movements seemed to slow down for a second after her statement or at least Talida felt like that. But maybe it was also all just in her mind like she knew so many things were.

She knew by now that she experienced the world differently, with sounds being more pronounced and certain spaces, especially the proximity to human beings, feeling much tinier to her compared to how others seemed to experience them. So she wasn't sure if her statement had really made an impact or if she had just imagined it.

Her mother looked at her from behind her large glasses. She wore a slight frown on her face but otherwise did not appear upset. Mavis observed his elder sister while chewing, but didn't say anything. Talida's gaze quickly turned to Insoo, who had put his chopsticks down and seemed to wear an encouraging smile on his face. So Talida took a deep breath and went on. "We've just settled down and I like our home. And South Korea is nice, but," she gestured, "Seoul is so big. . . . Just in case you are thinking of moving again." She briefly glanced at her mother. Talida didn't want to make her sad, but she also did not want to move to Seoul.

Eventually, her mother nodded.

Mavis, who had been quietly, but quickly, eating his food as usual, lifted his head. "I want to stay," he announced.

Everyone around the table looked at the boy. His blonde afro bounced as he spoke with determination. "I want to dance with Ji Su."

Ji Su smiled at him. Mavis had spent several mornings and afternoons with him at the studio, observing the team as they practised for his dance videos and copying their steps whenever he got the chance.

Talida frowned at her brother and said, "But it's not just about you."

He frowned back at her. "And it's also not just about you!"

He was already raising his voice, and Akila knew that the next level was probably a verbal battle between the siblings. "Okay, let's stop here!" she interrupted them. "Let's eat and talk about it later."

Talida had teary eyes when she turned to Akila. She couldn't help it. "Whatever you say, I won't stay!" She stood abruptly, making her chair fall backward, and went into the house. A moment later she was in her room and slammed the door loudly, hoping that they all heard the anger in the bang.

She dropped onto her bed and stared at the ceiling. It wasn't that Seoul was such a horrible place. Sure, the city was huge, and she would always prefer the countryside. But Insoo's house felt like a home already and she felt comfortable around him, Ji Su, and the other friends frequenting the house. They had done many interesting things so far, and she liked the beauty of what she had seen.

But still, she couldn't deny that the feeling of being different was even more pronounced here. It wasn't a feeling she experienced when she was around those close to her, but as soon as she left and ventured into the outside world, she could feel it acutely. The eyes focused on her. The quiet comments. Of course, this had always been a part of her life and she didn't hate it. Although it was exhausting.

In Scotland, Michael had become her second half, someone who understood what she felt–the mixture of irritation and pleasure caused by the attention. They were so far apart now. Who would be her second half if not him? If they moved, what would happen? And what about Rose and Edith and their pretty cottage? How was it that her mother seemed to find it so easy to leave everything behind and not look back?

After lunch, Akila sat on the rooftop of Insoo's house and thought. It was sunny and there was warmth on her face. There was a wide bench made out of palettes with many pillows of all sizes below a small roof on top of Insoo's house, an area they were able to use now that the days were filled with the pleasure of higher temperatures. Sitting up here, Akila could take in the sweeping views across the many rooftops surrounding her and could even see the high-rise buildings further down the valley and the sparkling waters of the Han River, which wound its way slowly across the city.

Akila could relate to her daughter's emotions. Weeks had passed by and they were still in Seoul, when initially they had only been talking about a few weeks during Talida's and Mavis' holidays and a couple of days after that.

What should she do? She couldn't ignore Talida's preferences. It was impossible for her to feel peaceful happiness when her child wasn't fine. At the same time, it felt exactly right to be in this place at this time. And Mavis seemed happy too. How could she ignore that side of the coin?

Then there was the additional fact she couldn't ignore–the fact that her children were meant to be in school. She had started compiling homeschooling materials, but she wondered if such a model would work for them.

Rose was on the phone, smiling at her on the video call. "Everything is fine with your little cottage," she reported. "I think the garden looks so much better since I can decide what to do with it," she said in an attempt to tease her friend.

Akila grinned back at her and said, "Make sure it looks wild by the time we get back. You know I like it wild."

"Ahhhhhh! Naughty Akila. She likes the wild things!"

Akila couldn't help but laugh.

Rose was obviously in a great mood, being ready to joke around like that. She fixed her eyes on Akila. "But I thought this cottage was turning into your holiday home anyway, so you can let me have my way with your garden. You were meant to be back ages ago. What's the plan?"

Akila sighed. It took a while before she felt ready to respond. "No idea," she finally said. "I don't seem to know how to bring it all together and make it one coherent thing."

Rose looked at her with something that seemed to Akila to be concern, but also compassion. And that made her feel good, but also a little irritated, because she felt vulnerable when being looked at like that. She realised how much she despised it when she didn't know the answers to her own questions.

* * *

A week later, Mrs. Moon walked into the house. She rarely turned up without prior notice, so Insoo had never minded that his mother knew the password for his front door. Insoo had come home from another shoot the previous night, and it had been a rather slow morning for all of them.

Mrs. Moon walked in and stood, staring at the shirtless Ji Su, who was in the kitchen preparing coffee. Akila was next to him, setting up different dishes for their late breakfast. Mavis and his friend, Ji Min, ran past swinging paper swords and shouting at full volume. Noticing Mrs. Moon's eyes on them, they all stopped and stared back at her. Even Talida who had been stretched out on the couch reading, noticed the shift in atmosphere and lifted her head to check what was going on.

After taking in the scene, Mrs. Moon released a shaky breath and turned to her son, who had just come up the corridor from his room, observing his mother. "I will call you," was all she told him, and walked out.

Insoo hated the feeling of discomfort in his heart when he saw his mother's face. It was almost a feeling of guilt for how he was living. But why? When he was with them, when he came home and there were all the noises they made, he was content. But as soon as the world seemed to point fingers and frown at how he lived these days, all the contentment and the strength he was sure he had in him flooded out as if someone had pulled the plug. And how to say it when Akila and Ji Su seemed to be so sure about everything and didn't appear to harbour any of the worries that sometimes kept him from finding sleep?

Later, he sat on the couch in his parent's living room, not sure how he should go about this conversation.

"Insoo!" His mother stared at him with her pleading eyes, the ones that her son feared the most. "Things have just gotten better! Why wouldn't you shield yourself from further damage? Haven't we all suffered enough agony this past year?" She abruptly covered her face with one hand. "I'm not sure I can take it again . . . the fear . . . the worry. . . ." His mother took a deep breath and turned her back on her son.

He totally understood his mother's concerns because he'd thought about them a lot as well over the last few weeks. He was sure that the safer path was to stop. And all the worries he had about it were wearing him out. But he knew deep down that he didn't have the true determination it would take to end it.

* * *

Talida stared at her mother and hoped that she was able to put all her resentment into her eyes. "I told you!" she screamed at her. "I told you I don't want to change schools again! And I told you I don't want to move!" She felt tears rushing down her face like a flood. "See what happened!"

She threw herself against the door of the room that she occupied in Insoo's house and then put as much force as possible into slamming it shut. Inside the room, she felt that the space was too small for her boiling emotions, and she started grabbing clothes, books, school materials, anything she could get her hands on and ripped and slashed and threw.

When she was hot and out of breath, she didn't stop, but took hold of the pillows and the blanket on her bed and whirled them off the mattress. One pillow caught the light on the nightstand, and it came crashing down onto the ground with a loud sound that made her feel a sense of satisfaction.

The door opened and Akila stood in the doorframe. Talida could see the irritation on her mother's face. She knew that Akila didn't like it when someone let their emotions out without any consideration for the others around. At that moment, Talida hated her for it. Breathing heavily, she stood, part of the blanket and one pillow still in hand, glaring at her mother. Just when Akila opened her mouth and Talida was sure that she would say things that would defeat and hurt her instantly and leave her feeling exhausted and empty, Insoo appeared behind Akila and put one hand on her shoulder. Akila closed her mouth and looked at him in obvious confusion. He then wrapped his arm around her waist, gently pulled Akila out of the room, and closed the door. Seconds later, Talida was alone, not sure how she should feel about that. To some extent, she had wanted the collision with Akila.

After standing in the middle of the havoc she had caused for another few minutes, not sure what to do next, she sat down on her bed, letting her blanket and the pillow drop to the floor. How could it be true? How was it possible that Michael didn't want to be connected with her anymore in the way they had been connected for so long? How was it that he didn't want to feel the familiarity anymore? She couldn't wrap her head around it. The hole that he left was already growing inside her, showing itself with a painful clarity that left her paralyzed.

Insoo slipped into her room without making a sound, just like the cat she often compared him to–quiet, observant, and only approaching when he wanted to. Insoo carefully sat down next to Talida.

Feeling embarrassed about the uncontrollable way she was sobbing and about her running nose, she turned away from him. But when the tears didn't want to stop and she felt as if the hole that was growing inside her would consume her, she pulled her legs up onto her bed and rested her head on his thigh. Lying there with her head in his lap, she kept her eyes tightly shut.

* * *

Akila sat on the rooftop, glaring at the view. It was a glare, she knew because she was so upset that her heart rate was still so fast after several minutes of sitting motionlessly that she could not find it in herself to enjoy the panorama she usually appreciated so much.

It felt so bad whenever Talida and her collided, even more so because it didn't happen a lot. But when it happened, it was a full-blown storm of emotions. Akila asked herself if Talida felt what she had felt for a while during puberty–the need to put distance between her mother and herself. It had often resulted in her being incredibly irritated with Katarina, followed by a feeling of guilt for feeling that way.

Was Talida going through the same thing? Right now, she didn't like her mother very much, and that made Akila sad. She wondered how responsible she should feel about what had happened with Michael. Was her way of life to blame?

Ji Su came up the small metal staircase and sat down next to her. Although she had the full view of the front yard and the steep road beyond the wall that surrounded Insoo's house, she had not noticed when he arrived and walked through the gate. He briefly flashed a smile at her, then just sat, letting his gaze travel over the city in front of them.

Akila thought about how a person was always quite alone with their feelings, no matter how much one tried to make others understand. Still, it was soothing her heart a little when Ji Su put his arm around her.

The next morning, Talida walked out of her room and into the kitchen. Her mother was there preparing her coffee as usual. Talida stood for a moment, observing Akila. It was strange to experience the mix of emotions she felt at times, the deep affection and, at the same time, a longing for something else, maybe something a little more conventional. She wasn't exactly sure what she wished for sometimes.

Talida sighed deeply, then strode over to her mother and hugged her, putting her cheek on her strong back. She closed her eyes.

Akila, only now realising the presence of her daughter, slowed down, then stood completely still.

After a long moment, Talida said, "Let's just stay." She took a deep breath. "Anywhere is fine. Homeschooling is fine."

Akila turned around and hugged her daughter tightly. She noticed the sound of defeat in Talida's voice. And she knew that after a while she would have to pick up the topic again. But for now, she wasn't sure if she had any words in her that would make Talida feel better, so she just held her, kissed her, and asked her what she wanted for breakfast.

* * *

Weeks passed and warmth spread across Seoul's streets, causing the city's inhabitants to seek cooling shade whenever possible.

Insoo's house was still filled with the same sounds that made him feel content and scared at the same time. But he had learned early in his life how to live with conflicting emotions, and even now it made it possible to carry on: When Akila put on her music, and Mavis and Talida danced and jumped through the living room. When Ji Su unleashed his unbelievable laughter at the world. It all made him feel like it was worth carrying on.

Ma Ru had managed to secure a couple of new interesting deals for him. His fanbase was growing. Critics praised his latest work. Insoo knew that he should be as happy as his manager about the progress they were making. But the truth was that he experienced a sense of doom when he was alone as if something lurked just beyond his comfort zone waiting to pounce at him.

He wasn't sure why. Was it because of his mother's pleading eyes or because some of his acquaintances, colleagues, and even fans had openly shown their disapproval of his lifestyle? Why should it matter? He wasn't sure.

Collision

Ma Ru looked at Akila and Ji Su. They were sitting in the front yard, deep in conversation. Music was playing and Mavis, Akila's son, was sitting on the ground with another boy, probably of similar age, laughing and chatting animatedly.

They hadn't even noticed him opening the gate and didn't seem concerned with anything other than what was going on in their tiny world.

Ma Ru couldn't help but envy them a little.

But he pulled himself together and reminded himself why he was here. Things needed to be set straight.

Since Akila's first visit had gone so wrong, and especially since their conversation when he had asked her to leave, their relationship had been rather reserved. She seemed to avoid him as much as possible, although she was always extremely polite whenever they ran into each other.

In any case, Ma Ru knew that they simply looked at the world with different eyes and that they had different values. She constantly seemed to question the direction in which Insoo was to go and made him hesitate or turn the other way.

And these days the house was full of noise every time he stopped by, children running around, Ji Su inviting his dance crew over as if the house was his, and Akila frequently sitting at Insoo's desk with her laptop as if it was her workspace now.

Too little time for Insoo to focus.

And today what he had expected, but also dreaded, had happened. Pictures of Ji Su and Insoo were all over the internet. Insoo's image still depended a lot on the sex appeal so many women associated with him, and the rumours about him living with a much older, foreign woman and with Kang Ji Su were damaging in the scariest way. Would they go through the whole ordeal of making the headlines again, only this time in the worst way imaginable?

And here Akila and Ji Su sat, looking content, happy to be with Insoo. Of course, who would not be? Ma Ru couldn't afford for the brand they had built all these years to be broken into pieces within hours. This had to stop today.

He took a deep breath and walked over to where Akila and Ji Su sat. They'd pulled their chairs close to the old wooden table that had been in the front yard since Insoo's birthday and were focused on a laptop, taking notes and exchanging thoughts on what they saw.

They both looked up in surprise when he greeted them politely and offered a bow. Ji Su stood briefly to return the gesture of respect and bowed too. Akila nodded her head slightly, acknowledging his respectful, but also distanced greeting.

"Mr. Kwon. Welcome," Akila said, offering him a seat next to her.

The short man could barely hide his irritation. How was it that she always sounded as if this was her house and he was the guest passing by?

Ji Su paused the video they had been watching. Ma Ru got a glimpse of Ji Su and the dance crew he was working with on the screen. They'd probably been working on his dance project. The realisation that they were sitting in Insoo's front yard working on making Ji Su successful while Insoo's career and well-being were in danger because of their careless behaviour angered him.

"Has your agency contacted you?" Ma Ru addressed Ji Su after he had settled down on the very edge of the chair Akila had offered him. The surprised look on Ji Su's face told Ma Ru what he had been suspecting. The other man didn't know yet.

Akila and Ji Su exchanged a quick glance. Then Ji Su asked, "What is going on? Where is Insoo?"

There was urgency in his voice, which Ma Ru noticed with some satisfaction. So he did care, after all. Akila wore a frown on her face and her eyes were wide. Ma Ru said, "I cannot believe that your agency is taking this so lightly. This is not a joke. Or at least not for Insoo. . . ."

"Mr. Kwon, can you stop talking in riddles and tell us what's going on?" Akila interrupted, her voice sharp like a razor blade.

Ma Ru swallowed, slightly taken aback. It still shook him, the way she could change when angered. He turned the laptop that was on the table in front of them so that he could type Insoo's name in the search engine. The images turned up almost instantly. Ma Ru's earlier fury returned and he fixed his cold stare on Ji Su. "What were you thinking?" he asked, not able to keep his voice steady.

Akila and Ji Su both looked at the screen in obvious disbelief. Then Akila put her hand on Ji Su's shoulder and faced Ma Ru. Her eyes remained wide, but her expression was unreadable, much calmer than Ma Ru had expected. "Where's Insoo? He left for the shoot in the morning. Does he know about this?"

Ma Ru shook his head. "Not yet, but as soon as he looks at his phone and sees my message, he will. I didn't want to distract him. But I am already discussing it with the production company of the program he is shooting for." He glanced at Ji Su, wanting to make him understand how responsible he was for the mess. "This is bad for him. The production company was already thinking of dropping him because of the earlier headlines. This might be the final push they need. You are not an amateur. What were you thinking?" His voice had gotten louder towards the end of the sentence and he realised that he was out of breath.

Ji Su didn't seem to have heard him. He was still looking at the pictures on the screen and he bit his lower lip, seeming unsettled and worried. Akila had her eyes on him and, seeing his reaction, moved closer and put her entire arm around him. Mavis and his friend had stopped playing, looking at the adults with questioning expressions on their faces. Akila frowned at Ma Ru. "Keep it down! There is no need to make a scene in front of the children."

* * *

Ji Su gazed at Akila. "My phone," he said and she stood up quickly, fetching Ji Su's phone from the other end of the table. He took it, checked the display, and looked up at them. "My agency has called several times."

They hadn't heard the phone, too absorbed in what they were working on. He dialled the number and stood up, too restless to sit any longer.

While Ji Su talked on the phone, Akila took her phone and called Talida, who was out with Seo Hui and Hae In. "Talida, Ji Su, and I need to go see Insoo quickly. Can you guys come over and be with Mavis and Ji Min?"

"What's going on, Mama?" the girl sounded worried.

"Some story about Insoo and Ji Su is out. Tell Seo Hui and Hae In to check online. Not sure how bad it will get."

"'Kay. . . ."

"I will call you later. Don't worry too much."

"We are coming home," Talida responded.

Akila hung up the phone and then went over to Mavis and Ji Min to let them know that they were leaving but that Talida was on her way. She fetched her keys from the kitchen counter. Her heart was beating fast, but her mind was completely clear. Kwon Ma Ru was standing by the time she came back from inside the house, a stern expression on his face. "What do you think you are doing?" he asked her. "There is no way you two can go near Insoo on the set right now."

She stared at Insoo's manager for a moment, wondering whether what she felt was true dislike. The man had turned into someone she would rather not have to see. She decided to do her best to ignore him. Ji Su was pacing, still speaking on the phone.

Akila hugged Mavis and smiled encouragingly at Ji Min. "Take care of yourselves for a few minutes. Talida will be here in a few."

She gave Ji Su a sign and he nodded, following her with the phone pressed to his ear.

"Keys," she mouthed at him and he pointed at his black leather jacket on the back of the chair. She picked up the jacket and they walked toward the gate.

"Ms. Akila! Kang Ji Su!" Mr. Kwon shouted, and Akila thought how it was completely unsuitable for the short man in the meticulous suit to behave that way. "This is unacceptable! What do you think you are doing?" Ma Ru hurled his words at them.

Ji Su was already walking through the gate, making an effort to focus on the conversation on the phone. Akila turned, blocking Mr. Kwon's way out. "What!" She was truly angry now and worried for every minute that passed, which increased the chances of Insoo being confronted with what was going on with no one around to catch him if he felt like falling.

She fumbled for the car keys in Ji Su's jacket and unlocked the car which was parked outside Insoo's gate. Ji Su got in on the passenger's side. As Akila moved to get into the car on the driver's side, Insoo's manager suddenly grabbed her arm but let go immediately as she looked first at his fingers on her skin and then into his eyes.

"You are making it worse if you go there now!" he exclaimed. "Can't you see that I just want the best for him too?"

Akila was slightly shaken by Mr. Kwon's human side showing up unexpectedly when she had just decided to dislike him without any regrets.

She took a deep breath and then retorted, "And can't you see that leaving him alone just now is exactly what we shouldn't do? I can't believe you came *here* instead of rushing to be with him, even if Mr. Park is around." She stared at him for a moment longer, then turned and got in the car, starting the engine as soon as she was in.

Ji Su said, "Yes, agreed," in Korean, and hung up. He just stared ahead without looking at her, his head resting on the car seat. Again, he bit his lip and Akila, who glanced at him briefly as she took the winding, steep roads towards the highway, knew that he was truly worried.

✶ ✶ ✶

Insoo and his female colleague were in the middle of the scene scheduled for the day when something changed. He didn't notice at first, totally immersed in the emotions he was feeling as the character he was impersonating. He held her, feeling all the pain that came with not being able to be with her. They both cried.

But there was a moment when he became aware of the slight sense of restlessness and redirected focus that seemed to be taking shape around him. And his concentration disappeared. He was distracted by something he could not yet name. His partner had noticed, and she looked up at him with questioning eyes and raised eyebrows.

He shook his head ever so slightly and mumbled, "Not sure...."

They stood up straight and looked around, then at the director, who seemed to have just received a message from a smart-looking man in an expensive blue suit. Insoo could see the frustration on the director's face.

"Break for now!" came the call an instant later, and the majority of the crew on set seemed as confused as Insoo was while others appeared to know something, whispering and glancing at each other. *Did they also look at me?* he was wondering when he heard the director call his name. He didn't sound pleased.

"What's going on, Insoo?" his colleague asked, worried. They all knew how shaky his part as the male lead in the drama was since the scandal surrounding his eating disorder and his comments on the industry.

"I really don't know," he responded before he made his way toward the director, whose face was a mask of barely contained anger.

The director, a short, rather round man with a beard and greying hair, had stood up already and was motioning for Insoo to follow him. A sense of fear gripped Insoo. This wasn't a good sign. Insoo briefly signalled to a worried-looking Mr. Park to wait and set out to follow the director.

The other man in the blue suit followed them, too, and they ended up in front of Insoo's dressing room trailer. With a jolt, Insoo remembered that the man, whose name he did not know, was representing the production company working with them on the drama. Insoo's heart beat hard in his chest while he unlocked the trailer.

Inside, the director slapped Insoo's dressing table with the baseball cap he had worn, apparently to relieve some of the boiling emotions he had been keeping inside. "Don't you have any brains?" he growled at Insoo, who was truly unsettled. "I told you to lay low!" the older man shouted at him. "Is this your definition of that? Last time you had people's sympathy but this time. . . ."

The man in the suit had noticed Insoo's confused expression and released a sarcastic-sounding little giggle, which Insoo thought was unsuitable given how elegantly he was dressed. "Director, I don't think he knows yet." With one fluid movement, he removed his large smartphone from his inside pocket and typed then showed Insoo the screen.

Insoo looked. At first, he didn't understand what he was seeing, but then, with a rush of heat that made his ears and cheeks feel extremely hot, he recognized what the pictures were. The man scrolled for him, watching him with a tiny, ironic smile plastered to his face. Or so it seemed to Insoo. And Insoo saw it all, the physicality and intimacy of the images hitting him. He suddenly felt so weak that he had to sit down. His breath was going shakily because his heart seemed to be stumbling, not remembering how to pump blood properly. His face was on fire. Was that how shame felt?

He covered his eyes with one hand and let out an unstable breath. Someone was talking to him, but he couldn't listen–didn't want to listen. For what? It was all useless anyway.

"Naturally, you are dropped. We were very clear that we wouldn't accept any further scandals."

Was it satisfaction he heard in the other man's voice? Was he happy to see him defeated? He tried to zone out and not hear the voice.

Someone touched his shoulder. He started, ready to jump–ready to run. It was the director. "Insoo. . . ."

Was there pity in his eyes?

Insoo was suddenly furious–so furious, that he realised in a split second that he might not be able to contain the energy that was building up inside him. He couldn't explain exactly what pushed him over the edge, it all happened so fast. The sleek man in the suit, looking at him as if he were a piece of trash. The director, looking at him as if he was to be pitied. Who were they to look at these images and dare judge him for it? He stood suddenly and the unexpected force of it made the director stumble backward with a surprised and helpless gasp.

"No need to get emotional," Insoo heard out of the sly man's mouth, who was looking down at his white shirt where he'd noticed something that needed to be brushed off. "You should have been more careful. Anyway, I don't get it. You can have any girl you like. Why go for . . . that. . . ." His tone was deeply dismissive when he uttered the last word.

Insoo knew that he was strong. The many years of Judo, all the injuries, and all the daily workouts had shown him the abilities and the boundaries of his body. So when he extended his arm, grabbed the elegantly dressed man by his collar, and pushed him against the dressing table, he knew what he could do and what he wanted to do. He heard no sound other than hot blood rushing through his veins and pulsing in his ears. And it felt good, seeing how the man's face changed when he realised that he was unable to move. It felt good to be the one to decide what to do with this person. The first blow didn't hit the man's face but the mirror next to him which exploded into dozens of shards. And just like the mirror crumbled, all the man's confidence seemed to crumble, and he lifted his arms over his head in an attempt to protect himself from Insoo.

Good. Insoo's fist was up for a second blow when there was a sudden movement in the air and something hit him so hard that he had to let go of the man and stumbled to the side. Insoo turned and sought his balance as quickly as possible, worried that a second attack might come.

But the person who stood in front of him, chest heaving and jaw set, was the person who was in the pictures with him. Ji Su was looking at him but didn't say anything. It was Akila, who appeared behind him, whose lips were moving. Slowly, the sound came flooding back to him and Insoo could hear her say, "Insoo, let's just go … please." She came over and took him by his wrist, pulling him with her. And he followed, suddenly feeling defeated.

Insoo caught a glimpse of the director in one corner, looking sad as he slowly sat down on the bench that stretched along the entire side of the trailer.

The man in the suit mumbled with a shaky voice, "You will regret this. You people can't be allowed to live."

Akila stopped on her way down the steps and laid her wide, unwavering eyes on the man. The man flinched, making an effort to move away from her. She didn't take her eyes off the man. Still holding Insoo by his wrist, she slowly turned around to face him fully. Her features expressed something that Insoo had never seen before in her, and it scared him that he had unleashed it.

Ji Su appeared again and, squeezing himself past them, blocked Akila's way back into the trailer. He took her hand, pulling her and Insoo along and out into the sunshine.

Insoo was blinded by the sudden warm light. It was unbelievable that a day like this had existed all around him, given how he had felt inside the enclosed space of the trailer. There were people outside, obviously wanting to know what was going on. They had probably heard the commotion or seen the images online by now. Or both. Insoo felt as if his legs might not be able to carry him anymore. But before he could fall, Ji Su had put his arm around his waist and steadied him. Mr. Park appeared in front of him and created space for them to walk through the small crowd. Insoo felt humiliated walking with Akila and Ji Su past the people who were all looking at them, and he couldn't help but stare at his feet.

How did they make it off the set, into the car, and all the way home? Insoo couldn't remember later. Once they were inside his house, Mavis and Talida came running. Seeing him, they wrapped their arms around him and held him tight until he gently, but determinedly, freed himself of their embrace. Even Tae Oh was there, having left his own shoot to be with him. All their eyes were full of concern, which sickened him. He had to run to the washroom. Grabbing the toilet bowl with both hands, Insoo threw up until there was nothing left and then heaved some more, feeling as if he was spitting out his organs too.

Eventually, he had no energy to go on, so he sat down next to the toilet with his head resting on the cool tiles on the wall behind him. The storm around him had picked up in intensity again and it was howling at full volume, this time taking him down, he was sure of it.

* * *

Evening light splashed the walls of the living room with golden liquid. Akila was sad to see the beauty and not be able to appreciate it. It was one of the wonders of this world, the way light created spaces–valleys and hills on walls, in trees, or on water. But today, there was a silence in the house that couldn't be filled by the light.

Ji Su sat next to her on the couch, his head resting on the back of the sofa, eyes closed. Talida sat on the other side of her with her brother's head in her lap. Akila was relieved that Mavis was finally asleep. She had tried to protect him from witnessing all the craziness of the day and the intense emotions, but he had refused to leave with his friend Ji Min.

Akila sighed and put her arm around Talida, who was reading a book she had picked up in Mr. Kim's bookshop the other day. Akila admired her daughter for being able to find refuge in stories at any time, in any place.

Ji Su moved slightly and Akila glanced over at him. He had been very quiet the entire day, his jaw tense, biting his lip frequently, his shoulders squared and his bounce even more pronounced as if he was daring the world to come at him. He seemed ready to take everyone down on his own. Even the meeting with his agency was something he had faced alone, declining her repeated offer to accompany him. Akila wondered what was going on inside his head. She knew almost nothing about his family and his broader circle of friends. How were they reacting to the scandal?

And a full-blown scandal it was by now, only a few hours after it had started. It was different this time. Akila felt it. The pictures that were out there for everyone to see, comment on and share were of a much more intimate nature. And because these were two men, they were of a much more explosive nature too. Why? She wondered. Why did it seem to matter so much?

Further, the man in the blue suit had not hesitated to take action. By the end of business hours that day, Insoo's agency had been informed that there would be an assault charge against the young actor.

After coming out of the bathroom, Insoo simply locked the door to his room and stayed in there for the rest of the day. No one had been able to persuade him to open the door again, not even when Akila asked him to let them take a look at the cuts on his right hand.

There had been insane activity outside Insoo's room, though. Mr. Kwon turned up, as expected, in a furious state of mind having heard of Insoo's attack on the man from the production company. But Insoo didn't open the door for his manager either, and Mr. Kwon left to deal with the media, the assault charge and the many messages that were coming in from other partners Insoo was working with.

Late in the afternoon, Tae Oh left to prepare for the next day. Akila promised to keep him updated. Earlier, he had taken several calls from worried or upset friends and acquaintances. Akila was grateful for how good he was at protecting his friend, for his calm demeanour and the words he chose.

Early in the evening, Mrs. Moon stormed into the house, totally distressed after not being able to reach her son. She didn't speak to any of them, except to ask where Insoo was. After that, she banged on Insoo's locked door for several minutes, but her son didn't respond.

Mr. Kim, who had walked in after his wife at full height and quiet, as usual, eventually pulled Mrs. Moon away from the door and held the hysterical woman until she finally calmed down a little. Akila walked over to them and offered them a seat as they were still in the corridor in front of Insoo's room. That was when Mrs. Moon screamed at her. "I told you to get out of my son's house! What are you all still doing here, ruining him!" She shook off her husband's hands and looked up at Akila with fiery eyes.

Ji Su, who had returned from his meeting by that time, stepped in between them. "Mrs. Moon," he said. "I think that is enough."

It was probably in an impulse that she slapped him with all her might across the face because after she did, her eyes went wild and she crumbled again, apparently only held upright by Mr. Kim's hands on her shoulders. Mr. Kim apologised and then guided his wife out of the house, almost carrying her.

Still looking at Ji Su, totally quiet on the couch, Akila wondered what he felt when Insoo's mother had hurt him as if he was responsible for the whole situation, and she inched closer and rested her head on his shoulder. He stirred and opened his eyes briefly to look at her. Then he stretched his arm out and pulled her closer. He closed his eyes and was motionless again. When had Kang Ji Su ever slowed down, except maybe to catch his breath for a second? For all the months Akila had known him, she had never seen him like this.

When Insoo didn't come out of his room the next day, even after they asked him several times, Ji Su broke down the door. By then, Mr. Kwon had come to the house to discuss the most urgent damage control steps but hadn't been able to because Insoo didn't respond to any of his knocks on the door.

Mavis and Talida were out with Seo Hui, who had offered to spend time with them and had picked them up right after breakfast. Akila didn't want the two of them to see Insoo in whatever state he was in. She was scared. What if they had waited for too long? What if he was already . . .?

Seeing the thought in her eyes, Ji Su shook his head. "He doesn't have the balls to do that," he said and sounded as if he meant it.

Still, when Mr. Kwon's knocks didn't result in any reaction around mid-morning, he stood in front of Insoo's door for a long moment, then clenched his fists and kicked. Wood cracked and, with the second kick, the door burst open.

Akila followed Ji Su into the room, telling herself that she had to be prepared for anything, her legs shaky. But the bed was empty and Insoo stood at the door of his bathroom, hair wet and towel in hand, looking shocked at the sight of the broken door and the sight of their eyes on him.

"I was just coming out," he muttered, avoiding their gaze.

Ji Su glared at him. "Then why didn't you say anything?" he addressed him. "Do you think you are the only one affected here?"

Insoo looked back at Ji Su and Akila felt as if a wall was growing out of the ground and separating the two men.

Insoo picked up his shirt from his bed and pulled it on while walking past Ji Su, who didn't take his eyes off him, and past Akila, whose heart ached.

* * *

Ma Ru and Insoo sat down in the living room. There was silence for a moment as the manager Insoo had worked with for almost his entire career tried to collect his thoughts and set the right agenda for this meeting. His intention was to avoid just collecting the broken pieces of their work, turning them this way and that, and mourning. Rather, he wanted this meeting to be constructive and forward-looking. But it was hard not to feel bitter about the fact that the many hours, months, and years of dedication were being torn apart by the audiences, by the industry, and, ultimately, by the choices Insoo had made.

Ma Ru knew that it made no sense to blame the young man for what had happened. It would only result in more pain. Still, hadn't he said it all before? Hadn't he asked all of them to stop? And not only once? He found it difficult not to point his finger at them, and say, "I TOLD you so!"

He didn't do any such thing and, after a moment, he cleared his throat and addressed Insoo. "Let's begin by discussing the current situation and what our next steps should be."

Ma Ru didn't wait for Insoo to agree and simply started summarising. As he described the extent of the damage, Insoo, who had a vacant look on his face from the moment he came out of his room, seemed to slump and shrink on the couch where he was seated.

By the time Ma Ru finished explaining which deals he'd lost and what the assault charge and a possible additional lawsuit for causing lasting damage to the image of the program he had been acting for meant for the actor's career, Insoo had turned even more pale. His head rested in his right hand. The reality of it all dawned on him. It was probably over. Hitting that man in the blue suit, him not getting a grip on his emotions early enough, had caused the real damage.

Ma Ru stopped talking and observed his client, the client he had invested most time and energy in during his entire professional life. The only client he had allowed himself to grow fond of.

He cleared his throat again, feeling as if there was a large obstacle stuck there, making it hard to speak. "Let's discuss what our next steps should be."

Insoo didn't move. Had he even heard him?

Before Ma Ru could add anything, Ji Su appeared in the living room. "That's enough," he said quietly. "Why don't you come back later to discuss the steps?"

The manager's irritation rose. Again, these people were here to interfere. Didn't they see what was important now? He sat up as straight as possible in the chair and faced Ji Su. "This is of utmost importance! Surely, you understand that!" he shot at him.

Ji Su's shoulders were broad and his hands clenched into fists. His jaw was set and his eyes were dark. He looked like he was ready to kick him, just like he had kicked the door earlier.

"Can't you see that now is not the right time?" Ji Su's voice was loud, reflecting what his body already displayed.

Akila walked into the living room behind him. "Mr. Kwon, I think Ji Su is right. Just give Insoo some more space. I am sure that there are certain measures you can take without him involved. I've seen how effective you are." Her voice was steady and calm.

Now she is even trying flattery, he thought. *Shameless woman!*

"Ms. Akila, I have really had enough of your interference," he said, and Insoo stood up so suddenly that all of them froze, startled by the unexpected movement. The tall man left the house without another word.

For a long time, the three of them just stayed where they were. Then, Ma Ru slowly stood up and said, "I will be back tomorrow morning. Please respect my wish to have privacy with Insoo so that I can discuss what is to be done without any interruptions."

Neither Akila nor Ji Su responded to his words, but they made way for him as he walked past them towards the front door to leave. *Good!* he thought, feeling as if he had regained some of the control that was needed to handle this mess.

* * *

It was past lunchtime when Insoo returned to the house.

Ji Su and Akila had wondered what they should do and were restless waiting for him. He had left his phone in his room, switched off. He hadn't eaten and probably hadn't taken any fluids either. Both of them were worried that this meant a relapse for Insoo.

When lunchtime came, they cooked, but neither of them had an appetite, and the food remained untouched and turned cold.

Feeling like she was unable to do anything, not even work, Akila climbed the metal stairs to the rooftop and sat overlooking the city. She had sat for quite a while when she eventually recognized Insoo, who drove in through the crowd of people in front of the gate. Relief washed over her like a large wave, and she stood up to climb down the stairs.

By the time she was down, he had already entered the house through the front door, which she had left open. Inside, she found

Ji Su and Insoo facing each other in the kitchen. Seeing their expressions and how tense their bodies were, she hurried over, all of her earlier relief swept away by fear. Her tummy turned hard and began to hurt instantly.

"I ask you again, do you think you are the only one affected?" Ji Su shot at Insoo. "What is going on with you?"

Insoo's back was rigid, his shoulders so squared that Akila thought that he might snap in the middle. He glared at Ji Su for a long moment, obviously trying to work out his emotions, maybe even trying to work out what to say. It seemed to be a real fight raging inside him.

He pressed his lips together and closed his eyes abruptly. Then Insoo slid down the wall and covered his face with his hand. "What do you want from me?" He addressed them both. "Do you want to drive me crazy? Ruin me?" His hand ran over the top of his head in a gesture of helplessness. "My life is not meant to be like this!" he shouted at them.

Akila looked down at Insoo, and her heart contracted painfully. She took a deep breath. "It's time to leave," popped up in her mind, and she knew that the decision was made.

Ji Su stood a few metres away with his arms dangling on both sides, frozen in the moment. They glanced at each other and the expression of complete disappointment she read on his face made her extremely sad–so sad that tears sprung up where there had been only a desert seconds before.

Not saying a word, Ji Su picked up his jacket with his phone and keys, and walked past Insoo, who was still sitting on the floor, forehead in his hand. He walked past Akila, whose cheeks were now wet with tears. And after putting on his shoes, he walked out through the front door that still stood open and into the sunshine. Akila watched him moving away from them with the bright light reflecting in his pitch-black hair, his bounce determined.

Tokyo

The spacious hotel room was designed in the usual muted colours of international business hotels. The designers of this particular accommodation had chosen different shades of brown and green and modern box-shaped furniture in line with what seemed to be the taste these days. Akila could have been anywhere, in any big city around the world. For a moment, the anonymity of the place washed over her and left her feeling empty.

She still had two hours before the dinner would start and was trying to get into the mood for the conference she was attending. It was a great opportunity, dinner with a selection of experienced coaches on the first evening, and meeting professionals from various fields who all seemed eager to exchange their experiences, thoughts, and connections.

She was scheduled to lecture the next day, mid-morning, and was slightly nervous about it. Previously, she would have been excited and energised on top of feeling nervous, but the last couple of months had left her shaken, and she noticed that it was harder for her to block her thoughts from wandering off into the less sunny landscapes of her mind.

Almost three months. How had she moved through those weeks?

When she was with the children, she rarely felt the vast empty space in her brain, and there were many moments when she was simply happy. But in places like this, where anonymity seemed the theme that shouted at her from every corner, she felt numb. With the numbness, it became difficult to focus on anything, her brain being too busy blocking out the flood of heavy emotions.

When the scandal around Insoo and Ji Su had blown up to its full extent three months ago and the impact began to hit everyone around the two men like cascades of energy ripples being sent out from the centre of an explosion, Akila had already left the country with Mavis and Talida. She hadn't been willing to expose the children to the flood of emotions that came pouring in from all around them from family, friends, acquaintances, colleagues, and strangers. The media. Companies Ji Su, Insoo, and even Akila had worked with. People who had no connection to the incident around Insoo, Ji Su, and herself at all, but who had to add their words to the debate.

Some of those words were supportive, especially from family and close friends. Others were harsh and shook her to her very core. It was intense. It was mind-blowing. It triggered her in the scariest way.

She was reminded of the time when someone had put up posts about her and Insoo and how suddenly everyone had an opinion about her, how even strangers had felt that they had a right to ask the most invasive questions and make comments about the most intimate topics around her relationship with Insoo. Akila still didn't understand how it worked. How certain things pushed masses of people to react in the strongest ways and to add layers and layers of words until it felt as if the person who was the subject of discussion was buried deep down below all those layers of noisy words and began to suffocate slowly–until the true essence of them was gone, wiped out by other people's emotions.

Alone in her hotel room, Akila remembered how the hardest part of the Ji Su and Insoo scandal had been seeing Insoo become an empty shell. It was as if the day Ji Su walked out of the house, Insoo had left too. Not physically. His body was still present. But mentally and emotionally, he had disappeared and there was no way to get to him. And when Mrs. Moon and Ma Ru took over, Akila experienced a sense of helplessness and exclusion that left her exasperated and exhausted.

She knew there was nothing to be gained from asking herself if she should have stayed or if there was more that she could have done for Insoo. She knew it was useless, yet these questions still popped up in her mind from time to time.

She'd stepped out of the shower, hair still wet, looking through the tainted big windows across Tokyo with all the blinking lights illuminating the night. "Mono," RM's first solo mixtape was playing nonstop in the background. She felt the sad and thoughtful songs completely reflected what was inside her.

The knock on the door was unexpected, and for a moment she wondered if it was all in her imagination. Her heart pounded a little faster and she trembled slightly by the time she reached for the handle and pulled the door open.

Insoo looked so tired that she was reminded of the first days of meeting him–that time when things had been really difficult for him.

Insoo gazed at her only for a split second when she opened the door. And while she was still shocked by the paleness of his skin, by the shadows below his eyes, and by the darkness inside his eyes, much more than by the fact that he was standing in front of her, he crossed the space between them.

Later, when she stood in the elevator on her way up to join the dinner, she thought about the sense of helplessness she'd experienced at that moment and how truly intimidating it had been. It was like a piece of a puzzle that had been missing for a long time and finally snapped into the empty space where it was meant to be.

"Sorry," he whispered, covering her neck and face with kisses and gently pushing her back into the room. Still not able to say a word, not sure what to make of it all, Akila felt as though he was seeking ways to eliminate all physical boundaries between them.

In movies, they always play such scenes in slow motion. Especially in a South Korean production. Minutes would pass by, emphasising the different emotions the heroes and heroines experience as they realise who has suddenly appeared in front of them.

In reality, the moments that shape us the most often last only seconds, and we don't have time to let them sink in and decide how to act. We merely react, boiling emotions making it hard to see clearly. And then the moment passes. Only much later might we come to recognise what that moment meant for us.

Akila milled over all this while standing in the elevator that was taking her to the restaurant where the reservation for the conference's evening dinner had been made. She felt lightheaded and was wondering how she would get through the hours ahead of her. She was already very late, but having woken up next to Insoo and taken in his face, still without any colour in it, but much calmer in his sleep, she had the sense that she wouldn't be able to digest it. She had experienced an overpowering urge to put some space between them. *Was this how Ji Su felt the day he walked out?* she asked herself. Whatever the case, here she was, in the elevator on her way to join a dinner that she had no interest in anymore.

* * *

It had been a long time since Insoo had slept so deeply. He woke up in the empty hotel room and was confused at first. Where was he?

But then he saw the note on the nightstand next to the bed and everything came rushing back at him.

He hadn't seen Akila in three months, and reading her note with the messy, slanted handwriting that explained why she left him alone sleeping set something in motion inside him. He was suddenly afraid that he might be overpowered by what he felt in this lonely and dark hotel room. He covered his eyes with his arm for a moment, wondering why he felt so overwhelmed. How could relief be such a painful experience?

Wanting to put an end to his brooding, he pushed himself out of the bed and entered the bathroom. He avoided his image in the large mirror that covered the wall above the sink and stepped into the shower, turning the hot water on. He closed his eyes and let the water run over his head for several minutes.

After he got out of the shower, he stood in front of the floor-to-ceiling windows that offered a spectacular view of the shining night lights. Tokyo was a bit of a crazy city. Thinking about it, it was actually the right place for them to cross paths again. He wondered if their crossing paths again would lead to walking on together or moving on their separate ways.

* * *

Ji Su let his gaze slowly wander across the thousands of lights of the city. He was high up and able to let his gaze sweep across Seoul. It was a great feeling, to be able to see all the blinking lights but be completely removed from the intensity of it all. The bird's eye perspective was what he needed.

For a long time, he just looked, slowly moving his gaze, never stopping. He was unable to stop moving, but he also wanted to delay it for as long as possible, the moment he would reach the spot where he had to take the steps back down into the maze of Seoul, into the many narrow alleys and wide streets, into the mass of people, vehicles, smells and emotions. He wanted to remain a little longer up here, suspended above it all, even if the wind was freezing.

When Akila had messaged him to say that she would be in Tokyo for a conference, he had been unsure what to do. It wasn't impossible for him to see her while she was in Japan. In fact, he still had many connections in the city from his boy band times, so he could have turned the trip into something more and maybe even secured another interesting deal for his channel, which was doing incredibly well these days. But he had hesitated, and after trying to not think about it for two days, he had replied that he was unable to make it.

She understood. He knew that she would. Too much was still shifting inside him, making him feel like he would overflow most of the days.

Ji Su sighed and removed his phone. He clicked on his chat with Akila and stared at the image she had sent him earlier. His heart was doing something even now as he allowed himself to look at the picture again. It was Insoo, sleeping. "Look who turned up. . . ." Akila had written below the image. "Ji Su, are you sure you can't make it?"

He took a long, deep breath and closed his eyes. Then, he suddenly realised how stiff his fingers had become with the cold and the way he held the phone, almost as if he wanted to crush it. Quickly, he slipped it back into the back pocket of his jeans and then jogged to the spot where he was able to take the stairs back down into the city.

While Ji Su was running, almost flying down the many steps and steep and narrow alleyways that took him back into the city, the resolve he had been looking for formed inside him. And by the time he had reached his parked car, he knew that he would book the flight to Tokyo.

It was morning when Ji Su reached Tokyo. He walked in the middle of the crowd of so many living beings, all with different thoughts, desires, and fears. All of them with tears and smiles. The place still intimidated him slightly, even after the countless concerts and interviews he had given here in the past when he was still part of the boy band. The city seemed to inhale life and exhale loneliness. Or was it the other way around? He was never quite sure.

On his way to the hotel where Akila was staying, he let his gaze wander. He felt a tightness in his chest as if it was hard to breathe because his heart and lungs were already filled with something else and there wasn't enough space for oxygen. A blazing ball of energy had been growing day by day over the last couple of weeks. Weeks that eventually turned into months. Months when he hadn't seen Insoo face to face but had only watched the news about him—the articles about the assault charge. The news about him being dropped from the program he had been shooting. The heavy fine he would have to pay for causing damage to the program. The discussions online about his violent and extravagant tendencies, about his being led astray by others. By the time it turned truly nasty, Akila had already left the country with Talida and Mavis. He had taken them to the airport, holding on to them tightly in the spacious departure hall, holding them one by one, feeling as if it might be hard for him to continue moving after they were gone.

He had stood in the hall for a very long time after the three had left, still seeing them walk away with Talida firmly holding Mavis' hand. The boy had been crying silently all the time with tears and snot covering his face.

But Ji Su wasn't someone to stop for too long and, therefore, the moment passed and he was able to walk out of the hall, get into his car, and drive home.

It was strange, being back in his flat, a place where he'd spent almost no time for the last months. He didn't know what to do with himself at first, so he wandered around, gazing out of the windows at the city outside.

It was the next morning when his doorbell rang. He opened his eyes and realised that he hadn't made it to his empty bed and had slept on the couch. Feeling unusually heavy, he slowly sat up and then stood and made it to the front door. He simply opened it without even checking who was outside.

It was his mother. She looked up at him and, after scrutinising his face for a moment, she lifted her left hand and cupped his cheek gently. He didn't want to let out what was welling up inside him at her touch, so he quickly moved aside and gestured for her to come in.

A while later, she stood in his living room-come-kitchen and looked out of the windows at the city, just like he had done the previous evening. He was preparing coffee for them. When he walked over to hand her the cup with the steaming hot brew, he wondered if she looked older than the last time they had met or if it was the way his feeling drained made the world look faded. Including his mother.

She glanced at him briefly and mumbled, "Thank you," when accepting the coffee from him. Then she turned back to stare out of the window.

Ji Su sat down on his couch, sipping from his cup carefully and wondering what his mother was thinking. Over the last couple of years, they hadn't met often, only occasionally, when she could find the time and didn't have to worry about her husband's anger for meeting with their disgrace of a son.

CEO Kang had accepted his son's years of fame with the boy band but made it clear that he expected him to complete his military service like every true man would and then get ready to join him at the company. Ji Su did not. He completed his service when the band took a break for several other projects the different members wanted to work on, but once back, he applied for the lead in an online series and didn't even go home to greet his father. He got the part and the attention was considerable, given that it was a small production and given the fact that it was a boy love drama.

His mother met him for coffee just after the series premiered. She sat opposite her son, looking tired and beautiful at the same time, as always. Her gaze focused on the people passing by outside, and she kept turning her wedding ring between her fingers absent-mindedly. It made Ji Su feel uneasy.

Eventually, she looked at her son and said, "You cannot come home anymore. Your father. . . ." She stopped herself from completing the sentence, and it was the first time in his life that Ji Su saw up close how his mother fought back tears. He knew that she used to cry. He had seen the sparkling tears in her eyes before, but she had always done the crying behind closed doors and made sure that he didn't get to see it. Being confronted with the sight of her, with how she tried to balance her tears, fighting hard for them not to fall made him feel unspeakably lonely.

Ji Su remembered that meeting on the day she spent with him in his apartment, looking out of his window. She drank from her cup slowly, almost passively, as if her mind was far away. Then, she suddenly placed her coffee on the windowsill next to her and removed a packet of cigarettes from her handbag. She shook one cigarette out of the box, removed a lighter, lit, inhaled, and blew the smoke into the room while leaning with her back on his window. She did the whole thing with such a deliberate intensity that it seemed like an act of ultimate rebellion. Ji Su gaped at his mother. Was she finally ready to fight?

Noticing the look on his face, she tried to smile but didn't speak. And he did not ask her to.

They spent the first part of the day like that, in silence. Words only came with time, after they had cooked and eaten and after she had smoked again and had blown the smoke into the room with her small mouth.

She asked him, "Is this very bad for you? The pictures online and everything about it?"

He responded while shaking his head slowly. "Not in the way it is bad for Insoo. My image is different. People already knew I was doing things my own way. So my fans are different and so are the people I work with. And I am not that big of a deal in the industry anyway."

She looked at him as if she wanted to tell him to stop lying.

He sighed and turned his head to the other side and bit his lip. What did she want him to say? That it hurt? That the negative comments got to him, even though he was far less affected than Insoo was? That he felt empty because it was as if the attention was a storm that had blown them apart, and now they were scattered all over, each on their own. That he hated the whole thing and the fact that it had happened so quickly as if they had no backbone to keep them upright for a bit longer? Ji Su put his face into his hands and waited for the sensation washing over him to pass.

When his mother sat down next to him, very close to him, he stood up and moved away from her. The last thing he wanted to do was to let his emotions come out and overpower him. It took a while for him to get himself under control, but he finally turned around and looked at her with dry eyes. She seemed very tiny on the couch, with her own dry eyes on him.

* * *

Now that he was on the way to the hotel where Akila was, the last months suddenly felt surreal to Ji Su.

After his mother's visit, he had spent a dreamless, pitch-black night in his empty bed. And then he was in motion again. As was his nature, he moved through the weeks, then months, working on his channel, focusing on his dancing, and accepting deals, when the worst of the shitstorm was over. He was contacted by small production companies that worked in more unconventional ways and was offered quite interesting projects. He appeared in shows, responding to questions and sharing opinions. On some days he felt as if he was constantly dancing, singing, posing, and talking. But never talking about Insoo and never about the scandal. It was the one topic his agency made clear no one could mention.

He spoke on the phone with Akila a few times, and they promised each other that they would meet. But when remained unsaid. Ji Su felt as if they both weren't ready to face each other and deal with everything that had happened.

What remained was to watch Insoo from a distance through new posts online, through shows that featured the story, and through Tae Oh who sometimes updated Ji Su on what was going on. It was hard to face these updates, especially the ones Tae Oh gave. Insoo was extremely quiet, he said. Mrs. Moon had a nervous breakdown, he reported. Kwon Ma Ru was working hard but looked tired.

Ji Su was afraid to hear the news at times but couldn't stop himself from asking. And it felt weird to see their names feature in the same headlines for weeks on end but to never speak to Insoo once.

After a couple of weeks, the public attention slowly shifted to other topics until, eventually, one day there was no news on Kim Insoo and his dramatic lifestyle. It became so quiet that it was as if Insoo had ceased to exist.

Ji Su didn't know what Insoo had done for all the weeks that no one knew what was going on with him and where he had disappeared. Even Tae Oh hadn't been able to give Ji Su any updates.

Strange, he thought, this mixture of affection and anger that he had carried with him all this time since the day he had walked out of Insoo's house.

Ji Su stood in front of the hotel, looking up at the many floors and at the large lobby, which was welcoming and spitting out guests through two big glass revolving doors. After a second of hesitation, he walked towards the entrance, and while he joined several other guests entering the hotel, he pulled out his phone from his back pocket and checked his messages.

Akila had written. They were currently in the restaurant on the top floor having some food. It was a relief to Ji Su that Akila mentioned Insoo and food in the same sentence. He had often wondered how Insoo was getting on with his meals and had worried that he'd stopped eating again. Reading her message gave Ji Su hope that it was maybe not as bad as he had thought.

He joined a group of loud, chatty guests in one of the elevators and made his way up to the restaurant. His heart was trying to find a way to jump out of his chest, to burst his ribcage open and run away, and was trying to do so with more and more desperation the closer he got to his destination.

When he finally got there, he strode into the bright, spacious room, which rang with the usual noises of human conversation, low music in the background, and cutlery and plates being moved. A waitress in black and white appeared in front of him and asked politely if he was looking for someone, having noticed how his gaze travelled across the large space and how he scanned the tables by the floor-to-ceiling windows. Ji Su bowed and smiled slightly, but absentmindedly, already making his way across the sea of other tables toward the one table that mattered to him—a table right by the window and in one corner of the restaurant.

He spotted her almost right away—the unruly hair, the wide black tunica below the long, rusty-red coat, and the large glasses that reflected the sunlight. Akila saw him coming, and the look on her face made him walk faster. She stood up and was already in his arms by the time he came to a halt in front of the table. The ball of energy inside him that had been growing for weeks threatened to explode, and his chest was heaving, trying to get air into his lungs. He held on to her to steady himself, to gain some composure before he could look at Insoo. When he finally did, Insoo was standing too, tall and thin, unhealthily pale, and eyes hidden behind his large sunglasses. Ji Su embraced him and Insoo hugged him back, wrapping his long arms around him tightly, hiding his pale face in Ji Su's hair.

Later, much later, Akila and Insoo would tell Talida and Mavis how this was the first and the only time that they saw Ji Su cry in public. It was a quiet and soundless way of crying, almost as if he didn't notice that his face was wet with salty tears.

* * *

Mrs. Moon slowly walked through the empty apartment. A few boxes and items still waited to be picked up in one corner of the living room. The place had an amazing view over the city, which she admired from the window. Insoo stood next to her, silent as usual, letting his gaze travel across the many houses and streets spread out below. Mrs. Moon glanced at her son.

The realisation that she had no idea what he truly felt or thought most of the time had shaken her up. The last few months had forced her to face the fact that she had probably not known how Insoo felt for a very, very long time. And even now, after having accepted that she had been in love with her version of him and ignored the person he had grown to be, she asked herself why. Why had he made the choices he had made and let all this happen?

It wasn't easy to admit, but Mrs. Moon had a hard enough time working through the jungle of emotions that came with the admission that she didn't understand her own child, this beautiful being that she had created.

And here she was, in this apartment that used to be owned by Kang Ji Su and that had been sold just two days ago. She had asked Insoo to let her see the place where the young man had lived.

She wasn't sure what she was hoping for–maybe getting a better understanding of this person who seemed to be so very important in her son's life.

Just the day before, they'd walked through Insoo's old house, which had also been sold, in a similar fashion. She hadn't been able to shake off the feeling of panic, the sense that Insoo was disappearing–that he was making every effort to become invisible and that he would slip through her fingers if she didn't hold on with all her might.

Today, she felt better, although she was worried about the lunch. What would she say and feel? What would they think of her?

Her phone vibrated. Mr. Kim was calling to let them know that he was on the way to the restaurant. Mrs. Moon hung up and sighed deeply in an attempt to calm her screaming heart.

"Let's go," Insoo said gently, and his fingertips touched her arm briefly. Mrs. Moon looked up at her son and tried to detect something in his eyes–a message for her that would make her feel more prepared for what was coming. But he was already turning away, and she had no choice but to follow.

* * *

Ji Su stood next to his mother outside the restaurant. The wind blew across the street, moving the clouds over the strip of sky he could see between the rooftops. Sunlight and shadows chased each other over the facades of the buildings around them and on the pavement in front of them.

He looked at Akila, who stood on the other side of his mother staring at the sky. His mother fidgeted, straightening her dress and smoothening down her hair, which she had held together in an elegant knot on the back of her head. Next to Akila, she seemed even tinier than usual, and Ji Su wondered how such a small being could have so much strength to keep going inside her.

They had decided to send Mavis and Talida on a day excursion with Seo Hui and Tae Oh and make this a lunch during which anything could be said without having to think about what the children would feel about their words.

Ji Su looked around in search of Insoo, Mrs. Moon, and Mr. Kim. He had no idea how this meeting would go or what he would say to Insoo's parents. So far, their brief encounters had been rather dramatic, and he hoped that he wouldn't have to say things that caused tension.

"There they are," Akila said, and Ji Su followed her gaze to look at Insoo, who was walking next to his father. The resemblance hit Ji Su immediately. Insoo was in every aspect a product of his parents. Ji Su took in his breath. If that was true, how much of his parents did he carry inside himself without even knowing it? How much of him was his father and how much was his mother?

Ji Su watched Insoo and his parents coming closer and thought about the fact that, although Insoo was an amazing mixture of his mother's and father's features, his mind was his own. He was making his own choices, even if it wasn't easy. And who he was showed in his eyes as they all faced each other, making introductions in English and Korean, shaking hands, and bowing politely.

They walked into the restaurant together, where Ji Su had reserved a table a few days ago.

* * *

Days later, Talida sat on the long, low bench at the back of Ji Su's spacious practice room. Music bounced off the walls, and over the beat, the head of Ji Su's dance crew shouted out numbers to help with the perfect flow of the dance moves. Mavis was in the first row, right in front of the big mirror, his blonde afro bouncing just like the music as he moved along with the other dancers. Talida smiled to herself while observing her brother. He had always been the more physical of them, and it amazed her to see how much he had grown and how sure he seemed to be about what was right for him.

She inhaled deeply. She was due to leave Seoul on her own in two weeks to join her new school in Scotland. It was a boarding school, and she would only join for her final year and to sit for the exams, but she was excited and looked forward to sitting in a classroom again after having done homeschooling all the time they'd spent in Seoul. Rose and Edith had agreed to have her over for the shorter holidays and to be there whenever she needed any immediate support.

Talida felt as if she was going to live her life by her own rules from now on, and it was amazingly liberating. It wasn't that she wouldn't miss her family. Akila, Mavis, Insoo and Ji Su would all remain here in Seoul. She knew that she would want to see them and wouldn't be able to for a while. She knew that she would miss her conversations with Insoo and Mr. Kim at the bookshop. She would miss Ji Su's crazy laughter and her brother's bustling presence. She would miss how Akila had deeper thoughts on everything in this world, something that irritated her to the core on some days and that she was extremely grateful for on others. She would miss the friends she'd made in Seoul and, funny enough, she would miss the city itself, with all its contrasts, all the good and bad. What she felt for Seoul was something similar to what she had felt for her birthplace, Nairobi.

Talida thought of one of RM's songs about Seoul. He sang:

"Saranggwa miumi gateun marimyeon, I love you Seoul,
Saranggwa miumi gateun marimyeon, I hate you Seoul . . ."

"If love and hate are the same word, I love you Seoul,
If love and hate are the same word, I hate you Seoul . . ."

Those lyrics resonated with her entire being.

Talida continued to watch the dance practice, but inside her, a colourful mixture of images, moments from the last few months, whirled past her and she felt slightly dizzy at the sight of everything that had happened since the day her mother had decided that they would leave Nairobi around 2 years ago.

How was it possible that such a storm of events could suddenly be set into motion by just one single decision a person made–a decision that resulted in so many other things happening for so many people?

If that was a given, what would happen to her life and the lives of those she cared about, now that she had decided to move to the boarding school in Scotland? Talida felt her stomach lurch with excitement and a little fear. Whatever was coming her way, she would make sure she would enjoy the ride!

Loud cheers and clapping from the crew forced her to let her thoughts go and return to the world around her. Practice was over and the dancers were hugging and patting each other's backs, all sweaty and with big smiles on their faces. Talida assumed that the session had gone well. Ji Su, who had been outside the studio for a meeting, entered the room and, after greeting everyone and briefly chatting with the crew's instructor, he came over to where Talida sat.

"Talida!" he said with a broad grin while sitting down next to her. "Let's wait for Mavis to get changed. Then we can go and pick up Insoo."

Talida returned the smile wholeheartedly and nodded. She felt elated at the thought of their short trip to a warm, sunny place for the next couple of nights. They had all agreed that they needed some time out of the city, just the five of them, without any distractions. She put her head on Ji Su's shoulder, who looked very pleased with her gesture of affection.

Insoo had started working with his father at the bookshop a little while ago. Whether that would be what he would do for the rest of his life remained unknown. Talida had seen that both her mother and Ji Su had agreed with Insoo's decision not to move back into his former acting career. There was too much at stake for Insoo. He still had trouble eating properly and remained in therapy.

Talida briefly thought of Mr. Park, who had been so attached to Insoo, but especially of Kwon Ma Ru. The short, brusk man had looked so sad the last time Talida had seen him, she almost felt sorry for him.

They had sold Insoo's house, which hadn't been easy–not because there were no buyers, but because they all felt so at home there and had a hard time imagining they could find a better place to stay. But one evening, when they had all been in the kitchen together, Insoo had said, "I really need to sell the house," and nothing more. Talida had noticed the quick exchange of glances between Akila and Ji Su and they all conceded without any further objections.

Selling Ji Su's apartment had been a much easier decision to make because no one, not even Ji Su himself, was very attached to the place. Talida thought that she spotted a sense of relief in Ji Su on the day the apartment was officially sold and handed over to the new owners.

Their new home was closer to the studio Ji Su used as a base for his projects these days and wasn't too far from Mr. Kim's bookshop either. It had been an interesting sensation, looking at places around Seoul and, all together, settling on the place they would call home going forward. The whole thing truly felt like the definition of the word "family" to Talida.

They hadn't decided what would happen to the small cottage next to Rose's and Edith's in Scotland, so for now, they would keep it, although it meant more financial planning for them. Talida wondered when she had grown so much now that she was actively involved in the day-to-day running of the family and spotted a lot of unspoken things and thought about stuff like finances. It was great, but also slightly weird.

Mavis had gotten changed and was jumping with exhilaration like a bouncy ball as they walked out of the building to get a taxi and pick up Insoo. Then they would meet Akila at the airport, who had been on the other side of the city for mentoring work. Talida walked between her brother and Ji Su and savoured the feeling of belonging.

Tiny grains

Months later, Joyce walked along the small road with her hands in the pockets of her coat. The cool autumn air was already biting her hands. She asked herself if she would ever get used to Germany's weather. They had moved months ago, and still, the extreme change of seasons got to her.

She followed her son, who made his way toward the playground. His steps were still a little wobbly, his little arms remained outstretched for balance and his lips were pursed, reflecting the energy and concentration it still took him to manage all those steps. He eventually reached the playground and went straight for the sandpit.

There were other children and parents, but Joyce found space on one of the benches where the rays of sunshine reached and from where she could see her boy playing in the sand. She let the sunlight run over her face and closed her eyes for a second.

Although it was her husband's birthplace, Germany wasn't a place where she could spend her whole life. Once it was possible, she wanted to move back to Nairobi. She had made her plans with Akila. They would meet again in Kenya and let the sun shine on their backs when they were old and wrinkly and had done whatever they needed to do in this life.

But at present, she was simply grateful for the medical support they received in this cool, organised country for their little boy without having to spend their last savings. As the months passed, she started feeling more at home, and the pressure she had experienced as a confusing fog that filled her head and heart ever since Sam had come into this world under such dramatic circumstances slowly began to decrease. It was funny how her priorities had changed with Sam. Suddenly it was all about him being well and almost never about her own needs. It was as if she could only start thinking about herself once he, the most crucial part of her, was fine.

Despite all the noise around her, or because of the noise around her, she felt peace.

Sam was eating the sand, his entire face covered with yellow-white tiny grains. Joyce couldn't help but laugh, dipping back her head, her teeth sparkling in the sunlight. And then she recognized the sky that stretched over them like a vast, crystal-clear blue canvas. It was the most beautiful sight she had seen in a long time.

* * *

Rose stood in the middle of the garden that lay behind Akila's small cottage. It was autumn, and the vines that covered the high fence that marked the border between this and the next garden shone in the most beautiful range of colours, everything from scarlet red, maroon, green, yellow, and orange. It was as if the fence had caught fire in the late afternoon light.

Rose shivered slightly, realising that it was getting colder much faster and that winter was probably only a few weeks away.

She had spent the afternoon clearing Akila's garden, raking the leaves that covered the grass below the trees, and cutting back the roses next to the terrace. She stored the old garden chairs that they had spent so many evenings on in the shed and moved the table away.

Rose looked up at the blue sky above her. It was completely clear and she could see a bussard with widely spread wings riding the wind.

Edith walked into the garden through the glass doors of the cottage and put her arms around her, warming her back.

She kissed her cheek, then rubbed it softly with the end of her sleeve. "You have dirt on your face, honey." Rose touched her skin and felt the small grains of black soil between her fingers.

Standing very close to each other, they watched the evening take over the garden. Shadows grew longer and deeper. Colours faded. Slowly, the blue above them turned into pink and golden grey. The first stars sprung up.

* * *

Hours later, in a different part of the world, Akila lay on her back, letting her hands run over the warm sand. The sun was low, and there was a golden light in her eyes that made her squint.

It was uncomfortable, so she closed her eyes completely and let the friendly darkness behind her eyelids embrace her. Millions of tiny grains of sand tickled her on her arms, shoulders, and legs, and a few had found their way into her navel and covered her belly.

The sound of the ocean came closer, retreating again every few seconds. She listened to the rhythm for a while.

There were additional sounds she made out. Loud laughter and squeals. Mavis and Insoo were playing football by the water where the sand was soaked with salty water and hard enough to let the ball roll at high speed. Talida was jumping in and out of the waves. She had spent almost the entire day in the water.

There was a light earthquake in her tiny, warm world when Ji Su let himself drop into the sand next to her. She turned her head and looked at him with the one eye that wasn't directly in the sunlight.

Lying on his back, he grinned at her and stretched out his arm over the sand. She did the same and the tips of their fingers met. Akila gazed up at the stunningly blue sky stretching above her, and at that moment, she was sure that she could feel how the world was round and how everything connected in an endless cycle.

Featured Music and TV Shows

Music

Kang Ji Su's playlist:

Anna of the North - "Lovers"
Canyon - "Lights Out"
Noel Gallagher & High flying birds - "Lock all the Doors"
TXT feat. Seori - "Lovesong"
Childish Gambino - "Feels like Summer"
Seori - "Lovers in the Night"
Loud Luxury feat Brando - "Body"
Kranium feat Ty Dolla Sign & Wizkid - "Can't Believe"
Tarrus Riley feat Shenseea & Rvssian - "Lighter"
Soolking feat Dadju - "Melegim"
Burna Boy - "Wonderful"
Rayvanny feat Diamond - "Tetema"
BTS - "So What"
Ice Prince - "Oleku"
Sauti Soul - "Extravaganza"
Popcaan - "Inviolable"
Masego - "King's Rant"
RM, Suga & J-Hope - "Ugh!"
Crudeplay - "In your Eyes"
TXT - "Thursday's Child Has Far to Go"
George Micheal - "Freedom"

Kim Insoo's playlist:

Seori feat. eaJ - "Dive with You"
Just a Band - "Probably for Lovers"
BTS - "Mikrokosmos"
Masicka feat Tarrus Riley & Dunw3ll - "Corner"
TXT - "Can't You See Me?"
Romain Virgo - "Rich in Love"

Kang Insoo & Lee Sang - "Wish for You"
Tarrus Riley - "Superman"
Disclosure feat Sam Smith - "Latch"
Noel Gallagher & High flying birds - "Dying of the Light"
Sauti Soul - "Train to Zion"
Mafikizolo - "Ngeke Balunge"
Lauryn Hill & Bob Marley - "Turn Your Lights Down Low"
Masego & FKJ - "Tadow"
Hui - "Who am I"
TXT - "9 ¾ (Run Away)"
Sun El Musician feat Sino Msolo & Omi Kobi - "Proud of You"
L' Indecis - "Soulful"
Koffee - "Lockdown"
Kamauu feat Adeline - "Mango"
Agust D - "People"
TXT - "Loser=Lover"

Other songs Akila, Talida & Mavis listen to:

(Special mention in the chapter "A dog and a song") Sarabi feat. Juliani - "Sheria"
(Special mention in the chapter "Tokyo") RM - "Seoul"

Anderson .Paak - "Tiny Desk" (live concert)

Mafikizolo - collection of their songs
Erykah Badu - "Tyrone" & other songs
RM - "Mono"
Joss Stone - collection of her songs

Korean series

Bad Guys - Vile City
The Lies Within
Strangers
Where Your Eyes Linger
Something in the Rain
To My Star (seasons 1 & 2)
Itaewon Class
My Mister
The K2
Descendants of the Sun
Semantic Error
Korean actress specifically mentioned: Bae Doona

Glossary

Swahili/Sheng

Matatu: Vans of all sizes, mostly colourfully painted, which are used as the public transport system in Kenya

Mzungu: A caucasian person

Matoke: Cooking bananas

Upcountry: English term to describe the Kenyan countryside, where many Kenyans who live in the city grew up and still have family

Korean

Banchan: An array of side dishes, can comprise of vegetables, fish and meat

Miane: One way of saying "sorry" in an informal way (Sounds sometimes almost like Biane when spoken)

A note on Korean naming conventions:

In Korea, the surname is mentioned first, then the first name.
Example: Lee Tae Oh. Lee is Tae Oh's surname, Tae Oh his first name.

Typically, a woman keeps her original surname upon marriage, which is why Insoo's parents have different surnames, Mrs. Moon and Mr. Kim. In a conventional setting, the child will take on the father's surname; in this case Insoo was named Kim In Su.

Acknowledgements

Thank you.

This book was written with Nomzamo and Noel, but also with Biko and "Baby" Leo in mind. All the stories were inspired by real people I have had the pleasure of meeting while being on my own personal odyssey called life. Every single encounter has been an inspiration and an opportunity for growth.

Thank you to my lovely step mother Sabine Verk-Lindner, to my wonderful friend Jihyun 'Mia' Hong and amazing Nomzamo for being my first test readers. Thank you for all your encouragement, energy and dedication.

Thank you Elayna Fernández for popping into my life at the right time so that you could help me turn this dream into reality, a real book that one can hold in their hands.